Anna King was born in the East End of London and grew up in Hackney. Now married, she lives in Kent with her husband and her two children. She is the author of four previous novels, *Life Is Just a Bowl of Cherries*, *Ruby Chadwick*, *A Handful of Sovereigns* and *Bow Belles*.

Also by Anna King

PALACE OF TEARS

Anna King

WARNER BOOKS

A *Warner* Book

First published in Great Britain in 1997
by Little, Brown and Company
This edition published in 1998 by Warner Books

Copyright © Anna King 1997

A CIP catalogue record for this book
is available from the British Library.

ISBN 0 7515 1815 8

Typeset by Palimpsest Book Production Ltd
Polmont, Stirlingshire
Printed and bound in Great Britain by
Clays Ltd, St Ives plc

Warner Books
A Division of
Little, Brown and Company (UK)
Brettenham House
Lancaster Place
London WC2E 7EN

To my sister Teresa Deere (née Masterson),

my brother-in-law Chris

and my niece Francesca May Deere.

ACKNOWLEDGEMENTS

With grateful thanks to my sister-in-law Barbara Guntrip for providing me with the valuable research books needed to write *Palace of Tears*.

CHAPTER ONE

The parlour was clean and tidy. The motley assortment of worn furniture shone, thanks to a liberal application of beeswax and elbow-grease. From the open fireplace red lumps of coal glowed brightly, the reflecting light spreading over the scrubbed, cracked linoleum and the coconut mats scattered about the floor. The solid oak dining table, scarred from years of abuse, was covered with a white cotton cloth, and in its midst sat a vase filled with hyacinths, their golden colour adding the final touch of homeliness to the normally drab, dismal room.

Sitting in one of the battered, brown armchairs that rested either side of the fireplace, Nellie Ford cast a critical eye around the room, then nodded, satisfied that all was ready for her daughter's homecoming. A smile softened her face as she visualised the forthcoming visit.

When her daughter Emily had first started work as a live-in maid at the home of George and Rose Winter, an elderly brother and sister who occupied a Georgian house in Hackney, Nellie had thought life would become unbearable without her daughter's presence. And at first it had been. Mind you, the seven shillings and sixpence that Emily gave her out of her nine-shilling wage was a godsend, though on her last visit home Emily had seemed restless, talking about leaving the Winters for good and finding a job that paid decent wages. But Nellie knew the real reason behind her daughter's desire to come home. It wasn't that she was unhappy with the Winters – they were a lovely old couple, and they thought the world of Emily, who over the years had become a companion to them, taking over the running of their household with the ease of one born to it. Oh no, the only reason Emily wanted to come home was because she was worried about her mother, even though Nellie constantly reassured her that she was all right.

A sudden movement from upstairs, where her husband Alfie lay sleeping off the effects of last night's drunken binge, brought Nellie's head up sharply, her eyes suddenly fearful. Then, as the sound receded, she visibly relaxed, her entire body slumping with relief. Resting her head against the back of the chair, she let her eyes roam over the mantelpiece. The carriage clock showed that it was nearly nine-thirty. She still had a good forty-five minutes before she had to leave for work. Above her head the floorboards creaked noisily, and again she felt a tightness grip her stomach, a feeling that was quickly followed by one of irritation at herself. What was she worrying about!

Good Lord, with the skinful he'd had on him last night, paid for with the last of her housekeeping money, he'd probably sleep the day away, or at least long enough for her to get out of the house before he woke up. And once Emily was home, he'd behave himself and leave her in peace. As she gazed into the roaring flames, her lips moved silently, repeating her thoughts. Peace . . . that's all she wanted from life now.

2

Once, many years ago, when the beatings had first started, she had dreamed of running away to find a new life for herself and her two children, yet always Alfie would cry and tell her how sorry he was and that he'd never do it again. And she, fool that she was, had believed him. She had also still been in love with him then, ready to forgive and forget, always finding excuses for his behaviour. As time went on, and her love for the man she had married began to die, she had visualised meeting another man, one who was strong enough to stand up to her husband and take her and the children away to a better place, a better life.

But that hazy image of a man had never materialised and, even if he had, she doubted if she would have had the courage to grab at the chance of happiness. She would have done once, but years of mental and physical abuse had turned her from a spirited young girl into a cowed, beaten, defeated woman. Now, at thirty-nine, she no longer dreamed of finding happiness; all she craved from life was peace . . . peace of mind, and a release from the never-ending assault on her tired body.

Heaving herself out of the comfortable armchair, she groaned silently as her body reminded her painfully of last night's beating.

Her eyes flickered to a framed, gilt-edged photograph of a sombre couple, hand-in-hand on their wedding day, and she felt her lips begin to tremble.

How could she have known that the handsome, kindly young man who had courted her so charmingly would turn into a foul-mouthed, vicious bully? Her gaze moved past the man's image and rested on the girl. She saw herself as she had been then – so young, so full of life and optimism for the future – and as the memories became stronger, it was as if she were looking back at a stranger. Where had that girl gone, the girl who had always had a laugh on her lips and a spring in her step? Had she ever really been that young?

As tears of self-pity threatened to overwhelm her, Nellie gave a brisk shake of her head. What did that matter now, she chided herself? Going over the past was a fool's pastime. You couldn't change what had already happened. All anyone could do was carry on, and hope that one day things would be better.

And things would be better, once Emily arrived back home, and not just for the afternoon either, but for three whole weeks. Her step suddenly lighter, Nellie walked quickly into the scullery to check on the stew she had prepared for dinner, thinking that at least something good had come out of this awful war.

Because if the Winters hadn't become mortally afraid of being hit by one of those new Zeppelin bombs, then they would never have thought of closing up the house in Hackney and moving to a relative's house in the country. Just until the end of October, Mr Winter had told Emily, going to great lengths to explain that it was for his sister's sake they were having an early holiday.

Well, Nellie didn't care what the reason was, all she cared about was the prospect of having her daughter to herself for three whole weeks; and Emily was being paid her full wage while her employers were away. Oh, they were good people, the Winters, but what mattered most to Nellie was the hope that one day, at one of the frequent social gatherings at which the Winters entertained their friends, her Emily would meet a young man, a kind, decent young man from a good background.

And it could happen, it could. Her head bobbed up and down on her shoulders, as if trying to reassure herself that her dream would one day come true. It wouldn't have happened in her younger days, but now, with the world seemingly turned upside-down by this dreadful war, the boundaries between the lower and upper classes were finally showing signs of being torn down and thrown aside. Of course there would always be divisions between the rich and the poor, but the need to bow and tug the forelock in the presence of the gentry was fast becoming a thing of the past. Any changes now would come too late to benefit Nellie, but she would put up with anything as long as her daughter was happily settled.

And her Lenny, of course. Her conscience pricked her, as if remonstrating with her for omitting her son from her thoughts. At least that was one young soul whom the war wouldn't claim, for her only son wasn't quite right in the head. Yet he hadn't always been that way.

Up until he was nine, Lenny had been the same as any other lad his age. Then, one day, while out playing with his friends, he had fallen from a high wall, hitting his head on the cobbled pavement. At first he seemed to recover, but as he grew older and his body began to fill out and expand, it became obvious that his mind wasn't developing with the rest of his body. Now, at seventeen, he still had the mentality of a nine-year-old. Oh, he wasn't a simpleton. He could read and write and add up well enough, but only within the capabilities of a child. The most heart-rending part of his disability was the fact that he was fully aware he wasn't like other young men of his age. Not that there had been many young men to compare him with, these last two years, she thought sadly, thinking of the boys – because that's all they were – who had dashed to join up in the early, heady days of the war. But on the whole Lenny seemed happy enough; and he had a job. It wasn't much of one, just running errands for the stall-holders down Well Street market, where he was well known, but it gave him a sense of self-esteem, and the bits and bobs he brought home with him had saved them from going to bed hungry on many occasions.

Entering the small scullery, Nellie shivered. Even with the large pot of stew bubbling on top of the gas oven, the stone-floored room was icy-cold. Stopping only long enough to check that the gas jet under the pot was still alight, she made her way back to the warmth of the parlour, her thoughts returning to her daughter and the worry that she would give up her secure job, and with it the only chance she would have of finding a suitable husband.

Oh, stop worrying, she chided herself. Her daughter had a good head on her shoulders, and knew when she was well off. A lot of women in service were leaving to find work in the factories and on the trams, now that the majority of able-bodied men were fighting overseas, but it wouldn't last. Why, look at how the men had joined up in their thousands at the start of the war, almost trampling each other in the rush to aid King and country, confident that the war would be over by Christmas. The battle of Ypres had put paid to that hope. Then there had been that awful night last year when those terrifying, cigar-shaped objects had rained their bombs down on the East End, flattening houses and killing hundreds. There had been other raids since, but so far this part of Homerton had been lucky to escape the deadly missiles. But for how long?

When the war had first started, Alfie had been working in one of the warehouses in Bush's, the chemical factory in Ash Grove. Being in full employment, and confident that at thirty-eight he wouldn't be called upon to sign up, he had ranted on about the unfairness of limiting the age of enlisted men to thirty, even though there had been nothing to stop him from joining up voluntarily.

It was around this time that he had started staying

out all night, giving Nellie reason to believe that he had found another woman. She could still remember the joyous relief she had felt, for with him absent from the double bed, the beatings had stopped. During that peaceful period of time, Alfie had even been nice to her, as if compensating her for his sudden lack of interest. As if she'd cared!

Then, ten months ago, just before Christmas, he'd come home with a face like thunder to tell her he'd been given the sack for stealing. Shouting and swearing his innocence, he had stormed out of the house, not getting back until the following afternoon. It was shortly afterwards that he began staying in at night, his mean eyes watching her every move, as if waiting for the right moment to strike, his spiteful tactics sending her nerves on end in fearful anticipation of what was to come.

But he kept his hands to himself until 1st March, when conscription for single men up to the age of forty-one came into force, with married men being given two months' reprieve. The beatings had resumed that very night. In June, Kitchener, along with the entire crew of the *Hampshire*, went down after the ship hit a mine off Scapa Flow. So died the man whose picture and pointing finger had forcibly reminded the men of England that their King and country needed them. Kitchener's death had sent shockwaves through the British Isles. Yet still England and the Home Counties maintained the patriotic fervour that had sent men in their thousands to join up – until 1st July, when at a place called the Somme 19,000 men, many of them the eager, young men of 1914, were systematically mowed down by the Germans' guns, their deaths adding to the 50,000 men who had already been crippled or maimed in one way or another.

Now, four months later, the slaughter was still going on, and elderly men, veterans of the Boer War, were calculating that soon both sides would have to dig in for the winter. Meanwhile back home, men who hadn't so far heeded the call-up were being tracked down with the aid of the electoral register, and thrown head-first either into combat or into prison, there to await court martial and, if found guilty, the firing squad. And that one upstairs was nearly out of his mind with fear. As well he might be.

There were plenty of conchies hiding behind closed doors, protected by loving wives and mothers, but they, like her husband, couldn't hide for ever. It was only a matter of time before Alfie's name came up on the electoral register and, when it did, the police would come knocking on their door.

And when that day came Nellie would cheer. Yes, she would. She'd hang out the flags and dance in the street as they carted him away.

Closing her eyes she prayed that day would come soon, for she didn't know how much more she could take. A deep sigh came from her parted lips. How much easier it would be if only she could confide in someone. But she had made the decision early on in her marriage to keep her troubles to herself; and especially to shield her children from the truth of what went on in their parents' bedroom.

Nor could she herself turn her husband in to the authorities. Oh, she'd thought about it the moment the new conscription laws came into force. She'd gone so far as to walk down to the police station in Mare Street, but once outside the imposing building her courage had deserted her. She knew, too, that there were many women in the street – women whose husbands and sons were away fighting in France – who would be only too eager to do the job for her, and were just waiting for her to give them the word. But she couldn't do it. She wanted Alfie gone, prayed for him to be gone. And though she knew she would be fully justified in getting rid of her husband in any way she could, Nellie's conscience would never give her any peace if she had a hand in his arrest . . . and maybe in his life, if he was sent overseas.

A sudden movement upstairs brought her out of her day-dreams. Oh, God! He should have slept for at least another hour. Nibbling at the corner of her bottom lip, she wondered whether to make a dash for it or stay and face him. She had a cleaning job in Morning Lane to go to, but that wouldn't make any difference to him if he came down and found her gone and no breakfast waiting for him.

Hating herself for her cowardice, she quickly laid the table, wincing painfully and holding her side where her husband's boot had found its mark the previous night. The sound of his heavy boots crashing across the floorboards above galvanised her into action. He was always hungry when he woke up, and these days, with the threat of conscription hanging over him, the slightest thing would set him off into a murderous rage. Agitated now, she ran back into the scullery and quickly put a large copper pan on top of the hob, put a dollop of dripping into its cavernous depth and took two sausages from the larder, together with two eggs, courtesy of Mrs Riley, who kept three chickens in her back yard four doors away.

Frantic with haste, Nellie broke one of the eggs, tears filling her eyes as the bright yellow yolk mingled and spread over the sizzling egg white, but there was nothing she could do; these were the last two eggs in the house.

The pounding footsteps were coming closer, then the back door banged noisily as her husband made his way to the outside toilet. Almost frantic with haste, she sliced two thick pieces from a crusty loaf, smothered them with marge, poured out a mug of strong tea, placed the eggs and sausages on a tray and carried it into the parlour, laying it down carefully on the freshly starched table-cloth, her heart hammering with every trembling action.

'What's this?' The gruff, angry tone brought Nellie's heart leaping up to her throat. 'You've broken me bleeding egg, yer stupid cow.'

Backing away, Nellie clutched at her neck, as if for support.

'I'm sorry, Alf. I . . . I didn't expect you up so soon. I was in a hurry to get your breakfast ready so you wouldn't have to wait . . . Look, if you like, I'll go and see if I can get another egg off of Mrs Riley . . .' Her voice faltered at the murderous glare in her husband's bloodshot eyes.

'Shut yer gob an' leave me in peace,' the loud roar silenced any further effort on Nellie's part to placate him. For the next few minutes, the only sound in the room was that of loud slurping and belching as Alfie Ford consumed his meal with gusto. With a final stomach-churning belch, he pushed back his chair, rubbed his ample belly and surveyed the woman standing before him. Christ! What a bleeding mess. Look at the state of her. The skinny, haggard woman, wearing a shapeless grey dress that hung on her slim body, her brown hair scraped back into a scraggly bun, bore no resemblance to the pretty, shapely young girl he had married all those years ago; she looked old enough to be his mother. Disgusted by the sight of her, he turned his gaze away and said roughly, 'Well, don't just stand there staring at me like a bleeding idiot, go down ter the corner shop an' get me five Woodbines. I'm gasping fer a fag.'

Taking the dirty plate from the table, Nellie stuttered nervously, 'I'm sorry, love, I haven't any money till I finish my cleaning job today. I could fetch you some on my way home . . .'

The wooden chair went crashing back, upturning on the cracked lino and scattering one of the straw mats. With a swiftness that no longer surprised her, Nellie found herself clutched roughly by the arm.

'Please, Alf, not again. You'll kill me one of these days. I can't take much more, Alf, I can't take much more . . .'

A heavy fist shot out, catching her a violent blow just behind her ear. As her head rocked back on her shoulders, a loud banging came from the other side of the partitioned wall.

'You all right in there, Nellie?' her neighbour, Dot Button, shouted through the thin wall. The strident voice caused Alf to drop his arm. He had to be careful, he wasn't liked around these parts, especially by the women whose men were away fighting. They would think nothing of shopping him to the local police if Nellie gave the word, especially that old cow next door. She never missed an opportunity to remind Alf that her precious husband Jack, who was older than Alfie, and her son Bert had joined up without any prompting from anyone. More fool them, he thought viciously. Though if he was married to that harridan next door, he might be tempted to join up himself. He smiled grimly at his sudden flash of humour, the smile slipping almost at once as he thought of Emily's forthcoming visit.

With his daughter living at home for three weeks, he was going to have to be on his best behaviour, because his Emily wouldn't stand for any nonsense. Even as he fretted about the long days ahead, he couldn't help feel a surge of pride in his daughter's fiery temper and strong character. If only his wife displayed some of the same attributes, he would respect her a lot more. As it was, she was easy prey . . . Yet even mice could turn, if goaded sufficiently. Reminded of his precarious position, Alf let go of the slim form. Yet, even knowing the power she had over him, he couldn't resist giving her a brutal push that sent the unfortunate woman crashing awkwardly against the corner of the heavy table.

'Yer keep yer mouth shut, understand,' he hissed viciously. 'What goes on between me an' you is private. It's family business, nothing ter do with anyone else. One word outta yer to that nosy cow next door, an' I'll do fer yer.' Picking up his heavy jacket from where he'd flung it over the back of his chair, he thrust his arms into the sleeves and buttoned it up over his shirt and braces, all the while keeping his eyes on the still figure sprawled on the floor.

Snatching his cap from the peg on the back of the door, Alf wrenched the door open and stormed out into the cobbled street, just as Dot Button was coming out of the adjoining house. The stout woman barred his way, her black eyes filled with animosity.

Hugging her woollen shawl tighter around her ample curves, she sneered, 'Think yer a big man, don't yer, Alfie Ford. Well, it doesn't take much ter knock seven bells outta a defenceless woman, yer bleeding coward.'

'Get outta me way, yer old cow, an' keep yer nose outta my business. Besides, I ain't touched 'er. Yer can ask 'er if yer like . . .' The burly man tried to push past the obstacle in his way and found himself being shoved backwards. Taken by surprise, he stumbled, his heart jumping in sudden fear at the prospect of falling flat on his face in the street. Already curtains were twitching behind the windows of the long row of terraced houses. Another few minutes and the whole street would be out in force.

'Don't give me that load of old cobblers, I know what's going on . . . Yeah, that's right, yer get yerself off, yer miserable bastard.' Dot's voice echoed after him. 'An' if yer know what's good fer yer, yer keep yer hands off poor Nellie, or the next person yer try it on wiv'll have a bayonet pointing at yer belly.'

Bursting with rage, Alfie Ford had no option but to walk off with as much dignity as he could muster, but there was no escaping Dot's strident voice.

'Yer should be over there with the rest of the men, like my Bert an' Jack. They're real men, they are, not jumped-up little piss-pots like you.'

Alf walked on, his heavy boots crunching over the cobbled pavement, his whole being seething with rage at the scathing words, while his frantic mind tried to find a way out of his predicament.

That his days were numbered he had no doubt. Because, if the police didn't track him down, then one of those bitches in the street would shop him soon. It was a wonder they hadn't done so already. Beads of sweat broke out on his face and neck at the prospect of going to war. He had read about the fighting in the trenches, and the poison gas that the Germans were now using. But it was that crack about facing someone armed with a bayonet that caused his very bones to turn to jelly. If only the new conscription law had stopped at forty, he would have been safe. As it was, he still had a good eighteen months before his forty-first birthday. There was no way he could hide for that amount of time. Tears of anger and fear stung his eyelids. Bugger that bloody Kaiser and his army, which was dug in so deep in the trenches that it would need a miracle to blast them out. Taking off his cap, he nervously ran his fingers through his greasy, thick black hair.

Soon he would be forced to choose between prison or joining up, and from what he'd heard about the way

13

conchies were treated by their fellow prisoners, he'd be better off in the trenches.

Once at the end of Wick Road he gazed with longing at the Tiger on the corner of Sydney Street. The pub wasn't open yet, and even if it had been, he couldn't have gone in. But he stayed where he was, his eyes fastened on the stout, closed door. He needed a drink, needed one badly, but he hadn't a penny to his name. Rubbing a hand over his stubbled chin, he was about to wander off, when he saw a tall, thin man coming out of St Mary's and St Dominic's Church, which was adjacent to the pub. Alf's face broke into a smile of greeting as he recognised Freddie Little, an out-of-work painter from the next street.

Keeping the smile pasted to his lips, Alf waited until Freddie came abreast of him, studiously ignoring the look of alarm that leapt to the other man's face.

'Freddie, me old mate, 'ow are yer.'

'All right, Alfie,' the man answered, while trying to walk on.

''Ere, 'ere, what's this, not got time fer one of yer mates, Fred.'

Knowing himself to be trapped, Fred Little groaned under his breath. Alfie Ford was no friend of his, or anyone else's for that matter. Their only claim to friendship was the fact that they had both so far dodged the call-up. But not any longer. Fred had had enough of hiding, and of putting up with the scathing comments that were hurled at him every time he stepped out of doors, and he had just come back from the recruiting office. Even there he had been met with ill-concealed contempt.

'Took yer time, didn't yer,' the sergeant had said derisively. 'What happened, given up hoping it'll all be over before yer was dragged in?'

Still, Fred had done it now, and curiously enough the relief he felt was overcoming his fear of the trenches. He had popped into the church for a few minutes, just to say a prayer or two for moral support, but now he was wishing he hadn't bothered. If he'd gone straight home he wouldn't have run into Alfie Ford.

Two women passed by, their eyes accusing.

'Lost somefink, 'ave yer, mate,' one of them sneered.

'Perhaps you'd better go down ter the 'ospital an' see if they've got any backbones going spare.'

Casting a malevolent glare at the women, a look that was returned with a vengeance, Alf grabbed the smaller man and steered him towards the pub. Keeping a vice-like grip on the silent painter's arm, Alfie kept up a stream of idle chatter to keep Fred occupied until the pub opened its doors.

Fred offered no resistance. After all, he told himself, it would be the last time Alfie Ford would be able to get a free drink out of him.

CHAPTER TWO

''Ere, drink this, it'll make yer feel better.' Dot held a mug of steaming tea to Nellie's trembling lips. 'Gawd help us, Nellie, why don't yer shop him, or if yer don't want ter do it, there's plenty round here who'll do it fer yer, me included.'

Weakly Nellie shook her head, much to the frustration of her neighbour. 'I can't, Dot,' she said quietly. 'He's my husband, when all's said and done, and I can't turn him in to the authorities. Besides . . .' she added lamely, 'he's not always like this . . .' Her voice trailed off miserably as she realised how inane her words sounded.

Dot stared at her friend, then blew her cheeks out in exasperation. She couldn't for the life of her understand why Nellie refused to talk about her troubles, even going so far as to deny there was a problem, when the whole street knew what was going on. Knowing it was useless to pursue the conversation, Dot slurped noisily at her mug of tea and asked, 'When's yer Emily coming 'ome?'

At the mention of her daughter's name, Nellie's face broke into a smile.

'This afternoon, probably about two. Oh, Dot . . .' she sighed heavily, 'I really miss her, but she's better off where she is. The Winters are a nice old couple, and kind with it. Miss Rose is always giving Emily her old clothes. Well, I say old, but some of the stuff is almost brand-new, hardly been worn some of it. And Mr Winter is always giving her books to read. Good books too, not those dreadful, cheap novelettes you can buy for a penny, but Dickens, Thackeray and Tolstoy – all the books I read as a child, but I never thought Emily would have the chance to read them. Dot, about Emily coming home . . .' Nellie hesitated for a moment before carrying on. 'The thing is, she doesn't know about my problems, and I'd rather she didn't find out. She's already talking about leaving the Winters and coming back home for good, and . . . and as much as I'd love to have her by me every day, well, like I said before, she's better off where she is.'

Nellie's anxious eyes strayed to the stout woman, as if begging her to agree, and Dot, a loyal friend for nearly twenty years, forced a smile to her lips and replied gently, 'I know what yer mean, Nell, I know what yer mean.'

Inwardly, despite her soothing words, Dot was seething. That bit about the books had brought it home to Dot just how different their upbringing had been. She, like most of the women in the street, had attended the local school, but Nellie had been taught in a convent school. She wasn't one for confidences or gossip, but she had told Dot about her parents dying when she was very young and being brought up by two maiden aunts. The women had been Catholics, hence the convent-school education.

When the Fords had first moved into number fifteen, everyone had taken to the young, affable cockney man, while steering clear of his quiet, well-spoken wife. A lot of the women had unfairly classed Nellie as being stuck-up, declaring that she wouldn't last long around these parts. But they had been proved wrong. In all the years Dot had known her, Nellie had never tried to lord it over anyone in the street – not like some, she thought darkly, like Ida Wilson at number nine, before her thoughts returned to Nellie. In fact today, by mentioning the books, was the first time in a long while that Nellie had referred to her background. It was funny, really, how both Nellie and Emily spoke so nicely, while Lenny was a true cockney, just like his father. Though that was the only thing that father and son had in common.

Still, it wasn't to be wondered at. Emily had been with the Winters since she was fourteen, while Lenny had been brought up with the market traders in the East End. Draining her mug, Dot looked with pity at her friend. She looked worn out, poor cow, but what woman wouldn't be, married to that pig of a man?

Alfie Ford wasn't one of your usual wife-batterers – at least those sods were open about what they did. No, Nellie's husband did it on the sly, when there were no witnesses to his brutality. The vicious bastard always made sure he didn't mark Nellie where it could be seen. And though Dot herself had never actually seen any bruising, she'd heard enough over the years through the thin terrace walls to know that her friend was being abused, and she'd made sure the rest of the neighbours knew too. She'd like to bet that beneath her clothes Nellie was black and blue. But what could Dot do about it? If only Emily would come home for good, that would put a stop to the beatings. For the nineteen-year-old girl would never put up with her father's brutal treatment towards her mother. And poor Lenny, bless him, didn't seem to have a clue about what was going on, though

Dot sometimes thought that he wasn't quite as simple as Nellie imagined.

Any further speculation was cut short as the front door banged open to emit a smiling young man, his arms filled with a large cardboard box from which the browning stalks of an overripe cabbage was hanging. At the sight of his mother and neighbour sitting so quietly by the roaring fire, Lenny Ford came to an abrupt halt, the smile sliding from his open, handsome face. At seventeen, he was a tall young man, his body, like his father's, thickset and muscular, but here the similarity ended. There was a gentleness about Lenny that was completely lacking in his father. Now, looking at the surprised faces of the two women at his entrance, his lips began to tremble as the familiar feeling of inadequacy hit him like a physical blow. Slowly lowering his precious gift onto the table, he turned to the two women and said in a trembling voice, 'He's hit you again, ain't he, Mum?'

Immediately, all her pain was forgotten as a wealth of emotion rose in Nellie's breast at the sight of her son's distress. How long had he known what was going on? Dear Lord, what could she say to take that look of pain and helplessness from his eyes? Putting aside all other thoughts but her son, she came towards him briskly, saying, 'Don't be silly, Lenny, nobody's hit me. Whatever put that idea into your head?' Her eyes held his anguished gaze steadily.

Behind her she could sense Dot fidgeting angrily in the chair, clearly bursting to refute the outrageous lie. Ignoring her friend's agitated state, Nellie walked towards the table. Picking out the mouldering cabbage, she lifted up two large oranges, also the worse for wear, and peered in obvious delight into the interior of the box.

'Oh, Lenny, you clever boy. You must have worked hard this morning to get this much.' Glancing over to where Dot was still glowering, she called out cheerfully, 'Look, Dot, look what Lenny's brought home for us. There's oranges and some apples. Oh, and see here, there must be about three pounds of potatoes at the bottom of the box.' Beaming up at her son, she touched his arm lovingly.

'You're a good lad, Lenny. Now, why don't you go upstairs and have a little nap. You must be tired, you've been up since five. I'll bring you up a mug of tea and a sandwich before I leave for work.'

His face dejected, Lenny pulled his arm away, all his earlier happiness evaporating. Walking slowly over to the door, he hung his cap on one of the four pegs, together with his jacket, and then, his face set, he said stiffly, 'I might be a bit slow in the head, Mum, but I ain't stupid.' Before Nellie could respond, Lenny turned his head towards Dot and said, 'He did, didn't he, Mrs Button. Me dad's been getting at her again, ain't he?'

Disconcerted by his straight talking, Dot was momentarily lost for words. But not for long. Gathering up her shawl from where it had fallen to the back of the chair, she eased herself to her feet and looked the young man straight in the eyes.

'Yer know, Lenny, I've always said yer wasn't as daft as people make out. Now I know I was right. An', yes, yer dad's been at yer mum again, the bleeding swine . . . An' it's no use yer trying ter shut me up, Nellie Ford,' she shot out fiercely as Nellie made to interrupt. 'The lad's got a right ter know what's going on in his own house.' When Nellie continued to stare at her with mournful eyes, Dot became uncomfortable, but she wasn't sorry for speaking out. Someone had to look out for Nellie, because she wouldn't do it for herself.

Hugging the shawl tighter around her shoulders, she

determined to say one last thing before leaving. Addressing herself to the tall young man, she said firmly, 'Now look here, Lenny. Your Emily's coming home today. You tell her what's been going on, an' between the two of yer, yer should be able ter help yer poor old mum, 'cos I tell yer this. If someone don't stop that pig of a father of yours, he's gonna end up doing yer mum some serious damage one of these days.'

Still neither Lenny nor Nellie made any reply, both of them feeling out of their depth at the unexpected confrontation forced upon them by their determined neighbour. When the front door had banged shut and they were alone, Lenny slumped into the armchair, his face contorting as his immature mind tried to grapple with the problem that had been thrust into his lap. Watching him, Nellie had to restrain herself from pulling him into her arms, much as she had done when he was a small boy. In spite of his bulk, he was still that same boy, despite his desperate attempts to act like a grown man. He had even gone so far as to beg her to let him join up, as if, by putting on a uniform, he would magically be transformed into the man he craved to be. Oh, the times he had come home nearly in tears because someone who didn't know him had called out after him in the street, cruelly deriding him for being safely tucked away at home, and he, poor soul, had been unable to defend himself. Aware that she was becoming maudlin, and suddenly remembering the job waiting for her, Nellie said briskly, 'I've got a cleaning job to go to, Lenny. I'm late enough as it is. Now look, you get yourself up to bed while I fix you something to eat. And don't worry about what Mrs Button said, she's only being over-protective. She's a good friend, is Dot, none better, but she's a habit of poking her nose into other people's business. Go on now, get yourself up the stairs . . .'

'Mum, you can't go on letting him treat you like this . . .'

Angry now, Nellie whirled on him.

'That's enough, Lenny. I don't want to hear any more about it. Now then, Emily should be here about two, and with a bit of luck I'll be back home before her. And listen, Lenny,' she took hold of his hands firmly, 'not a word about what Mrs Button said. Do you understand me, son? Not a word; promise me.'

His eyelids flickering rapidly, his shoulders hunched in defeat, Lenny shook his hands free and made for the stairs. Mrs Button was right. Someone had to help his mum, and he couldn't do it, but Emily would know what to do. Emily wasn't afraid of anyone, least of all their dad, whereas he . . . Tears of shame stung at his eyes as he climbed the wooden stairs to the small bedroom he had shared with his sister, until Nellie had decided they were getting too old to share the same bed and had bought a second-hand truckle-bed from the market. How he and Emily had fought over who would keep the bedroom, but it had been Lenny, always the first to capitulate in an argument, who had ended up sleeping on the rickety bed in the farthest corner of the living-room. Which was the safest place to be, with his father coming home stinking drunk at all hours of the night, cursing and shouting as he crashed and bumped his body against the furniture in the darkened room, while the young boy huddled further down under the threadbare blankets, praying that he would escape his father's attention, until his mother came down and helped the belligerent, staggering figure up the stairs.

He had been so excited when Emily had told him that she was going into service. All he could think of at the time was that he would at last have a room to himself. But, like most things in life, the reality was rather different from the day-dream. For a start, he hadn't realised that he would miss his older sister so much. The small house had seemed even smaller without Emily's presence, and what little laughter there had been in the fraught atmosphere of his home had disappeared completely the moment Emily left it. Then there were the noises and muffled arguments coming through the paper-thin wall of his parents' bedroom every night, always ending with the sound of a hand or fist connecting with bare flesh, and then silence.

The first time he had run away, Lenny had been caught by the local bobby and hauled back home. That escapade had earnt him a thrashing from his irate father, and it was only the intervention of his mother and Mrs Button that had saved him from serious injury.

The next time he had left home, he had been more careful, keeping a watchful eye out for the sight of a blue uniform. For three days he had wandered the streets, picking up a few pennies from stall-holders and shop-keepers by running errands, and curling up on a bench in Victoria Park at night, until guilt at knowing how his mother would be worrying, plus an empty belly and stiff joints from sleeping rough, had driven him home again. That time his father had merely given him a hefty clout round the head, which had knocked him off his feet and halfway across the room, before the burly figure had stomped off down to the pub.

Over the years there had been many more occasions when the young boy, unable to cope with the tension and the presence of the surly brute who was his father, had packed a few things into a carrier bag and taken off without a word. He soon became quite adept at looking after himself. During the day he would find a few hours' work at one of the various markets, and at night there were plenty of run-down hostels where you could get a bed for a couple of coppers – that is, if you weren't too fussy about the company, or the filthy mattresses strewn around the hard, dirty floors. For an extra penny, you could get a lumpy pillow and a moth-eaten blanket, but Lenny never bothered with those so-called luxuries. Inevitably, though, the novelty would wear off and he would start to miss his mother, so back home he would go, until the next time.

But he couldn't spend the rest of his life running away every time things got too much for him to cope with. He was a man now . . . But that was the trouble – he wasn't a man, he would never be a man, not in the proper sense of the word.

Slumping onto the single brass bed, Lenny stared down at his hands, his whole body churning with emotion. It wasn't fair. Why was he like this? He had tried to act like an adult – nobody would ever know just how hard he had tried – but he just couldn't do it. His sister was the one who possessed all the courage and gumption that were lacking in himself. He knew it, everyone in the street knew it. Brushing back a lock of fair hair from his eyes, he looked at the open door. Down below he could hear his mother bustling around the scullery preparing something for him to eat before she went out. In his mind he pictured his father's big fists punching that frail, defenceless body and he shuddered. He hated him . . . hated his dad with a force that frightened him. And yet, sometimes, when he was in a good mood, his dad was kind, and then Lenny loved him. Confused and tired, he tried to grapple with his tortured emotions. You couldn't love someone and hate them as well, could you? Wearily he shook his head. There was nothing he could do at the moment. He'd just have to wait until Emily came home. Emily would take charge . . . Emily always took charge. A sudden thought came to him, bringing his back up straight. He could go and meet her from the house where she worked. He knew the way. He'd been there on several occasions, when he'd helped out in the gardens for a couple of bob. A smile lit up his face. That's what he'd do. As soon as his mum left for work, he would go and meet his sister and tell her what was going on. Like Mrs Button said, someone had to look after their mum. Excited now that he was going to do something positive, he waited until Nellie had brought him a sandwich and a mug of tea. Gulping down the last dregs from the mug, he finished off the cheese sandwich and laid down on his bed, his ears pricked for the sound of his mother's departure. In his mind he went over the quickest route to his sister's place of employment.

If he cut through the back turnings and across Victoria Park, he could reach Gore Road in about twenty minutes. Comforted by his plan, his eyes began to flicker with tiredness and, somewhere between listening for the front door to bang shut and working out what he was going to say to his sister, he fell into a deep sleep.

CHAPTER THREE

'Emily, Emily, Miss Rose is calling for you.' The small girl dressed in a plain grey dress, over which rested a starched white pinafore, raced down the narrow hallway, almost knocking over the tall young woman who was crossing the hall, her arms full of freshly ironed linen.

'For goodness sake, Mary, you nearly had me over. Look where you're going in future, and stop your shouting. I've told you before about that.'

The small girl tossed back her head defiantly, her pert face taking on a look of resentment.

'Well, it won't matter after today, will it? This is me last day here, an' I won't be sorry to see the back of this place. There's loads of work going, now the men are away fighting. I can easily get a job in one of the factories, and it'll pay more than the measly few bob I get here.'

Trying hard to hang on to her temper, Emily Ford hugged the laundry closer to her chest and replied harshly, 'Well, you haven't finished here yet. And if you want your wages, you'd better get on with your work. There's still the drawing-room and bedrooms to clean before the dust-sheets go over the furniture, so you'd best get on with it, unless you want to stay on after your time.' Mary Dawkins, maid to the Winters since she'd left school, flounced off down the corridor.

Emily watched her go, her expression thoughtful, before leaving the hallway, her steps taking her towards the room known as the Study. Turning her back to the brown mahogany door, she knocked it open with a swift thrust of her buttocks and entered the room.

It was a large, airy room and Emily's favourite, for it overlooked the long, winding garden and the small orchard at the back of the three-storey house. At this time of year, with winter beginning to set in, the trees were bare, as were the rows of flower beds. But in the late summer months, when the trees were heavily laden with apples and plums, and the flower beds were bursting with a riotous assortment of colours, Emily would open the wide, glass doors and drink in the fresh sights and smells of nature at its very best. And always she would find herself wishing that her mother and Lenny could be here with her. The only view from the back to-back terraced house in Fenton Street was of their neighbour's yard backing onto their own.

Walking swiftly, she crossed the room and laid the sheets and linen on the corner of the long window-seat adjacent to the patio doors, intending to sort the laundry into individual piles.

Instead, she eased herself onto the plush red upholstery and, resting her arm on the windowsill, gazed out over the barren garden. She shouldn't have gone for Mary like that, especially knowing it was her last day. But that was the exact reason why she had spoken so harshly to the younger girl. Sighing softly, Emily cupped her chin in her palm. She wished this was *her* last day. It wasn't that she was unhappy here. Both Mr Winter and his sister Rose had always been very kind to her, but after nearly six years in service Emily was restless, and a little resentful. She was supposed to have a half-day off a week, and one whole day every fortnight, yet today would be the first time she had been home in two months.

She was very fond of her employers, but sometimes she felt they were taking advantage of her good nature. Miss Rose in particular had become very clinging during the past year. The elderly woman was terrified that a bomb would drop on the house. She jumped at every loud noise, and many a night Emily had had to leave her bed to sit with the frightened woman until she fell asleep. It was because of his sister's fears that Mr Winter was shutting up the house for a few weeks. But who could tell if they would return at the end of the month? If Miss Rose got herself settled comfortably at her cousin's house in Surrey, then Emily's employers might well decide to remain there until the war ended; and by the looks of it, that could be years away. Stifling a yawn, Emily found herself hoping that the elderly couple would stay on at the Surrey house. That way she would be set free without feeling guilty about leaving them.

Turning her head slightly, she looked over her shoulder at the grandfather clock in the corner of the room. It was ten-thirty already, and she had a dozen things to see to before the house was shut up for the duration of its owners' absence. And, according to Mary, Miss Rose was asking for her, even though Emily had only left her a short while ago. And it wasn't only Miss Rose who was constantly taking up her time. Mr Winter, too, seemed to be depending on her more and more these past few months. If someone were to ask her to define her job now, she would be hard-pressed to give an answer. When she had first started at the house, it had been as a maid of all work. Back then there had been two other maids, a cook and a housekeeper to run the household. The cook had left three years ago, having found herself a more lucrative position, and Emily, then sixteen, had been asked to take over her duties until the post could be filled. Eager to please, she had made such a good job of the cooking that somehow the post of cook had become hers, without the extra wages to go with it.

Mrs Banks, the housekeeper, had been the next to leave, her departure rather hasty, after a heated altercation with Mr Winter. Emily had never found out what the row had been about, and she hadn't even realised she was slipping into the woman's shoes and taking on her duties as well. It had just sort of happened. Then last year Betty, the under-housemaid, had upped and left and was now, so Emily had heard, working as a bus conductress. Like the other servants, Betty hadn't been replaced although, to be fair to the Winters, they had advertised the post in the *Hackney Gazette*, but so far there had been no replies. Nor would there be, not with the way things stood at the moment, with factories and businesses crying out for women to take the men's place on the work front.

Now Mary was leaving too, and if the Winters did stick to their plans and return at the end of the month, Emily would find herself running the house single-handed. Which would please her mother no end, for Nellie was inordinately proud of her daughter's rise in status. The fact that Emily had only been given a five-shilling rise to compensate for the extra work didn't seem to matter to Nellie. Emily had broached the subject of getting more help with Mr Winter, but each time she was told that the matter was in hand, and there it seemed set to remain. She heartily wished that her employers weren't so kind, because then she would have been able to hand in her resignation with a clear conscience. But as things stood, and feeling a genuine affection for them both, she found herself bound by loyalty and obligation to stay with them for as long as they needed her.

Then there was her mother to think of, who seemed desperate to have Emily remain where she was. Thoughts of her mother brought a worried frown to Emily's face.

In spite of assurances to the contrary, Emily knew things weren't right at home. Her dad was up to his old tricks again, she was sure of it. Shaking her head slowly, she thought back over the years before she had come here, her eyes hardening as she recalled the strange noises coming from her parents' room during the night. Once, nearly out of her mind with fear, she had banged on the wall, shouting at her dad to leave her mum alone. It had gone eerily silent, but the noises had stopped. She never heard them again, but every morning she would come downstairs, holding a bleary-eyed Lenny by the hand, not knowing what to expect, and there would be her mother, standing in the scullery or laying the table for breakfast, a smile on her face as she pulled her children against her stomach for a morning cuddle.

As the memories became clearer, Emily's blue eyes misted over. It was a ludicrous situation. Everyone in the street knew what was going on, yet the subject was never discussed. Nor would it be, while her mother continued to shield the man who had systematically beaten her for years. If only her mother would confide in her, bring the whole sorry business out into the open, then Emily would be able to do something positive. Still, she comforted herself, her mother would be safe for the next few weeks at least, and during that time maybe, just maybe, she could talk some sense into her. It would be easy enough to find somewhere else to live for Nellie and Lenny, and if need be she, Emily, would leave this lovely house and move back in with her family. As much as she felt obligated to the Winters, if it came down to a choice between them and her mother . . . Well, there wasn't any choice, was there?

Aware that time was getting on, she moved restlessly. Oh dear, she really must get a move on. The quicker she was finished, the sooner she could get home. But it was so comfortable sitting here in the quietness of the room, looking out over the garden.

It was another twenty minutes before she picked up the laundry once again and made her way across the landing and up the two flights of stairs that led to Miss Rose's room.

'Ah, there you are, Emily,' Rose Winter said querulously. 'Didn't Mary give you my message?' The elderly woman was seated on a padded chair, looking at Emily through the reflection in the gilt-edged mirror of her ornate dressing-table. Turning around, she tilted her head a little in order to look up at the attractive face that she was so fond of. Emily was wearing a plain navy dress with narrow white frills at the neck and cuffs, the latter having been added by Emily herself to relieve the severity of the dress that was also her uniform. Her chestnut hair was plaited and pinned to the back of her head, but as always tiny tendrils of hair had escaped the grips and lay in soft wisps on her forehead and cheeks. Rose Winter never tired of looking at the lovely face, with its large blue eyes and the smattering of freckles across the bridge of the pert nose. Today, though, she was feeling her age, and the affection she felt was tinged with envy. Envy and a sense of desolation for her own youth, which was gone for ever.

Aware of the scrutiny, and striving to keep her voice even, Emily replied quietly, 'Yes, she did, Miss Rose, but as you know there's a lot to be done before you and Mr Winter leave.' She would have liked to add, 'And only me to see to it all, because Mary is neither use nor ornament today,' but instead she said, 'I came as soon as I could.'

'Yes, yes, I know you're busy, dear.' The sharp blue eyes beneath the mass of white hair stared up at Emily. Rose Winter was entering her seventieth year, and although she was often to be heard declaring that she would soon be 'pushing up the daisies', she was going to remarkable lengths to ensure that she didn't meet her maker just yet. And when her time came, she wanted to go peacefully in her sleep, not blown to smithereens by a bomb. Just thinking about the danger brought a tremor to her bones. The sooner she was out of London and installed in her cousin's house in Surrey, the safer she would feel.

Giving herself a mental shake, she tried to remember why she had sent for Emily, her memory failing her for a moment. Then, as comprehension dawned, a thin smile came to her lips.

'Has Matthew arrived yet, dear? He said in his letter he would be here about eleven. Oh dear, you don't think something might have happened to delay his coming, do you?'

Seeing the old woman's plight, Emily felt her irritation fading. The poor soul was so frightened of being hit by a flying bomb that she was in grave danger of dying from a self-induced heart attack.

Taking hold of the trembling hands in hers, Emily said soothingly, 'Now then, Miss Rose, you know Captain Winter will be here as soon as he can. Besides, it isn't quite eleven yet. Why don't I get Mary to make you a cup of tea while you're waiting. It'll settle your nerves.'

The white head bobbed in agitation. 'Yes, yes, that's a good idea. Oh dear, I'm sorry, Emily, you must be eager to get home. I'm sure your mother is anxious to see you, though how we'll manage without you for three whole weeks I don't know, I'm sure. Now, have you remembered that Captain Winter will be staying here during his leave?' Without waiting for an answer she hurried on, 'Once he drops us at Victoria Station he will be coming straight back here, so you can hand over the keys to him. I don't know as yet how long he will be staying, but I shall remind him to drop the keys in on you at your home before he leaves, so that you can open up the house in time for our return.'

Her eyelids fluttered nervously. 'Dear me, Emily, this terrible war, I do so worry about Matthew. He's the only child of our dear brother . . . You remember me telling you about him, don't you, Emily?' When Emily nodded, the elderly woman carried on, 'He was killed at Khartoum when Matthew was five. My poor sister-in-law never got over his death. I think she only clung to life for the sake of Matthew, because once he reached adulthood she simply gave up on life. Poor Matthew was quite lost for a while. We were so pleased when he married, such a lovely woman she was. George and I were terribly upset when she died, and Matthew was devastated. We feared for his sanity at the time. But, as they say, time heals all . . . Though I'm not convinced of that particular piece of logic.'

Emily watched the wrinkled eyelids flutter, then close, and for a moment she thought Miss Rose had fallen asleep. She was about to leave the room quietly when the quivering voice halted her.

'Oh, I nearly forgot, there's a parcel for you . . . over there on the bed. No opening it, though, until you get home. It's a surprise.'

Emily looked over at the four-poster bed and the bulky parcel that lay on the quilted eiderdown, her heart sinking rapidly as she realised that, once again, yet another inducement had been made to keep her here. Maybe she was being unfair and the gift was being offered simply out of kindness, but she couldn't help wondering if they knew what had been on her mind for the last few months.

It seemed that every time she plucked up the courage to speak out, one of them would either praise her or give her yet another gift, while telling her how they couldn't manage without her.

Taking the parcel, which Emily surmised contained more items of clothing from the trunk in the attic where Miss Rose kept her old clothes, she smiled.

'Thank you, Miss Rose, but you mustn't keep giving me presents. It's not as if I work for nothing.'

The old lady waved her hand dismissively. 'Tush, there, child. I'm only too well aware that the money George and I pay you is nowhere near what you could earn in one of the factories, especially now, when so many of our poor young men are away fighting. Still, there's no shortage of women waiting to step into their shoes, though it'll be a different story when the war is over and the men come back home. The government may be grateful now, but they won't let the women keep jobs that rightly belong to the men. Oh, don't pay me any attention, dear. I know you're far too sensible to consider such an action. You run along now, and see George and collect your wages.'

Was there a warning in the lightly spoken words, Emily wondered, and for a moment she experienced a flash of anger. Then she looked into the faded blue eyes and saw the uncertainty mirrored there, and once again she relented. After all, she reasoned to herself as she hurried out into the long hallway, there was no point in upsetting Miss Rose now, when the problem could well resolve itself. She would wait until the end of the month to see how things lay, and in the meantime she would make the most of her unexpected holiday, for she wasn't likely to get another chance of three weeks' paid leave. And while she was home she would see how the land lay between her parents. Her dad might be able to put on a front for her usual few hours' visit, but he'd be hard-pressed to keep it up for three whole weeks. Placing her bundle on the hall side-table, she ran lightly up the two flights of stairs to the large den where George Winter spent most of his time.

Knocking once on the heavy panelled door, she heard a gruff voice bidding her to enter and twisted the carved doorknob. This room, like the Study, was large and airy with a high, embossed ceiling. Around the walls stood solid book shelves, each of them crammed to overflowing with an assortment of books, some lying flat, some stacked neatly and others left open, their binders splayed untidily where they had been put down at an open page and forgotten. At the far end of the room rested an enormous oak desk, also covered with a multitude of books, and sitting behind the disordered array sat her employer – his face, like his sister's, smiling fondly at her as she made her entrance.

'Ah, there you are, my dear. I was just about to ring down for you.' George Winter was a man of stocky build, with kindly blue eyes and a shock of grey hair that was for ever falling over his forehead and obliterating his view of his beloved books.

Getting to his feet, he came round the side of the desk and took her hands warmly, repeating the words his sister had uttered just a few minutes before. 'Whatever will we do without you, Emily? I only wish we could take you with us . . . Oh, don't be alarmed,' he laughed merrily at the stricken look that came to her face. 'I've no intention of kidnapping you and dragging you off to the wilds of Surrey. Though if you weren't such charming company, and pretty to boot, we wouldn't be so reluctant to let you out of our sight.'

The clear blue eyes twinkled merrily in the deeply lined face, bringing forth a loud chuckle from Emily's throat.

'Well now, I mustn't keep you talking any longer, my dear. I'm sure you've a dozen things to attend to before you leave.' Pushing aside a small pile of books, he picked up two brown envelopes. One had Emily's name written clearly in George Winter's bold handwriting, the other, intended for Mary, was unmarked. Holding both envelopes out to Emily, he waited while she put the envelopes into the pocket of her skirt and then, clasping his hands behind his back, he walked over to the bay window that overlooked the gardens below. Clearing his throat loudly he said, 'You'll find a month's wages, as promised, also an extra two pounds. The two pounds constitute a rise of ten shillings a week. I only wish it could be more.'

Behind him, Emily stared at the profile of her employer, her hand involuntarily going to the side pocket of her skirt. Oh Lord, this wasn't fair. It was as if the pair of them had the power to read her mind, and were doing everything possible to dissuade her from leaving them.

This was borne out as George Winter added solemnly, 'We . . . that is, my sister and I, realise that you could easily earn twice what we pay you, including the raise. And neither of us would harbour any ill-feeling should you decide to leave our employ. With Mary gone, you will have to run the house single-handed, for I doubt we'll be able to get any help.' He gave a short, nervous laugh. 'It seems as though the days of the servant are over. Or maybe Rose and I have simply outlived our time. Everything has changed so much since the war started, it frightens me at times. Even our monetary system has been altered. Oh, I don't suppose it bothers

36

you over-much if you're paid in silver, sovereigns or paper money, but then you are young, and the young always adapt to change much more quickly and easily than the elderly. But I can't get used to a paper pound, and a paper ten shillings. It just doesn't seem like real money to me.' He shook his head and sighed heavily.

'The world . . . that is, the world that we grew up in, has gone. And I doubt it will ever return; at least, not in our lifetime.'

Emily stood silently, her eyes fixed on the broad back by the window, and again her mind shouted: It's not fair, it's not bloody fair. They were playing on her good nature, and on the genuine affection she felt for them. But even as she silently ranted against the unfairness of the situation, she knew she couldn't just walk out on them. She was bound by her own sense of honour to remain here for as long as she was needed. Not trusting herself to speak, she mumbled a hasty thank you and fled the room. Once out on the landing, she took a deep breath and straightened her shoulders. She was being silly, getting herself worked up into a state. What she had to do was get on with her work, and push everything else to the back of her mind.

There'd be time enough during the next few weeks for her to think about her future. For now she had a job to attend to, and it wasn't going to get done on its own. Giving herself a mental shake, she lifted her head and walked purposefully down the carpeted stairway. The rustle of the two envelopes in her pocket reminded her that she had to give Mary her wages. Then again, she would be wise to hang onto it for a while longer, until Mary had finished the tasks allocated to her before leaving.

Humming quietly, Emily went in search of the young maid.

CHAPTER FOUR

The morning passed swiftly in a whirl of last-minute packing and checking to see if the Winters had everything they needed for their stay in Surrey. Mary had received her wages and left, not even stopping to say her farewells to her employers, nor to Emily, who watched her departure with envious eyes. It was gone twelve o'clock when Emily finally waved the elderly couple, driven by their nephew, off from the front step. And it took another two hours to finish covering the furniture and make sure that the guest room was in order for Captain Winter during his stay.

Tired now, she made her way wearily to her room in the basement. Eyeing the comfortable single bed with its gaily patterned quilt, she resisted the impulse to lie down for a moment's rest. The way she was feeling, she couldn't trust herself not to fall asleep. Opening the single wardrobe, she took out three dresses, four blouses and two skirts, all hand-me-downs from Miss Rose over the years, and laid them carefully in the battered suitcase she had arrived with six years ago. Looking at the expensive clothing brought a spasm of guilt spiralling through her body. With a loud grunt she quickly closed the lid of the suitcase, determined not to give in to sentimentality.

'Damn it,' she spoke aloud to the empty room. 'It's not as if they were given to me out of charity. I've worked bloody hard over the years.' Yet she couldn't quieten her conscience. She wasn't the type to take gifts, no matter how small, as if it were her due. It simply wasn't in her nature.

Grabbing the case, she walked up the small flight of stairs to the first landing, then groaned as she spied the bundle left lying on the hall table. It was too bulky to fit into the small case – she would just have to carry it under her arm. Putting the case down with a thud beside the table, she took her coat off the wooden coat-stand by the door and quickly thrust her arms through the sleeves, then jammed on her felt hat, poking a large hat-pin ruthlessly through the felt and out the other side. Glancing up at the grandfather clock, she saw that it was gone two o'clock and tutted impatiently.

Her mother would be expecting her home any minute, but she couldn't leave until Captain Winter returned to pick up the keys. Though why Mr Winter couldn't have had a spare set of keys made she didn't know.

Impatient to be off, Emily pulled open the heavy front door just as the gleaming black Daimler pulled up at the kerb. A smile of relief lit up her face as she skipped down the three stone steps towards the khaki-dressed figure behind the steering wheel of the motorcar.

'Hello, Emily. I'm sorry I'm late. The traffic was awful, but then it always is at the weekend.' Captain Matthew Winter smiled at the tall young woman. 'I expect you're in a hurry to get home. Are they all your things?' he asked, nodding towards the case at her feet.

'Well, either that or I'm running off with the family heirlooms,' Emily laughed, pointing to the parcel held tightly under her arm. A large grin spread across the man's face, while his grey eyes took in every detail of the face that had become so dear to him. It wasn't a beautiful face, in the conventional sense, yet the deep blue eyes and pert nose set in a face strong with character exuded a beauty that was sometimes overpowering. He could see wisps of chestnut hair beneath the dark green hat and wondered what it would look like left free to fall in waves around the lovely face. She was wearing a fitted coat the same colour as her hat, and it stopped short of her ankles, just skimming the tops of her black-buttoned boots.

'How long are you home for?' The question drew him from his scrutiny and, stepping out of the car, he walked to her side saying ruefully, 'Just a weekend pass, I'm afraid. I rejoin my regiment on Monday.'

'Oh . . . oh, that's a shame,' Emily said, trying to hide her impatience to be off. Her mum would start to worry if she didn't get home soon. 'Well, I'd better get a move on, before my mum sends out a search party for me.' She laughed awkwardly. Aware of his penetrating gaze, she felt her cheeks begin to burn and added hastily, 'Your room is ready, and there's enough food to last you a few days, though you'll have to catch the milkman if you need any milk.' Over his shoulder Emily caught sight of a tall figure running across the park, his arm waving to catch her attention. Seeing Emily's eyes focused behind him, Matthew turned his head, his mouth falling into a smile of welcome as he recognised Emily's brother.

'Hello, Lenny. Have you come to escort your sister home?' he asked kindly. He felt sorry for the young boy trapped in a man's body.

'Hello, Captain Winter.' Lenny grinned at the uniformed man for a minute, before turning to Emily. 'I was going to come earlier, Em, but I fell asleep, only I didn't know I was asleep till I woke up.'

Before Emily could answer, Matthew, his voice choked with amusement said lightly, 'Well now, how would you like a lift home. I'm not doing anything, and I'd be more than happy to drive you both home in comfort.'

At these words, Lenny's face lit up in a picture of pure delight, his blunt features pulling and stretching in anticipation of the treat in store for him.

'Oh, Em . . .' he breathed in wonder. 'Could we? Could we, Em? I've never been in a car before.' His eyes, filled now with longing, looked to his sister for confirmation, fearful that she would turn down the offer of a ride in the gleaming black car. And Emily, seeing the earnest, mute appeal in the clear blue eyes, nodded.

'Thank you, Captain Winter, that's very kind of you. That is, if you're sure you have time.' The words were hardly out of her mouth when, with a whoop of pure delight, Lenny, not wanting to waste a minute, clambered into the motorcar and settled himself comfortably on the long, red leather seat.

Emily looked up at Matthew and laughed. 'It seems he's taking no chances on you changing your mind.' She was about to lift her case, when Matthew also bent down, and for a moment their hands touched. At the feel of his hand on hers, Emily jumped as if she'd been burnt.

Noting her reaction to his innocent touch, Matthew's heart leapt in dismay. Well, what did you expect, man, his inner voice shouted at him. Why, you're old enough to be her father. Yet, when he was near her, he didn't feel his thirty-six years. He had been married for five years when Emily had first come to work at his uncle's house. He had been visiting with his wife when the fourteen-year-old girl had first started work. He could still remember how she had held her head high, determined not to show her nervousness, her eyes as wide as saucers as she'd gazed in wonder at the her new

41

surroundings. Over the years he had watched her grow into a proud, independent woman, but it wasn't until this past year that he had realised his true feelings for her. And the knowledge had both shocked and shamed him. At the time, Mary had been dead only a year and he'd been weighed down with guilt. First, for being disloyal to his wife's memory and, second, for hankering after a girl young enough to be his daughter.

He had carried his tortuous emotions onto the battle-fields in France, not caring if he lived or died. Yet while men dropped in their hundreds around him, he remained standing, unscathed among the bloody carnage, his eyes and ears assailed by the sight and screams of his battalion as they lay already dead, or dying in agony. As their blood had seeped into the French soil, some, merely boys, had called out piteously for their mothers, while he stood helplessly, unable to do anything to alleviate their suffering, and ultimately their deaths. The stark, searing memory was with him still, and would be until the day he died. He still couldn't understand why he had been spared. For the last year he had been stationed away from the field of combat. But on Monday he would be returning to the battlefield; maybe this time he wouldn't be so lucky.

'Are you all right, sir?' Emily's voice jerked him from his reverie.

'Sorry, Emily,' he smiled at her anxious face. 'I was wool-gathering. It must be a sign of old age creeping up on me.'

'Oh, Captain Winter, you're not that old.'

Emily's reassurance wasn't quite what he had hoped for. Still, serve him right for fishing for compliments, he thought ruefully.

As they walked towards the car, Matthew nodded towards the smiling Lenny, who was absorbed with the dashboard of the motorcar, and said softly, 'Has he had any trouble . . . ? I mean, in regard to him not being in uniform. Oh, now then, Emily, don't get on your high horse, I meant no offence,' he said hastily as he sensed the sudden stiffening of the body beside him. 'I realise that the people in your street understand, but to others, who don't know Lenny . . . Well, all they see is a seemingly healthy man who should, in their eyes, be doing his bit for King and country.'

Taking hold of her arm he moved closer, his head bending down towards hers. 'People can be cruel, Emily, especially if they think they have a grievance. I've seen men – good, kind brave men, who, because of their beliefs, refuse to fight, refuse to kill or injure another human being – being taunted and physically abused for their beliefs. Not all conchies are cowards. In fact, many of them are, to my mind, a lot braver than most. For it takes a special courage to stand on one's own against the surging masses.'

Seeing the worried expression in Emily's eyes he straightened up, ran a hand through his short, cropped hair, put his peaked cap squarely on his head and smiled. 'Well now, enough of all this gloom and doom. I'm sorry if I've alarmed you, Emily, I just thought you should be warned. Now then, I've taken up enough of your time for today. We'd better join Lenny before he bursts with impatience.'

On the short journey to Homerton, Emily sat silently, her eyes fixed on the road ahead, while Lenny chatted away excitedly. Matthew's views on conscientious objectors had hit a raw nerve in her. Had he been hinting at her dad's refusal to join up? Almost immediately she dismissed the idea. Captain Winter would never resort to sly innuen-does. Besides, he probably didn't even realise that her dad was now eligible for service. She was just being over-sensitive. Sensitive and ashamed at her father's cowardice. And he *was* a coward; a coward and a bully. Suddenly the prospect of three weeks at home wasn't quite so appealing. She was still brooding when Matthew finally pulled up at the top end of Fenton Street.

Lenny groaned in disappointment.

'Oh, Captain Winter, can we have another ride along the street, please?'

Matthew turned his head to look at the earnest face, his heart going out to the young man. The way things were going with the war, he wouldn't be surprised if Lenny ended up with a rifle thrust into his hands. After all, what did the top brass care about a man's mental ability – it was their bodies they were after. Just more cannon-fodder to feed to the never-ending bombardment of guns.

'Come on, Lenny, and stop pestering Captain Winter.' Emily's voice cut into his thoughts. Dragging the reluctant Lenny out of the car, she turned to Matthew, a smile of gratitude on her lips. 'Thank you, sir, it was very kind of you to drop us home, we're very . . .'

A loud shout from behind Emily brought her head jerking round and a wide grin to her mouth. There, running towards them, her calf-length skirt flying nearly up to her knees, was Doris Mitchell, her friend from childhood.

'Cor, bleeding hell, Em, I've been chasing yer all down Morning Lane. Didn't yer hear me calling yer?'

'Of course I didn't, silly, else I would have answered,' Emily laughed back at her friend. Then, remembering Matthew, who was waiting patiently to be off, she turned to him and said, 'This is Doris, an old friend of mine, Captain Winter. She works in the munitions factory at Woolwich Arsenal.'

Matthew smiled a greeting, his gaze taking in the

bright yellow face and the ginger hair that was protruding from beneath a gaily coloured scarf. It was the task of filling shells with the high-explosive TNT that produced this bizarre coloration. Because of this side-effect, the women and girls employed in munitions work had earnt themselves the nickname of 'canaries'. Aware that he was staring, he said quickly, 'I'm very pleased to meet you, Doris,' extending a hand towards the suddenly flustered young woman. 'You're very brave to be doing such dangerous and unpleasant work. I trust you are amply compensated for the risks you take.'

For a moment Doris's face remained blank, then, feeling a hard dig in her ribs, she grasped the gloved hand and replied brightly, 'Eh? Oh, yes, thank you, sir. I'm earning four times as much as I did before the war.'

'That's splendid, splendid,' the dark head nodded at her. 'Well, I must be off.' Turning back to Emily he said, 'I'll drop the keys back on Monday on my way to the station. It will probably be sometime in the morning. Will that be convenient?' As he spoke he wondered if Emily had thought it strange to be asked to stay on at the house to hand the keys over, when it would have been much simpler for her to have left them next door with the Simptons, his uncle's neighbours. What would she say if she knew it was his idea, and the reason for it to enable him to see her, to be with her, no matter how brief a time? Well, he had come unstuck, hadn't he? Because his planning hadn't included the arrival of Lenny. But perhaps if Lenny hadn't been there, she would have refused the offer of a lift.

Suddenly he felt a great need to be by himself. What did it matter? What did anything matter in these uncertain days? Come Monday he wouldn't wait around for a last glimpse of Emily, but would simply put the keys through the letterbox of her house without knocking.

45

There was no use in adding to his torment, or in saying something he would later regret.

'Yes, that will be fine. If I have to go out, just leave them with my mum.' If she had been on her own, Emily would have wished him good luck and told him to look after himself, but under the watchful eyes of Doris and Lenny, she felt awkward and had to content herself with a friendly smile at the man who had always shown her kindness.

Encouraged by the warm smile, Matthew was tempted to linger a while longer, then he thought better of it. He could see that Emily was anxious to speak to her friend, and once again he was painfully aware that this was yet another part of Emily's life from which he was excluded. Forcing a smile to his lips, he said cheerfully, 'I'll say goodbye then, Emily. I hope to see you on Monday, but if not . . . Well, take care of yourself. And you, Lenny,' he called to the downcast young man who was still watching him hopefully, his doleful eyes clouding over as the shiny Daimler sped away down the street.

'Coo, he's a bit of all right, ain't he, Em.' Doris gave Emily a playful nudge in the side. 'No wonder yer don't want ter leave service, though I still think you're daft, stopping on there when yer could be earning decent wages, instead of that miserable pittance yer gets from them Winters.'

At her friend's words, Emily felt a moment's irritation, then quickly shrugged it off. Doris didn't mean any harm, she simply spoke whatever was on her mind. She always had done, even as a child. Slipping an arm through Doris's, she pulled her friend closer and said, 'For your information, miss, I've just been given a raise. Oh yes, you can gawp.' She bobbed her head in front of Doris's face. 'I'm getting another ten shillings a week, and I get all my meals and a room to myself, plus I get perks.'

She now held out the parcel that Miss Rose had given her and, smiling broadly, said triumphantly, 'I haven't opened it yet, but I'll bet it's some decent clothes, not the Ridley Road rubbish . . . Oh, Doris, I'm sorry, I didn't mean . . .'

Her face crumpled in dismay as she realised her gaffe. All the women in the street bought their clothes from Ridley Road, Roman Road or Well Street market. Her eyes flickered over her friend's cheap woollen coat, then travelled down the length of her own body and the thick, moss-green, three-quarter-length coat with its black velvet collar, another gift from Miss Rose. She groaned silently. How could she have been so tactless, and she hadn't been home five minutes? Eager to make amends, she was about to apologise further when a light punch to her shoulder sent her off-balance. As she tottered backwards, she reached out and grabbed at Doris's arm to steady herself.

'Gawd, you should see your face, Em,' Doris laughed infectiously. 'You should know I don't get insulted easily. Bleeding hell, if I was that sensitive, I wouldn't have taken a job in munitions. Yer should hear some of the things I'm called, an' the looks I get from people in the street.' She gave a loud chuckle. 'Some of them cross the road when they see me coming. They probably think I've got something catching. Still, bugger them all, that's what I say. Anyway, it doesn't matter what I wear, I'd still look like second-hand Rose, or rather second-hand Daffodil . . .'

'Oh, Doris, that isn't true, you . . .'

'Never mind all that,' Doris cut in impatiently. 'D'yer fancy coming out tonight? Only Tommy and Andy have just got back from the Isle of Wight. You remember, they've just finished their basic training. I told yer on your last visit. Anyways,' she carried on, not giving

Emily time to answer, 'they're going out tonight to celebrate, yer know, kind of their last chance of freedom. Andrew said they're thinking of going ter the Empire. It should be a good night. How about it, Em, will yer come with us?'

Her anxious eyes were fixed on Emily's face, willing her to say yes. Although she and Emily had gone to the same school as Tommy and Andrew Carter, and had played with the boys in the streets after school, she knew that the invitation to her had been made out of kindness. It was Emily they both wanted to see, and behind her bright smile and laughter, Doris was hurting inside. She had loved Tommy Carter since the first day of school, but he – like his brother – had only ever had eyes for Emily. And now, looking as she did, well, there wasn't a hope in hell of Tommy taking more than a brotherly interest in her. Still . . . as long as she could be near him, even if he only had eyes for Emily, she would take comfort from his presence. Especially now, when she didn't know if she would ever see him again. A moment's panic assailed her. What would she do if he was to be killed in action . . . Oh, God, she wouldn't be able to bear it.

'Doris?' Emily was looking at her with concern.

'Oh, don't take any notice of me, Em, I'm just tired. It's a long journey back and forward every day, but the money's good, and yer know how I'm fixed, with me dad not able ter work.'

Harry Mitchell had been struck down with rheumatism over ten years ago. Now, in his fifties, he was almost crippled with the disease. His wife, and Doris's mother, had died some years earlier and now the proud man had to rely on his daughter to feed and clothe him, as well as to keep a roof over their heads.

'So, what about it? Will you come with us tonight? Tommy said they'd be leaving about seven.' Seeing the look of uncertainty on her friend's face, Doris pleaded, 'Oh, please, Em. It's their last night. Gawd knows when we'll have the chance to see them again.' She quickly quashed the thought that she might never see either of the two young men again. That was too terrible to contemplate.

Seeing how much the evening meant to Doris, Emily relented. She could do with a night out, and Tommy and Andrew had always been good company. She deliberately shut her mind to the reason for the night out. Tommy and Andrew would be all right, she assured herself, nothing was going to happen to them. Not wanting to dwell any further on morbid thoughts, she nodded her head.

'All right, Doris. But I'll have to make sure it's okay with my mum. She might have made other plans, seeing as it's my first time home in two months.'

Delighted, Doris threw her arms around Emily's neck. 'I'll call for yer about half-past six. See yer, Em.' Then she was off, running to the terraced house at the far end of the street.

Emily turned to face her brother, who was still lounging against the dusty brick wall.

'What's up with you, Lenny?' she demanded, thinking her brother was still sulking at not being able to have another ride in Matthew's car. But Lenny had only just remembered the reason for going to meet his sister, and now he was torn with indecision as to whether to tell Emily what had been going on in her absence or to honour his mother's plea to keep silent. The decision was taken from him as the front door of their house was flung open and his father came charging towards them. Seeing his daughter, Alfie came to an abrupt stop, his eyes suddenly wary. Then he was pushing past Lenny, his face averted from his daughter's accusing stare.

Without a word Alfie stalked off down the street, his actions betraying his agitation. Afraid for the worst, Emily ran into the house, her heart thumping wildly. There, sitting in the armchair, was her mother, her hand covering her eye. On hearing the soft footsteps she looked up, her face breaking into a smile of welcome.

'Emily, oh, Emily, I've missed you, love. Come in, come in, and I'll put the kettle on.' Ushering her daughter into the parlour, she almost ran into the scullery, all the while keeping up a rambling dialogue from the other room. 'And then, this morning,' she ended cheerfully, 'I went and walked into a blasted cupboard while I was at my cleaning job. Lord, it did hurt. Caught me right in the eye. I've had some remarks today, I can tell you. Still, while they're gossiping about me, they'll leave somebody else alone.' She came back into the parlour carrying two mugs of tea, her voice and step faltering as she watched Emily pick up a brown envelope from the table. Without a word, Emily drew out a long white feather, her eyes glittering with anger.

'So . . . He's finally dropped his guard, has he? I've often wondered when he'd get careless enough to mark you for everyone to see. I'm only surprised it hasn't happened before. How many of these have come through the letterbox while I've been away?'

Slumping onto one of the hard chairs, Nellie shook her head wearily. 'That's the first one he's seen, I . . . I've managed to keep the others from him.'

Crumpling the feather and envelope into a tight ball, Emily threw it contemptuously into the fire. Pulling out a chair, she hitched her knees under the table and picked up the steaming mug of tea.

'How many others?' she demanded, her anger increasing at the sight of her mother's eye, which seemed to be swelling with each passing moment. 'Come on, Mum, I want to know what's been going on, and I'm not going to be fobbed off, not this time.' Then she jumped as Nellie's lips began to tremble. She was about to go to her mother's side when the sound of quiet laughter came to her ears. Shocked into silence, Emily watched in amazement and fear as Nellie began to laugh. Softly at first, then louder and louder until Emily, becoming frightened, ran and grabbed hold of Nellie's shaking shoulders.

'Stop it, Mum. Stop it, you're scaring me.'

Nellie pushed at the restraining hands and sniffed loudly. 'Oh, I'm sorry, Emily, it's just that I've suddenly thought of Mrs Riley's chickens. They're going to be awfully cold this winter, because the amount of feathers that have come through that letterbox must mean the poor little things have been plucked bare.'

She looked up at Emily with watery eyes, not knowing if she was still laughing or crying, but when her daughter's arms enfolded her, she gave a loud moan and buried her face in Emily's neck.

By the open doorway Lenny watched the emotional scene, his eyes filled with anguish. Then, with a despairing shake of his head, he turned and ran, before he humiliated himself further by breaking down and sobbing like the child he was doomed to remain.

CHAPTER FIVE

'Are you sure you're going to be all right, Mum? I don't like leaving you on your own, and anyway, I don't really feel like going out. After the day I've had, all I want to do is curl up by the fire and rest.'

Emily looked over to where Nellie was sitting by the fire, her attention on her needlework box and the pile of worn socks on her lap waiting to be darned. Careful to keep her face averted from the pitying glances of the two young men and Doris, who were standing awkwardly by the door, Nellie said firmly, 'For goodness sake, Emily, how many more times do I have to tell you? I'm fine, and I'll be a lot better once you've gone and given me a bit of peace and quiet to get on with my sewing. Besides, Lenny will be back as soon as his stomach reminds him he's had no dinner. You know what your brother's like.'

Emily bit down hard on the retort that hovered on her lips. Oh yes, she knew only too well what her brother was like. And, as much as she loved him and sympathised with his plight, she found it hard to forgive him his periodic disappearances whenever life became difficult. She could understand his actions when he was younger, but not now, not when his mother needed him at home to act as a buffer between her and the brute she had married. Because even though Lenny might be childlike in his mind, his build and strength were more than a match for Alfie Ford. All Lenny needed was the confidence to stand his ground against his father – just once, that's all it would take – because, like all bullies, Alfie would soon back off once he knew there was a danger of finding himself on the wrong side of a heavy fist. But it was no good Emily voicing her thoughts. Her mother would be horrified at the idea of her son, her little lad, as she still thought of him, squaring up to his own father, however much the situation warranted it.

'Your friends are waiting, Emily.'

Realising that it was pointless to argue, and knowing her mother was embarrassed by her friends' presence, Emily picked up her clutch-bag from the table, her fingers opening and shutting the clasp nervously. She felt bad about going out and leaving her mother on her own, after what had happened earlier, though what Emily had witnessed was probably an everyday occurrence. That would explain why her mother had recovered from her short burst of crying so quickly and had fobbed off any further probing by her anxious daughter. As much as Emily didn't want to admit it, the plain truth was that her mother was so accustomed to being used as a punchbag that she no longer thought anything of it. But even though Nellie seemed resigned to her brutalised state, Emily had no intention of letting it continue, which was why she was reluctant to leave her mother on her own. For all she knew, her dad might well be keeping an eye on the house, just waiting for Emily to leave before he showed his face.

A surge of anger flowed through her, and it wasn't

all directed at her absent father. Threaded through the animosity was a feeling of pity and shame. Shame that her mother could let herself be used in such a way. God! If any man ever raised his hand to her . . . Then she looked at the bowed head and the anger vanished, leaving in its place a deep sense of guilt for having judged her mother so harshly.

Bending down to kiss the smooth cheek, she whispered, 'I won't be long. I'll be back home as soon as the show is over. And if Dad comes back in the meantime, you tell him I'll be bringing Andy and Tommy back with me.'

Straightening up she said aloud, 'Don't have any supper, Mum. I'll bring some fish and chips home with me. Or would you prefer some pie and mash?' A broad smile came to her lips as a look of disgust passed over Nellie's face. Her mum had never been able to stand the sight of the thick parsley sauce that smothered the traditional pie and mash. And she was the same herself. Every time her dad brought some home, Emily and Nellie would carefully avert their eyes from the gooey mess, as both Lenny and Alfie tucked in with relish. 'Don't worry, I was only joking. I'll bring you a nice bit of cod, or would you prefer plaice?'

'I'll have whatever you can get,' Nellie said testily. 'Now get yourself off, before those three start climbing the walls with impatience.' She nodded her head in the direction of the three figures standing by the door, all of whom immediately jumped guiltily. Forgetting her own troubles for a moment, Nellie let her gaze linger on the two young men.

She had known them since their childhood, yet at this minute she hardly recognised them. The fact that they were twins came as a surprise to most people, for they were as different as chalk and cheese, both in appearance and in manner. Nellie could still remember seeing them when they were toddlers.

Andrew, so sturdy with his mop of blond, curly hair falling over his face, and Tommy, as thin as a whippet and his hair as black as coal. They didn't look much different now. Andrew's heavy build and blunt features belied his nature. He was a quiet, shy man who had always seemed older than his years, whereas Tommy, with his slim build and dark hair, had always been the dare-devil, the cheeky rogue who could talk his way out of trouble as a boy and now, as a young man, could, as the saying went, charm his way out of hell and into heaven. As long as she'd known him, Tommy had always had a smile on his lips and a gleam of laughter in his dark blue eyes. Though Nellie had often wondered if his happy nature was simply a façade to compensate for the total lack of affection shown to him by his mother. Of the two brothers, Andrew was the one Ida Carter adored, lavishing all her love on that particular son while having as little to do with her other son as was humanly possible. Through no fault of his own, Tommy Carter was the living image of his father, both in looks and personality, and the unfortunate lad had paid dearly for his startling resemblance to the man who had left his wife and sons to fend for themselves many years ago.

Both young men had had their hair cropped so short that their heads looked only one step away from baldness, but it was the uniform that had completely transformed them, from the small lads who had seemed to be for ever in and out of her parlour when Emily was still at home into grown men. They were wearing tight-fitting khaki uniforms, with puttees wound around their calves from the tips of their highly polished boots, and their peaked caps held self-consciously by the tips of their fingers.

Then Tommy, his eyes alight with mischief, came towards Nellie, smiling.

'How about getting your glad rags on and coming with us, Mrs Ford? I've always fancied going out with an older woman.'

Despite herself, Nellie laughed out loud. Looking into the deep blue eyes of Tommy Carter, eyes that were filled with kindness, she felt suddenly young again. Flapping her arm at him she cried happily, 'Get along with you. Why, you'd run a mile if I was to take you up on that offer.'

Emily watched the happy banter, her own lips spreading into a grin of delighted amazement. Why, her mum was flirting with Tommy, and he, the cheeky devil, was playing up to her.

Oh, it was good to see her mum happy. She looked ten years younger at this minute. With a sudden shock Emily realised just how pretty her mother was. Or could be, if her dad wasn't around to put added years on her. There came to Emily then an overwhelming determination to make sure that her mother was never hurt again, even if it meant turning her dad over to the authorities. She was surprised to realise that she could consider such an action without any compunction on her part. For years he had made her mother's life a misery. Now it was time he had a taste of his own medicine; it was no more than he deserved.

When the door closed after them, Nellie stared long into the fire, the smile still in evidence on her face. He was a nice lad, that Tommy Carter, and kind. His brother Andrew was nice too, but in a quieter sort of way. But Tommy . . . Well, he'd broken a few hearts in his time, and without even trying. For a few moments she thought of Ida Carter, and wondered how any mother could treat her child as she treated her son. Then she shrugged.

She had enough troubles of her own without taking on anyone else's. As she bent to her sewing, she saw again those mischievous eyes, which had taken her back all those years, and found herself humming a tune beneath her breath.

CHAPTER SIX

'Look, if you don't want to go out, just say so. I don't mind staying in with your mum.' Tommy Carter, his face sombre now, looked to his brother and Doris for support. 'We could get some drinks from the off-licence, and later on go out to the chip shop.'

Emily was quick to see the look of disappointment that flashed across Doris's face. Her friend had gone to considerable pains for this evening out. She was wearing a royal blue coat, which Emily hadn't seen her in before, and had carefully arranged her hair beneath a wide-brimmed beige hat. She had also applied a liberal amount of face powder in an attempt to disguise the yellowish tinge of her skin. It was a brave effort on Doris's part and told Emily, more clearly than any words, that her friend wasn't as inured to spiteful remarks as she made out. Anxious not to spoil their night, Emily hastily reassured them.

'No, it's all right. I mean it's good of you to offer, but she'll only feel guilty if we stay in with her.' Nibbling at her bottom lip she said, 'Look, just wait a minute while I see if Mrs Button can come in and keep Mum company

58

while we're out. Lenny will probably be home soon, but I can't depend on him, and I'd feel easier in my mind if I knew she had someone with her.'

Flashing a reassuring smile at Doris, Emily quickly knocked at the house next door, and after a few words with her neighbour she came back to the small group.

'There, I said it wouldn't take long,' she smiled in relief. 'Only it wasn't any use me going out if I was going to spend the whole evening worrying. It would have spoiled the evening for everyone.'

They were at the end of the road when they saw the tram. Quickening their steps, they hurried to the tram-stop, with Doris waving her arms frantically to attract the attention of the conductor. Laughing and out of breath, the four clambered onto the platform, then, seeing that the bottom deck was full, they climbed the spiral stairs to the top deck of the tram.

'Phew, that was close.' Doris flopped down onto the slatted wooden bench, pulling Emily with her. Craning her head, she turned to the two young men seated behind them. 'D'yer know who's on tonight?' she asked, her glance flitting from one to the other. Then she let out a bellow of a laugh, which caused heads to turn and brought a smile to the face of everyone within hearing range. 'Bleeding hell, I can't see who I'm talking to under them hats. It's a wonder you ain't black and blue from walking into lampposts with those things on yer bonces. If all our soldiers wear them in battle, and the Germans have their funny helmets on, it'll be like playing blind man's bluff.'

This remark brought a loud burst of laughter from her now captivated audience. Encouraged by the attention, Doris spent the rest of the short journey entertaining her friends and the other passengers. But when an elderly man, sitting at the front of the tram, called out, 'Yer wasting yer time in munitions, luv. Yer could earn a fortune on the stage,' Doris's head jerked back, her good humour momentarily lost, as the man's words painfully reminded her that, despite her best efforts, she had still been recognised as a 'canary'. Emily was quick to notice her friend's fleeting discomfort and took hold of Doris's hand, giving it a reassuring squeeze. Poor Doris, Emily thought fondly, she wasn't as tough as she made out, and Emily loved her all the more for it.

When they arrived at their destination in Mare Street, all four left the tram smiling, with cries of 'Good luck an' God bless yer, lads' directed at the uniformed figures, who smiled back awkwardly before steering the two girls across the busy road and into the foyer of the Hackney Empire.

'Don't they look smart, Em?' Doris and Emily were standing by the kiosk while the men bought their tickets. 'I hardly recognised them this evening when they knocked on me door. And back there on the tram . . . Well, I felt sort of proud and sad all at the same time. D'yer know what I mean, Em?'

Emily smiled fondly at her friend and nodded.

'Yes, I do know, Doris. I feel the same way myself, but we mustn't let it show. They're probably scared stiff right now, I know I would be. So it's up to us to make them forget what's in store for them, by giving them both a good time. Aw, give over . . .' Emily pushed against Doris, who was looking at her with raised eyebrows. 'You've got a mucky mind, Doris Mitchell. You know perfectly well what I mean.'

'What's all this about a mucky mind?' Tommy had come up on them from behind, a wide grin on his face. 'Does this mean you'll be sending us off with more than a goodbye kiss?' Turning to his brother, who had bought the tickets and was walking towards them, he called out cheerfully, 'Here, Andy, our luck's in. The girls are planning to give us a good send-off . . . Ow, that hurt.' The plaintive cry, and the exaggerated rubbing of his arm, where Doris had landed a well-aimed punch, caused more heads to turn in their direction.

'That's enough, Tommy.' Andrew Carter, his face set with disapproval, had walked up behind them.

The smile slid from Tommy's face. 'I was just having a laugh, Andy,' Tommy answered flatly, all traces of merriment gone now as he faced his brother. 'There's no harm in that, is there? Because there'll be precious little to laugh about where we're going.'

Both girls looked at each other awkwardly, then Emily reached out and pulled lightly on Andy's arm.

'Come on, Andy, and you too, Tommy,' she appealed to them. 'You don't want to spend your last couple of days arguing, do you?' Staring up at the two grim faces, she sighed heavily and, turning to Doris, said impatiently, 'This reminds me of when we were at school. Do you remember, Doris?' She nodded at her friend, her eyes silently imploring her to help defuse the situation.

'Course I do. Blooming hell, it wasn't that long ago.' Jerking her head towards the two men, Doris said briskly, 'One minute the best of mates, the next knocking seven bells out of each other. Well, all I can say is, yer ain't changed much, neither of yer. And if yer going ter stand here arguing, then me and Emily'll go and see the show by ourselves and leave yer to it.'

The two men looked at each other guardedly, then grinned.

'We weren't arguing, were we, Andy?' Tommy glanced at his brother for confirmation.

'Course we weren't. Just having a good-natured difference of opinion, that's all.'

'Well, all I can say is, I hope I'm never around when

you have a good row,' Emily laughed, relieved that the short-lived argument had been nipped in the bud so quickly.

They were halfway up the red-carpeted stairs to the sixpenny stalls when Tommy darted back down to the foyer, returning minutes later with a box of Nestle's chocolates and a bag of Clarnico sweets.

The next two hours were spent in pleasurable enjoyment watching and listening to the singers, jugglers and an organ recital. But the highlight of the evening came in the shape of Harry Weldon, a burlesque character comedian, well known in the East End, whose anecdotes brought a pink tinge to the cheeks of the more delicate ladies in the audience.

It was nearly ten o'clock when they alighted from the tram in Well Street singing an off-key version of 'Bill Baily, won't you please come home', and ignoring the conductor's aspersive comment that they couldn't find a right note between the four of them.

'What shall we do now?' Tommy casually flung his arm round Emily's shoulders, pulling her against his side. 'It's too early to go home. How about going for a drink? I'm gasping for a beer. How about it?'

Emily looked into the handsome face only inches from her own and smiled. Swivelling her head, she was about to ask Doris what she wanted to do when she caught sight of her friend's face in the bright glow of a lamppost. The smile wavered, then died on her lips. Doris was staring past Emily at the slender figure beside her, and the look of hurt in her eyes caused Emily to look away at the other uniformed figure. What she saw in Andy's face brought her head down in confusion.

Oh, Lord! Oh, dear Lord! She had known these three people since early childhood. They were her friends, her dear friends. She had never thought of them as anything else and had imagined that they felt the same way. But she hadn't imagined the hurt looks mirrored on both Doris's and Andy's faces.

The full import of her discovery sent her head spinning in bewilderment. Doris had never said anything to suggest that her feelings for Tommy were other than those of simple friendship. And Andy, the way he had looked at her . . . The pain she had seen in his eyes . . .

Again she whispered silently: Oh, Lord, what am I going to do? Tonight had seen the end of a harmless friendship for, knowing what she did now, even if she kept her knowledge silent, things could never again be the same between them. And this realisation brought a deep sadness to her heart.

Determined not to let the evening end on a sour note, she swallowed hard, put the smile back on her face and said brightly, 'I'll come for a drink, but it'll have to be a quick one. I promised my mum I'd bring her home some supper.' Moving away from Tommy's side, she linked arms with Doris, while making a great show of stamping her feet and blowing her cheeks out against the cold night air.

'I think I'll go home, if you don't mind.' Doris pulled free from Emily's grasp, her face showing no sign of the turmoil raging inside her. 'It's been a long day and . . .'

'Whoa, hang on there, Doris.' Tommy came loping up to her side. 'We can't go without you, can we?' he appealed to Emily and Andy, who were now standing awkwardly by the kerb. 'How can we have a laugh without you, Doris? Why, you're the life and soul of the party, ain't she, Andy? You tell her, she'll listen to you.' When no answer was forthcoming, Tommy screwed up his eyes, looking from one silent form to the other, sensing that something wasn't right. Never one to keep his feelings to himself, he said, 'What's up? Have I missed something, 'cos you lot look like someone's just died.'

For the second time that evening Andy stepped forward, saying sharply, 'That's enough, Tommy, give it a rest. You never know when to stop.'

Seeing that another argument was looming, Emily leant closer to Doris and, keeping her voice to a whisper, said, 'Please, Doris, come for a drink with us, otherwise they'll be at each other's throat in a minute. We can have a talk later, but please, for now, don't let's spoil this evening.'

Beside her, Emily could feel the tension emanating from Doris's silent form and, knowing her friend's temper, braced herself for the worst. Then she let out a silent sigh of relief as Doris, who had recovered her aplomb, threw back her shoulders and cried in her usual strident voice, 'Here, what's all this? Yer bring us girls out for a night on the town and end up leaving us out in the cold, and dying of thirst. If you two want to fight, yer can do it later or, better still, save yer energy fer the Germans.'

The two men remained glaring at each other for what seemed an eternity, then Tommy, always the peacemaker, slapped his brother heartily on the back and grinned.

'Come on, Bruv, no more arguing, eh? Doris is right, we'd better save our energy fer the Germans.' Reluctantly Andy nodded, still not entirely mollified, but willing to let the matter drop. Then he gave a rueful smile at his brother, unable to remain angry with Tommy for long. With the atmosphere back to normal, Emily began to wonder if she'd imagined her earlier impression. But when Tommy made to put his arm round her shoulder, she immediately linked arms with Doris, to prevent any pairing off with either of the two men.

By now the October evening had turned bitterly cold

and it was with great relief that the four of them hurried into the warmth of the Kenton public house, just a short walk from their street.

Being a Saturday, the pub was packed, so it was left to the two men to push their way through the smoke-filled crowd, with Emily and Doris following close behind. Above the sound of a piano, played with gusto by an unseen figure at the far end of the tap-room, and a rousing rendition of 'My old man said follow the van' bellowing from the well-oiled throats of the working men who crowded the saloon, Tommy shouted, 'You two go into the snug. I'll send your drinks in to you . . . Oh, what d'yer want?'

'Shandy for me, please, Tommy. What about you, Doris? Do you want your usual gin and tonic?' Emily turned to her friend, then cried out angrily as a burly man, much the worse for drink, cannoned into her. 'Watch where you're going, will you.'

The man twisted his head to see who was behind the angry voice, the scowl dying on his lips when he saw the pretty young woman, her blue eyes glaring at him.

'Sorry, luv, can't hardly move in 'ere.' Rubbing a grimy hand over his stubbled cheek, he inched closer. ''Ow's abaht letting me buy yer a drink, sort of like an apology. 'Ow abaht it, darlin'.'

Before the indignant Emily could answer, Doris had elbowed her aside. 'How about you taking a running jump, before I call out ter me friends,' she said fiercely, her head nodding towards the uniformed backs of the Carter twins.

Following her gaze, the man's eyes flickered nervously. Shoving his hands into the pockets of a grubby overcoat he muttered, 'Sorry, didn't mean any 'arm. Just being friendly, that's all.'

'Yeah, and the rest. Go on, piss off, yer dirty old bugger.'

'Doris, there's no need for that,' Emily protested, immediately feeling sorry for the hapless man who had unsuspectingly walked straight into Doris's line of fire. It was clear from the forbidding look on Doris's face that she was in a high temper and had just been waiting for an opportunity to take it out on someone. And the apologetic stranger, who was now beating a path to the door, had simply been in the wrong place at the wrong time.

Grabbing a couple of seats at an empty table in the snug, the girls sat themselves down, making a great to-do of putting their handbags on the round table and fussing with their hats, while they waited for their drinks. Finally, when they ran out of things to occupy themselves with, Emily looked at Doris and sighed heavily.

'Look, Doris, we've known each other too long to be messing around like this. I didn't think we had any secrets between us, but obviously there's something going on with you and Tommy . . .'

'Leave it, Em. I don't want to talk about it, all right!'

'No, it isn't all right.' Emily leaned forward, keeping her voice low so that the other women in the snug couldn't hear their conversation. 'I had no idea you felt this way about Tommy until this evening, or maybe I imagined the dirty look you gave me back there in the street.'

'I didn't give you a dirty look . . .'

'Well, it certainly wasn't friendly.' Emily waved away the protestation. 'Look, Doris, if I'm wrong about Tommy, and it's something else you're angry with me for, then please tell me, because I'd hate to fall out with you and not know the reason why.'

''Ere yer are, girls. Drinks from the boys in uniform.'

Tutting impatiently, Emily rose from her seat to collect the two drinks, studiously ignoring the wink levelled at her by the portly barman.

Putting the glasses down on the table, she resumed her interrogation.

'Well, are you going to speak to me or not? Because I'm not going to let it drop. I value your friendship too dearly to let it go that easily.'

'All right, keep your voice down. I don't want the whole pub knowing me business,' Doris snapped. Picking up her glass she took a long swallow, glanced across the table at Emily's determined face, then gave a low chuckle, but there was no humour in the sound. Placing the glass back on the table, she drew imaginary circles on the shiny surface with her finger, then sighed. 'You always were a bossy-boots, Emily Ford. Sharp too – there's not much gets past you, is there? All right, so now you know. I'm surprised you didn't pick up on it before. Aw, sod it, what am I worrying about? He'll be off soon, so it doesn't really matter how I feel, does it?'

Tears sprang to Doris's eyes, and with an angry, impatient gesture she quickly wiped them away with the back of her hand.

Watching her friend's distress, Emily felt her own eyes begin to moisten. In all the years she had known her, Emily had never seen Doris so vulnerable, so unsure of herself, as she did now. Reaching over the table, she took hold of the trembling hand.

'Oh, Doris, I never knew, I never even guessed. I mean, all these years, you and Andy and Tommy . . . Well, you've all been like sister and brothers to me. And I thought you all felt the same way.' When the hand was pulled roughly from her grasp, she felt as if Doris had reached out and slapped her.

Taking another long swallow of her drink, Doris shuddered. Seeing the look of hurt on Emily's face, she gave a watery smile.

'Don't worry, Em, it's not your fault,' she smiled bravely. 'I just thought . . . Well, hoped, really, that maybe as he's going off to France in a couple of days, he might . . . you know, suddenly see me as more than just a friend and fall madly in love with me.' Her voice had taken on a deprecatory tone, but the self-mockery only served to make Emily feel even more guilty. And Doris's next words almost brought her leaping from her chair.

'I always was a stupid cow. I mean, what bloke's going ter give me a second look with you around? Even two like Andy and Tommy, who might be going off ter get themselves killed, don't want ter spend their last couple of nights in the arms of someone like me . . . Oh, sod it!' With a still shaking hand Doris picked up her drink, but such was her distress that the glass bumped against her teeth, spilling a few drops of the gin down the front of her royal blue coat.

'Oh, Doris, don't . . . Please, don't run yourself down like this. Here, take my handkerchief, you can . . .' Conscious of an enquiring look from two middle-aged women sitting behind them, Emily said icily, 'Yes! Can I help you?' Whereupon the two women bridled indignantly, snorted a muffled rejoinder and returned their attention to their drinks.

'Oh, Em. I wish I could do that.' Doris was laughing quietly through her tears. 'I swear yer could bring a charging lion to a halt with one of your looks, and so polite as well. Your posh voice is more effective than my common one. I can never argue without swearing.'

'Rubbish!' Emily answered self-consciously, relieved to see that Doris was outwardly back to her old self. But behind the smiles Emily knew that her friend was hurting inside. Doris's unexpected revelation had only served to remind Emily just how much she had become estranged from her old life and her friends. If she had been living at home and working in a factory or shop, she would have known how Doris was feeling. Yet would she be happy working in either of those places? Especially now, after all these years of being her own boss, even if she was overworked and underpaid. And wasn't she secretly proud of her education and of mixing with the gentry, even if it was in the capacity of a servant?

The years spent with the Winters had given Emily a confidence and a maturity that she would never have achieved working in a factory, or as a counter assistant in one of the large department stores. But never in a thousand years would she even have considered working in a munitions factory. Yet perhaps, if she had been at home, she might have dissuaded Doris from doing so. She was deeply worried for the safety of her life-long friend. The dangers of working with TNT were one of the worst-kept secrets in England. But the powers that be had no cause to worry, not while girls and women like Doris, filled with patriotic convictions, continued to risk their health – and, in some cases, their lives – to keep the wheels of the war machinery rolling.

Oh, dear, this silent meditating was making her head spin. What with the worry for her mother, and now Doris and the Carter twins to be added to her list of problems to be resolved, Emily was beginning to wish she'd stayed where she was. She needed to talk things out properly with Doris; they both did. But not here, where their conversation could be overheard. Bending her head forward she said, 'Look, Doris, we need to talk, but not here. How about you staying the night at my house, though we'd have to sleep in the parlour? But I don't mind if you don't.' Seeing the doubtful expression on Doris's face, she urged quietly, 'Please, Doris, it'll be like old times. What do you say?'

Under the pretence of blowing her nose, Doris sniffed loudly before saying, 'Yeah, all right, as long as me dad don't mind being on his own all night. But only if yer dad ain't home. No offence, Em. Your mum might not mind getting a belting, but I ain't that keen on being near a bloke too handy with his fists.'

The insensitive, cruel remark only served to remind Emily that Doris was still angry and looking for a chance to lash out at someone. Well, it wasn't going to be her! Her face set in anger, Emily glared at the young woman opposite her.

'That was a bit nasty, wasn't it, Doris? It was also uncalled for.' Emily seemed to be grinding out each word with extreme caution. The last thing she wanted was to fall out with her best friend, and if the remark had been directed at herself, she would probably have let the matter drop. But no-one was going to have a sly dig at her mother and get away with it; not even Doris.

The moment the words were out of her mouth, Doris wished with all her heart she could take them back. She was very fond of Nellie Ford. She could even say she loved the woman who had been like a mother to her, after the death of her own mother. How could she have said such a dreadful thing?

Emily watched her friend impassively. The only signs of Doris's agitation were the nervous swallowing in her throat and her refusal to meet Emily's accusing stare.

For something to do to fill in the awful silence, Emily rose and walked to the bar, returning with a gin for Doris and another shandy for herself. Almost before Emily had laid the glasses down, Doris picked hers up, downing the contents in one swallow.

'Thanks, Em.' Her voice sounded gruff, almost dismissive, but when she raised her head Emily could clearly see the remorse in Doris's grey eyes, and immediately her own anger melted away.

When the last bell sounded, they rejoined the twins and the four of them stepped once again into the cold street, heading for the nearest fish and chip shop. Their arms filled with their supper wrapped in newspapers, the four young people made their way to Fenton Street, laughing and teasing each other playfully as if they hadn't a care in the world. As they turned off the main road and into their street, their laughter suddenly faded, then stopped altogether. The street was filled with their neighbours, mainly women standing in small groups, their heads and shoulders covered with thick shawls against the cold night air. Through a gap in the crowd Emily saw the white ambulance, and for a moment her heart seemed to stop in her breast. One of the women turned, saw Emily and the others, and began walking towards them. But even before the woman reached the silent group, Emily had bounded away, her legs pumping wildly, her chest heaving and her mind praying over and over again: Not my mum . . . Please, God, not my mum.

CHAPTER SEVEN

The semi-darkened ward was hushed in silence, save for intermittent coughing from the patients tossing restlessly in the single brass beds that flanked both sides of the long room.

At the top end of the ward the night Sister, seated behind her desk, was studying her patients' charts by the soft glow of a table lamp. Every now and then she looked up, her eyes going to the second-from-last bed at the end of the ward, and to the couple who sat in silence on either side of the narrow hospital bed.

When the last chart had been read, she pushed her chair back quietly, picked up the lamp and walked softly across the wooden floor, stopping at each bed to ensure that the occupant was sleeping soundly. Her years of practice made her progress silent, before she stopped at the only bed that still had its wall light on.

'Why don't you go home and get some rest?' she murmured, her gaze directed at the young woman holding the hand of her mother, her shoulders slumped in weariness. 'I understand you wanting to stay, but really, there's nothing you can do at the moment. What your mother needs most is rest, and the best way you can help her is to get some yourself, otherwise you'll be of no use to her at all.'

When no answer came she looked at the young soldier seated on the other side of the bed. 'Could you talk some sense into her?' she appealed quietly to the dark-haired man. 'If there was some good to be had from her being here, I would say so. But, given the amount of morphine she's had, Mrs Ford is going to be asleep for quite some time. So there's nothing to be gained by sitting here on a hard chair, when you could both be tucked up warm in your beds.'

Tommy glanced up at the Sister, his normally cheerful countenance sombre, his eyes and body heavy with fatigue. He was sitting with the top half of his body bent forward, his elbows resting on his knees and his hands clasped as if in prayer.

'I'll see if I can talk her into going home,' he said quietly. 'But I can't promise it'll do any good, she's . . .'

'Don't talk about me as if I'm not here,' Emily's voice cut into Tommy's words. Shifting slightly on the hard wooden chair, she turned her head to look up at the ward Sister. 'She is going to be all right, isn't she? I mean, I know the doctor said there was no serious damage done, and all she needed was rest, but, I mean . . . Well, look at her, she . . . She looks dreadful.' The last words ended on a sob, but even as Tommy started to rise from his chair to comfort her, she straightened her shoulders, gave a very unladylike sniff and in a more composed voice said, 'If you can give me your word that my mother is in no immediate danger, then I'll do as you say and go home and get some rest.'

Sister May looked down into the deep blue intelligent eyes and nodded.

'I give you my word, Miss Ford. Your mother has

taken a terrible beating,' she saw the young woman flinch before lowering her head. 'But as far as the doctors can tell, there's no permanent damage to any of her internal organs.' The Sister hesitated for a moment, wondering if she should ask if there was a likelihood of the same thing happening again, before rejecting the idea out of hand. Mrs Ford was only one of the many hundreds of women who were daily beaten up by their spouses. The more severe cases ended up in hospital. Their husbands would invariably turn up, looking suitably sheepish, some clasping a bunch of cheap flowers, thinking that their gesture would show them in a better light to the hospital staff. And the women would look delighted and let themselves be taken home by the very men who had put them in hospital in the first place.

She had seen the same thing happen so many times that she should be immune to it by now. But she wasn't, and never would be. How could these women let themselves be abused without retaliation, knowing full well that another beating was inevitable, once their husbands' initial shame disappeared? She had long since given up trying to understand, but she could never get used to it.

Emily stood up slowly and stretched her aching back. She had lost track of the time, but knew it must be the early hours of the morning. Quietly thanking the Sister for her kindness, she let herself be led down the long, eerily silent ward by Tommy.

Once outside Hackney Hospital they both shivered, their bodies involuntarily coming together in a bid to keep warm.

'What time is it?' Emily asked, her teeth chattering with the cold. Pulling up the wide collar of his overcoat round his ears, Tommy placed a protective arm around Emily's shoulders and looked at his watch under the pale amber light of a street lamp.

'It's just after three. You should be able to get a good few hours' sleep before going back. Lucky it's not too far to walk home, though in this cold, it'll probably seem longer.'

As they began the walk home, Emily leant her head against the scratchy material of Tommy's overcoat and said tiredly, 'It was very good of you to stay with me, Tommy. Especially now, when you've so little time left at home, but I am grateful. It made it easier somehow, you being there.'

Tommy hugged Emily closer to him and gave a short laugh. 'Give over, Em. You make it sound like you've dragged me away from a good old knees-up. I'd only have been at home asleep. Besides, what are mates for, eh?'

Emily smiled up at the handsome face. She could see why Doris loved him; he was very lovable, was Tommy Carter, though his next words drove the smile from her face.

'Look, Em,' he started awkwardly, 'I know it's none of me business, but . . . well, what are yer going to do about your dad? Yer mum can't keep taking beatings like that. Why, the poor thing can't weigh more than six stone at the most, an' once yer go back ter work, she'll have no protection, 'cos, Lenny, as big as he is, can't do much. He . . .'

''Ere, d'yer want a lift, mate?'

Tommy and Emily turned eagerly at the sound of the rough cockney voice. A large van, piled high with fruit and vegetables, had pulled up beside them.

'We wouldn't mind, mate, thanks,' Tommy said gratefully. 'If yer could drop us off at the Kenton pub, that'd be a great help.'

'Right yer are then. Come on, jump in the pair of yer. It'll be a bit of a squeeze, but it ain't that far ter go.'

Quickly walking round to the passenger side of the van, Tommy got in first, then pulled Emily up beside him. On the short journey Tommy and the driver chatted like old friends, with Tommy telling the man about the *friend* they'd been visiting in hospital, while Emily sat pressed tightly against the door of the van, thankful that this cheerful man didn't probe the reason why this *friend* was being visited at this ungodly hour of the morning.

Her thoughts turned to Lenny, as she wondered where he had got to. He certainly couldn't have returned home in her absence. If he had, then somebody would have told him what had happened, and he would have been up at the hospital like a shot. More than likely he had run off again. But this time his absence was for the best, for all concerned, because there was no telling how Lenny would react if he saw the brutalised state of his beloved mother. He might very well turn tail and flee, unable to deal with the horrific sight of his mother's injuries; or the sickening revelation of his father's cowardly action might be the catalyst that turned him from a timid young boy into a raging, vengeful stranger, hell-bent on seeking revenge for the horrendous beating of his defenceless mother.

Despite Emily's earlier thoughts on the subject, now that there was a chance that Lenny would finally turn on his father, she found herself sickened at the image that her mind threw up. It would be tantamount to winding a child up into a rage, then putting a sharp knife into his hand. And once the rage and bloodlust had subsided, what then? Emily shivered and silently dismissed the notion from her mind. Her father would pay for what he had done, but not at the hands of his innocent son. If there was any retribution to be meted out – and there would be – she would be the one to make sure that Alfie Ford paid for what he had done this night. Her forehead creased with worry, Emily tried to work out how best to handle her brother when he returned from his wanderings.

Within ten minutes the van had pulled up outside the darkened doors of the Kenton. The driver, a short, middle-aged man, jumped down from his seat and ran around to open the door for Emily.

'Thank you, it was very good of you to give us a lift,' Emily said gratefully. And not only for the lift home, but also for cutting short the painful conversation that Tommy had started. She was too tired now to make any definite plans. For now, her best course of action was to ensure she got a good night's sleep.

'Thanks again, mate,' Tommy was saying, while shaking the driver's hand. Then, jerking his head towards the closed pub, he laughed, 'It's a shame they don't stay open all night. I could just do with a drink right now.'

''Ere, wait a minute, son, I've got just the thing. 'Ang on while I get it.'

Tommy looked at Emily and shrugged.

''Ere yer are.' The man had returned carrying something in his hand. ''Ave a drink on me, son, an' good luck ter yer,' he added gruffly, shoving a small bottle into Tommy's hand.

When Tommy looked down and saw the bottle of brandy, he made to give it back. 'Oh, leave off,' he protested. 'I can't take this . . . Here, at least let me pay yer something for it.' As his hand went into his pockets, the man laid a restraining hand on Tommy's arm.

'Take it, son, please. Yer'll be doing me a favour.' Lowering his voice, the man gazed down at his feet and murmured, 'Me son is over there somewhere, don't know where. We . . . that is, me and the missus, we got one of them telegrams after that balls-up at the Somme. Missing in action, it said, an' not 'eard a word since. Me missus . . . Well, she ain't 'ardly said a word since, just keeps looking out fer the postie every morning, while me . . .' His shoulders lifted in despair. 'Well, I've put away more of that stuff,' he nodded towards the bottle of brandy, 'than I care ter think abaht. So do me a favour an' put yer money away.'

Deeply moved by the man's story, both Tommy and Emily found themselves at a loss to know what to say. As the man went to climb back into the van, Emily ran after him and impulsively kissed his stubbled cheek, then, once more huddling herself against Tommy's body, she waved the man goodbye and they walked off.

As Emily fumbled in her handbag for her door key, Tommy wondered if Doris and the neighbours had tidied up the place. He could still see it now – the upturned table and chairs, the smashed crockery, and Nellie Ford lying among the debris, covered in her own blood, as still as death as the ambulance men crouched down beside the limp form, before lifting her gently onto a canvas stretcher. He could still hear Emily's screams as she'd tried to wake her mother up, and only the presence of Mrs Button had calmed Emily down, as she'd helped her up into the ambulance to accompany her mother to the hospital. He, Andy and Doris had caught the late-night tram and had waited with Emily while the doctors had seen to Nellie. After what had seemed an interminable wait, one of the doctors had assured Emily that her mother hadn't sustained any serious injury. But Emily hadn't believed him, and who could blame her? Even with the blood washed from her face and body, Nellie Ford had looked at death's door.

Doris and Andy had waited with them at Nellie's bedside until gone one o'clock, when Emily, suddenly remembering Mr Mitchell, had immediately pleaded with Doris to go home to her father. Tommy remembered Doris looking at him, almost as if . . . Aw, bloody hell, what was he thinking of? Doris was a mate. Still, it was no wonder his thoughts were jumbled, with all that had happened during the last eight hours. Andy had gone with Doris to see her safely home, and of course to see mum. Tommy's mouth twisted into a wry smile. She must have been hovering at the window for hours, waiting for Andy to get home. Not him . . . Oh, no, not him, just her darling Andy. As far as she was concerned, she had only one son, and Tommy was just an irritant that she would soon be rid of. As he felt the tears well up behind his eyes, he hurriedly wiped them away with the back of his hand. He must be more tired than he thought. He'd known his mother had no affection for him, even at an early age, and it hadn't bothered him then, so why should it worry him now? Liar, his mind shouted at him. You care, you've always cared.

'Thanks, Tommy, you've been a tower of strength tonight, but you'd better get off home. Your mum will be worried about you.'

Jerked out of his maudlin thoughts Tommy smiled wryly. 'Give over, Em. Yer know how me mum feels about me, or if yer don't, yer must be the only one in the whole bloody street. I wish now I'd joined up the minute I turned eighteen, but she created such a fuss, even threatening to kill herself if we joined up – that is, if Andy joined up. She wasn't worried about what I might do. Me and Andy were relieved when conscription came in. It gave us the perfect excuse to enlist. Not that we wouldn't have anyway, but . . . Well, you know Andy, he doesn't like to upset anyone, and it didn't seem right, me going off without him. We've always done everything together, an' that's always got right up her nose as well,' he said, following Emily into the house, again praying that someone had thought to tidy up the mess before Emily's return. At once his fears were unfounded.

Dropping his cap onto the now upright table, he glanced round the room, relieved to discover that someone had indeed set the place to rights. There was even a welcoming fire blazing in the grate.

'Oh, look, Tommy, there's a note from Doris.' Emily was standing close to the fire, a small slip of paper in her hand.

'Dear Emily,' she began to read aloud. 'Me and Mrs Button have tidied up a bit. Get some sleep after you've read this, and I'll be round later on. If you don't want to stay on your own, come round to my house and let yourself in. You know where the key is. Don't worry about waking me up, just climb in beside me, as long as you don't put your cold feet on my back. See you later. Love Doris.'

'Oh, that was good of her, and Mrs Button, it must have taken ages to get the place tidied up, it . . .' Her voice faltered, and she knew she was near breaking-point.

Seeing her distress, Tommy moved towards her. 'Come on, Em,' he urged gently. 'Yer mum's gonna be all right. What yer need is a good night's sleep, but Doris is right, yer shouldn't stay here by yerself, just in case yer dad decides ter come home. I don't suppose he will, not after what he's done, but . . . Well, I'd feel a lot happier if yer weren't here on yer own. Speaking of which . . . Where's Lenny?' He looked round the room as if expecting the young man to be hiding somewhere.

Sinking her weary body into the armchair, Emily shook her head tiredly.

'He'll be all right. It's not the first time he's gone missing. Though you'd know more about his habits than me, wouldn't you, seeing as I'm hardly ever at home.' Resting her head against the back of the high-backed chair she said softly, 'He was with me when I arrived home this afternoon, and . . . Well, you saw my mum's eye when you came to pick me up earlier. Anyway, Lenny got upset and bolted for it. I expect he's gone to the Mission house and scrounged a bed for the night. Though as things turned out, I'm glad he wasn't here, he couldn't have coped. I dare say he'll be back for breakfast.'

Seeing Tommy standing awkwardly in the middle of the room she added, 'For goodness sake, if you're stopping for a while, at least sit down. You don't have to stand on ceremony here, not after all these years.'

A relieved grin spread across Tommy's face. He didn't want to leave Emily on her own. With a bit of luck she might fall asleep in the chair, then he would be able to stay and watch over her. As he went to take off his coat he remembered the bottle of brandy in the deep pocket. Taking it out, he asked hopefully, 'D'yer mind if I have a drink, Em? I feel like me insides are frozen solid.'

Emily nodded.

'Don't be daft, you don't need my permission. In fact, you can pour one out for me,' she said recklessly.

Tommy's surprise at the unexpected request soon turned to one of gladness. A couple of glasses of brandy would quickly send her to sleep. Taking two chipped glasses from the wall dresser, he poured out two good measures of brandy and handed one to Emily, then eased himself down into the armchair opposite. They sat in companionable silence in front of the fire, both immersed in their own private thoughts. Now that the immediate drama was over, Tommy's thoughts turned to the coming Monday, when he and Andy, together with hundreds of others, would be crammed aboard trains carrying them to Dover, and from there to France. He was no coward, he never had been, but he couldn't control the fear that was gnawing away at his innards. He found himself pouring out another brandy, and when Emily wordlessly held out her glass, he silently filled it.

The bottle was almost empty when Emily tried to pull herself out of the sagging armchair, but the unaccustomed brandy had turned her arms and legs to jelly. Realising how silly she must look, she began to giggle, then her merriment turned to tears as the effects of the past few hours finally caught up with her.

When she felt Tommy's arms around her waist she fell against his body, grateful for and comforted by his embrace.

Then she was holding him close and felt his arms tighten around her waist. As they gently slumped to the floor, her mind sent out frantic signals for her to struggle free, to tell Tommy to let her go. But she was feeling so safe, so secure in his arms, and the combination of the warmth from the fire and the effect of the brandy had taken hold of her senses, banishing all reasonable thoughts. She felt hands removing her clothes and feebly tried to stop what was happening, but there was no power in either her limbs or her voice.

At the last moment, she made a final, weak effort to push Tommy away.

The wandering hands stopped, and Tommy's face loomed over hers, his eyes filled with such pain and longing that she stopped struggling. And when he whispered, 'Please, Em . . . please,' she gave up trying to fight him and lay back, her eyes tightly closed, but not tight enough to stop the single tear trickling down her cheek.

CHAPTER EIGHT

A loud, persistent knocking at the front door broke through Emily's heavy sleep. When she tried to open her eyes they felt as if the lids were weighed down by an invisible force. Her head too ached abominably, and her tongue felt as if it were glued to the roof of her mouth. When she tried to move from the confines of the armchair, she found herself as weak as a kitten.

When the knocking became more frantic, she summoned all her strength and, with her hands gripping the sides of the chair for support, rose unsteadily to her feet. As she stood, a heavy overcoat slipped from her body to the floor and, as she stared down at the dark grey garment, recollections of the previous night came flooding back. So it hadn't been a dream after all. Oh, dear God, how could she have allowed such a thing to happen?

Still in a daze, she walked slowly to the door and opened it, wincing and screwing up her eyes against the glare of the sudden daylight.

'Bleeding hell, Em, yer had me worried. I was just about ter get some help ter break down the door. I've been knocking fer ages.' Doris swept past the bemused Emily and into the house. 'I thought fer a minute yer old man had come back home and . . .' She stopped in mid-sentence, her eyes going to the empty brandy bottle and the two glasses lying in the hearth. But it was the overcoat that claimed her attention, an overcoat just like the one Tommy had been wearing last night, and which was now lying in a heap on Emily's parlour floor. The implication caused her heart to race and brought a tightness to her throat.

Steady on, girl, she warned herself silently. There's probably a simple explanation, don't go jumping to the wrong conclusions. Striving to keep her voice normal, she bent down, picked up the brandy bottle and gave a shaky laugh.

'Been having a party, Em? Yer might have invited me. After all, I am yer best mate.'

Still standing by the door, Emily opened her mouth to speak, but no words were forthcoming. She couldn't tell Doris what had happened, she just couldn't. If Doris hadn't confided how she felt about Tommy, then Emily would have been glad to share the burden of guilt and shame that she was now experiencing. But not now. How would it look to Doris, if she found out that only hours after telling her life-long friend about her true feelings for Tommy Carter, that same friend had slept with the man she loved? Suddenly Emily's head cleared. Doris must never know what had happened between her and Tommy. It hadn't been planned. If that driver hadn't given Tommy the bottle of brandy, they would have been content with a cup of tea before Tommy left. As it was, they had both needed comforting, – she because of her worry about her mother, and Tommy because of his fear of what lay in store for him in France.

'Well! Cat got yer tongue, Em?' Doris was staring at her, her grey eyes mirroring her uncertainty.

Emily, sensing her friend's pain, pulled herself together, saying hoarsely, 'Be a pal, Doris, and put the kettle on. I'm dying for a cup of tea. You wait until I see that Tommy Carter. He said the brandy was for medicinal purposes, but he failed to mention the after-effects.' As she talked Emily came slowly over to where Doris was standing and held her hands over the dying embers in the grate. 'We managed to get a lift home from a man on his way to Spitalfields, and you know what it's like these days, people only have to see a man in uniform and he's immediately a hero in their eyes. When he dropped us off, he gave Tommy that brandy. Lord, if I'd have known I'd feel this bad, I would never have touched the stuff. But, well, Tommy was feeling a bit low, the same as me, but for different reasons, and I didn't like to chuck him out, not after he'd stayed with me at the hospital. I don't remember much after the second glass, until you woke me up by knocking seven bells out of the front door. Still, at least he had the decency to cover me up with his coat before he left, otherwise I'd probably have had a stinking cold as well as a hangover.'

With each word Emily uttered, a dull pain pulled at the very heart of her. She didn't like lying, for any reason, and she had never lied to Doris before. But what good would it do to tell the truth? What had happened here last night would never happen again, so why cause Doris unnecessary pain, when there was nothing to be gained by it?

Standing close to Emily, Doris felt her body slump with relief.

There yer are, yer silly cow, she silently berated herself. Fancy thinking a thing like that about Emily. Oh, there was more than a few names she could mention who would have been only too pleased to offer their services to a man like Tommy, but not her Em. Why, she'd probably never even kissed a man, let alone . . . ! Feeling guilty about her earlier uncharitable thoughts, Doris immediately became all bustling solicitation.

'Here, don't stand around like a fart in a trance. Sit yerself back down while I make that tea.'

Emily let herself be guided into the armchair, making no protest when Tommy's coat was laid back over her shivering body. While Doris was busy in the scullery, Emily let her mind drift back to the early hours of the morning.

After it was over, they had both held each other and cried. Of the two of them, Tommy had been the most upset, blaming himself and calling himself names that Emily had never heard before, asking her over and over again to forgive him. When they had both calmed down, they had dressed silently and shyly, avoiding each other's gaze as they performed that simple, private act. Before he'd left Tommy had settled her in the armchair by the fire and covered her up with his overcoat, kissed her softly on the forehead and let himself silently out of the house. She didn't know how long she had sat there, unable to move, or even to think straight, before falling into a troubled sleep until Doris had arrived.

'Here yer are, girl, get that down yer.' Doris had appeared by her side, a steaming mug of tea held out to Emily. Gratefully taking the hot beverage, she sipped at it, careful not to burn her mouth. 'Shall I get the fire going again, Em?' Doris was hovering over her, anxious to be of help.

Emily shook her head, then winced as a shaft of pain shot across her forehead.

'Ooh, my head hurts something dreadful,' she groaned.

'I'll never, ever get drunk again . . . And no, don't bother with the fire. I'll be going up to see my mum as soon as I've washed and changed my clothes. What time is it anyway?' Craning her neck gingerly, she looked at the mantel clock and gasped. 'Ten o'clock, goodness, I can't have slept that long.'

Doris laughed. 'Well, yer have, so you'd best get yer arse up out of that chair and get a move on. Yer mum will be wondering what's happened ter yer.'

Twenty minutes later, her head still throbbing painfully, Emily left the house with Doris by her side.

'Maybe they'll give yer something at the hospital fer yer head,' Doris said gaily. Then, looking across the street she added, 'Look, there's Tommy. He's probably come looking fer his coat.'

Emily felt a moment of panic. Please, please, God, don't let him say anything about last night, she prayed silently. Her stomach churning nervously, she turned and smiled weakly at the approaching figure.

'Good morning, Tommy,' she managed to say calmly. 'Have you come for your coat? I was going to bring it over after I'd been to the hospital.'

Tommy looked from Emily to the smiling Doris, and back to Emily once more. Although she was smiling, her eyes were clearly pleading with him not to mention what had happened between them. As if he would, in front of Doris . . . or anyone else for that matter. He felt bad enough about his actions as it was.

'Here, give me the key and I'll fetch it fer yer.' Doris held out her hand to Emily for the key.

When she'd gone, both Tommy and Emily looked awkwardly at each other, neither knowing what to say. Emily could feel her face burning with embarrassment at the memory of them together. Here now, in the cold light of day, what had happened seemed sordid, even dirty, and nothing like the warm, comforting feeling that had led to them finding solace in each other's arms in the rosy glow of the blazing fire.

Shuffling his boots uneasily, Tommy said awkwardly, 'Look, Em, about last night, I . . .'

'No, Tommy, don't . . . don't say anything, please. We were both drunk, and I was just as much to blame as you.' Behind her she heard her front door being pulled shut and said quickly, 'It never happened, Tommy. Do you understand? Last night never happened. I don't ever want any reference to it again.'

'Here yer are, Tommy,' Doris said cheerfully, holding out the overcoat to the bewildered young man. Giving him a none too gentle nudge, she added slyly, 'And the next time yer feel like getting a woman drunk, come and knock on my door. I'll be more than willing ter drink yer under the table.'

'Look, I don't want to appear rude, Tommy, but I'm anxious to get to the hospital.'

'Oh, oh, all right, Em.' Tommy was busily donning his coat, glad of something to do to hide his tortured emotions as the two women walked away.

'Here, yer was a bit short with Tommy,' Doris said, a hint of suspicion once again rearing its ugly head.

Quick to realise her mistake, Emily shrugged. 'Was I? I didn't mean to be. To tell the truth, Doris, I've still not recovered from last night and, like I said, I'm anxious to see my mum. I'll see Tommy later and apologise for being so abrupt.'

Doris was only too happy to take Emily at her word and when, some twenty minutes later, they entered the ward, they were chatting easily together.

Nellie was waiting for them, propped up on what seemed a mountain of pillows. She managed a crooked smile at the two young women as they made their way down the aisle of the ward. Seated in a chair by the bedside was Dot Button, her normally cheerful face subdued, and sporting a livid bruise beneath her left eye.

Sighting Emily and Doris, the stout woman rose awkwardly to her feet.

'Well, I'll be off then, Nellie,' she said quietly, averting her eyes from Emily's gaze.

'Oh, all right, Dot, it was good of you to come and see me. I should be home in a few days, God willing.'

Dot buttoned up her coat and tied a plaid scarf over her head, tying it in a knot under her chin. God willing! That was a good one. Where had Nellie's God been last night, when that swine of a man had nearly beaten the life out of her?

'Oh, don't go on our account, Mrs Button,' Emily said hastily.

Dot, all bustling motion, picked up her shabby handbag from the bed and nervously fidgeted with the brass clasp.

'No, it's all right, Emily, I was about ter go anyway.' Giving up her chair to Doris, Dot came round the side of the bed and stood in front of Emily, her eyes filled with guilt. Keeping her voice low so that Nellie couldn't hear what was said, she muttered, 'I was only gone a few minutes, love, I swear it. Yer know I wouldn't leave yer mum on her own, not after yer'd told me what'd happened. But yer mum said she'd like a cup of cocoa, only she didn't 'ave any, so I popped next door to get some of mine. Then I stopped ter visit the lav, an' when I got back, 'e was already laying into yer mum. He must 'ave been watching the 'ouse an' seen me leave. I tried ter stop 'im, love, 'onest, an' I gave 'im a good clout round the 'ead with the coal shovel, but the bastard just kept . . .' A sob caught in Dot's throat, and the sight of the robust, indomitable woman in such distress cut Emily to the quick.

'Oh, don't, Mrs Button, don't,' Emily cried, placing an arm round the broad shoulders.

'Dot, what is it, what's wrong?' Nellie was watching them through the narrow slits of her bruised eyes.

Hearing the agitation in her friend's voice, Dot pulled away from Emily. Like all cockneys, she wasn't one for demonstrative behaviour. Briskly now, she turned towards the bed.

'Nothing's the matter, Nellie Ford. Now yer just take it easy, an' do what them doctors tells yer to. An' don't let them nurses boss yer about. Right little tin gods they are. One of them tried ter throw me out,' she nodded at Emily. 'She did, the little madam. Well, I soon told her where ter go, didn't I, Nellie?'

'You did that, Dot,' Nellie smiled affectionately at the indignant woman. Even Emily, as worried as she was about her mother, couldn't help smiling at the image of the nurse trying to force her authority on Dot.

'Yes, well, I'll be off now, Nellie, but I'll be back later.'

'Thanks again for all your help, Dot, and don't tell Lenny anything just yet. Emily can see to him later, there's no point in worrying the poor boy.'

At the mention of her brother, Emily raised enquiring eyes to Dot, and when the woman gave an imperceptible shake of her head, Emily remained silent.

She waited until the bulky figure reached the end of the ward, then, with an exclamation of annoyance, she said, 'Oh, dear, I meant to ask Mrs Button to get some milk for me, only the milkman will have finished his rounds by the time I get home.'

Dot was waiting for Emily outside in the corridor.

'Right, love, I won't waste time,' she started abruptly.

'The truth of it is that nobody's seen 'ide nor hair of young Lenny since yesterday, but I couldn't tell yer mother that, could I? She's enough on 'er plate as it is. Anyway, I told 'er he'd rolled up outside me 'ouse this morning, an' I told 'im she'd got a day's cleaning work. Gawd knows where he really is.' Hitching up her ample breasts a notch further, she added grimly. 'I'll tell yer something else, while I'm at it. I'm off down the Hackney nick to press charges, I think that's what it's called, against yer old man. The way I see it, yer mum'll never do it, so I'm gonna make it me business to see he gets banged up. And if I can't get 'im on an assault charge, then I'll shop 'im fer being a conchie, so don't try an' stop me, Em, 'cos me mind's made up.'

'I've no intention of trying to stop you, Mrs Button,' Emily said, her voice ominously quiet. 'I'd planned to do the same thing myself. If they don't take any notice of you at the station, then I'll come with you later.'

'Oh, don't you fear, love, they'll take notice of me, I promise yer that. But if I do get any malarkey from the coppers, then I'll get the whole bloody street up there, 'cos the lot of them are just waiting fer a chance ter put yer dad away . . . And I'm sorry if that offends yer, love, but yer know me well enough ter know I don't mince me words – but the truth of it is, yer dad ain't liked round our part of the world. So, anyway, like I said, I'm off ter the cop shop, but I'll keep a look-out fer young Lenny, an' if I find him, I'll take him home with me till you can fetch him.'

'Thank you again, Mrs Button. My mum's very fortunate to have a friend like you . . . And I'm truly sorry you were hurt in trying to defend her.'

Dot gave a short laugh and pointed to the rapidly closing mauve eye.

'What this – pshaw! That's nothing compared ter the wallop I gave him. It's just a pity I didn't hit the bastard a damn sight harder. I might 'ave saved yer mum from . . .'

Emily waited while Dot pulled a none too clean handkerchief from her coat pocket and gave her nose a resounding blow, to cover up what she saw as a sign of weakness. Emily had the strongest inclination to throw herself into the redoubtable woman's arms, but she resisted the temptation. Like her neighbour, she too wasn't one for demonstrative behaviour.

Besides, she couldn't afford to waste time in self-indulgence, nor could she weaken in regard to her father. If she had her way, Alfie Ford was going to go away for a very long time.

'I'll stay with Mum for as long as I can, Mrs Button, and I'll come and see you as soon as I get home, to find out how you got on at the station.'

Dot was about to say something further, then stopped. The steeliness in Emily's blue eyes for a moment sent a chill up the older woman's spine. Nodding at the silent young woman, Dot turned and hurriedly left the hospital.

Behind her Emily took a deep breath and retraced her steps down the ward, and the nearer she came to her mother's bed, the faster her heart began to thud against her ribcage. For in the harsh, October sunlight her mother's injuries looked much worse than they had done last night.

Keeping a tight smile glued to her lips, she bent over and kissed her mother's forehead, saying softly, 'Sorry about that. How are you, Mum?'

'Oh, I'm fine, love, I'm fine,' Nellie answered, her gaze kept firmly on her daughter. She was very fond of Doris, but she wished that Emily had come by herself.

She hadn't minded Dot coming to see her – she was a comfort, was Dot – but she felt embarrassed and ashamed to be seen by anyone else, even though she knew what had happened to her wasn't her own fault. Oh, she knew well enough that some would argue that point, saying that if she'd stood up to her husband, instead of letting herself be used like a doormat all these years, then she wouldn't be lying here now. But it was easy to be judgmental when you were standing comfortably on the outside looking in.

Turning her head carefully, she looked at Emily, who was putting a small bunch of flowers into a vase on the bedside locker, taking her time over the simple task in order to get her emotions in check.

Dear Lord! How could he have done such a thing to a small, defenceless woman? All Emily's worst fears had been realised last night when she'd found her mother in a bloodied heap on the parlour floor. Oh, why had she gone out with Doris and the Carter twins? The whole evening had ended in disaster. She deliberately shied away from the memory of Tommy Carter. That episode in her life was over and done with. What she had to do now was look after her mother and make sure that her father never again had the opportunity to harm her mother. Pulling the visitor's chair out from under the bed, Emily sat down and took her mother's cold hands in hers. Under the shapeless hospital nightdress Emily could see a mass of bruising on her mother's arms and above her chest. Some bruises were faded, but most of them were the result of last night. She was afraid to look too long at Nellie's face, not because the bruised eyes and split lips upset her – she'd got over that shock last night, and had wept enough tears then, and again later on in the early hours of the morning; she doubted she had any tears left to shed. No, the reason she didn't want to dwell on her mother's injuries was because she was afraid. Afraid of the murderous feeling that kept sweeping over her; that hatred, so overpowering that it frightened her. She had never realised until this moment that she was capable of such intense, white-hot rage, especially against her own father. May he rot in hell, wherever he was.

On the other side of the bed, Doris stared at mother and daughter, her face filled with angry indignation.

'Fine! How can yer say yer fine, Mrs Ford? Bleeding hell, yer look a right state.'

'Doris!' Emily protested, but Doris was determined to have her say. 'Don't Doris me, Emily. Look at the pair of yer, tap-dancing round each other, pretending everything's all right. I mean, Gawd help us, I've seen boxers down the Mile End gym after twelve rounds look in better nick than yer mum does.'

Bristling with outrage, Doris was about to say more when a nurse appeared by the bed.

'I'm sorry, but morning visiting hours are over, you'll have to go, I'm afraid.' The nurse, the same one who had tried to get Dot to leave, stood her ground now, determined not to have her authority flaunted again, especially by two girls who were clearly much younger than she.

'Says who?' Doris looked up aggressively at the starchily dressed figure.

'Doris, please, don't cause a fuss, dear,' Nellie spoke wearily. She felt so tired, she just wanted to sleep, and sleep. Summoning up a semblance of a smile, she reached out and patted Doris's hand fondly. 'I'm very tired, Doris. Please don't think me ungrateful, but I'd like to get some rest.'

As Doris rose to leave, the nurse visibly relaxed, glad to have been spared another confrontation. Not that she would have backed down, not again. Even so, she stepped smartly out of the way of the girl with the bright orange fringe, which was visible beneath her gaudy scarf, and the yellow-tinged skin, which signified her trade as a munitions worker. Everyone knew they were a rough bunch.

'I'll catch up with you outside, Doris. I just want a quick word with my mum.'

When they were alone, Emily again took hold of Nellie's hands and asked softly, 'Why, Mum? What set him off this time? Or have things got so bad that he no longer needs an excuse?'

'Oh, don't, love, not now,' Nellie pleaded weakly, her hands beginning to tremble in Emily's tight grip.

'All right, don't get yourself into a state,' Emily said hurriedly, cursing herself for being so insensitive. But, as she made to leave, Nellie, a sudden worrying thought coming to her, pulled herself painfully up on the pillows and grabbed at Emily's arm.

'He was after your wages . . . He knew you were getting a month's wages. Lenny let it slip. I would never have told him.' Her voice was becoming weaker as she valiantly tried to say what was troubling her. 'If . . . if he comes back, give the money to him, Emily. Please, don't try and keep it, he'll only get . . .'

'Hush, Mum, don't upset yourself. And don't worry about me, I'm not that brave. If he comes back, I'll let him have it, I promise.'

Satisfied that her daughter was in no danger, Nellie slipped back into a fitful sleep.

'Really, Miss, you'll have to leave.' The nurse had returned, grimly prepared to assert her authority, but Emily appeared not to have heard.

Her eyes hard, she swept past the surprised nurse and walked purposefully down the long ward, the heels of her patent boots tapping out a staccato beat on the polished floor.

Oh, she'd let her father have it, all right. Just let him show his face – she was ready for him, more than ready.

CHAPTER NINE

Victoria Station on a cold, October morning was teeming with heavily laden figures in khaki. Most of them, mere boys, crowded at the gates, their faces resigned. Some, with the initial excitement now swept away, were facing the harsh reality of the moment. Behind the smiles and boisterous bravado – an act put on for the benefit of loved ones, and of course to boost their own self-image – lurked uncertainty and fear as they were momentarily separated from friends and family at the barriers, while stern officials examined passes, before being allowed through onto the platform.

Over the general hubbub of noise the stentorian voice of a military policeman called out, 'Dover this way! Folkstone that way!'

Here and there small groups of uniformed figures, who had made the long, arduous journey from the North of England, lay pathetically on the hard ground, their bodies resting on their kit bags, sleep giving them some respite from their frightened, despondent thoughts. For these men there were no familiar loved faces to see them off, no reassuring hand to cling to before boarding the train.

Occasionally, a khaki-clad figure moved against the surging tide of bodies, his face beaming with relief at being granted an extra day's leave for some reason. And if any of them had been offered a five-pound note for each precious minute of that day, it would have been swiftly repudiated.

Hurrying through the entrance, Emily, Doris, Ida Carter and her two sons joined the jostling, surging crowd, the women hanging grimly onto their hats and bags, afraid of losing them in the mêlée, while the two young men by their sides kept up a never-ending stream of careless chatter, trying to hide their fear, and to still the awful gnawing in their stomachs.

The women were parted from the men at the barrier, before being reunited on the platform by the train that seemed to hiss menacingly, as if waiting to tear husbands from wives, sons from weeping mothers, and fathers from children, their eyes wide in bewilderment, asking where their daddy was going.

'Well, this is it then,' Tommy said, still striving to keep the occasion on a light note. 'Now then, ladies, I don't want any pushing or shoving. Just form a queue and I'll give yer all a goodbye kiss.' His eyes lingered for a moment on Emily, but it was his mother on whom his gaze settled, his eyes pleading desperately for some last-minute show of affection, but Ida Carter's attention was firmly fixed on Andrew. The snub wasn't deliberate, and that was the hardest part to bear. For as far as Ida Carter was concerned, Tommy might as well not have been there. Yet the dark-haired young man had thought – no, prayed – that this time, when it might be her last chance to take him in her arms, she would recognise him as her son and give him a token of the love that she'd denied him all his life. Caught up in his own private thoughts, Tommy was unaware of the pitying glances of the girls and his brother, all of whom had seen the desolation in his eyes.

'Oh, son, son, what am I going to do without you?' Ida Carter sobbed as she hugged Andy fiercely to her breast. 'I can't bear it, I can't . . . Oh, Andrew . . . Andrew . . .'

Andy looked over his mother's head at his brother, and when those thin shoulders shrugged nonchalantly, a lump came to his throat. Bending down, he whispered in his mother's ear, 'Mum, don't go on, yer shouldn't have come. I told yer it'd be upsetting.'

Ida's small body jerked in surprise. Pulling away from the stocky figure, she looked up into his face.

'Shouldn't have come? What sort of a mother do you take me for, Andrew? As if I'd let my son go off to war without saying a proper goodbye.'

Her voice carried clearly, and when Emily saw Doris's face and body stiffen in anger, she quickly caught hold of her friend's arm, nodding her head warningly at her. His face grim, Andy once again bent his head and hissed fiercely, 'You've got another son too, Mum. Good God! I'd have thought that, today of all days, you could've at least given Tommy a hug, even if yer didn't mean it.' When his mother remained silent, he ground out between clenched teeth, 'Bloody hell. How can yer treat him like this? What harm has he ever done yer? Well, I'll tell yer this much, Mum. Either yer go and show some kind of affection ter Tommy, or yer'll find yerself with no sons. I mean it, Mum. Tommy's me brother, and I can't stand ter see him treated like this.'

Ida Carter stood still for what seemed an interminable time, and then, turning slowly, she looked at the slender, dark-haired young man and immediately felt the familiar revulsion take over her body. But this time her feelings were tinged with guilt. As Andrew had pointed out, Tommy had never done anything to deserve the way she'd treated him – and was still treating him.

She had loved him once, when he was a toddler and Sam, her husband, had still been with them. They had been so happy, the four of them, a happy, contented family, until the day Sam didn't come home from work. He hadn't even had the guts to tell her to her face that he had found somebody else. And when, some weeks later, he had returned for his things, she had followed him round the house, crying and pleading with him to stay, while he had studiously avoided eye contact before making a hurried, shame-faced exit; she had never seen him again. But he had left a reminder of himself behind. As the years had passed, and Ida had finally given up hoping that her husband would one day return, her love had turned to resentment, which in turn had grown into hate. And the poor, bewildered young boy found himself being cast to one side, while his fair-haired brother continued to enjoy their mother's loving ministrations.

Oh, Ida had fed and clothed Tommy, nursed him through childhood ailments, bathed cuts and bruises, but all with a detached anonymity that was far crueller than any physical abuse. In time Tommy had stopped trying to please the cold, distant woman; had stopped running to her, his small heart racing with pleasurable excitement, to show her the gold stars, earnt with painstaking work, pasted into his rough school book, his large eyes hopeful for a bit of praise. Those same eyes had filled with unshed tears as the prized school work was barely glimpsed at and was cast aside in favour of Andrew's efforts. Soon, he had stopped trying altogether, maintaining a show of indifference; but, though he put on a brave fare, the inner hurt had never gone away.

Now mother and son looked at each other, and for a minute Tommy's heart leapt with joy, then he saw Andy give the short figure a gentle push and immediately his hopes went crashing to the ground.

Forcing herself forward, Ida steeled herself to place her arms round the lean figure, but as she came nearer and Emily and Doris moved to one side to afford them some privacy, Tommy, his face set, said stiffly, 'Don't force yerself, Mum. You've never shown me any affection before. It's a bit late in the day ter start now, even if it is fer Andy's benefit.'

The rebuff startled Ida, and for a moment she had a wild urge to throw her arms round the grim-faced man, then she looked at him again, saw the hurt in his eyes and was momentarily ashamed. But it was no use. Every time she looked at this young man she saw only her husband, and with the remembrance came the pain of rejection, and bitterness.

She couldn't help the way she felt, nor could she pretend to a love that wasn't there. She wasn't made that way.

All around them, couples were holding each other fiercely. Children clung to their fathers' legs, while others squealed with delight as they were thrown playfully into the air, too young to know that they might never see the familiar, loved face again.

Emily and Doris stood silently, neither of them wanting to interfere in the Carter family's squabbles. The small group was being jostled on all sides, and when Ida returned to Andy's side, Emily stepped forward and gently put her arms round Tommy's neck.

'Take care of yourself, Tommy, and come back home safely, you and Andy.'

Tommy's arms wrapped themselves around Emily's small waist and pulled her hard against his body, desperate for some show of affection, some reassurance that he was loved and cared for. Against her ear he whispered,

'I'm sorry, Em, you know, for what happened.' As he felt her try to pull away, his grip tightened. 'Don't worry, Em, I won't ever mention it again. But I just wanted yer ter know that if . . . well, if anything happened because of . . . Well, I'd stand by yer.'

At his words Emily's body jerked in sudden fear. She hadn't even thought of the consequences of last night. Then she relaxed. You couldn't get pregnant the first time, everyone knew that. And there wasn't going to be a second time, so she had nothing to worry about.

When he let her go, they smiled at each other fondly.

'May God go with you, Tommy,' Emily said softly, before she was pushed none too gently to one side by an impatient Doris.

When Emily turned to Andy, Ida grasped hold of her son's arm possessively, her reddened eyes filled with anguish. She didn't want to share her beloved son with anyone, especially now, when their time together was so precious. When Andy roughly freed himself from his mother's clinging grasp, the hurt was so great that Ida felt like howling aloud. But she kept grimly silent, her eyes fixed steadfastly on the girl who was holding her Andy in her arms. And when she saw the joyous look on Andy's face, she closed her heart to the realisation that he had pushed his mother from his thoughts.

A few feet away Doris was standing close to Tommy, her tongue making idle chit-chat, her heart racing as she tried to pluck up the courage to tell her childhood friend her true feelings. The shrill blast of a whistle cut through the babble of noise, driving home the urgency of the time slipping away. Raising her eyes, Doris fixed her attention on the big white clock, watching as if spellbound the black minute-hand, which jerked round and round, eating up the time at what seemed an alarming rate.

'Well, this is it then, Doris. How's about a goodbye kiss

fer an old mate.' Tommy, about to pick up his heavy kit bag, stopped and grinned at the solemn young woman, his tone nonchalant, but Doris could hear the fear in his voice. Bracing herself, she threw caution to the winds, and with a deep breath she flung herself against the startled young man and threw her arms tightly round his neck.

Then, with tears raining down her face, she whispered urgently, 'I love yer, Tommy Carter. I know yer don't feel the same . . . but I had ter tell yer. I know I'm gonna feel a right idiot later, fer showing meself up like this, but I don't care. If this blasted war hadn't have happened, I'd probably never have told yer. But it did happen, and yer going away, and . . . and maybe this'll be the last chance I'll ever get. So I'll say it again . . . I love yer, Tommy. I'll always love yer, no matter what happens. So now yer know. Go on, yer can have a good laugh now, I don't care any more . . .'

Tommy, his face filled with amazement, gazed down at the bowed head and the plaid scarf that covered the unsightly orange hair. And strangely, it was the scarf, the camouflage behind which Doris hid, that brought home to him just how vulnerable she really was, despite her strident voice and vociferous chatter to the contrary. He was even more amazed at the sudden wealth of emotion that was surging through him. He shook his head, as if trying to clear his jumbled thoughts.

I love yer, Tommy Carter, I love yer. No-one had ever said that to him before. Oh, he knew Andy loved him, that went without saying. But to hear it put into words . . . !

A great lump came to his throat, and he could feel his eyes filling with tears, but somehow it didn't matter now to be seen crying.

Gently, very gently, he pushed Doris away and then, with shaking hands, he tilted her chin up so that he could see her more clearly. Even now, after baring her soul, her grey eyes stared back at him defiantly. The protective wall that she hid behind had once more come crashing down. Tommy stared down at the plain face wordlessly, not knowing what to say.

This was the girl who had won his prized marbles off him, beaten him in arm-wrestling, and bloodied the nose of the school bully after he'd tripped the young Tommy over in the playground, grazing his hands and tearing the skin off his palms as he'd tried to break his fall.

Now, looking at his childhood friend in a different light, Tommy swallowed painfully. Doris's unexpected declaration of love, although it had moved him deeply, hadn't kindled any reciprocal feeling on his part. He held her gaze, knowing just how hard it must have been, and the courage it must have taken to utter those words. And, oh how he wanted to be loved – needed to be loved. Yet as much as he craved for that elusive love he had never received from his mother, that same urgent longing that had been the catalyst of the disastrous night with Emily, he couldn't pretend to an affection he didn't feel. He thought too much of Doris to treat her so shabbily.

But he couldn't just leave her like this. He knew only too well what it was like to have love thrown back in your face – knew too the devastating pain of rejection. He felt Doris pull away and, without thinking, he grabbed her roughly by the waist, pulling her into his body. Neither of them knew afterwards who had made the first move, but they were suddenly holding each other close, as if they couldn't bear to be parted. Then, watched in amazement by the small group, they kissed fiercely, their tears mingling.

Emily watched the poignant scene, her own eyes filling with tears, while her lips spread into a quivering smile. Oh, she was glad for them, for Doris in particular. Now, even if the worst happened, Doris would always have this moment embedded in her memory.

For a brief second Emily's mind threw up the image of herself and Tommy lying by the roaring fire, but just as quickly she clamped down on the memory. She deeply regretted what had happened, but happened it had. Everyone made mistakes, and she and Tommy had had more reason than most to forget themselves in one wild, reckless moment.

Another shrill blast on an unseen whistle cut through the cold morning air. All around them soldiers, families and friends were frantically saying their last good-byes, snatching a last kiss, a last hug from a loved one. For some, it would indeed be the last kiss, the last hug. But for now the milling crowd of soldiers and civilians tried desperately to maintain an optimistic view, telling themselves that their loved ones would return. Others would die – it would be foolish to believe otherwise – but not their husbands, their sons, or their fathers. These precious men would remain immune to the bullets, cannons and bayonets and would return home unscathed. Thus prayed the mothers, daughters, sweethearts and wives.

The carriages were rapidly filling with khaki-clad figures leaning from open windows to grasp outstretched hands, or to plant a loving kiss on the cheek of babies and young children. Pandemonium ensued, as officials strode up and down the platform trying to maintain some kind of order.

Jostled on all sides, the Carter brothers, Emily and Doris strove to keep up a brave face, while close by Ida Carter sobbed uncontrollably.

Once inside the packed carriage, Tommy and Andy pushed and shoved their way to an open window.

'Look, there they are,' Doris cried as she raced along

the platform, followed closely by Emily and Ida. But the train was already pulling out of the station. Frantic hands were left empty as the train gathered speed. All around them the air was filled with the sound of quiet sobbing, as women and children stared after the disappearing train before making their way desolately back the way they had come. Back home to their small houses – their empty, cold houses – to carry on with their lives as best they could until their loved ones returned to them.

'Well, that's that then,' Doris sniffed noisily. 'No wonder they've nicknamed this station "The Palace of Tears". Bleeding hell, the sights we've seen would make a statue cry.' Shrugging her shoulders, she squeezed Emily's arm and added, 'We'd best get going. There's nothing to hang around for now, and I've got ter get ter work. They'll probably dock me wages fer being late, the tight sods. Not that I care. I'd 've given up a month's wages, rather than miss seeing them off.' Linking her arm through Doris's, Emily hugged her friend close to her side.

'I take it you told Tommy how you feel,' Emily said, smiling through her tears. Seeing the boys off had been more emotional than she'd imagined. She felt a genuine affection for both the Carter boys, but it was nothing compared to the love Doris had for Tommy, nor to the almost fanatical devotion that Ida Carter had for Andy.

Her voice still wobbly Doris grinned. 'Yeah I did, and yer know what, Em! He didn't push me away. In fact he . . .'

'You had no business being here.' Ida Carter, her face and eyes red and swollen, had come alongside them. 'I mean, it's not as if you're family, and that's what this occasion was meant for – family. As it is, you've robbed me of precious time with my son. Still, there's no point in harping on about it now. What's done is done and, like you said,' she inclined her head towards Doris, 'we'd best be getting ourselves home. If we all pool our money, we can get a taxi home, the same as we did to get here.'

Both girls stared at the small, slim woman in her tight, fitted black coat and hat, amazed at the woman's cheek. Bristling with rage, Doris thrust her chin forward, her eyes glittering with anger, and said grimly, 'Don't yer go getting all hoity-toity with us, yer old bat. Yer no better than I am, and certainly not better than Emily. She's a real lady, she is, and her mum. So yer can piss off home on yer own, 'cos I'm not sharing a taxi with the likes of you. In fact, I wouldn't share a far . . .'

'All right, Doris, all right.' Emily, her lips quivering with amusement, tried to keep her voice steady. Then she remembered how this woman had treated Tommy and her eyes hardened. Holding Doris tight by her side, she faced the indignant woman and, her voice dangerously low, said, 'You're a hard woman, Mrs Carter. Some might even say unfeeling. I certainly would. How you could treat your own flesh and blood, your own son, so cruelly, and on a day such as this, is beyond me. And regarding your request to share a taxi, I agree with Doris, so I'm afraid you'll have to make your own way home. Good day to you, Mrs Carter.' The two girls turned and left the older woman glaring after their retreating backs.

With a determined stride, the irate woman caught up with them and, grabbing hold of Emily's arm, she leant her face close and snarled, 'I won't forget this, young madam. And you can be sure I'll be having words with your mother about your attitude – that is, when she's finally released from hospital. Though I'll have to be quick to catch her in between visits, won't I?'

The sneering face turned to one of alarm as Emily moved closer, her actions becoming menacing. Then, to the delight of the silent Doris, Emily said clearly and precisely, 'Why don't you piss off, before you feel my hand across your face, you spiteful old witch.'

The older woman's jaw dropped in stunned amazement. Then, her lips twisted in rage, she screamed after them, 'A lady, eh? It didn't take you long to revert to type. Still, it's not surprising, considering the company you keep.'

She remained standing on the platform, still seething with rage, long after the two girls had disappeared from view.

While Emily's party had been pushing through the milling crowd, Matthew Winter's taxi had been pulling up at the entrance. Before the vehicle came to a complete stop, Matthew had already jumped from the running board onto the ground.

'Thanks,' he said impatiently, anxious to be off. The driver, an elderly man with a row of medals pinned to his chest, had kept up a running commentary during the entire journey. The man had served in South Africa, and when he wished Matthew 'Good luck, sir,' he knew the true worth of his words.

Matthew grasped the proffered hand and shook it warmly. Picking up his luggage, he walked into the station, his eyes darting to left and right, looking for a familiar face in the crowd. He had stopped off at Emily's house on the pretext of dropping off the keys to his uncle's house, only to be told by a rather stout lady from next door, who was sporting a livid purple eye, that he had just missed Emily, who was on her way to Victoria Station to see the Carter lads off. Hiding his disappointment, Matthew had left the keys with the woman, who had introduced herself as Mrs Button. With his own car left safely parked outside the house in Gore

Road, he had jumped back inside the waiting taxi and headed for Victoria Station.

Now he was here, all he had to do was find Emily. He hadn't the faintest idea what he would say to her. But what did it matter! As long as he saw her lovely face once more before leaving England, he would be satisfied.

Passing through the barrier onto the station, he pushed his way through a sea of khaki. Some, indignant at being jostled, turned to protest, their angry words dying on their lips at the sight of the tall officer.

Matthew pushed on, his anxious eyes searching the crowd for that familiar face. Then he saw her, but she wasn't alone. The light that came to his eyes dimmed as a young soldier caught Emily up into his arms. The sight of the two young people brought a sickening lurch to his stomach. Afraid that Emily would see him, Matthew turned quickly and walked down the station, getting into the first carriage he came to. Most of the seats were empty, the men on the station waiting until the last moment before boarding the train. Settling himself into a seat by the window, he stared out onto the teeming platform. Being what was known as a 'Return' – someone who had already seen action – the imminent crossing to France no longer held anything new for Matthew. No surprises, no expectations, only a fatalism that said; If a bullet has your name on it, it'll find you; if not . . . !

Yet though France held no new surprises, Matthew had always hated this part of the journey. He felt a genuine sympathy for the newly recruited soldiers, some looking barely old enough to shave, their faces alight with a dogged enthusiasm that covered the fear lurking beneath the brave façade.

But this time Matthew's thoughts were on Emily, and the disappointment that he was experiencing made him feel physically sick. His eyes brooding, he looked out of the grimy window, then quickly lowered his head. The last thing he wanted was for Emily to see him now. Because if she caught sight of him, she would probably drag her soldier friend over to meet him, and he couldn't have borne that.

A look of puzzlement crossed his face. That neighbour he had spoken to, what was her name . . . ? Oh, yes, Mrs Button. She had given him the impression that Emily, along with the ebullient Doris, was seeing off a couple of old friends. His lips twisted into a wry smile. Well! They had certainly seemed friendly enough. Suddenly Matthew felt old – old and dispirited.

A loud, shrill whistle broke into his thoughts, and grimly he shook his head, determined to put all thoughts of Emily from his mind. Even though he no longer worried about his own safety, his men were depending on him to bring them safely through the war.

'Excuse me . . . Oh, sorry, sir!' A young second lieutenant was leaning over Matthew to put his shiny new suitcase on the rack above Matthew's head.

'That's perfectly all right and, please, relax,' Matthew said kindly. 'There's no need for ceremony here.'

Nodding, the young officer sat down opposite Matthew, his face flushed. Taking a copy of *Punch* from his pocket, he tried to lose himself in the articles.

Sensing that the second lieutenant needed to be left alone, Matthew sat back, rested his head, closed his eyes and waited for the train to pull out.

They had been travelling for twenty minutes before he opened his eyes. They were now running through the outskirts of London. More and more green patches flashed by, as the train hurtled on its way to Dover. When the houses began to thin out and disappear from view, Matthew raised his eyes to the young man seated opposite him. The copy of *Punch* now lay unnoticed on his lap. The young officer, whom Matthew surmised had come straight from the Army Academy, was staring out of the window, his palm supporting his chin, his elbow resting on the narrow windowsill. Suddenly, uncontrollable tears welled up in his eyes. He glanced at Matthew, who quickly dropped his gaze to save the poor man from any further embarrassment. The young officer bit his lip, picked up the copy of *Punch* once more and held it before his face.

The poor bastard, Matthew thought sympathetically. But there was nothing he could do. To offer any commiseration would only add to the man's discomfort.

Settling back once more, Matthew closed his eyes and waited for the train to reach its destination.

CHAPTER TEN

A week passed and still there was no sign of either Lenny or Alfie Ford.

True to her word, Dot Button had registered a complaint against Alfie, but she was unable to do the same on behalf of her friend Nellie. Despite all her arguments, the police sergeant was adamant. Only the person who had been the victim of an assault could press charges against their attacker, and as Nellie was unlikely to take such a step, Dot had left Hackney police station with a heavy heart. Her own injuries were mild compared to those her dear friend had suffered at the hands of that maniac, so even if the police did catch Alfie, he was hardly likely to be banged up for belting Dot in the face, painful though it had been. As the sergeant had pointed out, if they locked up everyone guilty of blacking someone's eyes, half the East End would be in the Scrubs. As for the business of Alfie refusing to join up, again she was out of luck. According to the sergeant, they could only act if the military police asked for their help in rounding up such men. And so far Alfie Ford seemed to have escaped their attention.

So it was in stunned disbelief that both Dot and Emily accompanied a determined Nellie to Hackney police station two days after her discharge from hospital, and there listened in delighted amazement as the normally placid woman, armed with a letter from the hospital doctor describing her injuries in detail, formally laid charges against her husband for committing grievous bodily harm to her person.

Now, with only a week of her holiday left, Emily was beginning to worry about what would happen to her mother, once she herself was no longer around to provide moral support. She had seen to it that the lock on the front door was changed, and a heavy bolt fitted to the top of the door. But she would feel a lot happier if Lenny was back home, before she left to return to the Winters. Yet apart from an occasional note, hastily written in Lenny's scrawled handwriting and dropped through the letterbox to assure them that he was well and would be home soon, neither of the two women had been quick enough to catch the errant young man on his brief visits, and Emily, as well as being worried, was also beginning to feel angry at his childish behaviour.

Nellie, too, was starting to fret about her son. This was the longest he had ever been missing from home, and these last few days had seen her walking the streets hoping to run into her son.

He had been seen in the East End markets, where he was well known, doing a few hours' work here and there, but despite the messages that Nellie had left for him with the stall-holders, asking Lenny to come back home, the seventeen-year-old young man remained elusive.

Now, on a bitterly cold October morning, Nellie was preparing to go out again.

'Oh, Mum, why didn't you wake me?' Emily, wearing a long white calico nightgown, her wavy chestnut hair tumbling about her shoulders, walked into the parlour. Yawning loudly, she hurried over to the fire where the black lumps of coal were just beginning to catch light. 'Bbrrr, it's freezing in here,' she said, her teeth chattering. Seeing her mother about to don her heavy coat, she protested, 'Hang on a minute, Mum, where are you going? Lord, it's not even seven o'clock yet.'

'I'm popping down Well Street to get a bit of shopping,' Nellie replied, her fingers doing up the large plastic buttons of her coat. 'There's a pot of tea made,' she inclined her head towards the table and the tray set for one. 'There's enough bread for some toast if you want some. I shouldn't be too long.' Then before Emily could stop her, Nellie was gone. A blast of cold air from the opened door caused Emily to shiver violently.

Hurrying back upstairs, she grabbed her cord dressing-gown from the bottom of the bed and, wrapping it round her shivering body, descended back down the stairs.

An hour later she was peering out of the window, anxiously biting at her bottom lip. It didn't take this long to buy a few groceries. Well Street was only five minutes' walk from here, and half the stalls wouldn't even be set up yet. 'Oh, Mum . . . Mum, where are you?' she murmured fretfully, her breath steaming up the window. Rubbing the glass clear with the back of her hand, she was about to turn away when the familiar figure of her mother came into view. Sighing with relief, Emily pulled open the door exclaiming, 'Mum, where have you been? I was just starting to get really worried.'

'Stop your fussing, Emily, I haven't been that long. Look, take this shopping and put it away, will you, while I get a bit of warmth from the fire. It's perishing out there.' Holding her hands out over the now blazing coals, she called over her shoulder, 'And put the kettle on, love, I'm dying for a cup of tea.'

When they were both seated either side of the fire, with mugs of steaming tea clasped in their hands, Emily asked quietly, 'Where did you go, Mum? And don't tell me you just went down Well Street. You've been gone over an hour.'

Taking a sip of the steaming liquid, Nellie looked over the rim of her mug and sighed.

'Why ask what you already know? Anyway, I didn't have anything better to do, and I can't sleep properly lately, so . . . !' Her slim shoulders rose and fell, her whole attitude one of utter dejection.

Seeing her mother looking so forlorn, Emily was torn between a desire to comfort her and to give her a good shaking. And as for her brother! Lord, but she'd give Lenny a skinning when she got hold of him. Unlike her mother, Emily, although worried, was certain that Lenny could look after himself. She also had a good idea of the reason behind Lenny's absence. She thought back to the afternoon of her return home, and the scene she had walked in on. She remembered, too, the frightened, almost shamefaced way Lenny had reacted before running off. An image of her brother's stricken face flashed before her eyes, and immediately Emily was ashamed of her harsh condemnation of the immature youth. He couldn't help it, poor devil. It must have been awful for him, seeing his mother's bruised face, and knowing that there was nothing he could do to help her. No wonder he had run off like he had. Wherever he was now, he was probably trying to make up a good excuse, as well as working up the courage to return home.

The rattle of the letterbox made both women lift their heads and look towards the door.

Emily reached the doormat first, picking up the brown envelope and turning it over to see who it was addressed to.

'Who's it for, love?' Nellie asked nervously. It was a special event to receive a letter. These days the postman was seen as a portent of doom. When he walked down the street, looking at the numbers on the rows of neat, terraced houses, women whose men were overseas peeped from behind net curtains, their hearts thumping, before heaving a sigh of relief when the uniformed man passed their door. But Nellie had no man away fighting, so who could have . . . ! She started to rise from the chair as Emily, the brown envelope held in one hand, pulled open the door and looked in both directions up and down the street.

'What is it, love?' Nellie called out anxiously.

Turning her head slightly, Emily held out the brown envelope to Nellie.

'It's another note from Lenny, though he doesn't usually bother putting it in an envelope. There's no stamp on it, so he can't be too far away. Wait till I get my hands on him, the silly begger, dropping notes through the letterbox and running off, instead of coming in and putting your mind to rest. He must know you've been worried sick about him.' Taking her coat down from the peg on the back of the door, Emily didn't stop to put it on properly, but pulled it tight around her shoulders. 'I'll see if I can find him,' she called out. 'He can't have got that far.'

Before she pulled the door to, she saw her mother take out a small scrap of paper from the envelope. Once outside the house, she again looked up and down the street, not knowing which way to go. Seeing Mrs Riley coming out of her house, she called out, 'Morning, Mrs Riley. Have you seen Lenny, by any chance?'

Mavis Riley, an energetic sixty-year-old widow, shook her head, her eyes curious.

'Sorry, Emily, I haven't seen the lad for well over a

week now. There's nothing wrong, is there, love? I'm not being nosy, but I couldn't help noticing he hasn't been at home, and he's not normally away for this long.'

Hugging the coat tighter about her body, Emily smiled. 'I know you're not being nosy, Mrs Riley, and no, there's nothing wrong – that is, I hope not.' Turning to go back indoors, she added, 'If you do see him, could you tell him I've been looking for him.'

'Aye, Emily, I'll do that. And tell your mum if there's anything I can do, just knock on me door, it's always open.'

Thanking the woman, Emily took one last look up and down the street before hurrying back indoors.

'There's no sign of him, Mum, and it's too cold to go running round the streets after him.' Dropping the coat over the back of the chair, she walked over to where Nellie was sitting in the armchair by the fire. 'What does he have to say for himself this time?' Emily asked, her eyes going to the note held in Nellie's hand.

Nellie looked up, smiling weakly. 'He says he's sorry if I've been worried, and he'll be home before you have to go back to work. In the meantime he's stopping at a friend's house, and . . . Oh! here, have a look for yourself.'

Taking the piece of paper, Emily scanned the scribbled handwriting. The note was in the same vein as the previous ones, short and to the point. Yet, there was something that didn't feel right . . .

Careful to keep her voice light she said, 'I didn't know he had any close friends, well, close enough to put him up for any length of time.'

'Oh, he has plenty of friends from the market, but as you say, I can't see any of them letting him stay longer than a day or two. He's probably been going from one house to another, stopping a night here and there . . .'

117

She stopped for a moment, her lips curving into a sad smile. 'He always sees staying with friends as a kind of adventure. Not that he would have stayed away this long, if you hadn't been here to keep me company. And, like he says . . .' she nodded towards the note in Emily's hand, 'he'll be back home before you have to leave.'

Leaning forward in the chair, Nellie smiled up at her daughter. 'You've only a week left of your holiday, and we've hardly spent any real time together. I was so looking forward to your stay, yet I've hardly had the chance to talk to you, what with one thing and another. So why don't you sit down, forget about your brother for now, and we'll make good use of the time we have left.'

Nellie waited until Emily was sitting opposite her in the sagging armchair before resuming their conversation. Keeping her tone light she said, 'Dot told me Captain Winter came looking for you. She remarked on what a handsome man he is. Tell me, has the poor man been seeing anyone, I mean, in the way of female companionship? After all, it's been a while since his wife died, poor soul, and he's not a young man any more.'

Emily's lips twitched in amusement at her mother's blatant attempt to try and elicit information from her concerning her employer's nephew. Folding her hands in her lap she leant forward, her eyes sparkling with laughter.

'You're about as subtle as a lorryload of bricks, Mum. And no, I don't know if Captain Winter has a lady friend. He doesn't confide in me about personal matters. I'm only the hired help, after all. As for him looking for me, well . . . There was no ulterior motive in his coming here. He merely dropped the house keys off before rejoining his regiment – unless of course he planned to whisk me off to some posh restaurant and propose to me over a glass of champagne.'

Nellie flapped her hands indignantly. 'I don't know what you're talking about, I'm sure. I was only stating what a nice man he was. Besides, what if I was dropping hints about his feelings towards you? All mothers want the best for their children, it's only natural.' Two bright spots of colour stained her cheeks as she defended herself against Emily's sardonic attack. Pulling herself further up in the armchair she added quietly, 'I want the best for you, Emily, and that means you having all the things I didn't, including a husband who will love and protect you. And if that man happens to come from a wealthy family, then so much the better.'

'Oh, Mum,' Emily breathed lovingly. Leaning over, she caught hold of her mother's hands. 'I know you only want the best for me, but if you're setting your heart on Captain Winter as a son-in-law, then you're going to be sadly disappointed. Like I said before, I'm only the hired help. Besides, I don't think of him in that way, nor does he of me, I'm sure. Anyway . . .' she gently shook the small hands chidingly, 'he's a lovely man, but he's also old enough to be my father.' As the hands jerked in hers, Emily's eyes clouded over. 'Speaking of which . . .'

Before Emily could finish her sentence, Nellie pulled her hands away abruptly. The last person she wanted to talk about was Alfie. Over the past few days Emily had constantly asked her mother why she had put up with him all these years. How could Nellie put into words the shame and guilt she felt, as if somehow it was her fault that things were the way they were between her and Alfie. No, she didn't want to talk about it, didn't even want to think about it. She'd done what she should have done years ago, and now it was up to the police to punish her husband. And pray God they would, and soon; for she wouldn't rest easy until she knew that Alfie was safely locked up, out of harm's way. Briskly now, she deftly changed the subject.

'You still haven't shown me the things Miss Rose gave you before she left on her holiday.'

Emily looked lovingly into the tired, almost haggard face, her heart leaping once again with pity at the bruising, which was fading but still clearly visible around the soft, blue eyes. The deep cut in Nellie's upper lip had almost healed, but how the rest of her mother's injuries were faring Emily didn't know, for Nellie was careful to keep her body covered at all times.

Emily's gaze took in the thin brown hair caught up into a scraggly bun fastened at the back of her neck, before travelling downwards to the dowdy, shapeless brown blouse and black hobble skirt above the scuffed boots, and a germ of an idea came into her mind.

Springing to her feet she said eagerly, 'I'll go and fetch them.' Within minutes she was back, holding the bulky parcel under her arm. Dropping to her knees, she deftly untied the string around the brown paper and opened the parcel outwards. Her delighted eyes looked down at the small pile of clothes.

'Ooh, Emily,' Nellie breathed in admiration at the collection of brightly coloured garments.

Leaning back on her heels, Emily began sorting through the dresses, blouses and skirts, her mind silently thanking Miss Rose for her kindness, while at the same time apologising for her previous uncharitable thoughts regarding the gift. Deftly sifting through the clothes, she picked up a dark red dress and held it up to the fire, her keen eyes looking for any faults in the soft, woolly material. Finding none she said briskly, 'Stand up, Mum. I want to see if this fits you.'

Nellie's eyes stretched wide at the sudden request.

Seeing her mother's bewilderment, Emily laughed,

'Come on, Mum, it's not going to bite you – at least I hope not. Lord knows how long it's been in the attic, because I've never seen Miss Rose wear it.'

Nellie rose obediently and let Emily hold the dress up against her thin body. It was a plain dress, the only adornment being a row of small, pearl buttons down the bodice, and the leg-of-mutton sleeves were years out of date, but to Nellie it was the most beautiful dress she had ever seen.

'It could do with shortening, and those sleeves will have to be altered, but that's no problem. Try it on properly, Mum, while I fetch the sewing basket.'

In a daze Nellie undressed, then, as if suddenly remembering, quickly slipped the woollen dress over her head and wriggled her arms into the long sleeves, letting the soft fabric fall over her slim hips to the floor, but not before Emily had caught sight of several deep weals across her mother's bare back.

Her lips tightened in anger. Then, swallowing hard, Emily carefully placed several sewing pins between her teeth, knelt down and deftly tacked the trailing material into an even hemline. When she had finished she carefully lifted the dress over Nellie's head and, settling herself into the armchair, began sewing up the hem with small, experienced stitches before unpicking the sleeves. As she watched Emily's fingers expertly altering the beautiful dress, Nellie's heart began to beat with pleasurable excitement.

It was now late afternoon. Emily washed and curled Nellie's hair with heated tongs, before allowing her mother to try on the finished article, after which the two women went upstairs. Nellie went quickly to the scarred wardrobe and took out her best pair, her only pair, of shoes. Pulling the ugly boots off, she slipped her feet into the black patent shoes, took a deep breath and looked at her image in the full-length mirror on the wall.

She hardly recognised herself in her new finery. And though her face still bore testament to her recent ordeal, it didn't look so bad now, not with her hair waved and falling around her cheeks and forehead. Her heart fluttering wildly, she ran her hands down the sides of her body, turning this way and that in order to get a better look.

Sitting on the double bed, Emily watched her mother's joy and felt a lump come to her throat. Why, oh why, hadn't she done something like this before, she asked herself? But she had, many times, though in the past her mother had always refused any of the garments that Emily had offered her. And the reason wasn't hard to figure out. The last thing her mother would have wanted was to make herself attractive while her husband was around. At the thought, Emily bowed her head, her heart full to bursting at the awful existence her mother had endured for years. Then her head snapped back up. That was all in the past now. With her father on the run, her mother could start a new life. Closing her eyes, Emily offered up a silent prayer. 'Please, God, wherever he is, keep him there, or let the police catch him and put him away. Don't let him come back into Mum's life. She's had enough, and she deserves to be left in peace.'

But the prayer gave her no comfort. Life was never that simple. Yet it was times like this – seeing someone that you loved happy, knowing that it was you who had made them so – that made it all seem worth while somehow. Now, if only Lenny would show his face, her mother's happiness would be complete. Emily could only hope that happiness wouldn't be short-lived.

CHAPTER ELEVEN

Later that evening, Lenny, his face flushed from running, swung open the heavy doors of the Red Lion pub in Stoke Newington. Uncertain of himself, he pushed his way awkwardly through the bevy of men, his eyes darting anxiously from left to right as if in search of someone. Then his face broke into a smile of relief. More confident now, he made his way towards a table at the back of the pub.

'Hello, Dad. I did it, I did what yer told me to.'

Alfie Ford looked up from his pint of beer at the grinning young man.

'Yeah, all right, don't go telling the whole pub our business,' he snapped, his eyes furtively darting around the packed pub.

The smile slid from Lenny's face.

'Sorry, Dad, I didn't mean ter . . .'

'Look, just sit yerself down, will yer,' Alfie said impatiently. Doing as he was bid, Lenny sat down on a rickety chair, his eyes downcast. Seeing his son's abject expression, Alfie gave him a hearty slap on the back.

'Gawd help us, son, yer look a right bleeding misery.

Now then, tell me what happened,' he said, leaning his head closer in order to keep their conversation private. Hearing the jovial tone, Lenny's face brightened.

'I did what yer said, Dad. I put the letter through the letterbox, then I ran fer it. I saw Emily come out, but she didn't see me. I was hiding round the corner at the top of the street.'

'Good lad. Now then, answer me truthfully. Yer didn't see yer mum, did yer. 'Cos yer know she'll only try ter stop yer if she finds out.' The moment the words were out of his mouth, Alfie realised what a stupid question it was. If either his wife or daughter had caught Lenny, his son wouldn't have been able to keep his mouth shut for long and he, Alfie Ford, would have been locked up in a cell by now. His hand tightened around the glass of beer. He still couldn't believe that Nellie had shopped him to the police. After all these years, and all he'd done for her, the bitch had gone and shopped him. All right, so he had gone over the top that night, but bloody hell, she had driven him to it. All he'd wanted was a few quid for some fags and a couple of drinks. But, oh no, she wasn't going to give Emily's hard-earned money to him to squander. That was what she'd said, the cow. Wait until Emily comes home, and ask her for it yourself, she'd added for good measure, knowing full well that their daughter wouldn't have given him a brass farthing, not after she'd seen the black eye he'd given Nellie.

Well, he'd given her a bloody sight worse later that night, hadn't he? And she had no-one to blame but herself, and Emily. 'Cos if they hadn't been so hard-faced and mean, if Nellie had handed over some of Emily's wages, then he would have gone off happy and nobody would've been hurt. Instead of which, all hell had broken loose, and when that nosy old cow from next door had barged in, he had totally lost control.

When he had fled the house he had been running scared, afraid for the first time at what he had done. He had watched unnoticed from the top of the street as his wife was carried into the ambulance, his heart sinking as he'd realised that this time he had gone too far. And it wasn't only Nellie who had suffered that night, the old bat from next door had copped it as well. Thinking of that moment when his fist had connected with Dot Button's eye brought a smile of pleasure to his unshaven face.

But the biggest stroke of luck had been running into Lenny in Bethnal Green Road. Mind you, it hadn't been as easy to placate Lenny as he'd expected. At first the youth had been angry and upset, the image of his mother's bruised face, as he'd run from the house, still etched in his memory. And even as Alfie had wheedled and apologised, his hands had been stained with Nellie's blood.

It had taken a lot of cajoling on Alfie's part, but finally he had managed to convince Lenny of his remorse, and of course had promised never to raise his hand to Nellie again. Afterwards it had been relatively easy to talk Lenny into staying with his father at a hostel in Mile End Road for a few days, laughingly saying that it would give the two women a chance to have a good old natter. And Alfie had also expertly managed to part the hapless youth from the small amount of money in his pocket. A week later, fed up with the cramped room and his son's inane chatter, Alfie had been wondering if it was safe to return home when he had run into an old workmate, who had taken great pleasure in informing Alfie that the police were after him.

Draining the last dregs of his beer, Alfie laid the glass heavily down on the round table. He still wasn't sure if the man had been lying, but he couldn't take the risk. The police didn't take much notice of domestic disputes as a rule, but there was a big difference between giving your wife a slap in the face on a Saturday night and nearly beating her to death. Left with only two choices, prison or enlistment, Alfie had quickly chosen the latter.

With a bit of luck he'd end up behind the lines, and if not – well, there was always the old dodge of shooting yourself in the foot. And if he was going to join up, he might as well take his son with him.

Lenny's eagerness to join up had been pathetic to see. Even Alfie, hard as he was, had felt a momentary jerk of shame at his son's excited willingness to take up arms and fight for King and country, but his brief spasm of conscience hadn't lasted long. Whatever love he had once felt for the boy had vanished the day he'd discovered that his son would never be right in the head. Now Alfie wanted vengeance on the woman who had forced him to put his life at risk, and what better way to get his own back than to take her darling son to war?

It had been easy enough to sign up. Although he had primed Lenny to lie about his age, when they had both presented themselves at the recruiting office, Alfie had held his breath when the recruiting sergeant asked how old they both were. But Lenny, his chest puffed out with pride, had looked the man straight in the eyes and said loudly, 'Eighteen, sir.' Though Alfie needn't have worried. By now the powers that be had become so desperate for new recruits that the age-limit was frequently breached, through the patriotic complicity of enthusiastic applicants and blind-eyed recruiting sergeants.

The medical, too, was passed without incident, and in a few days' time they would be heading for the Isle of Wight for their training period, and then . . .

'Are we gonna stay in the hostel tonight, Dad?'

Jerked from his reverie, Alfie looked into the bottom of his glass and grimaced. In a way, he would be glad when he donned his uniform. At least then he could be sure of a bed and decent food.

'I earnt a few bob down Roman Road today, Dad. I can get yer another drink if yer want.'

Wiping the back of his mouth with his hand, Alfie grinned and slapped Lenny hard on the back.

'Yer a good lad, Lenny . . . 'Ere, what d'yer reckon to that over there?' Following his father's gaze, Lenny looked across the crowded bar to the snug, blushing furiously when a heavily made-up woman, obviously the worse for wear, winked broadly at him over the rim of her raised glass. 'Bleeding 'ell, look at the state of it! I wouldn't know whether to shake 'er 'and, or throw 'er a bone.' Chuckling loudly, Alfie took the proffered florin from Lenny's hand and weaved his way through the crowd towards the bar.

Lenny watched him go, his eyes thoughtful. Remembering Mrs Button's words, he smiled. He wasn't as daft as people thought, and if his father had ever spent some time with his son, Alfie would have realised it. And though Lenny was frightened – well, scared to death of what lay ahead – he was also proud of himself.

For the first time in his life he was going somewhere he would be treated like an equal. He would have to be careful, though. Sometimes, usually when under stress, he would act like a young boy, but if he kept his mouth shut and copied the other men in the training camp, he should be able to bluff his way through without any trouble. And when he went, he would be taking his father with him. He had agonised for years over how he could make his adored mother safe from his father's brutal behaviour. Now he had done it. His mum would be safe from harm now, and that was all that mattered. Raising his eyes to the bar, he caught his father staring at him and smiled.

His dad thought he was so clever, but this time Lenny had got the better of him. For a moment he thought of his mother, his eyes misting over. He knew she would be worried about him, even with that last note he'd slipped through the letterbox, saying he would be back home before Emily left. That bit had been his dad's idea, in the hope that it would stop Nellie from pestering the stall-holders, trying to find the whereabouts of her son. Lenny felt bad about lying to his mother. But he couldn't have told her his plans. She would have stopped him straight away.

Still, it was for the best. In a few months' time he would be eighteen, then he would write again, telling her where he was.

He glanced up once more and saw his father making his way back to the table and thought grimly: No, I ain't as daft as you think, Dad. In fact right now, I don't feel daft at all.

CHAPTER TWELVE

'Oh, come on, Em, say yes. It would be great working together, and it would mean yer didn't have ter leave yer mum on her own. What d'yer say, Em? Yer could at least think about it.'

The two women were seated in a small booth in a fish and chip shop just off the Roman Road market. They had spent the best part of the morning browsing through the stalls, without actually buying anything, which was unusual for Doris, who loved nothing better than haggling with the stall owners in search of a bargain. But on this Saturday morning Doris had other, more pressing matters on her mind. Two days earlier, one of the women in the munitions factory had lost two of her fingers, when the TNT she was packing had gone off without warning. The experience had badly shaken Doris, causing her to rethink her profession. Not one to stand idle, she had set about finding alternative work. The idea of working on the trams had always appealed to her, but it would be a lot better if she could persuade Emily to join her. Taking another mouthful of plaice and chips, she chewed rigorously, her eyes fastened on the young woman opposite.

Seeing the pleading look in Doris's eyes, Emily shook her head in wry amusement.

'Good Lord, Doris, I'll say one thing for you, you're persistent, I'll give you that. You could talk a glass eye to sleep with your chatter. If you don't mind, I'd like to finish my dinner in peace.'

'Does that mean yer'll think about it? Oh, all right, I'll leave yer in peace,' Doris said, her face and tone filled with exaggerated acceptance.

For the next few minutes they concentrated on their meal, but as soon as Emily had laid down her knife and fork, Doris resumed her campaign.

'It's good wages – not as good as I get now, but at least it'll be safer. And I won't have that awful journey back an' forward every day. As I said, the money's not as good on the trams, but it's a lot more than you get, so what . . . ?'

'Doris, please, give it a rest,' Emily pleaded. Pushing away her plate, she leant her elbows on the marble-topped table and said, 'You know how I'm fixed. I can't just leave the Winters. They've been good to me, and, well, they depend on me . . .'

'Play on yer good nature, more like,' Doris interrupted.

'That's as may be,' Emily retorted. 'But there is such a thing as loyalty. Now, I'm not saying I won't leave them; in fact I've been thinking about doing just that for some time, but I'll have to wait until they find someone to take my place.'

Doris leant forward eagerly.

'Yer never said yer was thinking of leaving service. Why didn't yer tell me? I am yer best friend, ain't I . . . ? Oh, it don't matter . . .' She waved her hand in front of Emily's face. 'So . . . what yer saying is, yer'll leave the Winters as soon as they can get someone ter fill yer place,' she gave a short laugh. 'That'll take some doing, Em. Especially on the money they're offering. Still, I suppose there's plenty who'd do it for a roof over their heads, and a full belly – and I thought yer told me once it was bad manners ter lean yer elbows on the table.'

'What! Oh, yes, I did, didn't I?' Emily smiled affectionately at her friend. She was about to make a suitable rejoinder when a woman of about their own age appeared by their table, with a clean, wet cloth in her hand. Nodding towards their plates she asked, 'You two finished?'

'Yeah, we're finished, love. Here yer are,' Doris said cheerfully, holding her plate out for the waitress to take. The woman's eyes flickered over Doris's smiling face, before lowering her gaze to the yellow-tinged hands, her nose wrinkling in distaste. Doris was quick to notice the look and would have let it pass without comment, if the woman hadn't used the cloth she was holding to pick up Doris's plate gingerly, as if touching a dead rat.

'Don't worry, it ain't catching,' Doris spat out angrily, as she moved along the bench and out of the narrow booth. She had become accustomed to the hurtful looks and comments, and would have let the matter drop, but Emily, outraged at what she saw as an open attack on her dear friend, wasn't about to let the incident pass without notice.

Sliding along the bench, Emily stood up in front of the sullen waitress and said icily, 'How dare you treat my friend in such a disrespectful manner, you stupid, ignorant woman.' All chatter ceased as the other customers craned their necks to see what the disturbance was about. 'If you had any sense at all, you would realise what courage it takes to work in munitions. Women like my friend risk their welfare, and their lives, every day for this country and the men fighting overseas. They should be treated with respect, not scorn. What the hell do you think gives you the right to look down your nose at . . .'

'Leave it, Em, she ain't worth it.' Doris had hold of Emily's arm and was pulling her towards the door, but Emily hadn't finished.

Turning her attention to the owner, a burly, red-faced man who was staring at the scene, she said scathingly, 'Rest assured, sir, we won't be frequenting this establishment again. Good day to you.' The last thing she saw was both owner and waitress staring after her with open mouths.

Once outside in the market, Emily pulled out her gloves, angrily shoving each finger into its allotted place, her body still quivering with anger. Then she heard the laughter, softly at first, then rising to an infectious, full-throated bellow of glee. Spinning round she saw Doris, her hands holding her side, doubled up in mirth.

'Cor, blimey, Em, I ain't had such a good laugh since me Aunt Flo caught her tit in the mangle. Yer should have heard yerself in there.' Wiping her streaming eyes, she placed a hand on her hip and, in a pseudo-posh voice, said loftily, 'We shan't be using this establishment again. Bleeding hell, Em, it's a fish and chip shop, not the blooming Ritz.'

Emily stared at the figure convulsed in laughter and felt her own lips begin to twitch.

'Well, maybe I did overdo it a bit, but she made me so flaming mad, treating you like that. Did you see her apron? It must have had a month's chip fat on it, and she had the cheek to look down her nose at you.'

Arm-in-arm the two women walked slowly down the market towards the tram-stop.

'Yer know, Em, before the war, yer couldn't walk down the market – any market – without saucy comments and whistles flying after yer. Now yer could walk the length of Hackney Wick in yer drawers without risk of being molested.'

'You sound as if you're complaining.' Emily smiled.

Doris shrugged her shoulders. 'Being chatted up by the stall-holders used ter be half the fun of shopping down the markets. Mind you, yer still get the odd bloke who fancies his chances, even though most of them are coffin-dodgers, but it ain't the same.' Suddenly she shivered and huddled closer to Emily. 'I wonder where Tommy and Andy are right this minute? I hope neither of them is silly enough to try to be a bleeding hero. There's enough have done that already.'

'I know, I read the papers too, though just lately I've tried to avoid reading about the war. It's different now that men I know, and care for, are among those fighting. They're not just faceless uniforms any longer, but real people, just like Tommy and Andy – and Captain Winter.' Shivering inside her thick green coat, Emily pulled the cowl collar up around her ears. 'It's funny, but I never thought of Captain Winter being in danger. I mean, I knew he was away fighting, but I never dwelt on it. Maybe that's the best way to cope – not to dwell on things, I mean – but it's not so easy as it sounds.'

Seeing the tram rounding the corner the two women inched up closer in the queue, ready to repel any late-comers who might try to push in.

Once inside, Emily hurried to the front of the tram where she could see some empty seats. Sliding across the slatted wooden bench, she stared out of the window, deep in thought, while Doris made herself busy trying to find out about wages and hours from the young conductress.

Grateful for a bit of time to herself, Emily pondered on the future. She would dearly love to join Doris on the trams – that is, if there were any vacancies, but she still felt herself bound by loyalty to remain with the Winters until a replacement could be found to take her place. She didn't need Doris to remind her that it would be no easy task. And aside from worrying about her employers, she still had her mother to contend with. A mother who still clung to the hope that her only daughter would marry someone like Captain Winter – or even the man himself! Smiling to herself, Emily imagined what the captain would say if he realised that Mrs Ford had him down as a possible candidate for son-in-law.

'What yer smiling ter yerself for?' Doris nudged Emily in the ribs. 'If yer've something funny on yer mind, yer can share it around; we could all do with a bit of a laugh.'

Shaking her head Emily replied, 'No, it's nothing important, honestly.' As dear as Doris was to her, Emily knew that if she got wind of her mother's aspirations, she, Emily, would never hear the end of it. Later, as they parted company outside Emily's house, they made arrangements to go out for a drink later on that evening.

'I'll come and knock fer yer about seven. See yer.' Emily waited until Doris reached her door, then, with a final wave, she entered the house.

'Hello, love. Did you buy anything nice?' Nellie came out of the scullery, wiping her hands on a floral apron tied around her waist. Taking her coat and hat off and hanging them behind the door, Emily wiped a strand of hair from her eyes and looked up. Once again she was amazed at the change in her mother in such a short space of time.

Nellie was wearing a royal blue jumper and a black skirt that Emily had altered to calf-length, both garments from the parcel that Emily had brought home. Nellie had protested at first, alarmed at the thought of showing her ankles, even though it had been the fashion for many years.

'No, there was nothing I saw that I really wanted.' Flopping down in the armchair, Emily took off her boots and held her cold feet out towards the roaring fire.

'You'll get chilblains doing that,' Nellie said reprovingly.

Emily turned towards her mother and laughed.

'Don't you start. Doris has already remonstrated with me for leaning my elbows on the table in the café. I must be slipping into bad habits.'

Returning her daughter's smile, Nellie came towards the fire.

'And how is Doris? Is she still thinking of leaving the munitions factory? Maybe you could get her set up with the Winters? You keep saying you need help, and Doris was telling me the other night how good it would be if you two could get a job together . . .'

'Mum,' Emily sighed, blowing her cheeks out in frustration. 'You know as well as I do that Doris would never go into service . . .'

'There's nothing wrong with being in service,' Nellie interrupted sharply.

'I didn't say there was. But if Doris wouldn't contemplate it before the war, she's certainly not going to change her opinion now. Look . . . Oh, sit down, Mum, please.' She waited until Nellie, her face stiff, had reluctantly sat down before continuing. Then, taking a deep breath she said, 'Mum, I know you want me to stay with the Winters, and I know why. But it's not going to happen, Mum. No titled gentleman is going to visit the house, take one look at me, and immediately drop onto one knee and propose. It's a lovely notion, and I've often thought about it happening myself – usually when I'm day-dreaming, or engaged in some particularly tedious job. Or even to make the time pass more quickly. But it's pure fantasy, Mum. There's nothing wrong with dreaming, we all do it at some stage. There's no harm in it, as long as we keep a tight rein on reality.'

Lowering her gaze, Nellie bit down on her lower lip. Emily was right of course, but . . . Patting her daughter's hand, Nellie smiled ruefully.

'All right, love, you must do what you think best. But you will give them plenty of notice, won't you?' Seeing the reproachful look on Emily's face, she added quickly, 'I'm sorry, I know you wouldn't do anything underhand. Now I really must get on with my baking.' She had taken only a few steps towards the scullery when a thought entered her mind, which stopped her dead in her tracks. Spinning around, her hand going to her throat, she asked anxiously, 'You . . . you aren't thinking of joining Doris in the munitions factory, are you, love?'

Seeing the look of horror on her mother's face, Emily smiled broadly.

'Good heavens, Mum, of course I'm not. And if you could think that for even a minute, then you're crediting me with more courage than I possess.'

Left alone, Emily sank down into the soft cushions of the armchair, and with a contented sigh closed her eyes. Wriggling around to make herself more comfortable she murmured softly, 'Make the most of it, me girl, you won't get many chances to laze around after next week.' With her own advice ringing in her ears, and the soft voice of her mother singing in the scullery, Emily fell into a light sleep.

The following Tuesday when Nellie came downstairs there was a letter lying on the mat. Thinking it might be from Lenny, she picked it up eagerly, her face falling at the beautifully scripted handwriting. Placing it on the table, she called up the stairs, 'Emily. There's a letter for you. It must be from Mr Winter.'

'All right, I'm coming down,' a sleepy voice called back.

As Nellie stoked up the fire she waited for Emily to tell her the contents of the letter. She didn't have to wait long.

'They'll be home at the end of the week as planned. Well, Sunday afternoon to be exact.'

Nellie heard the disappointment in Emily's voice. More surprising, though, was the disappointment that she herself was feeling. She had become used to having her daughter at home and was now loath to let her go. She had come to terms with Emily's decision to leave the Winters' employ, and was now looking forward to having Emily home for good. Even so, she would still have to work out her notice and, once back in the large house in Gore Road, who knew whether she might not change her mind when she was back in the familiar, comfortable surroundings. Surprisingly enough, this thought disturbed Nellie more than she would have imagined; that, and the fear of being left on her own. Suppressing the gnawing anxiety that had suddenly gripped her, she said lightly, 'I'll get breakfast started while you read your letter.'

Once out in the solitude of the scullery, Nellie stood over the stone sink, her hands tightly gripping the cold, damp rim. Dear Lord, how was she going to manage without Emily's comforting presence? What if *he* was out there somewhere, watching, spying on her, just waiting for his chance to get her on her own? A wave of nausea spiralled up into her throat and she swallowed quickly, her eyelids blinking furiously as she tried to keep calm. When the spasm had passed she splashed her face with cold water, silently cursing herself for her weakness. As she set about making the tea and getting the breakfast ready, Nellie thought back to the day when she had walked into Hackney police station and she shivered. Her action had surprised even herself. She would never have believed she'd have the courage to report Alfie to the police. But, oh, how good it had felt. For the first time in her life she had been proud of herself, and when she had seen that same pride reflected in both Emily's and Dot's eyes, she had wondered why she hadn't done it sooner. Yet the very next day she had woken up in a cold sweat, terrified at what she had done.

The following week, when she had returned to the hospital for a check-up, she had discovered where her new-found courage had stemmed from. On her discharge she had been given a small bottle of medicine to alleviate the pain of her bruised ribs. She hadn't asked what it was, and had only taken it for a couple of days, but it had been long enough for the morphine to make her do something completely out of character. And sometime soon she was going to have to pay the consequences, for her husband would come after her, of that she had no doubt; it was just a matter of time.

'They're bringing a cousin back with them.' The sound of Emily's voice cut through Nellie's tortured thoughts. 'Apparently the woman, Cynthia Denton, has just lost her husband. Well, she hasn't lost him exactly. He was reported missing some time ago, and now he's been officially listed as dead.'

'Oh, the poor woman, how terrible.' Nellie, her face and voice bearing no sign of her inner turmoil, came back into the room to hear Emily's news.

Emily's eyes flickered as she read on. 'As she has no income, Miss Rose has suggested that she return home with them and take up residence in their house. She goes on to say that at last I'll have some help, but asks me to be understanding about Cynthia's role, as she isn't used to heavy work.' Throwing the letter down on the table, Emily sat down heavily on the hard-backed chair and began to drum her fingers on the table. 'In other words, I'll still be expected to carry on as usual, while this cousin of theirs flicks a duster here and there.'

Nellie's eyebrows rose at the hostility in her daughter's voice, her mind thankfully shifting from her own problems for the time being.

After a silent breakfast Nellie laid down her empty cup and said quietly, 'Now that they've enlisted the help of their cousin, it'll be easier for you to tell them you're leaving.'

Raising her eyes Emily asked, 'You really don't mind me giving in my notice, Mum?'

'No, I really don't.' Taking a sip of hot tea, Nellie smiled over the rim of the cup. 'I've thought about it a lot, and you're right. Mind you, there's still a chance of meeting a gentleman of means. I suppose if they can't find a taxi, they'll use the trams.'

Emily's earlier feelings of anger had quickly disappeared and, shaking her head, she said affectionately, 'Oh, Mum . . . You never give up, do you?'

Nellie smiled back, her thoughts racing. Even if Emily handed in her notice, it would be a month before she could return home. And if Lenny didn't come back, she would be on her own during that time. Feeling her hands begin to shake, Nellie quickly rose to clear away the table. It was only a month, she kept telling herself, just four weeks. She could manage until then. She continued to reassure herself for the rest of the day and throughout the long, sleepless night, but the fear had taken a tight grip on her mind and body; and it wasn't going to go away until she had Emily back home for good.

* * *

On Friday morning, as Nellie was preparing to go to one of her regular cleaning jobs, there was a loud knock on the door.

Thinking it would be the milkman, Nellie picked up the tin can by the door and opened it with a smile. Then the smile faltered, as she came face to face with a complete stranger.

'Good morning, are you Mrs Ford?'

'Um . . . I mean, yes . . . Yes, I'm Nellie Ford. How can I help you?'

The woman on the doorstep smiled.

'My name is Cynthia Denton. I believe my cousin, George Winter, has written to your daughter about me.'

'Oh . . . oh, yes, please, come in.' Slightly flustered, Nellie moved to one side to allow her visitor to enter. 'Please, won't you sit down.' When the woman was seated at the table, Nellie asked, 'May I get you a hot drink? It's very cold out today.'

'Thank you, that would be most acceptable. As you say, the weather is dreadfully inclement.' Taking off her leather gloves, Cynthia Denton laid them in her lap and smiled. 'Is your daughter at home, Mrs Ford? I'd like to make her acquaintance.' She gave a short laugh before adding, 'I'm sorry, I seem to have caught you at a disadvantage. I should have let you know I was coming on ahead of my cousins, but it was a last-minute decision on my part.'

'No, really, it's quite all right.' Recovering her aplomb, Nellie hurriedly put the milk can on the floor and said, 'Emily, my daughter, is visiting a neighbour. She'll be back shortly.' Almost before she'd finished the sentence, the door flew open to admit a smiling Emily.

'Bbrrr, it's absolutely freezing outside. It's a wonder Mrs Riley's chickens are still laying, they . . . Oh . . .'

Nellie came forward quickly, saying, 'This is Mrs Denton, Emily. You know, the Winters' cousin.'

'Oh, yes, how do you do.' Emily held out her hand in greeting, trying to keep the surprise from her voice. 'I'm sorry, I wasn't expecting you to call here. It had been arranged that I would get the house ready for the Winters' return.' A look of panic came to her eyes. 'Goodness, they haven't arrived back early, have they?'

Cynthia Denton gave a tinkling laugh.

'Please, Miss Ford, don't alarm yourself. As I was just explaining to your mother,' she inclined her head towards Nellie, 'I acted on the spur of the moment. It was very remiss of me, I know, but as I've arrived early, I might as well get acquainted with the house. After all, it is going to be my home.' Another tinkling laugh accompanied her words, but Emily was quick to notice that the laughter didn't reach the woman's eyes.

Taking stock of their unexpected visitor, Emily saw a slim woman in her thirties, dressed in a dark blue coat, adorned at the neck and cuffs with black fur. Beneath the blue hat was short, black, wavy hair that was tucked neatly behind her ears. But it was the eyes that caught Emily's attention. They were a greenish-yellow colour, which reminded Emily of a cat watching its prey. When she shivered, it had nothing to do with the cold. Their visitor was also taking stock, and she wasn't liking what she saw.

Cynthia Denton was thirty-five years of age. She was attractive and, like all women of her class, well educated. Yet despite her affluent appearance, Cynthia was on the verge of poverty. Her late husband, a lawyer by profession, had always kept her in a comfortable lifestyle – a lifestyle that was shattered the day he signed up. He had had a tidy sum put by, but over the two years he had been away, Cynthia, thinking that the war would end soon and that her husband would return to his profitable profession, had quickly gone through the nest-egg. The

141

dwindling fortune had caused her some alarm, but not sufficient to curb her spending. She had reassured herself that the money would be replaced, if not doubled, when her husband returned home and set up practice once more. The thought that he might be killed in action hadn't ever occurred to her. But since the telegram three months ago, she had cursed him every morning upon waking, for dying and leaving her in such dire straits.

Forced to give up her fashionable three-storey house in Kensington, Cynthia had swallowed her pride and returned to her former Surrey home. And since the day she'd arrived, her mother had never missed an opportunity to remind her daughter that she was in their debt.

When Cousin George and Rose had first written to ask if they could come to stay, Cynthia had been incensed, knowing that her mother would expect her to wait on them like a common servant. But their visit had turned out to be a blessing in disguise. Listening to their talk about the house in Hackney, and their problem with finding suitable staff, a problem with which her mother had sympathised, Cynthia had seen a way of getting out of the intolerable position she endured in her parents' home.

Her interest had been furthered by talk of Matthew, her ears pricking up at every mention of his name. She had met Matthew on several occasions at social functions, when they had both had partners. Now it seemed that they were both free. Of course, with Matthew away fighting, he might come to the same end as her departed husband, but she was willing to take that chance. She had nothing to lose, after all. There was an alarming shortage of men to be found these days, and every opportunity had to be grabbed at the first chance.

She had been confidently optimistic on the journey to

London, but now she wasn't so sure of herself. This lovely young woman, decked out in what was obviously cast-off clothing, but still immensely attractive on its wearer, was nothing like Cynthia had imagined. Of course her cousins had described Emily as being beautiful, but she had imagined that description to be clouded by affection. Nor was she the subservient creature that Cynthia had pictured in her own mind. This woman, who was holding her gaze without faltering, was clearly not the usual run-of-the-mill servant.

Still, the mother seemed pliant enough. Shifting her gaze, she said to Nellie, 'Forgive me for asking, Mrs Ford, but have you been in an accident?'

Nellie jumped, her face reddening at the sudden enquiry. But before she could answer, Emily, wanting their visitor to leave, said quickly, 'I'm sure you want to be on your way, Mrs Denton. Please don't let us keep you.'

Cynthia's head jerked back sharply at the dismissive tone in the young woman's voice, and though her natural instinct longed to give the young scut a good dressing-down, she warned herself to tread carefully. The last thing she wanted was to be left with her elderly cousins and a large house to take care of by herself. Then again, it wouldn't hurt to remind Miss Ford of the proposed change in her status.

'Yes, you're quite right, I do have a lot to attend to.' Rising to her feet she turned to Nellie. 'Thank you for the refreshment, Mrs Ford, it was much appreciated.' She smiled sweetly before turning to Emily. 'My cousins have told me all about you, my dear. They were most anxious that you should have some help around the house and, now that I'm here, I can relieve you of the more mundane chores, letting you get on with what I think is called the "heavy work": is that the correct terminology?'

Her face set tight, Emily answered, 'I believe so, though I have always considered all the work to be of equal importance – and would expect it to be divided so.'

Putting her gloves on with precise movements, Cynthia picked up her handbag and prepared to leave.

'If you would fetch the keys for me, I'll be on my way. I have a taxi waiting outside.' When the keys were silently handed over Cynthia said, 'Thank you. Though why Cousin George couldn't have had another set made, I can't imagine. Still, it has enabled me to make your acquaintance before you resume your duties. So much more informal, don't you think?'

Emily held the door open wide.

'Yes, well, I'll take my leave.' Somewhat disconcerted by Emily's aloof manner, Cynthia sought to adopt a friendlier attitude, deeming it best for the moment not to antagonise the girl.

Flashing what she deemed to be a bright smile, she said lightly, 'Thank you, Miss Ford. Oh, that does sound so formal, doesn't it. May I call you Emily?'

'Miss Ford will do, Mrs Denton.'

At the curt tone, Cynthia's hackles rose. Clutching her leather bag tightly under her arm, she looked towards Nellie, who was quietly watching the tense scene. Still adopting a friendly guise she remarked sweetly, 'What a beautiful blouse, Mrs Ford, and such a lovely shade of blue. I couldn't help noticing it the moment I entered. My cousin Rose had one just like it, though I haven't seen her wear it for a few years now.'

Emily saw the hurt, embarrassed look that crossed her mother's face and was instantly on the defensive. Her eyes blazing dangerously, she said curtly, 'Good day to you, Mrs Denton.'

At a loss for a suitable reply, Cynthia inclined her head, and with a sweeping movement she glided past

Emily and over the polished step, the door banging so hard behind her that she was forced to drop her haughty demeanour and step quickly into the street.

'I don't like her, Emily, but then I'm no good at judging character. You've only to look at your father to know that.' Nellie was staring out of the window at the figure getting into the waiting taxi.

'Don't worry, Mum, I didn't think much of her either.' Emily's voice was grim. 'Still, it makes matters easier, doesn't it? Because with Lady Muck in residence, I'll be able to give notice without any further misgivings. Oh, what's the matter, Mum, are you in pain?' The sight of her mother holding her stomach brought a fresh wave of anger to Emily's already agitated state. 'Is it because of her? You don't want to take any notice of the likes of that one, she's not worth upsetting yourself about.'

Nellie shook her head and took her coat down from the back of the door.

'No, love, it's nothing to do with our visitor, though I admit she was rather unpleasant. No, it's only my time of the month, something all women have to put up with . . . Emily! Emily, whatever's the matter, you've gone as white as a sheet.' Nellie looked in alarm at her daughter's pale face.

Quickly recovering herself, Emily forced a smile to her lips.

'It's nothing, Mum,' she answered lightly. 'Probably just wind. I shouldn't have eaten such a big breakfast.'

When the door closed after her mother, Emily dropped down in the armchair, her mind and stomach racing. With all that had happened these past weeks she hadn't realised she was late. Her monthlies were regular, always had been, but not this month. Feverishly calculating when she had been due, her stomach churned at the realisation that she was ten days overdue.

Yet even in the first frantic moments of her discovery her thoughts didn't turn to herself, or even to her mother and what it would mean for them. Instead she saw a smiling face with orange hair and heard a loud infectious laugh. It was almost as if Doris was here in the room.

Dropping her face into her hands, Emily began to rock back and forth whispering, 'No, no, please, I can't be, I can't. It was only the once, please don't let me be pregnant . . . please . . . !'

Even as she prayed she heard fragments of the familiar, chirpy cockney voice saying, 'You're me best mate, Emily . . . I love Tommy . . . I told him, Em, and he didn't push me away . . .'

Wrapping her arms round her waist, Emily groaned loudly as she continued to rock her body in anguish.

'Oh, Lord, I'm sorry, Doris. I would never deliberately have hurt you . . . I'm so, so sorry. Please forgive me, Doris . . . And please, please try and understand, and not hate me . . . please . . . !'

CHAPTER THIRTEEN

It was two days before Christmas and, as Emily rose tiredly from her bed, she thanked heaven that most of the festive preparations were already done and that, as in the past, she would be going home on Christmas Eve to be with her family. Though this Christmas it would just be her and her mother. Easing her legs over the side of the bed she yawned, then shivered as the coldness of the room hit her exposed skin. Reaching for her dressing-gown at the bottom of the bed, she quickly wrapped it round her shoulders, while her mind raced on the tasks that she still had before her. But all such thoughts vanished as her feet touched the icy floor and a wave of nausea rushed up into her throat.

Clapping a hand over her mouth, she tried to regulate her breathing, but it was no use. Running over to the washbasin, she just had time to remove her soap and flannel before throwing up. When the spasm was over she wiped her mouth and, wrinkling her nose in disgust, carried the basin at arm's length from the room and up to the first-floor landing to the water closet.

Later, when she was washed and dressed in a pale blue

work frock, she looked at the bedside clock and sighed. Only quarter past six, and already she felt as if she'd done a day's work. Giving herself a brisk shake, she took a last look at her reflection in the dressing-table mirror, tucked a stray curl into the bun at the nape of her neck and left the room.

Passing through the hall, she stopped for a brief moment to admire the huge Christmas tree, decorated with tinsel and coloured baubles, her eyes slipping to the small pile of gaily wrapped presents arranged at the foot of the tree.

She had decorated this same tree from the age of fourteen, a task she had always enjoyed, but this year the festive sight held no joy for her.

Walking into the icy kitchen she shivered violently, hurrying to get the iron range alight and some warmth back into her bones. This achieved, she set about filling the kettle for a much-needed cup of tea, when another wave of nausea swept over her. There was no time to race to the closet and she was forced to lean over the sink and retch miserably, thanking God that there were no witnesses to her wretched discomfort. She was reaching for a cloth to wipe her mouth when a voice from behind set her already frayed nerves jangling.

'Is there something you wish to tell me, Miss Ford?'

Emily jerked in surprise, her head swivelling round in panic, while her mouth opened and closed futilely.

Cynthia Denton stood behind the large wooden table, her hands folded over her stomach, her eyes staring fixedly on the young woman at the sink.

'Well, Miss Ford. I'm waiting for an answer.'

Something in the older woman's tone immediately set Emily's hackles rising. Slowly straightening up, she lifted her head proudly and said, 'I should have thought the answer was painfully obvious, Mrs Denton. I think in some social circles it is referred to as being with child, but as I've only ever heard that term used in romantic fiction, I'll be more direct. I'm pregnant, Mrs Denton, about three months by my reckoning. But then, you already knew that, didn't you?'

Cynthia Denton's hands tightened across her stomach, her eyes hardening at the flippant tone of the young woman on whom she was, unfortunately, at least partially dependent for the time being. Nonetheless, Cynthia had an overwhelming desire to raise her hand and wipe the infuriating smug look from that attractive face. Oh, if only this blasted war would end, then there would be no shortage of help to be found. As it was, she needed this chit of a girl, for without her she herself would have to see to the running of the house. And she hadn't left the drudgery of one house to endure more drudgery in this house. But she could wait. There would come a time when she no longer needed Miss Emily Ford, and when that day came Cynthia would take great delight in sending that young miss packing. For now she would have to tread very carefully. Swallowing hard, she wet her lips and said quietly, 'There you are mistaken, Miss Ford. I had my suspicions, of course, but never having had any children myself, I wasn't quite sure. But now that I do know, I have to ask what you intend doing?' Seeing the quizzical look in those blue eyes, Cynthia squared her shoulders and added, 'Do you intend staying on here until . . . well, until the baby is due, or is it your intention to return home?'

The quietness of the words, and the dignity with which they were delivered, caused Emily to lose some of her composure. She hadn't expected this reaction, not from Mrs Denton, whom she knew disliked her intensely. Then her head cleared. Of course the woman was being charitable, she didn't have much choice, did she? At the present moment, Cynthia Denton needed Emily for more than she herself needed this job. Her face set, Emily replied, 'My plans for the future are no business of yours, Mrs Denton. That depends on Mr George and Miss Rose. If, after hearing my news, they want me to stay on, then of course I will. I shall inform them of my condition after breakfast; unless of course you'd like to do the honours? Now, if you will excuse me, I have work to do, unlike some.' With a curt nod of her head she turned back to the sink.

The dismissive gesture was not lost on Cynthia. A wave of hate surged through her and she found she was clenching her hands so tightly that her nails dug into her palms, drawing blood. Breathing deeply through her nose, she turned to leave.

Emily's voice came after her.

'While we are being frank, I want to say that I know you dislike and resent me. The reason is obvious. You have no power over me, and that in itself must be very galling for a woman like yourself. But your feelings towards me don't matter. You see, Mrs Denton, I dislike you as much as you dislike me. The difference is that I can walk out whenever I choose. You, on the other hand, don't appear to have the same choices. But for now we seem to be stuck with each other. So until such time as our circumstances change, we had best make the most of a bad situation.'

Cynthia's back stiffened but she remained silent. With a graceful sweep of her head she walked sedately from the room.

Left alone, Emily slumped against the cold sink, her head bowed. What on earth had made her say such cruel things? It wasn't in her nature to be spiteful, even towards a woman such as Mrs Denton, who had shown from the start of their acquaintance that she resented Emily's standing in the house and the affection shown to her by the Winters. But there was something about the woman that brought out the very worst in her.

Still, Mrs Denton's question was a valid one. What *was* she going to do? She wasn't normally indecisive, but the shock of finding herself pregnant had knocked her for six. Even now, when she was throwing up every morning, she still found it hard to believe that she was going to have a child. Her mother had already said that she would look after the baby while Emily worked. But it wouldn't be fair to leave her with a small child, for what might be weeks on end. Besides, it was no good making any plans at all until she knew how her employers reacted to her news. If they did throw her out, she could take her mother up on her offer and apply for a job on the trams with Doris.

That is, if Doris was still speaking to her by then. Feeling somewhat subdued, Emily applied herself to her chores. After she had lit a fire in the dining-room and laid the table for breakfast she returned to the kitchen, her thoughts going back to the night when she had told her mother of her condition.

She had asked for, and been given, a day off at the end of November. She remembered well that Saturday, and how she had followed her mother round the small house, starting to speak, then changing her mind and rambling on instead about trivial matters. Finally her mother had asked her directly what was wrong and, in a flood of tears, Emily had unburdened herself. With her mother's comforting arms holding her tight, she had relived the night with Tommy Carter and the guilt she had since lived with. After the initial shock her mother had been wonderful, and had continued to lend Emily her support. Yet even though Nellie had shown no outward sign of hurt or disappointment, Emily knew that her mother was suffering.

Nellie still hadn't got over the shock of Lenny signing up, and Lord knows that had been a bombshell to them both, especially the way they had found out – a scrawled message on a scrap of paper inside a brown envelope postmarked France. Nellie had raced down to the nearest recruiting office, frantically explaining about her son's mental disability and begging the bemused sergeant on duty to locate and return her son to her. The man had been sympathetic but unable to help, saying wryly that the young man couldn't be that simple, or he would never have got past the officer in charge at the time.

Since that day Emily knew that her mother had been going through torment. Every day the newspapers were filled with fresh lists of casualties, which Nellie would scan fearfully, her face dropping with relief when she failed to find her son's name among them. She still couldn't understand why, or how, Lenny had summoned up the courage to lie about his age and bluff his way through the recruiting office. Emily, though, could see her father's hand in the affair – it would make more sense than the notion of Lenny thinking the whole thing up by himself. Neither of the two men had been seen since the night Alfie Ford had put his wife in hospital. It was too much of a coincidence to be ignored. But Emily had kept her suspicions to herself. She could see no reason to heap further worry onto her mother's shoulders. As it was, from Emily's point of view, both she and her brother, in different ways, had let their mother down very badly.

And now that Mrs Denton knew of her condition, she would have to tell Miss Rose, and she in turn, after a liberal dose of smelling salts, would inform Mr George. Sighing heavily, Emily rolled down her sleeves and picked up a silver tray containing Miss Rose's early-morning tea and a plate of lightly buttered toast. As Mr George always took his breakfast in the dining-room at nine o'clock prompt, she had ample time to see Miss Rose first before preparing the elderly gentleman's morning meal, though she wasn't looking forward to cooking the scrambled eggs, kidneys and bacon that he looked forward to in the mornings. Even the thought of greasy food made her want to gag. Then there was the porridge to make for Mrs Denton . . . Oh, get a move on, woman. She chided herself irritably for wasting time.

Rallying herself, she marched quickly from the warmth of the kitchen out into the chilly hallway and up the stairs leading to her employer's bedroom. Resting the tray on the carpeted floor, she took a deep breath, knocked once and entered.

'Actually, it wasn't half as bad as I'd imagined. Miss Rose was shocked – well, I expected that, but she took it much better than I thought she would. And Mr George – oh, he's so lovely, Mum. He was embarrassed at first, you know what men are like about these things, but afterwards he was more worried about me. Told me to put my feet up and have a rest.' Emily laughed at the recent memory, but the gay chuckle sounded hollow to her ears. All her chatter was simply a means of filling the silence. Every nerve in her body was screaming as she waited for the knock on the door that would herald Doris's arrival. For when that ordeal was over there was no-one left to tell her news to. Because that's all she seemed to have done these past months. Tell this person, then that one. It would have been quicker to take out an advertisement in the *Hackney Gazette*.

Then there were the neighbours to face. The women round here hadn't been brought up to be tactful. If they

153

had something on their minds, they came straight out with it. No hinting or double meanings with cockney women, and that suited Emily just fine, as she had never been one for subterfuge.

Her body tensed as footsteps thumped outside the door, then she relaxed as the wearer of the heavy boots moved on. With it being Christmas Eve, the street was even noisier than usual. Later on in the day, when the night began to draw in, many of the women in the street would don their thick shawls and coats and go down to the market in the hope of getting a last-minute fir tree, or a chicken for their Christmas dinner, at a fraction of its usual cost. If they were lucky they would find some bruised oranges and apples lying in the gutter with which to fill their children's stockings. Sometimes the ruse worked, but at other times, when the traders had had a profitable day, the women would come back weary and empty-handed, to be greeted by eager children wanting to know where their tree was. Their small faces crumpling as they realised that, once again, Father Christmas wouldn't be visiting them this year.

Normally Emily was sympathetic to the mood of the street, but on this occasion she was too wrapped up in her own thoughts to pay much heed to what was going on outside her front door.

'Have they heard from Captain Winter yet?'

A feeling of irritation stole over Emily. She knew the real reason that lay behind the innocent question. Trying to keep the exasperation from her voice, she sighed, 'Mum, don't keep on, please. I'm just as worried as you are about Lenny, but like I've told you before, there's nothing Captain Winter can do about it. Lenny could be anywhere over there. France is a big place, you know. Besides, Captain Winter doesn't write to me, so I couldn't ask, even if I thought it would do any good.'

Ever since Nellie had learnt of her son's enlistment she had tried everything she could think of to get him back home to safety. Her last hope had been Captain Winter, thinking that he might meet up with Lenny and use his influence to have him discharged from the army. Emily shook her head with impatience. The way her mother had asked, it seemed that she imagined there was only one spot where all the troops were converged, making it a simple matter for Captain Winter to find Lenny and send him home.

Nellie flushed and nibbled at her bottom lip, painfully aware how idiotic her request had been. Emily didn't understand, how could she? The concern she felt for her brother didn't come anywhere near the stomach-churning fear that a mother felt for her child's safety; no matter how old that child was. But she would understand one day. Putting Lenny from her mind, she asked quietly, 'Would you like me to stay, love?' Nellie looked anxiously at her daughter. Emily's face was pale and drawn, and Nellie wasn't sure if that was due to Emily's condition or to the task that lay before her.

'No, it's all right, Mum. This is something I have to do myself. And, knowing Doris's temper, it might be better if you weren't here when I tell her.'

Nellie's eyes widened in alarm.

'Good Lord, Emily, you . . . you don't think she'll turn violent, do you? I mean, well, you've been more like sisters than friends. Surely she'll understand.'

Emily's lips parted into a wry smile.

'From what I've heard, sisters aren't always renowned for their closeness. Anyway, it has to be done, and . . . and I want to get it over with. It's bad enough that I did what I did, but what makes it worse is that Doris still thinks I'm going to leave the Winters and apply for a job on the trams with her. She's talked about nothing else for months. Oh, Mum, I'm so confused. I don't seem to know what I want at the moment. One minute I want to stay on with the Winters, the next I want to come home for good. I just wish I could settle on what I want to do . . .' The words ended on a spiralling note that reflected her growing panic. She was visibly shaking at the prospect of facing Doris with her news. Telling her mother and her employers had been bad enough – but Doris! She shuddered, her hands and body twitching in agitation. Trying to hide her emotion, she held her hands out over the blazing fire, concentrating on the leaping flames, anxious suddenly to have the coming confrontation over and done with.

'What time is Doris coming?' Nellie's voice cut into Emily's tortured thoughts. Giving herself a mental shake, Emily looked up at the mantel clock and said, 'I'm not sure. I think she said her shift started at eleven and it takes over an hour and a half to get to Woolwich, so she should be here soon, it's gone nine already. When I saw her last week she said she'd pop in to see us before going to work today. That's why I came home so early. I had to get up at five this morning so that I could get everything done before leaving. Miss Rose was upset that I was leaving so early on Christmas Eve, because I normally stay on until after dinner. But I couldn't put off telling Doris any longer. I just want it over and done with.' Her haunted eyes stared up at Nellie.

'I should have told her straight away. I've had plenty of opportunity, since Mrs Denton came to live with the Winters. I don't like the woman, but at least her being there has made it easier for me to get time off. I've seen Doris half a dozen times since I found out I was pregnant, but I kept putting it off. Now keeping quiet has only made things worse. I never realised before what a coward I am . . . And I am, Mum, yes . . . yes I am.'

Her head bobbed up and down as if to drive home the truth of her words. 'And weak too, because I should never have let it happen in the first place. I could have stopped Tommy, he would never have forced me . . . But he looked so frightened, Mum, so lost and afraid. I've never seen Tommy like that before, he . . . he . . .'

'There, love, don't upset yourself, and don't be too hard on yourself, either. You're not the first woman to find herself in trouble, and I doubt you'll be the last.' Nellie stood over the armchair, her hands resting on Emily's shoulders. She too was dreading the moment when Doris found out about Emily and Tommy Carter. Like her daughter, she knew Doris's temperament only too well. If only the man responsible had been anyone else – not that she herself minded Tommy Carter as a son-in-law. It had been a dreadful shock to discover that her daughter was pregnant. But she had to admit, if only to herself, that seeing her dream vanish, of Emily marrying a man of means, had far outweighed her concern about the unwanted pregnancy. Though that was terrible enough, and there would be plenty of tongues wagging when Emily started to show. And the first one to come sniffing round the door in search of gossip would be that one over the road.

Visions of Ida Carter floated in front of Nellie's eyes, bringing a tight smile to her lips. Well, she'd be in for a shock when she found out who the child's father was, wouldn't she? Then Nellie's eyes clouded over. What was she thinking of? Ida Carter wouldn't care about Tommy becoming a father. Now, if it had been her precious Andrew . . . Still, it was no using getting into a lather at this early stage. Pregnancy was an uncertain state, as many a woman could testify. She herself had suffered two miscarriages and . . . Oh, dear Lord, what was she thinking of? Hurriedly sending up a silent prayer of apology for such a dreadful thought, she turned to the dining-table and began to rearrange the already neat table-cloth.

'When are you planning to write to Tommy?' she asked, her voice sounding far more casual than she felt. 'I mean, he'll have to know sooner or later. You don't want him coming home on leave and finding himself a father. It wouldn't be fair . . .'

Emily shifted uneasily in her chair. The same thought had occurred to her, but deep down she had hoped that maybe . . . Well, maybe there would be no need. A rush of guilt swept over her, a feeling that she quickly pushed aside. She wasn't going to be a hypocrite. She didn't want a baby. Lord, she didn't even want to get married. And if Tommy returned home safely, and she prayed God that he would, she wasn't going to be pressured into marrying him just for appearance's sake.

Keeping her gaze averted from her mother's worried face she said lightly, 'It wouldn't be fair to let him know by letter either, Mum. There's no telling how the news might affect him. I'd . . . Well, I'd much rather wait until he comes home . . . Oh, Lord, I have to go to the toilet again. I don't know whether it's nerves or . . .' She was halfway out of the chair when a sudden loud knocking at the door froze her in mid-air.

Nellie, too, experienced an alarming lurch in her stomach and, with a supreme effort, she smiled and said reassuringly to Emily, 'Don't worry, love. You've been friends since you were both children. I'm sure Doris will understand . . . but, I think I'll stay, just to be on the safe side.' Walking quickly to Emily's side, she patted the cold hand, then impulsively she leant over and wrapped her arms round Emily's stiff shoulders and gave her a hug, before crossing the few short steps to the front door.

'Wotcher, Mrs Ford. Hello, Em. Cor, it's all right for some, ain't it? Sitting in front of the fire, while the likes of me have ter go out and earn a few bob.' Doris swept into the room like a whirlwind. She was heavily wrapped up against the bitter December wind, in a herringbone coat and thick black woollen gloves and matching scarf, the latter pulled over her head and across the lower part of her face. 'Can't stop long, Em. I don't want me pay docked fer being late. Yer know what them tight sods . . . Oh, sorry, Mrs Ford.' She flashed an engaging smile at Nellie. 'Common as muck, that's me. Still, wouldn't do if we was all the same, would it?'

Nellie smiled back weakly.

'No, indeed it wouldn't, Doris.'

'Anyways, like I said, I can't stop long. The buses and trains'll be more packed than usual terday.' Doris chatted on, coming over to where Emily sat by the fire, unable to say a word. 'Ooh, it's lovely an' warm in here. I wish I could stay with yer, instead of going ter work.' Throwing back her head, she let out a raucous laugh. 'Gawd! I wished I'd been born rich instead of beautiful, then I wouldn't have ter worry about dragging me arse out of bed every morning.' In spite of herself, Emily smiled. You couldn't help but smile when Doris was around.

Doris grinned back at her friend, thinking, without a trace of jealousy, how lovely Emily looked in the red velour dress with its white lace collar and cuffs. As if she'd just thought of it, Doris leant towards Emily and said hopefully, 'Here, why don't yer come and meet me after work. Me an' some of the women are going ter the pub fer a bit of a knees-up, sort of like a Christmas party. I know it'll be late, but I'm sure yer mum'll let yer go, won't yer, Mrs Ford?' She looked at Nellie, her plain face wreathed in a wide grin. 'Eh, why don't you come an' all, Mrs Ford. We could do with a steadying influence, 'cos some of those old girls go barmy once they've had a few drinks.'

Seeing the solemn expression on both women's faces, Doris shuffled her feet awkwardly.

'Yeah, well, I suppose it would be a bit common fer you, Em. I just thought it'd be a laugh.'

Hearing the embarrassed uncertainty in her friend's voice, Emily started up from the chair, her own worries temporarily forgotten.

'Oh, Doris, that isn't it at all,' she protested.

'It's all right, Em. I don't mind, honest. Anyway, the reason I wanted ter see yer is I got those forms – you know, ter apply fer a job on the trams. I've filled it in fer yer, all yer've got ter do is sign it, then I can drop them off on me way ter work.' Seeing the puzzled look on Emily's face, Doris groaned, 'Oh, Em, yer ain't changed yer mind again, have yer?'

Sensing the turmoil that her daughter was going through, Nellie entered the conversation in an attempt to give Emily some precious breathing space.

'Didn't you sign on in munitions for three years, or the duration, Doris? Only I was under the impression that all work involving the war effort was entered into under those conditions.'

Doris grinned and tapped the corner of her nose.

'There's always ways ter get round that, Mrs Ford. Turning up late fer work once too often, for instance, or suddenly developing a nasty cough that won't clear up, and a doctor's certificate ter go with it. Ooh, there's plenty of dodges ter pull, if yer want ter get the sack.' A look of apprehension flitted across her face. ''Ere, yer don't think any the less of me fer planning ter pull a fast one, do yer?' She looked from Emily to Nellie. 'Only, there's plenty of others ready ter take me place, and besides, I've done my stint, so there's no reason fer me ter feel guilty.' Yet there was a sudden doubt in her voice.

'Oh, no, Doris. No, of course not, dear,' Nellie said hastily. 'As you say, you've done your stint, and that's more than I would ever have had the courage to do – isn't that right, Emily?'

Emily's head suddenly cleared. It was no use putting it off any longer. The sooner she told Doris her news and got it over with, the better. Taking hold of Doris's arm she said quietly, 'You'd better sit down, Doris. I've something to tell you, and it's going to come as a bit of a shock.'

Doris looked from Emily to Nellie in alarm.

'What's up? Yer both look like one of you's got some fateful disease . . . Oh, gawd, yer ain't, have yer, Em?' Letting herself be led, Doris collapsed into the sagging armchair.

'No, silly, of course I haven't.' Emily laughed shakily. 'But, well . . . Oh, Lord, this is terribly difficult, Doris. There's no easy way to tell you, so I'd better come straight out with it.' Taking a deep, shuddering breath, Emily blurted out, 'I'm pregnant, Doris, and . . . and Tommy's the father.' There, she had said it. The worst part was over. She felt Nellie by her side and instinctively moved closer to her mother.

Doris looked up at the two women in bewilderment, her mouth opening and closing in stunned confusion. Then, a trembling smile came to her lips.

'Get out of it. Yer're having me on, you . . .' Her voice faltered, then died at the troubled expression mirrored in both women's eyes. Lowering her gaze, Doris clenched her hands into fists. It couldn't be true, it couldn't. Then her mind shot back to the night when Mrs Ford had been rushed into hospital, and the state Emily had been in the next day. Squeezing her eyes tightly shut, the vision of

Emily – and of Tommy's coat lying on the floor . . . this very floor, in front of the self-same fire she was now sitting by – swam in front of her. Her hands began to tremble and, as the terrible truth began to sink in, she saw her world, and her hopes and dreams for the future, collapsing all around her.

Doris couldn't describe the feelings that were racking her body. But it hurt. Oh, God, how it hurt. And the cause of her pain was the one person she would have staked her life on – would have given her own life for. The sense of betrayal was crushing her, squeezing her chest so tight that she felt she was suffocating. And with the pain came humiliation.

She remembered clearly her declaration of love to Tommy on that windswept, cold platform barely three months ago. She remembered his stunned expression as she'd prattled on about how much she loved him, and all the time it had been Emily he had wanted . . . Huh! He hadn't only wanted Emily, he'd bloody well had her, hadn't he? And all the time Emily had kept quiet. She'd known, or had a good idea, that Doris was going to tell Tommy how she felt, and the cow had said nothing. Just stood by and watched her make a complete fool of herself. The memory of her actions sent her body squirming with embarrassment, while her face burned with humiliation as she silently relived her actions and words of that day. Her chin began to wobble, as she fought desperately to hold back the tears that she felt building behind her eyes. She wasn't going to cry, she bloody well wasn't going to make a fool of herself again.

'It only happened the once, Doris, and . . . and we both regretted it afterwards.' Emily edged forward cautiously, her hand going out, then stopping inches from Doris's bowed shoulders. Twisting her fingers nervously she went on, 'I know you must be feeling very hurt right now, and I know it seems daft to say this under the circumstances, but there's nothing between me and Tommy. Up until that night we were just good friends. The thought of being anything else had never occurred to either of us. And . . . and I've no intention of forcing him into marrying me, so you can still . . . Oh, Doris, please, don't look at me like that, please . . .'

Doris wasn't even aware that she was looking at Emily. The red haze that had descended over her eyes lifted, leaving her curiously numb.

Slowly, terribly and terrifyingly slowly, she gathered her bag from her lap and rose stiffly to her feet. She had to get out of here – had to get away from Emily, dear, kind, faithful, loyal . . . Oh, God . . . Oh, dear God . . . !

'Doris, Doris, please . . . Please, don't. Oh, don't, Doris. Look, sta . . . stay a while, I want to explain. I need to tell you how . . .' Reaching out, Emily caught hold of Doris's coat sleeve. The reaction was swift and dreadful to behold.

The feel of Emily's hand on her arm broke through Doris's calm exterior. Thrusting off the offending hand she swirled round, her eyes blazing with fury and hurt; eyes that were now also brimming with barely suppressed tears.

'Don't touch me – just don't touch me.' Doris's voice came at Emily, low and menacing, and matched the fury that was twisting the familiar face into that of a stranger; a dark and frightening stranger. 'It was that night, wasn't it. Wasn't it?' Her voice was rising out of control. Some part of her was yelling, telling her to stop it, reminding her that this was Emily, her friend, someone who deep down she knew would never intentionally hurt her. But the pain was too raw, too deep, to be ignored. She hardly recognised her own voice as the hurtful, cruel words spilled from her mouth.

'You bitch, yer bloody selfish bitch. You had everything – looks, a good education, and class. Oh, yeah, you had class, all right. I used ter be so proud ter be seen out with yer. But you weren't satisfied, was yer. Oh, no, yer had ter take the only thing I ever wanted, didn't yer, you . . . you . . .'

'Doris, please . . .' Nellie tried to step between the two women and was instantly thrust aside.

'Stay out of this, Mrs Ford. This ain't nothing ter do with you. It ain't yer fault that yer've got a slag fer a daughter.'

Both Nellie and Emily gasped in shock as the venomous words continued to pour from Doris's lips. Emily felt sick, physically sick, and would have fallen had it not been for Nellie's tight grip round her waist.

The cautionary voice in Doris's head continued to yell at her to stop this madness, but she was hurting badly, too badly to stop now.

'What did Tommy say, ter get yer ter drop yer drawers, Em? Not that old chestnut about going away ter fight and maybe never coming back? Gawd, I'd've thought yer were too clever ter be caught out by that one.'

The sneering words were too much for Nellie.

'That's enough, Doris. I know you're upset, but that's no excuse for your outrageous behaviour. And how you could even think such things about Emily, let alone say them, is beyond . . .'

'It's all right, Mum. Let her get it all out of her system, I don't mind.' Emily stood, white-faced but proud, and it was her stoic demeanour that, instead of pacifying Doris, lent fuel to her already heated rage.

Thrusting her head forward, she pointed a gloved finger at Emily's chest and hissed, 'Yer think yer so high and mighty, don't yer. Coming back down here from that posh house in yer posh clothes, thinking yer better than the rest of us. Well, I've got news fer yer, Lady Muck. I might be rough and ready and, yeah, I'm common, but at least I ain't a whore.'

When Emily remained silently aloof, refusing to retaliate, Doris lost her last ounce of self-control. Rushing forward, she raised her arm, screaming wildly, 'Slag, bitch, whore! I hate you, I hate you.'

Her upraised arm came sweeping down towards Emily's face, but before the intended blow could find its mark, Emily's hand shot out, grabbing the flailing arm and holding it in a tight grip.

'Get out, Doris, get out now. I know I've hurt you, but I'm not going to take this abuse. I don't deserve it, and deep down you know that too.'

Nellie stood nervously to one side, ready to step in if Doris retaliated with her fists. But her action wasn't necessary. Suddenly deflated, Doris's body slumped, all the fight gone from her. As if in a daze she moved slowly towards the front door. Placing her hand on the doorknob she stopped and then, without turning round, she said softly, 'I never want ter see you again, Emily, not ever, understand?' Turning her head, her eyes met Emily's. Swallowing loudly she added, 'I mean it, Em. I'll never forgive yer fer this, and I never want ter set eyes on yer ever again.'

'Doris . . .' Emily started after the retreating figure and found herself held in a vice-like grip.

'Leave her, love. It's the hurt talking. She'll come round, you'll see. Once the initial shock wears off, she'll be back. You know what Doris is like. Well, you should do after all these years.'

Emily didn't answer. Her throat was too full for mere words. Still shaking from the violent altercation, she crossed to the window and pulled the net curtain aside. Her vision blurred, she stared after the figure walking unsteadily down the cobbled road.

With her body bent against the sharp December wind Doris looked so defenceless, so vulnerable, that Emily had to fight down the urge to run after her. Leaning her cheek against the cold windowpane she whispered, 'Doris . . . Doris, come back, please come back.' And even though she knew there was no chance of her friend returning, she stayed at her post until the familiar figure disappeared from view.

CHAPTER FOURTEEN

The buses, as Doris had predicted, were packed solid, which did nothing to alleviate her already highly charged state of mind.

On arrival at Woolwich Square, Doris joined the seething mass of men and women waiting for the next bus, which would take them to No. 4 Gate of the Arsenal. The square was a hive of activity, with dozens of stalls, some decorated with fairy lights to promote the Christmas spirit, crammed into every available space in the busy road. Shoppers alighting from other buses carefully wended their way through the disorganised bus queue, making sure that the men and women waiting for the Arsenal bus knew they weren't trying to push in, but were merely attempting to get through to the market.

Somewhere in the distance, a choir from the Salvation Army was singing 'O come, all ye faithful', hoping that the festive cheer would prise loose change from pockets and purses and into their collecting tins.

Normally, Doris would either have joined in or rendered her own version of the Christmas carol, but today she was oblivious to the sights and sounds surrounding her.

The moment the bus came into view the crowd surged forward, fighting and pushing indiscriminately for a place on board. Loud curses came to her on all sides as she grimly battled her way through to the bus, only to be ejected, along with a dozen others, back onto the cold, frosty pavement. It was twenty minutes, and another two buses later, when Doris finally climbed aboard.

The bus was crowded to suffocation point, with men wearing flat caps and thick woollen scarfs tied tightly at their throats, hanging on all round the outside. No money was needed on this particular bus route, as it was almost impossible for the conductor to collect the fares amid such a mêlée. When the bus reached its destination, the occupants spilled out onto the pavement, joining thousands of men and women pouring in through the four gates, still pushing and shoving as they went their separate ways down the roads that led to the various buildings inside the Woolwich Arsenal.

The Arsenal was a huge place surrounded by a high wall and four gates, with sentries and policemen stationed at each one. Inside the walls lay scores of sheds, buildings, chimneys and even more walls, all covered with thick, black soot. There was a railway just inside No. 4 Gate, and sometimes, fearing they would be late for work, men would climb in between and over the tops of the wagons, risking their lives rather than have their wages docked.

It was a sight that Doris had witnessed for the last eighteen months; a sight she had grown to hate and fear. Caught up in the swarm of her fellow workers, she let herself be carried forward, her mind still back in Fenton Street on the soul-destroying news she had heard there.

Suddenly she was fighting against the tide of bodies, using her elbows and shoulders to forge a way through the crowd. Finding herself safely on the cobbled pavement, she leant back against some old boarding to catch her breath, and it was only when her heart began to beat normally that she made her way to a small café at the side of the road.

Carrying a tray bearing a mug of tea and two slices of toast, she found a vacant table and sat down. She couldn't face work today, at least not for a while. Perhaps if she felt better after her late breakfast she might return to the factory. It would be madness to attempt to work in the state she was in right now.

Picking up the steaming mug, she was alarmed to see how badly her hands were shaking. Thank goodness she'd had the sense to come here instead of going into work. She could have blown the entire building sky high if she had attempted to carry on as if nothing had happened. But something had happened. Something so . . . so . . .

She shook her head slowly, then, aware of curious eyes from the surrounding tables, she picked up a slice of toast and made a great show of normality, even though her stomach was churning and crying out in protest at the intake of the unwanted food. Doris wondered idly how she could eat at a time like this, yet when the toast was consumed she found that she was still hungry and returned to the counter for more.

Her light meal finished, she turned her head and stared out of the window, her mind going back to the scene that had taken place not two hours before. It seemed a lifetime ago, and in a way it was. Another life, another time; a different Doris.

Not wanting to dwell on the painful confrontation with Emily, she tried instead to trace her steps back to the first time she had come to Woolwich. It had been back in July 1915.

On 26th May of that year, a Coalition Government was formed and Lloyd George became Minister of Munitions. Posters and demonstrations, with the added support of the suffragette movement, began a campaign to recruit women for factory work. Caught up in a wave of patriotic fervour, Doris had signed on at Plumstead labour exchange, and had been among the first batch of girls and women to be employed at the Woolwich Arsenal.

Her first job had been working in the Old Fuse Factory, sitting around a long table gauging metal rings, before being taught how to handle the heavy machinery in a separate building. This room was vast, with long, narrow aisles leading between scores of machines, lathes and belts, the first sight of which had turned Doris's legs to jelly. Soon she was managing a facing machine with ease, turning and facing parts of fuse caps for the big shells destined for the Front. It was dull, repetitive work that she did without complaint for ten hours a day, six days a week. From there she had been put on working a capstan lathe, which was a bit more interesting to start with, but soon, as she became more adept with the machinery, this too had become boring.

After hearing some women on the bus home talking about their day in one of the so-called 'danger buildings', Doris had applied for the position of, and been taken on as, a canary.

The money had been the driving force behind her decision to undertake such hazardous work, for with her father unable to work due to his arthritis and bad chest, Doris had become the sole breadwinner. Harry Mitchell hadn't liked the idea of his daughter working with TNT, and there had been furious rows between the two, with Doris emerging triumphant. And she had enjoyed her work, seeing herself as taking an active and important role in the war.

But since the accident a few months ago, when one of the women had lost two of her fingers while handling a quantity of TNT, Doris had become aware just how dangerous her job really was. She was no coward, but the incident had shaken her badly. From that time on she had begun to think of moving on to another, safer line of work. And with Emily moaning about being stuck as a maid all her life, it had seemed a good idea for them both to start a new career together.

Emily!

As her thoughts returned to the present, Doris's eyes hardened at the memory of what she had learnt about her so-called friend.

How could she? How could Emily have done such a despicable thing? It would have been different if Emily and Tommy had started up a relationship beforehand. It was something Doris had always feared – Tommy noticing and falling for Emily. Every time they had paired up into a foursome with the Carter boys, Doris had held her breath in agonising anticipation, waiting for the moment when the two people she loved slowly became closer. She had steeled herself for the day they would announce their changed relationship, had rehearsed over and over again in her mind how she would smile and say all the right things, so that they would never suspect her true feelings. But it hadn't happened. Emily and Tommy had carried on being just good mates and, despite her cautionary attitude, Doris's hopes had begun to rise.

There had always been the danger that Tommy would meet, and fall for, another woman outside their close circle, but it had been Emily of whom Doris was most afraid. And she had been right.

Emily's face swam in front of her tortured mind,

followed by Tommy, as she had last seen him. Pushing that memory aside, she let her mind wander back down into the past, reliving different stages of her life in the company of Emily and the Carter boys. Then she and Andy disappeared, replaced by a vivid picture of Emily and Tommy together. Smiling at each other, whispering endearments, as they kissed and fondled in front of a roaring fire. She shuddered violently and felt the tears prick at the back of her eyes. She had imagined that scene, or one similar, a hundred times before. Only then she had been the woman in Tommy's arms.

Her stomach churned, and she felt a strange sensation tightening her chest. It was like a bad dream. Or like the time she'd had a bad case of flu some years back and had lain in a fever for days. She had heard her dad, Emily and Mrs Ford coming in and out of her bedroom, talking, sponging her down and sitting with her throughout the night, but somehow it hadn't seemed real.

She had forgotten about that, until now. Only this time it would take more than a week in bed to get over it. The way she was feeling now, she couldn't ever see a time when she would laugh again – or trust anyone again. And she had trusted Emily, trusted and loved her without question. The sense of betrayal continued to swamp her, overriding even her anger, which was at boiling point.

'You all right, love?'

Startled, Doris jumped, nearly knocking over the now empty mug. Looking up into the concerned face of the canteen waitress she mumbled, 'Yeah, yeah, I'm all right, thanks. Just having a bit of a day-dream.' Hurriedly leaving the canteen, she walked out into the street and once more hesitated. What was she to do? She had to go into work, she hadn't been paid yet, but she still felt shaky.

Spotting a familiar figure hurrying by she called out, 'Oy, Lucy . . . Lucy, here a minute.'

A young woman of about Doris's age hesitated, a wary look stealing over her plain face as she approached the woman in the herringbone coat with a blue scarf tied over her head.

'Yeah! Wha'dja want, Doris, I'm late.'

'I know yer late, so am I,' Doris said impatiently. Then, changing tack, she tugged on the woman's coat sleeve and said, 'Look, Lucy, I don't feel too well. Could yer clock me in? I'll be all right soon, but if yer could just . . .'

The woman pulled away in alarm.

'Leave orf, Doris. I'd get the sack if I was found out. No, no, I'm sorry, Doris, I can't take the risk – sorry.'

'Bleeding hell, I'm only asking yer ter clock me in, not nick the ruddy crown jewels . . . Oh, go on then, sod off, yer miserable cow.'

The young woman scampered away, and Doris immediately felt ashamed of her outburst.

'Lucy, I'm sorry . . . I didn't mean . . . Oh, bugger it.'

Her head drooped, then almost instantaneously she jerked her chin upwards. What was the matter with her! She was acting like some snivelling kid, hanging about outside the factory, afraid to go in. Well, bugger you, Emily Ford. I ain't gonna lose me job on your account.

With a determined step, she once again joined the seething mass of people and was soon entering the tall building at the farthest end of the Arsenal.

Once inside the freezing-cold changing-room, Doris quickly stepped into her boiler suit, slipped on her rubber boots and head covering and, grabbing a protective mask from an overhead rack, almost ran to the clocking-in machine.

Punching in her card, she noted with dismay that she

was over twenty minutes late. Turning over in her mind possible excuses for the supervisor, she was pushing open the factory door when the explosion happened.

In the space of a split-second she heard an almighty blast, smelt the acrid smoke and heard the women screaming. Then it felt as if a giant hand had lifted her from the ground and thrown her with ease against the far wall.

Her body collided with solid brick, she experienced a sickening lurch of fear – then nothing.

The smartly dressed middle-aged man sauntered casually down Fenton Street, his shrewd eyes darting from one side of the road to the other, obviously on the look-out for a particular number. Moving around a group of children who were playing hopscotch in the rapidly darkening late afternoon, he gave a grunt of satisfaction as he stopped outside number fifteen. Pausing just long enough to note the crisp, white net curtains and the gleaming ochre front step, the man lifted the brass door knocker and let it fall.

Inside the house Emily and Nellie were busy making some last-minute decorations, hanging paper chains and tinsel, in an effort to instil some Christmas spirit into their hearts. But, after the events of that morning, neither women was feeling in the least bit festive.

'I wonder who that can be? Were you expecting someone, love?' Nellie clambered down from the chair she'd been standing on, still holding a row of blue paper chains.

Emily shook her head.

'No, of course not . . . unless . . .' Her face broke into a wide smile as she hurried towards the door, hoping to find her friend standing sheepishly outside. Throwing open the door, she found herself looking at a stranger.

'Yes, can I help you?' she asked, puzzled by the stranger's presence.

Micky Masters, a senior reporter at the *Hackney Gazette*, tipped his fedora to the back of his head and emitted a long, low whistle at the sight of the tall, chestnut-haired woman. Confidently leaning against the door-jamb, he gave an engaging smile. That and the whistle always smoothed the way with the ladies.

'Miss Emily Ford?' he asked while at the same time moving forward, his foot raised to enter the house.

'I said, can I help you?' The icy voice froze him in his tracks for a moment, but not for long. He was too old a hand for anything to faze him for long.

Changing tactics he removed his hat and, holding it between his hands, said apologetically, 'Sorry, darlin'. . . I mean, Miss,' he amended hastily, adding, 'You are Miss Emily Ford, aren't you?'

Emily looked at him suspiciously.

'Yes, I am she. What do you want with me?'

Glancing up and down the deserted street, Micky Masters decided to forgo the charm and come straight to the point. She wasn't what he had expected, not round these parts.

Suddenly he wasn't so sure of himself. Maybe the office had made a mistake. This snooty little piece didn't look the sort to have friends working in munitions . . . Well, not on the factory floor. Though they were all getting into the act these days. Ladies were now working alongside their one-time maids but, as far as he knew, they hadn't been reduced to living alongside them as well. But his editor wasn't the type to make mistakes. And Frank Dobson, the head reporter, had been one of the first on the scene after the explosion. He had phoned his report into the office, along with the names of a few women who had been caught up in the accident. By virtue of a discreetly offered banknote, Dobson had obtained not only the names of the munitionettes, but also those of their next of kin. Doris Mitchell's form had listed two names to be informed in the event of an accident, the first being her father; but it was the friend that Micky Masters was most interested in. He was after a story, and fathers weren't always aware of what their daughters got up to outside the home, whereas a girlfriend . . . !

It was a pity it had happened today. Because what with it being Christmas Day tomorrow, no paper would be able to print the story until Boxing Day. But if he played his cards right, he could have a good front-page story for when the paper went to press. It all depended on what he could find out here, and what his fellow reporters dug up about the other women involved in the accident.

'Look, Mr . . . whoever you are. Will you kindly state your business. I'm letting all the cold air into the house standing here.'

Micky shivered and thrust his hands into the deep lining of his heavy coat.

'My name's Micky Masters. I work fer the *Hackney Gazette*, an' I'm covering the story about the accident at the Arsenal munitions factory, and . . .'

Emily's eyes widened in shock. Clutching at the door frame, she said hoarsely, 'Accident, wh . . . what accident? Oh . . . oh, come in, please.'

Micky walked gratefully into the warmth of the small house.

'Mum, Mum, there's been an accident at Doris's work.' Before Nellie could make a reply, Emily turned back to the man who had brought the news. 'What happened? Is Doris all right? Oh, please, please, sit down, you must be frozen.'

Emily chatted on, afraid to hear what the answer might be. Oh, God, if anything had happened to Doris

176

because of her, she'd never forgive herself. She should have waited before telling Doris, not blurted it out just before her friend went to work. Whatever had she been thinking of. To tell such shattering news to someone just off to a dangerous occupation, where one needed all one's wits about one, was nothing short of crass stupidity.

Clutching at the front of her dress she stammered, 'Is she . . . Is Doris all right, Mr Masters. Please tell me, is my friend alive?'

Seated awkwardly on the edge of a sagging armchair, Micky thought of the best way to handle the situation. When his editor had handed him this address, along with Harry Mitchell's, he had quickly decided to visit the friend first, hoping that the woman would have some snippets of gossip to impart about Doris Mitchell. He conceded that it was a tacky approach, especially as the woman in question had been engaged in work vital to the war. But human nature being what it is, it was gossip that sold papers, not stories about decent men and women going about their lawful duties. But this young woman watching him so intently, her lovely blue eyes filled with anxiety, didn't seem the type to engage in idle chit-chat, and even less likely to tell a complete stranger intimate secrets concerning a friend. Still, you never knew with people, they never stopped surprising him.

First off, though, he had better explain his primary reason for being here. Dangling his hat between his knees he said simply, 'I'm sorry, I thought you might already have heard. There was an explosion at the Arsenal munitions factory this morning. About a dozen women have been taken to hospital. I don't know the full story yet. Everything's been a bit of a shambles. The government is trying ter keep a lid on it, ter avoid panic in the other factories, but my editor did manage ter get some of the women's names. And your name was down in the files

177

as the person ter contact in the event of an accident.' He stopped here and looked up at the two women. 'Didn't yer hear anything . . . I mean, news like this usually spreads like wildfire.'

Dumbly Emily and Nellie sank down onto the hard-backed chairs, their hands automatically clasping each other across the table for support.

'You still haven't told us about Doris. Is she all right? Or have you come to tell us she's dead?'

'No . . . Well, what I mean ter say is, I don't know. But don't get your hopes up, love. Like I said, I don't know the whole story yet, but . . . Well, I do know one of the women died, but I don't know her name . . . I'm sorry, that's all I can tell yer fer now.'

Emily nodded and squeezed Nellie's hand tightly, unable to speak. Nellie patted the shaking hand and turned to the man, who had now risen to his feet.

'If you don't know anything, then why have you come here? I don't understand. What do you want of us?'

Micky took a large notepad and pencil from his inside pocket and looked at them expectantly.

'I was hoping you'd fill me in on Doris's background. Yer know, the usual things. What she was like, did she have any boyfriends . . . Oh, and if you have any photographs of her, that'd be great. People like that sort of thing.'

'You mean, something that will sell newspapers,' Nellie said, her voice turning cold. 'I'm afraid you're wasting your time here, Mr Masters. There's nothing we can tell you that would be of any interest to your readers. Now, if you'll excuse us, I'd be obliged if you'd leave. This has come as a great shock, and my daughter and I would like to be alone.'

'I understand how yer feel, Mrs Ford, but . . .'

'I doubt that very much,' Nellie interrupted him. Striding to the door she opened it wide.

'I'm authorised ter pay for any information . . .'

'Please leave, you're not welcome here.'

Micky shrugged his shoulders. There were other doors to knock on. Someone in this street would be willing to talk to him – someone always was, especially if there was money involved. If not, there was always the father. A good human-interest story, boring though it might be, was better than nothing.

Nellie closed the door hard behind him.

'What a dreadful man, he . . . Emily, Emily, love, what are you doing?'

Emily was putting her coat on, her movements jerky.

'I have to get to her, Mum. I have to find out if Doris is all right. I should never have told her about the baby, not when I knew she was on her way to work. I should have had more sense. We both know how dangerous her work is, and how she has to have her wits about her at all times. I don't know what possessed me to tell her; I must have been mad . . . No, not mad, just bloody thoughtless. Thoughtless and selfish. I was so concerned about unburdening myself, trying to ease my conscience, that I never stopped to think of the repercussions.'

'Hang on a minute, love, I'll come with you. I just want to make sure that man hasn't gone to bother Mr Mitchell. The poor man's chest and arthritis are always worse in the winter, and there's no telling what this news might do to him in his condition; not that that would worry a reporter on the hunt for a good story.'

Emily jumped guiltily. She hadn't even thought of Mr Mitchell. Oh, the poor man. First his wife and now . . .

'You wait here, I won't be long. I'll knock for Dot on the way down. She's very good in a crisis, is Dot, then Mr

179

Mitchell will have someone to keep him company while we go and find out exactly what's happened.'

Nellie was at the open front door, agitatedly tying a floral print scarf over her dark, wavy hair. Seeing the despair on Emily's face, she tried to comfort her. 'There's no sense in thinking the worse until we know for sure, love. You could drive yourself mad that way.' Giving a nervous laugh she added, 'If she is in the hospital, she's probably giving the nurses hell right now. You know how she hates to be bossed around. Anyway, we'll soon have her back home safely, you'll see.'

'If she's alive.'

Nellie pulled the scarf tighter, her face sombre.

'Alive or dead, we'll see to her. Whatever's happened, we'll see that she's taken care of – she's family.'

CHAPTER FIFTEEN

Pausing outside St Joseph's Hospice, Emily hunted around in her large canvas bag for her purse. Finding it at the bottom, she took out a sixpenny piece and handed it over to the smiling flower-seller.

'Hello, duck, you back again. That's the second time this week. Not that I'm complaining. Wish I 'ad more customers like yer.' A grimy hand swiftly took the shiny silver coin and deposited it in the pocket of a tatty navy apron. 'People in there don't get many regular visitors, poor sods. The relatives usually come once or twice at first, then don't bovver after that, 'cos them that goes in there don't ever come out again – a bit like the workhouse. Still, there's always the odd one, like yerself, who don't ferget their loved ones. Yer muvver is it?'

Bright, inquisitive eyes peered up at the tall figure. The woman's blatant, ghoulish curiosity brought a feeling of irritation to Emily, but she merely shrugged and took the small bunch of brightly coloured flowers from the flower-seller.

'Thank you,' she muttered politely, and walked quickly away.

She was about to enter the building when she heard her name being called. Glancing round, she smiled at the woman approaching her.

'Emily, my dear, back so soon. Doris is a very lucky young woman to have a friend such as yourself.' Sister Bernadette MacNally, the nun in charge of the hospice, held out her hand in greeting. She was a woman in her late thirties, with a thick Irish brogue and deep greenish-blue eyes. Emily imagined that beneath the nun's wimple rested curly red or auburn hair.

'Well, like I've told you before, the hospice is only a ten-minute walk from my workplace, and my employers have been very understanding. I don't suppose there have been any dramatic changes since I was last here?'

The grey-clad figure sighed regretfully.

'Not with Doris, at least . . . Oh, my dear, I'm very sorry, but I'm going to have to discharge her, and God knows I don't often have the opportunity to do that. The good Lord Himself usually takes my charges from me.'

Quick to note the startled expression that flitted across Emily's face, Sister Bernadette laid a comforting hand on her arm.

'The point is, Emily, there's nothing more we can do for her here. In fact, she should never have been admitted here. I only took her in because there was nowhere else for her to go, but I always imagined she would recover and want to leave of her own accord. A hospice is for the chronically sick, those who have no chance of recovering, and Doris doesn't fall into that category, I'm pleased to say. I didn't tell you before, but I was all set to discharge her months ago, but then her father died and she took it so badly. As you know, he was her only living relative, and to Doris's way of thinking she is now all alone in the world. But that isn't so, is it, Emily? She has you, and your mother. And may I say that you have both, and you especially, shown Doris more love and compassion than many a blood-relative I could mention. Oh, dear, I feel terrible about this, but . . .' The slim shoulders shrugged resigningly. 'I have a waiting list a mile long, and I cannot, in all conscience, allow Doris to take up a bed any longer, not when there are dying people desperate for a place to stay. And as I've already said, it isn't as if she had no-one to care for her – she has you.'

Shifting uneasily from one foot to the other, Emily raised her eyebrows and sighed.

'That may be so, Sister, but the point is she doesn't want me. In fact, she doesn't want anything to do with me . . . unless she's said something to you!' A hesitant note of hope crept into Emily's voice, then died as she acknowledged the sympathetic look on the nun's face.

'Is there no way you can heal the rift between you?'

The same look of curiosity that Emily had seen in the flower-seller's eyes was now reflected in those of the Irish nun. Yet not quite, for this woman was genuinely concerned for her patient's well-being. As if reading Emily's mind, the woman added apologetically, 'Of course, it's no business of mine why you two became estranged . . .'

'No, no, don't apologise, please.' Emily touched the nun's shoulder fondly, then deftly skirted around the painful subject and touched on another difficult problem that was facing her. 'The thing is, Sister, there is no home for Doris to return to. We tried – that is, my mother and myself, and a few of the neighbours, we all tried – to keep up the rent payments on their house, but money's tight all round, and I'm afraid we had to let it go. The council has already moved a new family into Doris's house. But there's room for her at our home. It just remains to convince Doris to move in with us. And seeing as she won't even talk to me . . .' She shook her head slowly, then in a brisker manner asked, 'When will she have to leave?'

Sister Bernadette's hands came together as if in prayer and then, raising her fingers to her lips, she said ruefully, 'I can keep her maybe for another couple of days, then I really must discharge her. I'm very sorry.'

'Well, don't be,' Emily reassured her. 'Maybe it's what Doris needs. She never was one to be coddled, but that was before . . .' Her voice faltered and she quickly pulled herself together. She was about to enter the building when the quietly spoken voice stopped her.

'She's in the garden, dear. Would you like me to tell her, or . . .'

'No, no, I'll tell her. I'm an expert at giving Doris bad news.'

Putting a brave smile on her face, Emily walked towards the lush green gardens of the hospice. There were several patients sitting in bath chairs on the immaculately cut lawn, one of whom was her friend.

'Hello, Doris,' Emily said cheerfully, ignoring the hostile look that immediately sprang into the grey eyes, the faintly scarred grey eyes that had almost been blown out in the explosion. Doris's last words to Emily, about not wanting to set eyes on her again, had been terrifyingly close to coming true.

Looking round, Emily noticed a small bench nearby and, keeping up a stream of careless chatter, she gripped the handles of the bath chair and wheeled it round so that it was facing the bench.

She half-expected Doris to wheel the chair around again, but the seated figure remained impassively silent. Heaving a sigh of relief, Emily eased her heavy body down onto the hard wooden surface.

'Phew, it's getting warmer. Not that I'm complaining, I hate the winter. Mum sends her love. She would have come with me, but she's got another job. You know Harry's fish and chip shop up Mare Street? Well,

Mum's working three afternoons, and two evenings a week – or did I tell you that on my last visit?' The young woman in the bath chair remained silent, her eyes now closed, but Emily knew that Doris was awake and listening to her. For a brief moment she was tempted to get up and walk away, walk away and never come back. But she couldn't do that. Despite Doris's attitude, she was still her friend, and Doris needed Emily now more than ever before. Still, perhaps if she copied Doris and stayed silent, it might just provoke her friend into acknowledging her. Minutes passed and still the figure, dressed in a garish candy-striped dressing-gown, remained mute and unmoving.

Lord, but she had a good mind to give Doris a firm shaking. Goodness knows, she'd tried everything else these past five months to get a response. Even if Doris were suddenly to open her eyes and scream abuse at her, it would be something. Anything would be better than this awful silence. Emily shifted uncomfortably on the hard bench and arched her aching back. Glancing upwards, she gave a startled jump as Doris's eyes found hers, but even as Emily opened her mouth to speak, the eyes closed tightly shut once more.

'All right, Doris, play your silly games. It doesn't bother me any more. But I'm not going just yet. I'll give you another five minutes, then, if you still haven't spoken, I'll carry on talking. Just rambling on and on, until you have to acknowledge me, even if it is only to tell me to shut up. And don't think you can out last until visiting time is over. Sister Bernadette told me that I can stay as long as I like.' The lie came easily to her lips and she was rewarded by a slight movement inside the ill-fitting dressing-gown. Did she imagine it, or had Doris smiled? No, it had probably been a trick of the light.

Settling herself in for a long wait and with nothing

else to do, Emily thought back over the last five months. Together with her mother, she had made a fraught journey to the munitions factory, and from there to the Woolwich Hospital, which was where, they had been informed by a sympathetic policeman, the injured women had been taken.

By the time they reached the hospital some hours after the explosion, Doris was being prepared for surgery and the two women hadn't been allowed to see her. One of the nurses had told them that, compared to the other women who had been on the floor of the factory when the explosion occurred, Doris had been very lucky. One of the young munitionettes, a girl called Lucy Williams, had died instantly. Even so, Doris's injuries had been bad enough to warrant surgery. Her upper body and face had suffered severe burns, which, although never life-threatening, had nonetheless been extremely painful.

At the first sight of Doris's injuries Emily had had to summon all her inner strength not to cry out. Doris had been barely conscious, dosed up as she was with sedatives and painkillers. But she had been able to tell Emily to go away, that she had meant what she'd said about not wanting to see her again. Shocked by Doris's appearance, and devastated by her cruel words, Emily had stumbled from the ward, breaking down in tears in a deserted corridor.

Nellie had stayed for over an hour at Doris's bedside, however, talking to and comforting the young woman who had been like a second daughter to her since her early childhood. On the long journey home, she had tried to comfort Emily, telling her that Doris was still in shock and didn't know what she was saying. But Emily had refused to be placated. Doris had known only too well what she was saying.

They had kept Doris at Woolwich Hospital for nearly

three months, after which she asked to be transferred to Hackney Hospital to be near her ailing father, who was also, by that time, a patient there. At that time the hospital had no available beds and had asked the nursing Sister of St Joseph's Hospice if they would take Doris in, until the hospital was able to admit her.

Tragically, Harry Mitchell suffered a stroke and died just two weeks after his daughter's transfer to the hospice, and Doris, thinking herself to be the cause of her father's stroke, had sunk into a deep depression. A depression that had lasted to this day.

Emily's eyes began to droop. It was so warm out here in the strong sunlight, and she hadn't slept well last night. Her eyelids became heavier as she struggled to keep awake.

Glancing down at her wristwatch, she noted with some alarm that it was nearly three o'clock. Despite what she'd told Doris about staying all day, in reality she had to get back to work. Both Mr George and Miss Rose had been very good these past few months, letting Emily have more time off than she'd ever had in her six previous years in their employment. But now there was Mrs Denton to take Emily's place in her absence. Emily's mouth tightened in anger. That woman!

Emily knew that she had placed another advertisement in the *Hackney Gazette* for a live-in maid, and not only there, but in several shops in the neighbourhood, putting small cards into shop windows for those not in the habit of reading the newspaper. And there wasn't a day that passed when she didn't make some sly remark or observation. Nothing that Emily could tackle her on outright – oh, no, the woman was too devious for that – but the insidious remarks and the sly looks were wearing Emily's temper thin. If she hadn't been pregnant she would never have put up with the woman's treatment.

But, much as she disliked admitting it, things had changed. She now needed her job. Miss Rose had already said that Emily could have the child with her in the house – as long as it wasn't too disruptive, of course. Her mother had offered to look after the child, if Emily decided to seek alternative employment, but that wouldn't be fair to Nellie, who was enjoying her new-found freedom and independence after the restrictive and abusive years with her husband.

No, Emily now needed to stay with the Winters. It was the only way she could envisage keeping her child close to her. But, as determined as Emily was to stay, so Cynthia Denton was determined to be rid of her. Emily could have taken her grievances straight to the Winters, but that wasn't her way. She had never been one to expect others to fight her battles, and she wasn't going to start now. The outcome would ultimately depend on whom the Winters were more fond of. And Emily felt sure that, after all these years, the friendship that existed between her and her employers was such that she need never fear for her livelihood.

Of course a lot would depend on the baby, and she could only hope that her child would be a contented one. Most of all, it had become very important to her to have her child grow up in that comfortable house, away from the drabness and poverty of Fenton Street.

The sound of the afternoon tea bell from the hospice building jerked Emily from her day-dreams.

'Lord, I was nearly asleep then.' She gave a soft laugh, and then, taking another look at the time, her manner became brisk. 'Look, Doris, I know I said I'd stay all afternoon, but I have to get back to work. The Winters have been very kind in letting me have time off, but I can't abuse that kindness. I've taken time off twice this week already and I . . .'

'Nobody asked yer to.'

The shock of hearing Doris speak nearly knocked Emily off the bench. Recovering quickly, she leant nearer the chair.

'Well, I see your disposition hasn't changed . . . Oh, now look, Doris, don't go pretending you're asleep again. All right, play it your way. I've neither the time nor the patience to humour you any more.' Her tone and attitude turned to sharpness. 'Now I've tried, my mum's tried and the nuns have been marvellous. We've fussed round you and been careful what we say, in case it upsets you, but there isn't time for that any more. So no more soft soap. I'm going to tell you how things really are, then it'll be up to you to decide what you're going to do.

'First off, Sister Bernadette is going to have to discharge you within the next couple of days. I know it might be a bit of a shock, but it can't come as a complete surprise. You must have known you couldn't stay here for ever. You know you can't go home, and you also know you'll be more than welcome to come and live with me and Mum. Of course, that would mean you'd have to put up with seeing me from time to time, when I come back home on my days off, but I should imagine that would be preferable to sleeping on the street.

'You would also have to see my child . . . Oh, yes, my child, Doris,' she said loudly, as the silent figure gave an involuntary jerk. Snatching hold of Doris's resisting hands, Emily stared hard into the grey eyes, which were filled at that moment with raw hostility.

'It's not going to go away. I'm having Tommy's child, and I'm not going to apologise for it any longer. It was a mistake, something I never planned to happen any more than Tommy did, but it's too late to change things now. And I'll tell you something else, while I'm at it. I'm sick to death of trying to appease you. These past five months I've grovelled and apologised, and done everything I could think of to get you to forgive me, but not any longer. All right, so you've had a lot to put up with these past months, and I don't just mean me and Tommy. You were in a terrible accident, and I can't begin to imagine what it must have been like. But you were lucky compared to your friends. So for the very last time, I'm sorry. Do you hear me, Doris? I'm sorry about what's happened. I never meant to hurt you, but it's done, and we both have to get on with our lives. And that's the last apology you're going to get out of me . . . Oh, to hell with you, Doris Mitchell.' With an angry, despairing cry Emily almost threw Doris's hands back into her lap.

'I'm going to work now and I won't be coming back here. I'll tell my mum you're being discharged in a couple of days, then you can work out with her what you're going to do. I won't be having any more days off for a while, so it'll be quite safe for you to go home with my mum for the time being. But, like I say, it's up to you what you do now. I've done all I can. Goodbye, Doris.'

Without looking back, Emily walked slowly across the lawn, half-hoping that Doris would call out after her, but no sound came. Holding her head high, she pushed open the hospice gate for the last time and walked out.

Doris remained motionless, her heart thumping wildly in her chest. They were going to chuck her out. What was she going to do? If her dad had still been alive, it would have been different. But he wasn't alive, he had died, and now she was all alone; alone and frightened.

But she needn't be. She had somewhere to go, but how could she go there after all that had happened? A feeling of panic swept through her entire body. Never before had she felt so helpless. Yet all she had to do was forgive and forget, and there was a home waiting for her. A place where she would be loved and cared for. But she couldn't forgive, and she could never forget – the hurt went too deep for that. Yet in spite of everything, she still loved Emily, but there was some part of her that refused to lay the ghosts of the past. She had said terrible things to Emily that night, called her names that could never be taken back, and in spite of all that, and her present condition, Emily had persevered in coming here. She hadn't missed a week since Doris's arrival, and Mrs Ford too had shown Doris nothing but kindness and concern. Doris had been able to talk to Mrs Ford, and had welcomed her visits – and would have welcomed Emily's too, if only she'd been able to forget the past. But she couldn't, she wasn't made that way.

Brushing her eyes with the back of a trembling hand, she bit down hard on her bottom lip. Whatever was she going to do?

Oh, Dad, I don't half miss yer. Hearing soft footsteps approaching, she froze, half-expecting to find Emily by her side. But it was only the orderly bringing round the afternoon tea. And Doris was more disappointed than she'd ever dare admit that it wasn't Emily.

CHAPTER SIXTEEN

On arriving at Gore Road, Emily was startled to find the doctor's car outside the house. Hurrying as fast as her condition would allow, she climbed the stairs to Miss Rose's room. Finding it empty, she was about to go to Mr George's study when Cynthia Denton appeared on the landing outside George Winter's bedroom.

'What's happened? Why is the doctor here?' The words tumbled breathlessly from her lips.

Behind the closed door Emily could hear muted voices, one of which was heavy and deep, and which she recognised instantly as that of the Winters' doctor.

'I'm surprised you are worried, Miss Ford. You haven't shown much concern for my cousin these past few months. If you had, you would have noticed that he hasn't been well of late.' Cynthia Denton saw Emily start to move forward and stepped in front of her, effectively barring the door behind. 'Please return to your duties, Miss Ford. If either of my cousins asks for you, I shall inform you immediately, but until such time I forbid you to enter this room.'

Emily's chest heaved with worry and anger.

'How dare you speak to me in that way.' Her voice was low and controlled. 'I have every right to go where I please in this house. It is you who is the interloper here, Mrs Denton, not me. Now kindly move aside, before I remove you forcibly.'

Cynthia's eyebrows rose, her lips curling into a sneer.

'Well, well, the veneer is slipping, Miss Ford. Be careful it doesn't slide too far. I don't imagine my cousins would be too pleased to discover what lies beneath your façade.'

Putting out her hand, Emily thrust the startled woman to one side.

'There you are wrong, Mrs Denton. Both Miss Rose and Mr George have seen all aspects of my nature over the years. My temperament and moods hold no surprises for them. Which is more than can be said of you, you scheming bitch. I know what you're after. I'm fully aware you're doing your level best to get me out of this house. For an educated woman, you haven't been too subtle about it. But your efforts will prove fruitless; both in removing me and in setting your cap at Captain Winter.' The older woman flinched as if struck, and for a brief moment Emily felt a pang of pity for her adversary, but not for long. She had too much to lose by turning soft; she had her own particular war to fight, and she couldn't afford to take any prisoners.

'All those veiled questions about Captain Winter, wanting to know everything but his shoe size . . . Oh, yes, I've heard you trying to worm information out of Miss Rose, and what I haven't heard for myself, I've been told by Miss Rose. She's quite alarmed, you know, by your sudden interest in her nephew. Because, in spite of your so-called social standing, your cousin doesn't think you're suitable for her nephew, and I can't say as I blame

193

her. All things considered, I think Captain Winter is safer where he is.' They stood glaring at each other, their faces only inches apart.

'You'll rue the day you trifled with me, madam. I have no intention of letting you get the better of me,' Cynthia hissed menacingly.

'Oooh, piffle,' Emily countered, her hand waving the air in a dismissive gesture.

The door behind them was flung open to reveal an irate man, somewhere in his fifties, with a shock of iron-grey hair that looked as if it hadn't seen a brush or comb in weeks.

'What in tarnation is all this racket? I have a sick man in here and he can do without your female caterwauling, as can I . . . Oh, hello, there, Emily, dear. I didn't realise it was you.'

'Dr Green, how is Mr George? I didn't know he was ill. He hasn't said anything to me, he . . .'

'There, there, my dear, don't go upsetting yourself in your condition. George didn't want to worry you, but . . . Look here, don't stand out there like a stranger, come in, come in. I'm sure your presence will do the old boy a world of good.' Leaning down he added wryly, 'And you can take Rose off my hands into the bargain. The woman's driving us both to distraction.'

Placing a fatherly arm around her shoulders, the doctor led Emily into the bedroom. Then, as if remembering the other woman's presence, he turned to Cynthia and said off-handedly. 'You, Mrs Whatever-your-name-is, make yourself useful, woman, and fetch some tea.'

Then the door was slammed shut once more, leaving Cynthia standing alone, her whole body seething with indignation and outrage at being treated in such a manner.

'Ooh, I'll see to you, madam, you see if I don't,'

she said to the empty landing, before reluctantly, and with great ill-humour, making her way down to the kitchen.

Inside the large bedroom George Winter lay raised on a mountain of pillows, protesting weakly to the doctor about all the fuss he was causing.

'Really, Alfred, all this palaver over a little turn. Stuff and nonsense, that's what it is; stuff and nonsense.'

'I'll be the judge of that, George,' said Alfred Green good-humouredly. Taking hold of the gnarled hand, he felt deftly for a pulse, his countenance showing none of the concern he was experiencing about his old friend.

Letting go of the wrist he said heartily, 'Now then, ladies, I think we should let George get some rest. After all, he's not as young as he was.'

'No . . . I mean, I'd like a word with Emily, Alfred. Just a few minutes, I promise I won't tire myself unduly.'

The doctor made as if to protest, then changed his mind. Ushering a flapping Miss Rose out of the room, he closed the door gently behind them.

'Come here, my dear,' George Winter said kindly, patting the side of the double bed. Sinking onto the soft mattress, Emily took hold of the wrinkled hands and clasped them gently.

'I'm so sorry, Mr George, I never realised you were ill. You should have said something.'

'There, there, child, stop your fussing. I know how worried you've been about your friend, and rightly so. It's no more than I would expect of you.'

'But I should have noticed. There's no excuse for my negligence, I've been very selfish. But I know now, and I'll take good care of you. I'll soon have you up and running about the place, you'll see.'

George's eyes swept lovingly over her face, then in

a quiet, dignified voice he said, 'No. No, you won't, child. My days of running are long gone, as indeed will I be soon.'

'Oh, sir, don't . . . Don't say such things, please.'

'Now, now, don't you start blubbering. I've had enough of that with Rose, bless her. Listen, my dear, I wanted a chance to speak with you, to tell you that you need have no fear for the future. I've always said you would be looked after, and I'm a man of my word; besides which, I'm inordinately fond of you.' He gave a short laugh and patted her hand.

'There, you see, just like a man. Can't come right out and say I love you. And I do, you know, Emily. I hoped that I would live long enough to see you married and settled down happily; and more so over the last months.' Emily knew only too well the significance of the words, and her head drooped forward onto her neck.

'Now, now, none of that.' George Winter's voice gained strength at Emily's obvious discomfort. 'I don't know the whys or wherefores of your present condition, nor have I any intention of prying at this late stage. What I do know is that you remain as dear to me now as you've always been. Nothing in the world could ever alter my high regard for you. The only reason I mention it now is because of my anger towards myself for letting this business of making a new will drag on for so long. You've been like my own child over the years and, like any parent, I want to ensure that my child, and the children of that child, are taken care of. To that effect I want you to phone old Palmers and get him here as soon as possible.

'The last will I made was over twenty years ago, when I was still young enough to imagine I would live for ever. But there you are, human nature doesn't alter, and I'm not the only man, or woman, who has put off making a will in the twilight of their years. Once one gets past a certain age, it seems as if it would be tempting fate to put one's affairs in order. I confess that is the sole reason why I have never made a new will. I imagined the ink to be barely dry on my signature before some calamity befell me . . .' The faded eyes suddenly became bright with unshed tears.

'Oh, Emily, I wish I could be brave about this . . . but . . . but I feel so afraid. You see, I don't feel old, not inside. Inside I feel just as I did thirty years ago, and there's so much I still want to do. Silly things, like certain books I've wanted to read and never quite got round to. One always says, I'll do it tomorrow, or I'll make a start next week. Only there comes a time when there are no tomorrows and . . . I . . . I don't want to die, child . . . I don't want to die.'

'Oh, sir, sir, don't, please don't.' Throwing herself into his trembling arms, Emily gave vent to her emotions. As the tears rained down her face, she was conscious of the sounds coming through the open window of the bedroom. The high-pitched voices of small children could be heard playing in the park opposite. An ice-cream vendor was shouting his wares, and in the distance the clip-clopping of horses' hooves resounded on the cobbled roads. A light breeze floated through the window, fluttering the white, freshly laundered net curtain that Emily had hung up yesterday, while the faint whiff of lavender polish filled the room.

As the sounds from outside seemed to intensify, Emily wondered how everything could be so normal, so everyday, when this dear man lay dying.

Life goes on. The words sprang unbidden to her mind.

What a trite, insensitive platitude that was; it was also painfully true.

Emily hugged the thin body tighter and laid her head against the frail chest; against the heart that soon would beat no more.

George Winter died at six o'clock that evening. He died with dignity and without pain in the company of the young woman he had loved and respected, a woman who refused to leave the elderly gentleman to face death alone, and put aside her own fear and grief to comfort him during his last moments on earth.

CHAPTER SEVENTEEN

Captain Matthew Winter didn't make it to his uncle's funeral, a fact much lamented by Rose Winter, who took her nephew's absence as a personal slight.

Her resentment, however, vanished three days later when Matthew arrived on the doorstep, dishevelled and unannounced, and deeply distressed at not being able to say goodbye to the uncle who had taken him under his wing at such an early age.

For the past two days Emily had been forced to witness the nauseating attention bestowed on the distraught man by Cynthia Denton, who appeared to have made it her goal in life to dog the uniformed man's every move.

Now Matthew's compassionate leave was over. He just had time to stay to hear the reading of the will, but what with Cynthia fawning over him, and his aunt's constant demands for attention, the hapless man resorted to the only solace that had seen him through the past forty-eight hours; he sought refuge in the kitchen, and in Emily's company.

'Oh, good morning, Captain Winter. You startled me. I didn't hear you come in.' Emily was bending over the hot stove, a tray of scones in her hands. Shoving the baking tray into the fierce heat of the oven, she closed the door carefully and straightened up, a welcoming smile on her flushed face. 'Sit down, sir, and I'll make you a pot of tea. I was about to take a tray up to Miss Rose, if you would prefer to take your morning tea with your aunt.'

'Good Lord, no,' the hasty refusal burst from his lips. 'I mean, well . . . Oh, look here, Emily, I know it's a dreadful thing to say, but if I spend another moment upstairs I won't be responsible for my actions.' Pulling out a chair, he lowered his long frame easily onto the hard seat.

Emily smiled at him in understanding.

'I know. Poor Miss Rose. She's hardly slept a wink since the funeral. She was all right up till then. In fact, I was amazed at how calm she was after your uncle's death. Dr Green said she was in shock at the time, and it seems he was right.' Placing a china cup in front of Matthew, she added sadly, 'He was a lovely man, and I miss him dreadfully. The house won't be the same without him.'

'I know. Not that I'd seen much of him or Aunt Rose over the past few years, but it was always a comfort knowing he was here if I needed him. He was a grand old boy and, like you say, he'll be sorely missed.'

Nodding silently, Emily carried on with her tasks, unaware that her every move was being watched with loving, yet sorrowful, eyes.

Matthew rested his hands, palms upwards, on the table, throwing his mind back two days. Even now he couldn't honestly say which had come as the greater shock: finding out that he had missed the funeral of his dearly loved uncle, or discovering that his beloved Emily was pregnant. He had assumed, in those first gut-wrenching moments, that she had married during his absence. A hasty marriage too, by the look of it.

Cynthia had soon put him right on that score. In fact, she had taken great delight in telling him that their maid had got herself into trouble, with no future husband on the horizon. *Their* maid. The cheek of the woman! He didn't know her very well, having only met her on a few previous occasions in the past, but, judging by these past couple of days, hers wasn't an acquaintance that he felt eager to renew. He wasn't a man to make judgments lightly, always preferring to look for the good in people, but as far as he could see, Cynthia Denton was a scheming, conniving bitch of the first order, who from the very moment of his arrival had made it embarrassingly obvious that she was interested in him. He squirmed uncomfortably at the thought.

He was at a loss to understand why his aunt and uncle had ever allowed the creature house-room, though his late uncle would have been loath to ask the woman to leave, always preferring a quiet life. Still, Matthew was surprised to find his aunt so smitten with this far-flung relative. Perhaps it was because she was still in shock. Even so, from what he had seen, Cynthia Denton seemed to have inveigled her way into the old woman's affection, and as the former had made no secret of her dislike for *the maid*, as she sneeringly put it, where did that leave Emily, now that his uncle was no longer around to protect her interests? Unless, of course, the old boy had made a new will recently. Ah, well, the family's solicitor would be arriving today for the reading of the will, so he and Emily would find out how the land lay soon enough.

'Would you like something to eat with your tea, sir? I could make you some toast, or a sandwich if you prefer. Lunch will be late today, what with the solicitor coming this morning.'

'What! Oh, no, thank you, Emily. The breakfast you gave me was quite ample.'

As she smiled and moved away, Matthew said haltingly, 'Emily!'

'Yes, sir?'

'Damn. Sorry, Emily, but I wish you'd drop this "sir" business, at least when we're alone. You make me feel like some damned relic from Victorian times.' When Emily smiled shyly, it was all he could do to stop himself leaping from the chair and taking her into his arms. There was so much he wanted to know. For instance, where was the father of the unborn child she was carrying so proudly? And, more importantly, did he intend marrying her? Because if the father wasn't interested, then he certainly was. Oh, Lord, what was he thinking! Emily had made it painfully clear that she didn't look on him in that way. And would he be prepared to take on another man's child? The answer came back swiftly. Yes, a thousand times yes. If the mother came willingly, he would take on a whole brood of fatherless brats.

He took a mouthful of the piping-hot tea, then, remembering Emily's conversation of last night, said, 'About Lenny, Emily. I wish there was something I could do, but I'm afraid . . .' He spread his hands wide in a gesture of helplessness.

'Oh, sir . . . I mean, Matthew,' she smiled shyly, 'don't be silly. I know there's nothing you can do for him. I shouldn't have mentioned it, it's just that my mum knew you'd be coming home and . . . Well, you see, she seems to think that the entire British Army is camped in one place over there and, being an officer, it would be easy for you to find him and send him home.' She looked away, embarrassed at troubling him with her problems when the poor man had enough of his own.

Draining his cup, Matthew sighed, his hand running absently through his mass of dark hair.

'Well now, Emily, your mother's not that far from

the truth, because it's a madhouse out there, a bloody shambles. Regiments and battalions being pushed further and further back, until some of them are meeting up with the new arrivals. Nobody seems to be where they should, and the wounded are fast outnumbering the able-bodied. It's chaos, complete and utter, bloody chaos.'

Emily lowered her gaze, uneasily aware that she had unwillingly evoked memories of the war, when the Captain should have been resting and forgetting, at least for his short leave, the carnage he had left behind and would soon be returning to.

Seeing her discomfort, Matthew reached out and took hold of Emily's hand and said warmly, 'Don't look so downcast, my dear. It's only natural you should be worried about your brother. I only wish I had the power to help. I like Lenny, and rest assured that if our paths do cross, I'll do everything I can to see he is safely returned home.'

A bell tinkled overhead, interrupting Emily as she was about to answer. Glancing up at the wall clock, she exclaimed, 'Goodness, he's early. The solicitor, I mean,' she said by way of explanation to Matthew. 'He wasn't due to arrive until twelve-thirty.' Removing her apron, she flashed a bright smile and left Matthew staring forlornly after her.

God, Emily, if you only knew the effect you have on me, you wouldn't smile so readily.

Out on the hall landing, Emily paused for a moment to tuck a wisp of chestnut hair behind her ear before opening the door.

'Morning, Miss. I've come ter see Mrs Denton. She's expecting me.' The shabbily dressed woman stared at Emily's puzzled face, afraid for a minute that she'd got the wrong address. When Emily remained mute, the woman clasped an equally shabby handbag more firmly, seeming to take comfort from the inanimate object. 'It's about the job, Miss – for a live-in help,' the woman added as Emily continued to bar her way. 'Mrs Denton wrote ter me an' asked me ter start terday.'

'I'll deal with this, Miss Ford. Please, go about your duties.' Cynthia, a satisfied smirk on her face, pushed Emily to one side while extending a welcoming hand to the relieved-looking woman on the doorstep.

'Fank yer, Miss. Fanks, ever so much. I'm much obliged.'

Realising what was happening, Emily turned sharply on her heels and made her way back to the kitchen, her cheeks flaming with anger.

'Emily, what's wrong! Sit down, dear, you look dreadful.' Matthew had risen from his chair in concern. Brushing past him, Emily bent down and pulled open the oven door, burying her head in the intense heat to hide her agitated state.

'Nothing's wrong, sir. Just that infuriating woman up to her tricks again.' The muffled reply brought a look of puzzlement to Matthew's face.

As suddenly as Emily's anger had appeared, so it vanished. Examining the partly baked scones, she pushed the tray back into the oven and said wryly, 'I'm sorry, Matthew. I don't know why I let myself be riled by that woman.'

The sound of his name on her tongue brought a sudden, glorious lift to Matthew's heart.

Oblivious to the officer's state of mind, Emily chatted on.

'Ever since she came here, she's been trying to turn your aunt and uncle against me. She was subtle at first, because of course she realised that she needed me to stay. I can't imagine Her Ladyship getting down on her knees to black-lead the grate, can you? Although from what your aunt told me, Mrs Denton was nothing less than a skivvy herself at her parents' home. But she certainly hasn't dirtied her hands since arriving here.'

Coming closer Emily leant her head towards Matthew, a smile pulling at the corners of her mouth. Nodding her head towards the door she added, 'That was the new live-in maid. Well, I say that, but she won't have been hired yet, nor will she be – at least not without Miss Rose consulting me first. In fact . . .' a grin spread her lips even wider, 'Mrs Denton may have done me a favour. You see, your uncle and aunt have been trying to get me some cleaning help since the war started. But that crafty piece thinks that if she finds someone to live in, there'll be no use for me, but that's where she's wrong. Any additional staff were always sought to help me in the house, not to replace me. Besides which, as far as I know, Cynthia Denton has no authority to hire staff. Oh, I know she's been spending a lot of time with your aunt this past week, and I know Miss Rose has been looking to her for support. Because as much as I would have liked to be with her more often, I simply haven't had the time to give her the attention she's been craving. Obviously your relative has assumed airs of grandeur, if she thinks she can hire and fire at will. Because that's what she's been after. To get rid of me, and get her hooks into . . . Oh . . . Oh dear . . .'

This time it was Matthew's turn to smile.

'It's all right, Emily. I know what you were about to say. Good Lord, I've never seen myself as a latter-day Lothario, but I'd have to be deaf, dumb and blind not to realise what the blasted woman is after.' And of course she would want you out of the way, my love, he added silently. Because what man would ever give Cynthia a second look with you on the horizon?

They exchanged a friendly, conspiratorial look, before Matthew reluctantly left Emily to get on with her work.

The solicitor had been and gone, thankful that for once he hadn't had to contend with hordes of relatives squabbling over the last will and testament of their dearly departed loved one.

Emily sat alone in the kitchen, mystified and hurt that she hadn't been asked to attend the reading. She was aware that she wouldn't have been mentioned in it, as the will had been made long before she had entered the Winters' employment. Even so . . . ! For the first time she questioned her position in this house. Miss Rose could have had Emily present if she had wished for her company at such a distressing time.

'Oh, stop being so sorry for yourself, lady,' Emily chastised herself in the empty kitchen. 'You know full well how Mr George felt about you. It wasn't his fault he left it too late to change his will. Miss Rose will see that you're taken care of, so stop worrying. It's all the upset of this past week, that's all. So don't go getting yourself all wound up and saying something that you'll regret later on. That's exactly what that odious woman wants.' But still the uneasy gnawing in the pit of her stomach continued.

The sound of raised voices from upstairs brought Emily's head swivelling round. Her mouth suddenly dry, she stood up and faced the closed door, waiting for it to open – waiting for . . . !

Doors slammed overhead, then running footsteps thundered down the stairs before stopping outside the kitchen. Emily waited, her heart hammering at an alarming speed inside her chest.

Then Matthew was standing in the doorway, his face filled with a multitude of expressions. Anger, pain, but most of all, shame.

Wetting her parched lips, Emily asked quietly, 'What is it, sir? What's happened?'

Hanging his head Matthew groaned.

'Oh, Emily. Oh, my dear, dear, Emily.'

Some part of her being recognised the depth of feeling in the words, but the practical side of Emily's nature came to the fore.

'I asked you a question, sir.'

Before Matthew could answer, another voice, familiar and jubilant, filled the air.

'I can tell you that, *Miss Ford*. Your services are no longer required. You are, of course, entitled to a week's notice. Please be advised that that notice is hereby served.'

The words resounded inside Emily's confused head. This couldn't be happening; it must be a mistake. Mr George had always told her she would be well cared for as long as she remained in their employment, and his sister had echoed those sentiments; not once, but many times over the years. And she had remained, hadn't she? Even though she had been bored and had wanted to be more in life than simply a paid drudge, she had stopped on, out of affection for them both. Even after last week, when her mother had again offered to look after the baby while Emily found another job – a job that would offer excitement, as well as more money, a job where she could have worked with people of her own age. And still Emily had refused, had almost thrown the unselfish offer back in her mother's face.

All right, so she hadn't relished the prospect of sharing a roof with Doris – a sullen, resentful figure who had slammed out of the house the day Emily had gone home

207

to tell her mother that Mr Winter had died. But most of all Emily had stayed on out of loyalty and a genuine affection for the elderly couple. *And this was her reward!*

There must be some mistake, because if there wasn't, then her faith in human decency would be shattered for ever. But wait a minute. Why had the Denton woman waited until now to sack her – why today?

'My late cousin made no provision for you, Miss Ford. We, that is my aunt and I, thought that George might have amended his will over the years, but apparently not. And that being so, there really is no reason for you to stay any longer. The new help seems quite capable, though if you wish you may stay on for a few more days to help her settle into the routine of the house. That option is entirely up to you. I'm sure my aunt won't see you turned out penniless into the street, though I shouldn't set my sights too high, if I were you. Rose has become very concerned with self-preservation lately, and of course that includes the money necessary to ensure that she has the best of comfort in her twilight years.' But Emily was no longer listening.

As she moved towards the stairs, she heard Matthew say in a tone she'd never heard him use before, 'Will you shut your spiteful mouth, woman. And you can wipe that smug look off your face. Because I'll tell you this now. Despite your success with my aunt – and God knows how you managed that, because she's loved Emily like one of her own – despite your scheming efforts, you are going to be disappointed. Because if Aunt Rose won't take responsibility for Emily's future, and that of her child, then I will. I'm not without my own resources. And furthermore I won't, as I imagine you'd hoped, be moving in here after the war. I have my own home to return to. That's if I come back, and . . .'

Emily slowly climbed the stairs, still unable to believe

that dreadful woman's words, even though Matthew hadn't actually refuted them.

Once outside Miss Rose's room, Emily hesitated, suddenly reluctant to hear, from her dear friend, what, in her heart she knew to be the truth.

Rose Winter lay on top of her four-poster bed feigning sleep. But, as Emily drew nearer, the wrinkled eyelids began to flutter in nervous agitation.

'Miss Rose. Miss Rose, please, I have to talk to you.' The frail body began to quiver as the eyelids slowly opened. But the faded blue eyes shifted nervously, unable to meet Emily's direct gaze. 'Is it true – what Mrs Denton tells me? Have I been dismissed? Because if so, then it's a cruel reward for all the years I've spent in your employ. Not the actual dismissal, though I can still hardly believe you would cast me aside so coldly, but the way in which it has been done. The subterfuge involved wasn't worthy of you, though I can still hardly believe that you waited until you were sure Mr George hadn't made a new will in which I would have been provided for . . . Oh, yes, Miss Rose, you can look all sorrowful, but it's the truth, isn't it? Even so, I would have thought that after all this time you would at least have had the decency to tell me yourself.'

'Really, Miss Ford. You are overstepping the grounds of familiarity in speaking to your employer in such a disrespectful manner. Remember your place, girl.'

Cynthia Denton had entered the room. Crossing swiftly to the bed, she took hold of the trembling hand and stared across at Emily, her eyes hard and jeering.

The woman's triumphant expression was bad enough, but it was the way in which Rose Winter grabbed the comforting hand and held onto it, totally ignoring Emily's presence, that caused the last vestiges of her patience to break.

'I was talking to the organ-grinder, not the monkey,' she snapped back angrily. Coming closer, Emily looked down at the wrinkled face and said calmly, 'People told me I was a fool to stay on here, when I could easily have found a job with more money, and prospects. But I wouldn't listen. You see, I thought you cared for me as a friend, a part of the family. God knows you told me so often enough. Or was that merely a ploy to keep me here? How many times did you suspect I was becoming restless? What did you do then? Think up a way of keeping me here? Did you conspire with Mr George? No, I can't believe that of him.' She shook her head slowly. 'Did you rack your brains for inducements, like the old clothes from the attic that I was so grateful for, or more words of praise and assurances of how much I meant to you both?'

Rose Winter's eyes brimmed with tears as she started to speak.

'That isn't so, Emily. Everything I said was true. You are . . .'

'There, there, Aunt Rose, don't upset yourself.' Cynthia hastily cut off her aunt's trembling words. God! She hadn't spent these last months, and especially the last few days, grovelling and worming her way into the old dear's heart just to have it all come to nothing at this late stage.

'Let her speak. Let her say what she really feels. Because I'm not leaving until Miss Rose tells me, to my face, that she doesn't want me here any more. I'm certainly not going to take your word for it, you hateful, deceitful woman.' Emily glared at her adversary, then, turning slowly back to the elderly woman, she said softly, 'If you want me to leave, then I'll go. I won't cause a fuss, because I know it's not your fault. Somehow, this . . . this creature has turned you against me. I want to know how.

How, after all we've meant to each other, you could turn me out without any explanation.'

A look of uncertainty crossed the lined face, then she felt her hand being squeezed and Miss Rose seemed to gain courage. In a quivering voice she said, 'I never lied to you, Emily. I did have, that is to say, I still have, a great affection for you. But as Cynthia pointed out to me, once the child is born you won't have the time to see to your duties – or to me. And I need someone to look after me, Emily. And . . . and you're a young woman who will want to get married one day, maybe to the father of your child, whoever he is. I never probed, did I, Emily? I never asked who he was, or condemned you for your indelicate state. I . . . know I said you could raise the child here, but I spoke hastily, without thinking the matter through. The fact is that I simply couldn't bear the thought of a young child in the house. All that noise and disruption. I'm old, Emily. I need peace and quiet, and I need family around me.'

Emily's body slumped. So that was it. The Denton woman had used Miss Rose's innate fear of being left alone to drive Emily from the house. There was no use in talking any longer. The sooner she got away from here, the better, before she broke down and lashed out with words that she would later regret. Besides, she wouldn't give that woman the satisfaction of seeing her brought low.

Gathering all her self-possession, Emily lifted her head and stared at the old woman she had loved – still loved, in spite of her disloyalty, and said, 'Very well, Miss Rose. I won't argue with you, except to say that I would never have left you alone. Even if I had a husband and half a dozen children around my feet, I would never have deserted you. But that's all academic now, isn't it? You've made up your mind, or should I say, you've had it made up for you. I wish you well, Miss Rose. I loved you and Mr George as if you were my own family, which is why I stayed on here so long. I see now that I was a fool to believe you felt the same way. I hope you have a long and happy life, though with the company you have chosen to see you through it, I very much doubt it. Goodbye, Miss Rose.'

She walked sedately from the room, her head held high, but once out on the landing she let her chin fall and fought back the tears that were stinging her eyes.

Behind her she could hear soft weeping, but she hardened her heart. It was no good trying to persuade Miss Rose to change her mind. Cynthia Denton had got her claws in too deep . . .

Going to her room, Emily was startled to find the shabby woman sitting on her bed with two brown carrier bags by her feet.

Hearing Emily approach, the woman leapt guiltily to her feet.

'I'm sorry, Miss. That other lady brought me 'ere an' told me this was where I was gonna be sleeping.'

Emily's lips tightened. This room had belonged to the previous housekeeper. It was the largest and most comfortable of the servants' rooms. There were two smaller rooms in the attic, one of which she herself had occupied when she first came to the house, which would have provided adequate accommodation. It was yet another example of the malicious spite in which Cynthia Denton seemed to revel. Emily was surprised to find how calm she was now feeling, and she experienced an urgent need to put this poor woman at ease. After all, it wasn't her fault.

'Please, don't be alarmed. I don't intend to cause any unpleasantness. If you will wait while I pack my belongings, I'll get out of your way and let you settle in, Mrs . . . ?'

'Oh, Lawson, ma'am. Mrs Lawson's me name.'

Nodding, Emily smiled reassuringly at the nervous woman and began packing her things. Ten minutes later she was ready to go, her movements sedate, almost lethargic. Perhaps she was suffering from the same shock that Miss Rose had experienced after the funeral. Perhaps she should ask Miss Rose for some of the pills Dr Green had prescribed for her. She wasn't aware she had made any sound until the woman stuttered, 'Pardon, ma'am. Did yer say somefink?'

Bemused, Emily turned to face her.

'Did I? How extraordinary. I don't remember speaking.' Then, putting out her hand, she said affably, 'Good luck in your new employment, Mrs Lawson. I hope you'll be very happy here . . . By the way, you said you were sleeping in. Well, obviously you are, or you wouldn't be needing my room. What does Mr Lawson think of your new arrangements?'

The woman was regarding her with puzzled eyes.

'I'm a widow, ma'am. Me 'usband was killed six months ago.'

'Of course, how stupid of me, I should have guessed. Well, goodbye again, Mrs Lawson.' Emily shook the woman's hand again. 'And good luck.' She avoided adding that Mrs Lawson would need it.

Carrying her suitcase, Emily took one last look round the hallway, her eyes straying up the long flight of stairs for the final time. Then she took a deep breath and opened the heavy front door. Descending the stone steps awkwardly, she reached the pavement and paused. It was as if she were waiting for something – or someone – but she didn't know who.

Shrugging, she lifted her case and began to walk

towards the park. Passing through the wrought-iron gate, she rested the suitcase on the grass for a moment before picking it up and walking on. She hadn't gone more than a few feet when she heard her name being called, and was both surprised and alarmed at the sudden surge of gladness that swept over her.

Lowering the suitcase back onto the grass, Emily waited until Matthew caught up with her.

'Lord, Emily, I didn't think you'd leave straight away.'

'I didn't think there was anything to stay for,' she replied much more coolly than she was feeling.

Disconcerted by her aloof manner, Matthew scratched at the back of his head, before hesitantly holding out a large brown envelope.

'You forgot your wages, plus a week in lieu of notice. Please take it, Emily, it's the least my aunt could do after the shameful way she's treated you.'

Taking the envelope from his outstretched hand, Emily uttered a low laugh.

'I've no intention of refusing it, sir. As you say, it's the least your aunt could do: besides which, I earnt it.' She was smiling again, smiling and nodding her head to put him at his ease. Yet she didn't feel like smiling. She wanted to cry – no, not cry, that was too . . . too . . . ! She wanted to howl, long and loud. And to scream and shout, and behave in the way Cynthia Denton had expected of her. Vulgar and common – she wished she was vulgar and common. She had found that such women were much happier with their lot. Maybe it was because they held nothing back. No silent resentment, no repressed anger. It all came out in a torrent of loud, and often foul, language. It must be wonderful to let go in such a way.

But Emily had been brought up as a lady. And ladies kept their inner feelings locked up inside themselves – to

fester and gnaw away at their very soul. Fortunately she
had also benefited from her early upbringing in Fenton
Street – that, together with Doris's vociferous company
over the years, had instilled in Emily an added strength,
a gutter instinct of survival that no well-bred lady could
ever hope to understand.

'Let me drive you home, Emily. You shouldn't be
walking in your condition.'

Now Emily did laugh out loud.

'Shouldn't be walking! You do have a sheltered view
of life, Matthew. Did you imagine I've been lounging
around with my feet up these past months? I've been
awake since six o'clock this morning. I've cooked, washed
a pile of bedding and hung it out to dry in the garden.
I've ironed a mountain of clothing, and been down on
my knees scrubbing the kitchen and bathroom floors.
The last of which I did early this morning. It doesn't do,
you see, to have the hired help littering the house with
buckets of dirty water and the like – it sets a bad tone.'

'Don't, Emily. Don't be like this, it doesn't become
you.'

'Doesn't become me! What does become me?' she
demanded fiercely. 'To be thrown out like yesterday's
rubbish? To be cast aside, like so much discarded clothing
that is no longer required . . . ?'

A pair of arms enveloped Emily, pulling her close and
directing her faltering steps towards a park bench. She
didn't even try to struggle free.

Instead she laid her face on the broad shoulder and
wept, quietly at first, then with shuddering sobs. She let
free all the hurt and anguish that seemed to be choking
her. Between sobs she poured out all that had happened
since their last meeting, the disjointed words tumbling
over each over in her haste to unburden herself. She
told Matthew about her parents, and about the brutal

existence that her mother had endured for years. Yet, even as she bared her very soul, there was one piece of information she kept back – the night she had spent in Tommy Carter's arms. That part of her life was too personal to share with this man – with any man. She simply said that the father was someone she was very fond of, but that she had no intention of marrying him. This piece of information was the only part that had truly concerned Matthew, and his hopes soared again now that he knew there was no immediate rival for Emily's attentions.

When the spasm had passed, she gently disentangled herself from Matthew's embrace, embarrassed now at the spectacle she had made of herself. Taking a white handkerchief from the pocket of her blue checked smock, she wiped her eyes and made a sound somewhere between a laugh and a hiccup.

'Goodness, I am sorry, Captain Winter . . . I mean, Matthew. It still seems strange calling you by your first name. It's a shame I won't have the chance to get used to it.'

'You could, you know, Emily. Get used to calling me by name, I mean.'

Her eyes widened slightly at the sudden change in Matthew's tone, and when his hand tightened around her fingers, a light began to push its way forward from the deep recesses of her mind. It appeared to be coming from the long end of a dark tunnel, and it kept coming closer and closer until, with a startled gasp of surprise, the truth exploded into sudden brightness, hitting Emily squarely in the eyes and almost blinding her. She felt her cheeks begin to burn and started to rise clumsily to her feet.

'I . . . I must be going, Captain Winter. Thank you for . . .'

Matthew too had risen, his face and manner seemingly at odds with each other, while he cursed himself for giving the game away. Now wasn't the time to profess undying love. Not here, where they were in all probability being spied on from the house opposite. And not now, when he wasn't sure of the future; or even if he had a future. In two hours' time he would be back on the train to Dover, and by tomorrow he'd be in France. Back among the dirt and squalor, the fighting and the carnage. But whereas before he had been in danger of falling into a state of apathy, now he had hope. Not much, he warned himself. He could return on his next leave and find Emily happily married, but it wasn't very likely. There weren't many eligible men around these days, which was doubtless one of the reasons why that flighty piece back at the house had set her cap at him. He guessed that he had been the sole motivation behind Cynthia's campaign to get rid of Emily. He shuddered inwardly.

God! He would rather face a Hun armed with a bayonet than the prospect of seeing *her* lying in his bed. But what was he doing standing here like a stuffed dummy, filling his mind with trivial matters when time was so precious?

Emily was standing awkwardly before him, her face pink and averted from his gaze. And suddenly he threw caution and common sense to the wind. This might very well be the last chance he had to tell Emily how he felt.

His heart pounding, and steeling himself for rejection, Matthew placed his hands on Emily's arms and said softly, 'I love you, Emily, and have done for some time.'

'Oh, sir . . . I . . .'

'It's all right, my dear, there's no need for you to be frightened. I'm well aware I'm old enough to be your

217

father – well almost.' He gave an embarrassed laugh. 'But I wanted you to know that, whatever happens, I'm here for you, no matter what. I don't expect you to return my feelings. Indeed, I'd be amazed if you did. But will you think about it, Emily? I'd take good care of you, and I'd look on your child as my own. You don't have to say anything now, but . . . but, as I say, think about it while I'm away. And . . . and if you could imagine spending your life with me, then you would make me a very happy man.'

He searched Emily's face for some sign – anything to show him that she wasn't completely revolted by the idea of marrying him. Then a sudden thought struck him. He hadn't mentioned marriage – oh, dear Lord!

With almost comic haste he spluttered, 'When I say spend your life with me, I meant to say, will you marry me? Good heavens, Emily, I hope you didn't think I was trying to take advantage of you.'

Now Emily did show a reaction, but not the one he had hoped, for she began to smile, and for an awful, heart-stopping moment he thought she was going to laugh in his face. Instead she laid her hand on his and said gaily, 'Well, if that was your intention, I would say you were roughly nine months too late.'

His breath exploded in a giant sigh of relief. If she could laugh with him, it was a start. Yes indeed, it was a start. He would say no more on the subject for now – except . . .

'Emily, listen. I won't push you for an answer now. I know it will take you time to come to terms with my proposal, but I want you to know that, whatever your answer, I intend to provide for you . . . Now, now, don't argue. This has nothing whatever to do with my feelings for you. I'm doing it because it is what my uncle would have wanted, what he would have done himself, if he'd had more time. And look . . .' he was rummaging in his trouser pocket, and when his hand emerged it was holding a key. 'This is a spare key to my house in Brixton. You know the address don't you?'

Emily nodded, unable to speak. It was like a dream. She couldn't take it in, and yet . . . Why did she feel so excited? So . . . so . . . happy, happy in a way she had never felt before? Oh, she needed her home, her mother, the familiar sights and sounds that would bring her back down into the real world. But Matthew was still talking, and she must hear what else he had to say. Matthew, Matthew. How easily his name came to her mind now. She felt the key being pressed into her hand.

'Take it, Emily, even though you will probably never have a use for it. It will make me feel better knowing that, whatever happens while I'm away, you need never fear being homeless. And I'll write to Palmer, the solicitor, as soon as I can, authorising him to send you a weekly sum during my absence. And if you won't take it for me, then take it for George, for he would have been deeply saddened to see you left without any recompense for all the faithful years you gave him.'

She couldn't answer, she was too full, too overcome with emotion to think straight right now. And when Matthew took her case and headed back towards the house, she followed him dumbly, like a faithful dog trotting after its master.

Leaving her side just long enough to collect the car keys from the house, Matthew helped the silent woman into the car. Running lightly round to the other side, he got in behind the wheel and started the engine. Then, with a wide grin on his face, he turned his head and waved towards the upstairs window, before releasing the brake and driving off.

Cynthia watched them go, her fingers curling into

bunched fists. Letting the net curtain fall, she remained standing, her eyes narrowing into tiny slits of anger.

She had won. That common piece masquerading as a lady had gone. Now she had all the time she needed in which to persuade Rose to sign over the house to her. She would ensure that her cousin didn't make the same mistake as her brother in failing to make a new will. She should be feeling very relieved and settled. Yet she hadn't quite got all that she'd hoped for.

Suddenly she turned, the sound of a tinkling bell echoing through the room, the room that had once been Matthew's on his visits. She could sense his presence in every corner, every part of the room, and at night she snuggled down in contentment in the bed he had occupied for so many years, her fertile imagination conjuring up the man himself to lie by her side. Well, she hadn't lost him yet. Oh, no, the last battle was far from over, despite the scene she had witnessed from the window. The bell sounded again, more urgently this time, bringing a grimace to her stiff lips. She was about to answer the summons, then she stopped.

Flopping in an unladylike manner across the bed she thought savagely, 'Let the old cow wait. I'm not her servant.'

Down in the basement Gladys Lawson sat uncomfortably on the single bed, her eyes fixed on the small bell jangling on the opposite wall. She was still waiting for someone to come and explain her duties to her, and was mulling over the angry scenes she had heard and seen in the short time she had been in residence. And when, some ten minutes later, with her nerves at screaming point and the insistent bell still ringing loudly, she placed her hands over her ears and wondered nervously what sort of a household she had landed herself in.

CHAPTER EIGHTEEN

Emily had only been home a fortnight, and already the atmosphere in the small house had become unbearable. Coming down the stairs, she awkwardly lowered her swollen body into the sagging armchair by the fireplace, carefully ignoring the figure seated in the chair opposite. She needn't have worried. The moment she sat down, Doris rose and left the room.

Emily least her head against the back of the chair and sighed. God! She couldn't take much more of this. It wasn't so bad when her mother was at home, for Doris spoke quite freely with Nellie. But left alone with Emily, she clammed up, avoiding being in the same room if at all possible. Emily's normally placid nerves were in tatters and she knew that her poor mother was exhausted, from trying to keep up a cheerful appearance, as well as from attempting to keep the peace between the two young women sharing her home. It wasn't right. Her mother had spent her life walking on eggshells around her father, and it wasn't fair to expect her to endure this oppressive atmosphere at this stage of her life. Especially now, when Nellie had just begun to realise how good life could be, without having to stop and think before she opened her mouth.

It was no good. She would have to have a word with Doris. And what would she say? Start talking to me or sling your hook? Doris, like herself, had nowhere else to go.

And yet that wasn't true in Emily's case. She squirmed uncomfortably on the threadbare cushion, her eyes darting almost furtively to the bedroom above, where the key that Matthew had given her was hidden among a mass of trinkets in an old biscuit tin that served as her jewellery box. She hadn't been able to bring herself to tell Nellie what had happened between her and Captain Winter for, as she kept reminding herself, it didn't seem real, and the more time went by, the more she began to think that she had imagined the whole episode. But if Nellie knew, then her hopes for her daughter would soar once more, and Emily wasn't going to risk disappointing her, for she didn't yet know how she felt herself.

He probably felt sorry for you, a voice in her head niggled at her. After all, the weekly sum he promised hasn't materialised, has it? And God knows she could have done with it right now. For as things stood at the moment, her mother was the only one working, and her wages barely covered the rent. Oh, she wouldn't have carried on taking money from Matthew, she wasn't made that way. But a little help until she was back on her feet would have made life a lot easier for them all. With an impatient shrug of her shoulders, Emily turned her thoughts back to the woman who had once been like a sister to her.

Before the accident her old friend wouldn't have tolerated the situation. She would have slept rough rather than stay under the same roof as someone she'd imagined had betrayed her.

But it was different now. Doris was different now. In fact, nothing seemed the same any more.

Moments later Emily's eyes flew open as the front door slammed. She hadn't realised she was falling asleep. Good Lord, she'd only just got out of bed. She made a feeble effort to rise, then decided against it. She didn't feel at all well. The lower part of her back ached something awful, and she was so tired. She imagined that if the house suddenly caught fire, she wouldn't have the energy to flee. Even the mundane task of brushing and twisting her long hair up into a bun at the nape of her neck was too much trouble now. Instead she had let it fall around her face and shoulders these last few days. She hadn't even bothered to get dressed this morning and was still in her nightdress. But who cared? There was no-one to see her disarray. She was rapidly settling into full-blown self-pity when the first pain struck.

She gasped, her eyes widening in shock as the contraction seized her stomach.

Minutes later another, more protracted pain brought her head down almost to her knees. Sweat began to break out on her face. Lord! She had asked her mother repeatedly what contraction pains were like, and how she would know when it was time. Her mother had smiled wryly and answered, 'You'll know, dear. Believe me, you'll know.'

And she was right. It felt as if a giant hand was inside her, clenching her innards into a tight ball.

When yet another pain struck, barely three minutes after the last one, Emily felt a wave of panic. Breathing shallowly, she raised her eyes to the mantel clock. It was only just gone nine o'clock. Her mother had gone down to the market, and from there she was going to see one of her old employers to find out if she could get some morning cleaning work. She might not be back for hours yet.

Trying to still the mounting fear, Emily attempted to reassure herself that it would be all right. Babies didn't come that quickly, or that easily. Her mother would be home in plenty of time.

The thought had barely crossed her mind when she was doubled up once more, and deep in her heart she knew she was in trouble. Her baby was struggling to be born and she was on her own.

Bravely she tried to rise from the armchair to summon help, but succeeded only in making it to the floor. Dot! She could knock on the partition wall for Dot. But no sooner had the idea entered her head than she remembered that her neighbour had gone away last night to spend the weekend at her sister's house in Essex. Whimpering like a wounded animal, Emily began to crawl towards the door, but she felt so ill, so tired. A sudden rush of warmth between her legs brought tears of mortification to her eyes. She'd wet herself.

Outside the front of the house she could hear women's voices as they exchanged a few minutes of idle gossip before getting down to their household chores. But she didn't really know her other neighbours that well. She always said good morning, when encountering one of them in the street, but that was about as far as her acquaintance with them went. And these past months she had been only too aware of their curious eyes, eager to know who was responsible for the child she was carrying. No! No, she couldn't crawl out into the street. It would be . . . well, undignified, and if nothing else, she still had her dignity. Then all such feelings vanished in a wave of searing pain and fear, as she began the fight for survival – for herself and for her unborn child.

*   *   *

'Wotcha, Doris, love. 'Ow's fings?'

'Oh, you know, Bert. Mustn't complain. An' it wouldn't do any good if I did, 'cos no-one'd listen.'

Well Street market was alive with activity. Despite the war, the East End stall-holders still managed to thrive, obtaining their wares from nefarious quarters to sell on to women who were always on the look-out for a bargain – war or no war.

The warm July air was filled with the smells of dead fish, warm meat, flowers and fresh – and some not so fresh – fruit.

'Yer found a job yet, duck?'

Doris started, the large, bright orange that she'd idly picked up from the stall slipping from her grasp to fall back among its companions.

'Nah, there's nothing going at the moment. Still, keep smiling, eh? That's what I say.'

She was about to move off when the stall-holder caught hold of her arm with a dirt-encrusted hand.

''Ere, just a tick, Doris. The reason I asked is 'cos I 'eard there's one going down at the baker's. Yer know the one. The Baker's Dozen down the end of the market, where we all get our rolls an' tea. Why don't yer go an' see if it's still going. Suit yer, that would, wouldn't it?'

'Thanks, Bert. I'll go along now an' ask. Thanks a lot. See yer.' With a cheery wave of her hand Doris walked off, appearing to head in the direction of the market bakery. But once out of sight of the helpful stall-holder, she crossed the road and continued to wander aimlessly through the market.

What was the matter with her? She had never been afraid of work, or anything else for that matter. But since the accident she had seemed to retreat inside herself, unable, or unwilling, to do anything more arduous than cope with the everyday mundane necessities of living.

At times she felt as if she were being sucked into a giant, dark void, a void that she had until now resisted. Yet she had the idea that if she were to succumb to the welcoming dark abyss, then she would be drawn down into a place from which she would never return – and the idea both appealed to and terrified her.

Every little mishap, even something as trivial as finding there was no milk for her tea, was enough to bring tears gushing to her eyes. She couldn't understand it. She'd never been one to let things get her down, yet now . . . !

''Ere, 'Arry. Wot yer done ter yer missus? I seen 'er just now crying 'er eyes out.'

'Yeah, well, the silly cow won't piss so much then, will she?'

This sally, which would normally have brought forth a howl of laughter, didn't even elicit a smile from Doris as she passed by the two labourers perched on a wall outside a terraced house, drinking strong, muddy tea from tin mugs. One of them, an elderly man in his fifties, looked up and gave an exaggerated wink at Doris. The unexpected gesture brought a sudden rush of colour to her pale cheeks and a jerking lift to her heart. Confused, she bowed her head and hurried on. Before the accident she would have dallied a while with the men, exchanging quips in harmless flirtation – *before the accident, before the accident*.

Stop it, stop it, her mind screamed at her. It was no good harping back to the accident. It had happened, and now it was over, and she had to move on, let it go – but she couldn't. She had tried, oh, yes, she had tried. But sometimes she didn't even know herself. Didn't recognise the miserable, moody, frightened, apathetic creature she had become. If she hadn't been living with the Fords, she would have given up altogether. And all her frustrations and spite had found a release in tormenting Emily.

Emily, her dear friend, whom she no longer hated, although she couldn't seem to tell her so. The apologetic words, words that she rehearsed over and over again in her mind each night, became locked in her throat whenever the recipient of her inner feelings appeared.

Passing a second-hand stall, Doris listlessly picked up a pale green blouse and a brown hobble skirt.

'Only five bob the pair, darlin'. Belonged ter a real Duchess, they did.'

Doris nodded, dropping the garments back among the untidy heap of clothes. If the owners of second-hand stalls were to be believed, the entire wardrobes of the nobility had ended up in the East End markets.

Inexplicably her throat tightened and the familiar urge to cry assailed her. She walked on, lost in her own deep, troubled thoughts, her footsteps taking her, like an unbridled horse, back towards Fenton Street. And as she listlessly dragged her feet along the uneven pavement, her mind again travelled back to the day of the accident.

Poor Lucy Williams, the girl she had asked to clock in for her, had died almost instantly, and Freda Hawkins, an older, more experienced woman, had died of her injuries two days later. Five other women had been treated for burns and shock, as she herself had, and Doris had been extremely lucky. It still wasn't clear what had caused the TNT to ignite. Either it had been a faulty batch, or someone had been careless; disastrously so. The explosion had occurred in the lower end of the factory floor, right behind the heavy entrance door, blasting it to smithereens, and fragments of the door had pierced Doris's eyes, almost blinding her. She had been lucky – she had to keep telling herself that. For the accident had happened in the very part of the factory where she herself had worked. If she had been on time that day . . . !

Her legs froze, and her heart began hammering inside her chest. Oh, my God! All this time she had been blaming Emily for everything that had befallen her, yet if Emily hadn't told her about the baby, if she had kept quiet just another day longer, then she, Doris, would have gone into work as usual. Would have been working alongside Lucy and Freda and . . . !

The weakness struck at her arms first, then at her legs, and for an awful, stomach-churning moment she thought she was going to pass out. Quickly she steadied herself. Why had she never realised that before?

And the answer came back swiftly. Because yer was too bleeding busy feeling sorry fer yerself. Well, now yer know. If it wasn't fer Emily, yer'd be lying six foot under right now. So get yer arse back home and start apologising. No, make that grovelling, 'cos yer've been a right bloody bitch these past couple of weeks; in fact, yer've been a right pain in the arse since . . . Oh, Gawd, she had ter get home, and could only hope that Emily wouldn't spit in her eye when she apologised. No, never. Emily was too much of a lady to do anything so coarse.

As if in a daze, Doris looked around her and saw that she was at the very end of the market, facing in the direction of Morning Lane. Shaking her head in bewilderment, she turned slowly and began to retrace her footsteps.

Cutting through one of the side turnings that would bring her level with Fenton Street, she heard raised voices and the sound of glass shattering, and without stopping to think she began to walk in the direction of the commotion. What she saw brought her to an abrupt standstill.

About half a dozen men, presumably from one of the nearby factories, were gathered outside a butcher's shop, some clutching thick sticks, others holding stones high ready to throw, their faces contorted with savage rage, their mouths shouting hate-filled obscenities. More glass shattered and a loud, jeering cry rent the air.

'Piss orf back ter Germany, yer bleeding Hun. We don't want the likes of yer over 'ere, spying on us fer yer murdering pals. Yer all butchers, the whole bleeding lot of yer kind.'

Fear struck Doris's heart at the almost demoniacal hatred she was witnessing. Then an elderly man, his head bleeding, his hands raised in a gesture of helplessness, ran from the shop, his quivering voice barely audible above the frenzied, clamouring noise.

Heirhart Noschke, a German Jew who had lived in England for over twenty years, ran frantically to and fro, his sweaty palms rubbing the front of his striped, blood-stained apron, his eyes filled with bewilderment rather than fear. He had taken over the butcher's shop from his father before him, and he looked upon England as his home, and the English people as his friends. He couldn't understand what was happening, couldn't comprehend the hate pouring from this small group of men, some of whom he knew and had passed the time of day with. Now they were looking at him as if he were some loathsome creature whom they were about to tread underfoot, with as much thought as they would crush an insect. Another stone found its target, hitting him squarely on the side of the temple. He wasn't quick enough to put his arms out to cushion his fall, and his face hit the pavement, his lower and upper teeth slamming together with a sickening crack that jarred his entire body. As hot blood gushed from his mouth, the men surrounding him cheered loudly, and it was that awful, inhuman sound that spurred Doris on.

Without stopping to think of her own safety, she stormed through the pocket of men, her raised hand punching and whacking indiscriminately, knocking caps from ducking heads as she waded into the startled mob.

'Yer bleeding cowardly bastards,' she screamed defiantly, 'picking on an old man on his own.'

'Stay out of it, love. That old geezer's a German. 'E ain't got no business being 'ere, spying on us fer 'is bleeding mates back 'ome, while our boys are out there being murdered by that bastard's relations.' One man strode forward, his chin thrust out aggressively, his whole bearing one of self-righteousness. He glared down at Doris with dark, menacing eyes, but she never wavered. Gripping her arm, he began to drag her away, but Doris's blood was up. Any influence that Emily might have had on her over the years was stripped away to reveal a wild animal, an animal prepared to fight to its last breath to defend the weak. Swinging her handbag, which was as usual filled to capacity with an assortment of junk, she brought it up and round, landing it with a resounding, satisfying thwack on the side of the man's head. With a string of obscenities the man staggered back, caught off-guard by the suddenness of the attack.

'Oh, yeah, worried about our soldiers, are yer, yer miserable fucking bastard. That goes fer the rest of yer, does it?' She spun round, her eyes blazing at the group of men who were now beginning to shuffle uneasily, an element of shame overwhelming then, their heads lowered against the ferocity of this young woman's gaze.

'If yer that worried, why ain't yer over there fighting alongside them? Nah, men like you lot wouldn't have the stomach fer a real fight. Yer only good fer beating up defenceless old men. Scum of the earth, that's what you lot are, scum of the earth.'

The man she had knocked sideways bent to pick his cap up from where it had fallen on the dusty road. Ramming it back on his head, he looked at his companions, then, seeing no help forthcoming, again sought to justify his actions. Stretching his neck up from the collar of his starched shirt, he ground out fiercely, 'We're no cowards. But someone has to stay behind to keep the factories going. You women can't do everyfink, though most of yer fink yer can.' The last words came out as a sneer. 'What we do is vital ter the war effort an' we don't 'ave ter . . .'

'Vital war work, my arse!' Doris screeched derisively, her hands placed firmly on her hips.

What would have happened next she wasn't sure, but in the distance the unmistakable wailing of a siren brought the men to their senses. Swiftly now they disbanded, all but the man Doris had struck with her handbag. Perched on his toes ready to flee, he snarled at her, 'Yer interfering bitch. If I sees yer around I'll . . .'

Doris threw her head back and laughed.

'Yer'll what, yer great big bag of wind. I ain't frightened of the likes of you. Go on, piss off before I land yer another one.'

With a final, threatening shake of his fist the man scarpered away, the wailing black Maria chasing after him and his companions.

Doris watched in some amusement as the back of the van opened and four burly policemen leapt to the ground, pulling out their batons before giving chase. Then her face altered, her chin wobbling as she realised just how close she had come to receiving the same brutal treatment as that poor old . . . !

Oh, my Gawd! She had completely forgotten about him. Whirling round, she ran to where the elderly gentleman was sitting on the edge of the pavement holding a blood-stained handkerchief to his mouth, seemingly unaware of his head wound, which was by now bleeding profusely.

'You all right, mate?' Even as she spoke the words she cursed herself for her stupidity. Of course he wasn't all bleeding right. A person could be lying by the side of the road with a dozen knives sticking out of their back, and some bright spark would come along and say, 'You all right, mate?'

Casting around her for something to stem the flow of blood, Doris let out an angry exclamation, lifted up her loose black skirt and, with much cursing and panting, managed to rip the white petticoat apart at its seam. But try as she might she couldn't tear a piece off to use as a bandage. Without stopping to think, she hastily pulled the petticoat down and over her feet. Bunching it up into a ball, she pressed the soft fabric against the man's forehead, effectively stemming the flow of blood.

'It's all right, it is clean.' Doris smiled wanly and then, placing a hand gently under his elbow, assisted the dazed man to his feet.

'Thank you, thank you for helping me.' The man's voice, which had a foreign inflection, quavered as he held gratefully onto her arms. 'I . . . I don't understand . . . These people are my friends . . . my friends. Why did those men hate me so? I've never done them any harm, never done harm to anyone . . . I . . . I don't understand. Why! I was born in Germany, that is true, but I'm a British citizen now . . . I don't understand.'

The feel of the man's trembling body brought a lump to Doris's throat. How could people be so cruel . . . so evil. When a hand came to rest on hers she jumped, startled by the warmth of the gesture. Swallowing hard she muttered, 'I'm sorry fer what happened ter yer, but we ain't all like that lot. They're scum, ignorant scum. Some people are so barmy about the war that they'd hang someone fer having German measles.'

Looking into the reddened eyes of the old man, it

was all Doris could do to stop herself from bursting into tears.

'You're a very brave girl, very brave. You put those men to shame. If . . . if I can ever be of service, please . . .'

Doris fidgeted with embarrassment. She was about to make light of her involvement and say, 'If ever I need a pound of sausages on the cheap, I'll let yer know.' But instead she said quietly, 'Don't be daft, I'd have done the same fer anyone. Anyone would.'

The grizzled grey head shook slowly.

'No. No they wouldn't, dear.' And there was such a wealth of despair in those quietly spoken words that Doris had to turn her head away.

Doors that had been ajar were now flung wide, as people rushed to help and involve themselves in the drama. As two women, obviously known to the butcher, began clucking round him, Doris looked up and said scathingly, 'Took yer time, didn't yer. What were yer doing while this poor sod was being beaten up – watching yer drawers drying on the line?'

The women had the good grace to look ashamed as they led the tottering man across the road and into one of the terraced houses opposite his shop.

As he was about to enter the house, the old man turned and mustered up a trembling smile at Doris, then the women closed round him and he was lost from sight. Not wishing to hang around for the police to return, she set off at a brisk walk.

She wanted to get home. Home to a welcoming cup of tea and a sit down. Home to Emily. Her steps quickened, and such was her desire to see her friend, the friend who had inadvertently saved her life, that by the time Doris turned into Fenton Street she was practically running. Yet when she came to rest outside the door of number fifteen she hesitated, memories of the past flooding her brain, reminding her painfully of the way she had behaved, and the cruel words she had spoken. She could hear herself screaming the words 'whore' and 'slag' at Emily's white face, and shame at the memory brought her head low. How could she have said those things? More importantly, would Emily be prepared to bury the hatchet and start again? Oh, she hoped so, because if not, if Emily turned away from her, then Doris would truly be all alone in the world – and she'd have nobody to blame but herself; herself and her big gob.

She felt shaky, and wasn't sure if it was a reaction to the fight she had been involved in or the prospect of facing Emily. She drew in great lungfuls of air and felt slightly better; not marvellous, but definitely better. She stared at the familiar front door, unsure now she was here exactly what she would say. Rubbing a hand over her mouth, she began to form the words in her mind, trying to find a good opening with which to greet Emily. After the first sentence it would become easier, she hoped.

Being a Saturday, most of the doors in the street were wide open and smells – some appetising, others less appealing – wafted from the terraced houses, in the sultry July air. Children swarmed in the narrow street, playing hopscotch, marbles and kiss-chase. A few of the older, more daring ones had fitted a rope to one of the lampposts and were twirling around it, shrieking and laughing as they enjoyed the start of the weekend.

The noise and the smells, together with the curious glances that Doris was attracting from two women gossiping on their doorsteps, propelled her into making a move. Pulling at a piece of string, she drew the key through the letterbox and inserted it in the lock. Then her face changed to one of puzzlement. The door seemed to be stuck. Pushing again, she realised that something was wedged behind the door. For an awful moment she thought that Emily had barricaded her out.

Aware that she was now a focus of attention, Doris redoubled her efforts – then gasped as she realised that it was Emily's body that was barring her way.

Using all her strength, she lent the whole weight of her body against the door, until there was enough space for her to squeeze through the narrow opening and into the house.

'Em . . . Em, are yer all right?' Gawd! There she went again, asking those stupid bloody questions. Dropping to her knees, she attempted to roll the prone figure onto her back. With much huffing and puffing the feat was achieved. 'Oh, Gawd, Em, yer look bloody awful. Hang on, mate, I'll go an' get some help.' She used the floor as leverage to stand up, only to be pulled down again by Emily's frantic hands.

'Don't . . . don't leave me, Doris. I'm scared, don't leave me, pl . . . Ooooh, Doris, help . . .'

Thoroughly frightened by now, Doris squeezed Emily's hand and rocked back on her heels. What was she going to do? She couldn't leave Emily in this state, but it looked very much as though her baby was coming – and coming fast.

'Hold on, Em, I'm just gonna get some towels . . . No, it's all right, I ain't leaving yer,' she gabbled as Emily's hands tightened around her wrist. 'I've got ter get some things from upstairs. Towels an' blankets an' stuff . . . an' . . . and I'll get the kettle boiling.'

'Wha . . . what for?' Emily's voice was barely audible.

'What fer? Well, ter . . . ter . . . Oh, Gawd, Em, I don't know. I ain't never seen a baby being born before, but I've heard women talking about it, and they always boil a kettle. Look . . . look, let me go an' get some help . . . Okay, okay, I'll stay with yer. But at least let me go an' get something to lay under yer, otherwise the poor little bugger'll bash its bonce on the way out.'

Casting a hurried glance at the heaving body, Doris quickly climbed the stairs, and was back within a minute holding a pile of towels, which she unceremoniously thrust between Emily's legs.

A sudden loud scream made the hairs on the back of Doris's neck stand on end. She watched helplessly as Emily drew her knees up to her chin. Her face was bathed in perspiration as the pain racked her swollen body.

The cotton nightdress was drenched in sweat, and as Doris attempted to pull it up round Emily's chest, she gave an unexpected chuckle.

'Bleeding 'ell, Em. No wonder yer having trouble. Yer've still got yer drawers on, yer silly cow.'

Through a haze of pain Emily tried to smile, and with the aid of Doris she removed her undergarments. Then she was bearing down, harder and harder.

'Ooooh, Doris, it's coming. The baby's coming . . .'

Her nails were digging into Doris's hand, but Doris hardly felt the pain. Her eyes widened in fascinated awe as the baby's bloody head began to emerge, then a moment of panic set in. Oooh, shit! What was she supposed to do now? Biting down on her lower lip, she gingerly caught hold of the tiny, slippery shoulders, terrified that she might do the child some damage. She was sweating as much as Emily now, as they both endeavoured to bring the new life into the world. Doris's hands slid, causing her to take a firmer grip, spreading her fingers to catch hold of the baby under its arms. And, with a feeling of wonderment, she eased the wriggling form onto the towels, where it proceeded to kick and flail the air in angry protest at being removed from its warm haven.

Laughing and crying, the two women looked at each

other, all past differences wiped out and forgotten in this moment of highly charged emotion. And then Doris carefully wrapped the child in a soft blanket and laid it almost reverently in Emily's arms, saying shakily, 'It's a boy, Em, a lovely little boy. And . . . and he looks just like his dad, poor sod.'

All Emily could say was, 'Oh, Doris, my dear, dear Doris. I've missed you so much.'

Doris gave a lop-sided grin, then slumped back onto her heels, her body spent.

Emily too was exhausted. She had never felt so tired in her entire life; nor so happy. Her cheeks damp with tears and sweat, she moved the blanket to one side and gazed down into the pair of deep blue, puzzled eyes that were surveying her warily.

An overwhelming feeling of love, so strong it could almost be termed violent, swept through Emily's battered, bruised body. Doris was right. There was no denying who the father was, for Tommy Carter's eyes were looking up at her and, in that moment of awe, Emily silently wondered where her baby's father was at this minute – and even whether he was still alive.

But instead of seeing Tommy's face, she pictured Matthew's and was filled with confusion. And when Doris asked hopefully, 'Can I have a cuddle?' Emily reluctantly relinquished the soft burden.

The moment the child left her arms, Emily's eyes began to droop and, try as she might, she couldn't keep them open. Telling herself that she would just rest her eyes for five minutes, she drifted off into a light sleep.

And there was Tommy, smiling at her, holding out his arms – then the image changed, and it was Matthew who was smiling, his arms thrown wide, waiting for her.

Tommy and Matthew – Matthew and Tommy. Their faces were so clear in her mind, then they mingled until only Matthew's remained, and it was his face she took with her into a contented slumber.

Doris gazed at Emily's peaceful countenance, and with a muffled cry she brought her face down to the child she was holding and whispered, 'You've got a son, Tommy, an' . . . and he's beautiful. I'll write an' let yer know as soon as I can. Mind yer, I'll probably get it in the neck from Em fer telling yer, but yer know me, I never could mind me own business. Oh, Tommy, yer'll never look at me now, will yer? But it doesn't matter, honest. Just so long as yer come back home safely. I'll help Em look after him, I promise, 'cos . . . 'cos I love his mum and dad more than anyone else in the world.' Raising her eyes in anguish, she sobbed quietly, 'Where are yer, Tommy? Where are yer? Oh, Tommy, please don't be dead. I can bear anything, as long as yer not dead.'

CHAPTER NINETEEN

It looked like the end of the world. As far as the eye could see, bodies lay strewn over the battlefield like so many discarded dolls, their heads lolling to one side, their limbs, if still attached, flung out haphazardly, seemingly at variance with the shattered, mangled torsos. Here and there, as Very lights exploded against the dark sky, other shapes, large and round, could be seen – the dead horses, brave creatures that had galloped into the hail of bullets and shells, trusting their masters to bring them back unharmed. As Tommy Carter stared out over the bleak, corpse-laden landscape he was reminded of a picture he had once seen at Sunday school: 'Armageddon', the end of the world.

And he had helped bring another life into it.

The letter from Doris was inside his breast-pocket, resting against his heart, a heart that had almost become dehumanised by the atrocities and senselessness of war. Almost, but not quite, for Tommy Carter was an optimist, who always managed to see the good side of people, the funny side of life.

But once over the top of the trenches, he, like thousands

of others, had to clamp down on human emotion, shut his mind to reasonable thought, for how else could he stick and twist his bayonet into another bloke's belly, then pull it out and carry on until the next German barred his path? Out there in No-Man's-Land, you had to stop yourself thinking the Huns were just ordinary blokes like yourself, with mothers, wives, sisters and girlfriends, all sitting at home and praying for their safe return. Blokes who, like yourself, enjoyed a pint, a laugh and a game of football, and had an eye for a pretty girl when out with their mates, while deep down inside they nurtured dreams and hopes for the future. They were all there, just one and a half miles away – the Hun, the Bosch; the enemy.

Squatting in mud-filled trenches, the young men and old, clutching their rifles, their hearts filled with apprehension and fear, wondered if the new dawn would be the last they would see. They would be experiencing all the emotions Tommy was feeling, which all the platoons, battalions and divisions camped here on the Ypres Salient were feeling. But you couldn't let yourself think like that, couldn't liken the enemy to yourself, daren't look them in the face as you plunged the cold steel into their bellies. For then you would see a human face, a real human being, and you wouldn't be able to do your job. Your job! Legalised murder, that's what it boiled down to, legalised murder – on both sides of the trenches.

And here, at Passchendaele, they didn't even have proper trenches. Just a load of shell-holes, lengthened and widened, and reinforced with sandbags to hide behind. When leaving your particular trench on night attacks, you had to ask which way to go, because often you didn't know where the next trench was. Then there was the diarrhoea brought on by drinking tea out of discarded petrol tins, and the agony of standing waist-deep in mud, while trying to empty water out of your trench with the aid of only a couple of bully-beef tins. Many of the men got trench-fever and trench-feet. The former left a man weak and listless, the latter nearly rotted his toes off.

The conditions were sometimes too terrible to describe, yet in spite of all the privations, the fighting went on. New arrivals were drafted into regiments that had sustained huge losses, swelling the ranks once more until the next battle.

The men in the front line were on duty for three to five days at a time. Then they would move back half a mile in support, and then further back, four or five miles away to billets, until it was their turn to return to the front line once more.

But there was laughter too, not least from the East End regiments, who kept their companions cheerful with their robust cockney humour. And the camaraderie was wonderful. Men he had never met before would share cigarettes, chocolate and food parcels from home with him. If one man was lacking in something, another would provide it with a grin, shrugging off murmurs of thanks, some replying that they were all in this together and that it would be a pretty poor show if they didn't look out for one another. Oh, yes, there was a good side, and thank God for it, because without it, many of the men would have given up by now.

They had been here since 31st July. It was now 26th October, and rumour had it that this would be the third, final push, marking the high tide of the British advance towards Passchendaele – a place he had never heard of a year ago, and which might now be his final resting place.

Oh, give over, man, he rebuked himself silently. You've been thinking that ever since the fighting started, and you're still here, aren't you!

Setting his back more firmly against the mud wall, Tommy looked down the long dug-out, where shadowy figures lay crouched or hunched up as he was, too wound-up to sleep, sunk in their own private thoughts as they waited for the dawn to break. And when it did, they would go over the top again, their combat boots trying not to get bogged down in the mud, but, worst of all, trampling over the bodies of their own men who lay out there, trapped in a battlefield where no stretcher-bearers could venture to bring them back for a decent burial. Weeks of attacks and counter-attacks, plus a seemingly non-stop deluge of heavy rain, had turned the battleground into a morass, and wounded men had been left to die in the stinking slime, their voices filled with despair as they realised the impossibility of being rescued.

Men like Alfie Ford. No! Not like Alfie Ford, because he had been a real bastard, and a coward. What little courage the man had possessed had soon disappeared, and two weeks ago, so the story went, one of Alfie's lieutenants had had practically to force the cowering soldier over the top at gun-point. Once out in the open, Alfie Ford had dropped to his knees in a vain attempt to avoid the bullets. Crawling on all fours, he had scrabbled along the muddy ground, his face alive with terror, then a shell had exploded a few feet away and he hadn't made it back – nor had the lieutenant.

This war wasn't only a living nightmare, it was, at times, a bloody shambles. The chances that four men, joining up at different times but known to each other, should meet up in the same stretch of France weren't as improbable as one might imagine. After all, the battle plans were mapped out by generals sitting comfortably ten miles behind the lines, holed up in some French château, playing out the war on a game-board. Moving soldiers and artillery over the board was like a giant game of draughts. It was no wonder then that platoons, brigades and battalions not only crossed paths, but intermingled. And in the confusion men stumbled along blindly, uncertain of their orders and where they should be, and ultimately men died needlessly, while the powers that be played on.

Yet it had been pure coincidence that the Carter twins had crossed paths with Lenny and Alfie Ford, for their battalions were separated by two miles of dug-outs spread out across the barren countryside of Ypres. Tommy and Andy, on their way for a few days' leave in the billets, had come across Lenny in the camp kitchen. The two men had joined a long queue for their first hot meal in days, when Lenny, his blunt features spreading into a wide grin of disbelief, had rushed up to them, grabbing their hands in delighted recognition. The three men had eaten their ration of watery stew, served up in tin cans, out in the open, using boulders as chairs. Tommy and Andy had remained solemnly silent as Lenny related his tale of having fooled the authorities into letting him join up. But his animation slowly faltered as, shame-facedly, he admitted that he hadn't been allowed to bear arms, but instead had been allocated to latrine duties. The sergeant in Lenny's battalion had spotted the young man's intellectual disorder and, out of compassion, had ensured that the fresh-faced soldier was kept well out of the line of fire.

The three men had parted soon after their shared meal, shaking hands and wishing each other well, and the Carter twins had watched Lenny walk away, subdued now, his shoulders slumped as he returned to his obnoxious duty.

Thinking of Lenny brought forth, as always, an upsurge

of pity. Poor Lenny! It was bad enough that his father's last cowardly moments had been witnessed, and were now talked about with contempt among his battalion, without having the further humiliation of being detailed to latrine duties, a job usually allocated to elderly, dependable men, who were excused most camp parades and left to get on with their work without supervision. It was essential work, yet it was doubtful that Lenny Ford saw it that way.

Tommy and Andy had met up with Alfie Ford only once, when the burly man, blustering and disavowing himself from any part in his son's enlistment, had sought out the twins, desperate to try to stop the story from spreading. He wasn't liked much as it was, but if the men in his battalion found out just how low he had sunk in order to get back at his wife, his life would have been made hell. But neither Andy nor Tommy had felt any sympathy for the man. It had been Andy, his eyes cold and accusing, who had cut Alfie off in mid-sentence, saying curtly, 'Piss off, Alfie. Go an' find another hole ter crawl into. You ain't welcome here.'

And Alfie had pissed off and crawled into another hole, only to be dragged out of it and ordered over the top. Now he lay out there somewhere, rotting along with hundreds of others. Tommy shook his head slowly, his steel helmet glinting dully in the dark, early morning. No! Even such a man as Alfie Ford didn't deserve a death like that. No man did.

The slight movement of his head set off a crinkling sound that Tommy felt rather than heard. Flicking open the button on his breast-pocket, he extracted the letter from Doris and stared down at it. He couldn't see the words, but he didn't need to. They were imprinted on his brain.

He had a child, a son, and he didn't know what to make

of it. He had received the letter almost six weeks ago, and as yet he hadn't replied. He had tried to write back, but each time his pen faltered, not knowing what to write, or who to write to. Should he reply to Doris, or to Emily? It was Emily who had borne his child, but she had kept quiet about it. She'd had nine months – no, make that seven months, he countered, because she wouldn't have known at first. But she'd had plenty of time since, and she hadn't written a word about it.

Oh, she had written to him, or rather to them both, her letters short and cheery, with not even a hint that she was pregnant. He had thought something was wrong when Doris stopped writing. Her first two letters had been much the same as Emily's, but her third had been more personal – nothing too flowery, for Doris wasn't the type for writing soppy love-letters, yet an element of intimacy had begun to creep into her writing. Tommy had replied quickly, surprised to find just how much he was looking forward to her next letter. But it had never arrived. Emily had continued writing to them both, and it was through her that they had learned of Doris's accident. Both men had immediately written to their old friend and received a short letter back from Doris, stating that she was perfectly all right and not to worry about her. But still there had been no mention of the baby; until now.

Tommy shook his head in bewilderment. He couldn't make it out. Couldn't understand why Emily had kept her condition such a closely guarded secret. He had told her he would stand by her, if there were any consequences of their brief night together. Had she been afraid that hearing the news would make him act rashly, or cloud his judgment and so put his life at risk? Or was it simply that she didn't want his support and his help, in any shape or form? His chin sunk lower until it was nearly touching his chest. He was surprised that his mother hadn't imparted the news. One of her main pleasures in life was seeing others in trouble, and the sight of Emily's swollen belly would normally have had her falling over herself to pass the news on. He gave vent to a long, silent sigh. Perhaps his mother had become more charitable in his absence, though it was more likely that she was too wrapped up in her worry for Andy to bother with anyone else.

Oh, his mother! Now there was a woman who could write. She'd written enough pages to fill a book. Not to him, though – oh, no, not a word to him. Andy tried to cover for her and spare his brother's feelings, by reading out the letters and starting them 'Dear Andy and Tommy', but Tommy knew differently. Oh! Oh, now, don't start feeling sorry for yourself, mate, his mind cautioned. You've enough to worry about. Don't make more grief for yourself. He moved restlessly, his mind shifting towards the coming dawn.

After this one, he would ask again about Blighty leave. He was due, his whole regiment was, but their requests had been turned down. Instead they had been granted a few days off behind the lines, but he didn't want to wander around France, he wanted to go home, now more than ever. He needed to get back home to sort things out with Emily.

'You all right, Tom?' Andrew's voice, barely a whisper, cut into Tommy's thoughts.

Smiling down into the darkness, he whispered back, 'Yeah, I'm all right, Bruv. I was just thinking about Blighty. Maybe we'll get some leave after this one. What d'yer reckon, Andy?'

Andy smiled back, his teeth and eyes all that could be seen in the dug-out.

'Don't get yer hopes up, mate. Anyway, let's get today out of the way first, eh? Mind you, if we do get some leave, the first place I'm heading for is the fish an' chip shop, then the pub.' A loud murmur of agreement from several soldiers nearby brought a grin to Andy's lips. Then, nodding towards Tommy's hand, he added quietly, 'You'll wear that out. It must be interesting, you've hardly stopped reading it ever since it arrived. 'Ere, Doris ain't proposed ter yer, has she?'

Tommy started, then put the letter back, and with a shaky laugh he muttered, 'Nah, nothing as serious as that. Just letting us know what's going on back home.' A sense of guilt assailed him immediately. In all their lives they had never kept secrets from each other, until now. But this business with Emily was too personal to share, even with his brother. In truth, he felt ashamed of his actions that night. He hadn't forced Emily. Oh, no, he mentally shook his head in denial, but even so he should have stopped, should have been the strong one. And there was another reason he hadn't told his brother. Although Andy had never said anything, Tommy had a sneaking suspicion that his brother had a soft spot for Emily, and if that were true, Andy wouldn't be passing him a cigar when he found out. No, like Andy had just said, let's get today out of the way first. There would be plenty of time to talk afterwards; when they were on their way home for a spot of much-deserved leave.

'You sure, Tom? You've been acting strange ever since that letter arrived, and . . .'

'Officer coming, put yer mucky pictures away, officer coming.' The whisper floated down to Tommy and Andy, and both men pulled themselves up slightly in order to make room for the approaching officer to pass. Instead the tall, distinguished man stopped at their side saying, 'Is everything all right, private?'

'Oh . . . oh, hello, sir. Yeah, I mean yes, sir.'

Tommy's head snapped round and up at the tall figure

wearing a heavy trench-coat and flat peaked cap, but he didn't attempt to stand to attention. All such procedures were rendered useless in the trenches; unless you wanted to have your head blown off by a German sniper. The officer standing over them wasn't in their regiment, the 1/13th Battalion, but attached to the 2/4th Battalion, which was camped in the trench about a mile down the line. But a lot of the officers took to visiting the dug-outs, stopping here and there to have a word with the men, by way of trying to keep morale high. And as officers went, this bloke wasn't bad. You could talk to this one, ask him questions, and even have a bit of a laugh. Still, you had to be careful not to overstep the mark, because when it came right down to it, he was still an officer.

Bearing this in mind, Tommy touched the tip of his helmet by way of a salute and said, 'I was just saying ter me brother, we're overdue for our Blighty leave, sir.'

Captain Matthew Winter gave a sardonic smile.

'I'm afraid there's nothing I can do about that, private. As regards Blighty leave, it appears that we are all in the same boat – or trench, in our case.'

Encouraged by the officer's friendly tone, Tommy cleared his throat and asked hesitantly, 'Sir, about Lenny . . . Erm, I mean, Private Ford. He won't have ter fight, will he? I mean, if things get really bad, he won't have ter . . .'

Matthew's eyes clouded over at the mention of Lenny's name. He had arrived back in France after his brief leave and been plunged head-first into the third battle at Ypres. Since then he had lost over half his original battalion, and three officers, two of whom had been good friends – and good men. It had been in a rare moment of rest that he had noticed Lenny, and for a brief moment he had imagined himself to be dreaming. But it had been Lenny, all right, there was no mistaking that open, guileless face, which stood out like a beacon among the weary, grim faces of his companions. And the way he had greeted him! Matthew could hear Lenny now, saying, 'Oh, Captain Winter, I ain't half glad ter see yer, an' another two of me mates are here an' all. Ain't that nice . . . I mean, it's nice having all me mates here with me.'

Nice! Good God! Matthew remembered looking out over the bloody battlefield, at the bodies of men and horses, their bellies ripped open by mortar fire, littered over the barren wasteland. He had looked then at his men, with their dirty, mud-caked faces, their eyes dulled by the constant bombardment of the ongoing battle. Then he had raised his gaze to Lenny, and the smile that was splitting the youth's broad face in two, and to his amazement had managed to smile back. Oh, Lenny. Poor, poor Lenny. Yet how he had envied the young man in that moment, for he had seemed utterly oblivious to the carnage surrounding him. He hadn't been involved in the fighting so far, thanks to a keen-eyed and compassionate sergeant, and Matthew had lent his weight to the man's decision, using his rank to ensure that Lenny stayed safely away from the immediate front.

Clasping his hands behind his back, Matthew glanced down at the soldier, another of Lenny's friends, and answered soberly, 'It's all right, private. Lenny will remain where he is. I've seen to it.'

Both Tommy and Andy breathed a sigh of relief, for even though Lenny Ford was only a year younger than themselves, they looked on him as a younger brother, a small boy caught up in a man's world.

'Thank yer, sir, that was good of you.' Tommy, his face earnest now, was looking at Matthew in gratitude. 'His dad copped it a couple of weeks ago, did yer know?'

Matthew's eyebrows rose in surprise.

'No, I didn't know. I'm sorry, private. I know what it's like to lose a friend . . .'

Both Tommy and Andy snorted in disgust.

'He wasn't any friend of ours, sir,' Tommy answered first, then went on to inform Matthew about the late Alfie Ford's character. And, as the man's brutal life was exposed, Matthew's eyebrows rose even higher, until they disappeared beneath the peak of his cap. Emily's father, by all accounts, had been a brute of the first order; she had told him something of her family's history but he hadn't realised it was that bad. But then Emily was a private person, not one to unload her personal problems onto others. Matthew had known of many men who honestly didn't see anything wrong with knocking their wives about, but to take one's own half-witted son into a bloody, merciless war . . . It beggared belief. Yet by all accounts, that's exactly what Emily's father had done. Well, that was one soldier who wouldn't leave a grief-stricken family behind him. He paused, uncertain whether to ask these two men any further questions. They knew, via Lenny, that he, Matthew, was the nephew of Emily's employer, as well as being a friend of the family, so to speak. But they hadn't attempted to get over-familiar with him, as some men would have done.

Matthew's gloved hands were clasped behind his back, the stiff fingers interlocked tightly. What the hell was he doing here? He had every right to be here, of course – all the officers visited as many dug-outs as possible prior to a battle. But this was the second time this week that he had ended up in here. Yet still he hesitated, the questions he dared not utter locked behind closed lips. He gave himself a mental shake. No, no, he would leave things as they were. He straightened up abruptly. Was he going mad? Of course he mustn't probe any further. Yet the dark-haired soldier . . .

Matthew was sure he was the same man he had seen with Emily at Victoria Station last year. The man who had held Emily in a tight embrace, the sight of which had acted as a physical blow to Matthew's tentative hopes. Was this man the father of Emily's child? Did either of these men even know of Emily's condition? Lenny didn't. If he had done, he would have said something. People of Lenny's simplicity couldn't keep secrets to themselves. Like children, they had to share their knowledge with others.

Oh, Lord, he must get on. Besides, there would be nothing gained by knowing if this good-looking, young – yes, damn it, young – man was responsible for Emily's condition. Oh, that was quaint terminology. Now, if he had been brought up like these men, he would have thought of it as being 'up the duff' or 'in the family way', or several even coarser descriptions. But no matter how it was referred to, it all boiled down to the same thing in the end – and he didn't for the life of him know why he was torturing himself about something that he was powerless to change.

'Is it still on fer six o'clock, sir?'

The fair brother was addressing him now, and Matthew, giving himself a shake, replied almost curtly, 'Yes, private, it's still on for six o'clock.' He sensed the sudden tension among the men, looked around him and added in a softer tone, 'Good luck to you all.'

And, hearing the genuine empathy in the captain's voice, Tommy and Andy replied warmly, 'An' you, sir.'

One wag, sitting only yards away, piped up, 'Any chance of a mornin' cuppa, sir? An' a good fry-up would go down a treat.'

And Matthew, his face split into a grin, answered back heartily, 'I'll see what I can do.'

'Thanks, sir.'

'And, good luck, men.'

'Yeah, good luck ter yer too, sir.'

The rough cockney voices started to come at him from all sides, bringing a surge of emotion to Matthew's heart. How many of these men would be alive this time tomorrow? But he couldn't allow himself to think like that. He had learnt early on in the war not to dwell on the eventuality of dying. Such thoughts were best put away in a corner of one's mind. That was the only way to keep one's sanity.

The dawn of 26th October was breaking. The men, some still cracking jokes, were leaning against the parapets, their guns by their sides. Officers walked up and down the duck-boards, having a quiet word with their men before giving the order to go over.

One soldier, the fear evident in his eyes, asked his companion nervously, 'What time is it, Charlie?' And the answer came back at him quickly, 'Why, you got somewhere important ter go, Nobby?'

Up and down the line men bantered with each other, endeavouring to keep their spirits up. Sergeant Grady of the 1/13th Battalion stopped in front of the Carter brothers and looked first at his watch, then up at his lieutenant and said, 'Five more minutes.'

And the lieutenant replied, 'Yes, that's what I have, sergeant.'

In the dug-out, Tommy and Andy gripped hands.

'Good luck, Bruv.'

'Yeah, you too, Tommy.'

Then they stood ready, their hearts beating wildly, trying not to think, not to feel. Despite the coldness of the morning, both men's hands were sweating. They were prepared for the order, yet when it came they both jumped.

'*Over. Over. Over.*' The order rang down the trench, being picked up and carried on down the line.

Then Tommy was up the ladder and over the top, with Andy by his side, as they raced across the open space, their booted feet slipping every now and then in the mud, although they managed to keep upright. They were both yelling, screaming wildly as they fired their guns, not knowing if the bullets were finding a target or simply being discharged into emptiness. On all sides screams filled the air, and it was impossible to tell if they were screams of bravado or pain. Shells exploded, ripping great holes into the mud-caked ground, throwing up lumps of clay and stones into the air.

Then Tommy was down, his feet tripping over a body in his path, and a loud cockney voice yelled, 'Get orf, yer clumsy bastard.'

Stumbling awkwardly to his feet, Tommy grinned and held out his hand.

'Sorry, mate. Here, upsadaisy.' Then the grin slid from his face as a stray bullet slammed into the man's face, instantly pulverising it to a bloody, unrecognisable mess.

'Oh . . . Oh, God . . . Oh, God . . .'

'Tommy, get going . . . Don't look, just keep going.' Andy was by his side, pulling him along. '*Move, Tommy, move.*' And Tommy moved.

They ran on, slipping and sliding, then they were fighting their way through barbed wire, before landing in the thick of the fighting. Figures were coming at them; the enemy. Tommy sprang forward, his mud-streaked face a mask of grim determination.

Lunge! Stick it in. Turn. Pull out.

Don't look down, don't look at the blood. Keep on fighting, keep on killing. It's them or us.

A German blocked his path, his gun aimed at Tommy's

253

heart, and then the gun dropped, its owner falling heavily beside it. Tommy glanced round at the soldier who had saved his life, but the man was already running on. Tommy didn't recognise him. Obviously the companies had overlapped again.

A hail of German fire sent Tommy sprawling for cover, and as he crawled along the shell-pitted ground he spotted a figure propped up by the side of a trench.

Recognising the uniform of one of his officers, Tommy carefully turned the man over just as a Very light exploded overhead, and saw that it was Captain Winter. The upper part of his body was covered in blood. At first glance Tommy thought the man was dead, and he was about to go on when he felt a hand pull weakly at his sleeve.

Helping the captain to sit up, Tommy looked wildly around for Andy, but his brother was nowhere to be seen. There were bodies littered as far as the eye could see, and in the near distance khaki figures were advancing towards the enemy line.

'It's all right, sir. Don't yer worry, I'll soon have yer out of here.'

Putting his bayonet down, Tommy placed his hands under the captain's armpits and dragged him into the relative safety of the dug-out, just as a shell exploded, showering both men in stones and fragments of mud and dust. Again Tommy muttered, 'It's all right, sir. Don't worry, I'll get yer back, you just lie . . . ' Another blast tore into the side of the trench and instinctively Tommy threw himself over the wounded figure. When the dust settled he grinned sheepishly. 'Sorry, sir. Hope yer don't think I was making a pass at yer!'

Despite the pain, Matthew felt his lips twitch into a semblance of a smile. This man reminded him of someone, someone he had once met . . . Oh, yes, yes, that young woman, Emily's friend. What was her name? Ah, yes, Doris. That was it, Doris. They would make a good pair, would Doris and Private Carter. And wouldn't that be convenient for him? God in heaven! What was the matter with him? How could his mind work along such lines at a time like this? They would probably both be blasted to Kingdom Come before the day was out. But, no. No! He couldn't let this man put his own life in jeopardy.

Struggling to speak, Matthew croaked out painfully, 'You must leave, private. Go on, that's an order, you . . .' His head flopped back, the effort of talking proving too much for him. Beads of sweat stood out on his forehead as the pain ravaged his body, and in his mind's eye he saw Emily, dear, sweet, kind Emily. Oh, she was kind, her letters were filled with kindness, a polite kindness. But he didn't want kindness, not from Emily. He wanted her love, and now he might never have the chance . . . the chance . . . Blackness descended, as black as the darkest night, and Matthew was lifted temporarily from the pain and fear of reality.

'Sorry, sir, I didn't hear yer. Besides, Lenny an' Em would skin me alive, if I was ter leave yer here on yer own. They think of lot of yer, them two. Sir, sir, wake up, sir, we . . . Oh, shit!' The exclamation was torn from Tommy's lips as yet another shell landed nearby.

'We're gonna have ter move, sir.' He had to shout now – the bombardment was getting heavier and frighteningly close. 'Look . . . look, put yer arms round me neck . . . Oh, oh, it's all right, sir, don't worry.' Tommy dropped his hands and the wounded man gasped in pain before lapsing once more into unconsciousness.

Matthew looked ashen in the glare of the artillery fire and Tommy bit down hard on his bottom lip. Bleeding hell! What was he going to do? He couldn't just leave the man here.

A shower of stones rattled down the side of the trench accompanied by the sound of heavy boots approaching. Swiftly Tommy turned, his bayonet held out in front of him, his body slumping in relief as his brother slithered into the trench.

'What the bleeding hell you playing at, yer silly bugger? I thought yer'd copped it . . . Oh, Gawd, is he dead?' Andy nodded his head towards the unconscious figure behind Tommy.

Leaning his rifle against the side of the trench, Tommy muttered grimly, 'Not yet, but he soon will be, if we don't get him back ter the first-aid post . . . 'Ere, that was a stroke of luck you finding me. I ain't half glad ter see yer, Bruv.'

'It wasn't luck, I had me eye on yer all the time. 'Ere, look, we ain't on our own.' Andy threw his arm out, gesturing to the far end of the trench, where a small group of soldiers had taken temporary shelter from the relentless bombardment. 'Where the bleeding hell did they come from?' The words were hardly out of his mouth when a giant mortar shell landed among the huddle of men, ripping limbs from uniformed bodies and throwing what was left up and over the side of the trench. Both Andy and Tommy had witnessed such scenes before, but it didn't detract from the horror, didn't stop the sick feeling from gripping their throats, or still the silent rage coursing through their bodies.

'We can't stay here. Cop hold of his legs, Tom, I'll take the top half.'

'But he's been hit in the chest, we . . .'

'Fer Christ's sake, Tom,' Andy bellowed. 'We ain't got any choice. The next shell could land right on top of us, just like that lot of poor bastards. An' I ain't hanging round here ter find out.'

As rough hands gripped his arms and legs, Matthew

tried weakly to protest. Not at the rough handling, but at the suicidal attempt to get him back to the safety of their lines. It was a hopeless task. It was one thing for a man to run and dodge bullets and shells across a mile of desolate, muddy wasteland, which could suck a man down like quicksand, but it was quite another to attempt it while carrying a dead weight. For once such a journey began they would be exposed, with no chance to run for cover. It was madness even to attempt such a thing. But they were going to! Oh, Lord, the bravery of these men. He couldn't let them do this; he had to try to stop them. He didn't want to be left here to die, alone and helpless, but he was an officer, and he had a duty to the men in the ranks.

'Leave me. Go . . . go on, leave me here. Th . . . that's an order.' He could barely hear his own voice above the noise of the guns.

'Ready, Bruv?' Tommy looked at Andy.

'Whenever you are, mate.'

Scrabbling out of the trench, Tommy took hold of the captain under his arms, while Andy gripped the leather boots tightly round the ankles. Shutting their minds to the perilous journey ahead, they started off.

Lenny, his face set against the awful stench, emptied the contents of one of the latrines into a gaping shell-hole, then grabbed a shovel and quickly covered the foul, evil-smelling mess with mud and gravel. This part of his duty done, he bent and picked up a sprayer from the ground and sprinkled the shell-hole and surrounding area in creosol and chloride of lime.

He was on his way to another latrine when a small band of injured soldiers staggered past on their way to the nearest first-aid post, leaning on each other for support. Despite the wound in his leg, which was bleeding profusely, one soldier grinned at Lenny and quipped, 'Yer must be working double shift terday, mate. We was all shitting a brick before we went over the top.'

Lenny reddened, then gave an embarrassed shrug and was about to move on, when another voice stopped him in his tracks.

'Yeah, all right fer some, ain't it? We could all pull that stroke, mate, pretending ter be a bit on the daft side ter get out of fighting, but some of us 'ave a bit more guts.' The private, his face ravaged with pain, his bloodied left arm hanging uselessly by his side, ignored the protests of his companions and thrust his face aggressively into that of the startled Lenny.

'Look at yer, yer spineless lump. I don't care if yer are a few sandwiches sort of a picnic. It don't take brains ter pick up a gun an' fire, or ter get stuck inter a fight. I've seen yer, walking round acting gormless. Well, it's paid orf, ain't it, an' yer right where yer belong, yer useless article, in among the shit. Yer muvver must be proud of yer!'

'Come on, Bill,' another man urged wearily, 'leave the lad alone, it's not 'is fault.' Turning to Lenny, he said tiredly, 'Take no notice, son. 'E don't mean it. Yer do a good job, an' we're all grateful, 'cos wivout blokes like you, we'd really be up ter our necks in it.' The man smiled kindly into Lenny's stricken face before moving on.

Lenny remained rooted to the spot, trembling in every part of his body. It wasn't the first time he'd had to put up with derisive remarks – because his job was normally carried out by elderly men, not strong, fit men like himself – but today was the first time he had experienced such hatred, such stomach-curdling contempt, and something inside him snapped.

Throwing the shovel and sprayer to the ground, he took to his heels, not knowing what he could do, just knowing that he had to do something – anything that would take away the gnawing self-loathing he had endured for the past three years. Up ahead was a first-aid post, and piled high to the left of the hastily constructed building lay a stack of stretchers.

They were all still waiting for the arrival of stretcher-bearers from the Royal Army Medical Corps, who were at present unable to get through the heavy artillery fire. Lenny eyed the stack of stretchers, the germ of an idea beginning to form in his fevered mind.

He was sick of being called a coward, of being jeered at, talked about, and once even spat on, but it was that crack about his mother that had finally proved too much to bear. She wouldn't know yet about his father, but he silently prayed that she would never find out about her husband's last moments. Lenny had witnessed the sickening scene, had heard the big, bluff man who was his father beg and sob, pleading to be allowed to remain in the trench.

Lenny felt no great sorrow at his father's death, for in the months they had been together, Alfie had not only allowed his son to be publicly humiliated, but had joined in the cruel taunts. No, he wasn't sorry his father was dead. At least now his mother was safe for good. She would never again know the feel of Alfie Ford's fists, nor the fear his presence had inspired.

His mother! Tears sprang to Lenny's eyes and he angrily dashed them away with the back of his hand. She was so grateful he wasn't involved in the actual fighting, and the letters that came regularly were filled with love and earnest entreaties, begging Lenny not to mind too much, and not to do anything foolish.

He looked up at the sky in despair. It was still dark, except for those moments when the blackness was illuminated by artillery fire. The bombardment seemed to be getting heavier, noisier – and Tommy and Andy were out there in the thick of it all. And Captain Winter, he mustn't forget Captain Winter.

He felt so useless, so . . . !

'Bugger it, I've got ter do something, I've got to.' The exclamation held all the frustration, fear and shame that Lenny had harboured against himself since the war had begun. Without stopping to think, he yanked a stretcher from the top of the pile and, gripping the wooden handles, began to run, dragging the stretcher behind him.

Tommy and Andy were lost. There were no landmarks to guide them, no helpful signs to let them know they were on the right path back to their own lines. Zigzagging as best they could to avoid the shell-holes, the brothers staggered on, the figure they held becoming heavier by the minute. They had no breath to talk, and even if they had, their voices would have been drowned among the unrelenting noise of the barrage. Every so often they had to stop and rest, to change ends, to exchange a reassuring smile, before picking up their cumbersome burden once more. As the mud and clay flew in the air around them, they realised that they were in as much danger from their own artillery as from that of the Germans.

Both men were almost on their knees, their eyes half-blinded by flying mud, when Tommy glanced up wearily and saw, almost in disbelief, the dressing station, the white-painted sign just visible in the early-morning light.

'An . . . Andy, l . . . look . . .' Tommy's voice came out as a strangled sob of relief.

Behind him Andy, suddenly infused with a second wind, gripped the captain's legs more firmly.

'Yeah, I . . . I see it, Bruv . . . I see it.'

Tommy, his arms feeling as if they were being slowly

wrenched out of their sockets, squinted at the two relay-bearers who were running towards them from the dressing station, a stretcher held between them.

'Bleeding hell, is it worth it?' Tommy muttered, as valuable time was wasted transferring the captain onto the canvas stretcher.

'Bet you two could do with a nice cuppa,' one of the relay-bearers shouted as they trotted off with their burden.

Hoisting his rifle more firmly over his shoulder, Tommy followed, his head turning towards his brother.

'Did yer hear that, Bruv, they're gonna give us a cuppa. Makes it all worth while, don't it?'

Andy smiled tiredly, his lips trembling with exhaustion. He wasn't a religious man, but now he raised his eyes upwards and was about to say a silent prayer of thanks, when a bullet from a German sniper took the back of his head off.

Tommy was still talking.

'I think we deserve the VC fer this, but I ain't greedy. A cup a tea'll do nicely . . .' He glanced back over his shoulder, then his stomach seemed to come up at a rush, filling his chest, his throat, cutting off the scream that was swelling his entire body. His mouth opened and closed futilely, whatever strength he had left draining from his arms and legs. He remained standing, too frozen with horror to move. Then he was screaming and falling, as he scrabbled his way on hands and knees to where his brother lay still.

'Andy . . . Andy . . . Noooooo.'

Sobbing, he tried frantically to raise the inert form, and when he put his arm under Andy's neck to lift him and saw what was left of his brother's head, he began to scream wildly.

Hands were trying to pull him away, but he fought

them, gabbling, 'No, no, yer don't understand . . . He's me brother. I can't leave him here, he's me brother . . . me brother. Andy . . . Andy, come on, Bruv. Yer can't be dead, I won't let yer be dead . . . Oh, Andy, Andy. Don't leave me, Bruv . . . Don't leave me. Pl . . . please don't leave me . . .'

Two miles further down the line, Lenny, his face red with exertion, staggered to the first-aid post, then flopped down on the hard ground beside the stretcher he had dragged across one and a half miles of desolate, shell-pitted country.

The wounded man he had saved reached over the side of the stretcher, wrung Lenny's hand and burst into tears.

'Gawd bless yer, mate. Yer saved me life. I'll never ferget yer fer this.' Then he was whipped away inside the first-aid post, still declaring his gratitude.

Lenny lay half-sprawled on the ground, a warm feeling spreading through his body. He was exhausted, cut and bleeding from the hazardous journey, and yet he felt . . . He couldn't put it into words for the moment, he just knew that he felt good. A huge grin spread over his dirt-streaked face, and without stopping for a further rest, he grabbed a stretcher that was lying on the ground outside the first-aid post and headed back the way he had come.

He had travelled almost half a mile before the word he had been searching for came to him.

The feeling he had inside him was pride. When that man had shaken his hand and said what he had . . . Well, Lenny had thought he was going to burst. For the first time in his life, he felt proud of himself.

When a mortar shell landed directly in his path, Lenny Ford died instantly. But in the moments preceding his death, he was a happy man.

*   *   *

Tommy found himself on the quayside, wandering in a daze in and out of the hundreds of wounded men lying on stretchers, on the ground, leaning up against Red Cross lorries, all bandaged heavily – all on their way home to Blighty.

Bewildered, Tommy tottered unsteadily along the edge of the quay and would have fallen into the sea, if a passing nurse hadn't grabbed his arm. Gently leading him away from the danger, the middle-aged nurse settled him against a nearby ramp before hurrying on.

How had he got here? He couldn't remember getting on the train, but he must have done. There was no other way to get to the quay except by train. And why was he here? He wasn't wounded – was he? Carefully inspecting his body, Tommy shook his head in bewilderment. What was going on? And where was Andy?

Then he was being herded up the gangplank onto a Red Cross boat. He wanted to protest, to tell someone he was all right. Then a sergeant came up to where he was lying and asked for his papers and Tommy knew, without knowing quite how he had managed it, that he was going AWOL, and a voice in his head told him to keep quiet, to play dumb, and it had worked. He was going home. Going away from the slaughter, the carnage, the stink and the misery.

He was going home – going home without Andy. Going absent without leave.

Going home to his mother!

On 6th November of that same year, Passchendaele was taken at a loss of 245,000 British lives. Some argued that it was too heavy a price to pay for a ridge and a burnt-out village, but by that time the generals were already planning their next battle.

CHAPTER TWENTY

'You're going to spoil that child, between the two of you. He only has to murmur and you nearly break your necks to see who can get to him first.' Nellie, her face bearing a look of exasperation, was seated by a roaring fire, her fingers busily clicking her knitting needles, from which a pale blue garment was beginning to take shape. Peering over her reading glasses, she looked at the two women kneeling either side of a fluffy new rug and anxiously watching the wailing infant while Emily changed his cotton nappy.

'It's still dry, so he can't be crying for that reason, and I've only just fed him, so he can't be hungry.' Emily looked at her mother for advice, her blue eyes clouded with worry.

With an impatient sigh, Nellie laid down her knitting and, pushing the two women to one side, picked up the red-faced baby and expertly laid him over her shoulder. Walking slowly back to her chair, she looked sideways and, when the tiny face broke into a lop-sided grin, she felt her heart melt with love. It had been hard at times, listening to the whispers and seeing the knowing looks follow her and Emily whenever they ventured out into the street. If it hadn't been for Dot Button, who had made it clear that anyone upsetting Emily would have her to answer to, the situation might have been a lot worse. But since the child's birth, almost five months ago, Nellie couldn't imagine life without him now. Cuddling the baby in her arms, she gently rocked him back and forth and soon the small eyelids began to droop.

'There you are,' she said in grandmotherly triumph. 'Nothing the matter with him. He's probably just fed up with you two always hovering over him.' Settling herself more comfortably she added, 'Why don't you both go out for a few hours, it would do you good. Go down to the pub for a couple of drinks. He'll be perfectly safe here with me.'

'No, it's all right, Mum,' Emily said quickly. 'I don't fancy going out, it's too cold.'

Casting a disparaging look at her daughter, Nellie turned her gaze to her sleeping grandchild.

'Maybe your mum's right, Em.' Doris had now moved and was sitting at the table. 'You've hardly set foot outta the house since His Nibs was born. We wouldn't have ter stay long, an' like yer mum said, it'd do us both good ter get out of the house fer a while.'

Emily sat down opposite her friend, her hand still clutching the dry nappy. She looked at Doris and marvelled again at how much she had changed during the past year. With the pigmentation gone from the front of her hair and from her face, Doris looked a different person. You could still see the scars round her grey eyes, but they had faded considerably since the accident. Her brown hair was now long and shiny and her complexion clear, and Emily found herself wishing that Tommy was here to witness the transformation in his old friend.

'What are yer staring at?' Doris demanded, her face

265

beginning to flush under Emily's close scrutiny. 'Have I got a bit of dirt on me face or somefink?'

Emily laughed.

'No, silly. I was just thinking how nice you looked, if you must know.'

Doris squirmed uncomfortably.

'Yeah, in a dim light.' She gave a self-conscious laugh. 'Well, yer coming out or not?'

Emily dropped her gaze, her fingers pulling at the soft material in her hand.

'I don't know, Doris. We can't really afford it, can we? And before you start,' she said quickly, as Doris made to speak, 'I'm not breaking into that money Captain Winter sent me. I know I was grateful for it, when it started coming after Joseph was born, but now you're working in the bakery, and Mum's working full time in the fish and chip shop, I don't feel right about spending it.' Now it was her turn to blush, as Doris gave her a penetrating stare. Folding the nappy into a neat square, she murmured, 'Don't look at me like that, Doris. You know I've tried to stop the money being sent, but that solicitor insists he can't stop the payments until he has written authority from Captain Winter. And I've written to Matt . . . I mean, Captain Winter, about it, but he insists it's only what I'm entitled to . . . Ooh, never mind, I don't want to talk about it any more, except to say that with yours and mum's money coming in, we're comfortable and . . .'

'I thought yer just said we couldn't afford ter go out. Make yer mind up, Em.' Doris grinned across the table.

'Oh, you,' Emily laughed and threw the folded nappy at her friend.

'Bleeding hell, Em,' Doris protested laughingly. 'Don't get inter the habit of doing that, the next one might have . . . 'Ere, who's that outside the window?' Getting up from her chair, Doris marched over to the front window and peered out. 'I could have sworn I saw someone lurking about out there,' she said, frowning as she let the curtain fall back into place. Then she brightened. 'Well, Dilly Day-dream, are yer coming out fer a drink or not?'

Emily hesitated, her eyes darting to where the baby lay contentedly on her mother's lap, then she shrugged.

'Oh, all right, but just the one. I'll have to get back in time for Joseph's next feed.'

'Do the lad a favour, Em,' Doris said patiently. 'Start calling him Joe, will yer. It'd be all right if yer lived somewhere posh, but yer know what it's like round here. The poor little begger'll be tormented rotten if yer keep calling him Joseph. He'll be for ever coming home with a black eye.'

Emily felt her body tense and quickly turned away. If she lived somewhere posh! Wasn't that what she was hoping for? Deep down didn't she nurture the hope that when Matthew returned, he would come for her. She hadn't given him any encouragement in the letters she wrote to him, just in case he was regretting what he'd said that day in the park. It was strange how her feelings towards him had changed, because while she had never looked upon him as anything other than her employer's nephew when she was with him, now that he was away, she realised just how much she missed his company. He filled her thoughts every waking day, and every night she prayed for his safe return, along with Lenny, Tommy and Andy. Mounting the stairs, she called over her shoulder, 'I'll get our coats.'

'I think I've put me foot in it.' Doris looked over at Nellie. 'But I wasn't being nasty, Mrs Ford, honest.'

Nellie glanced up, her face quizzical.

'Being nasty about what, dear?' she asked, her attention

fixed solely on the sleeping babe. Then, without waiting for an answer she said quickly, 'Oh, before I forget, could you knock on Dot's door when you go out and ask her if she'd like to come in for a while. The poor woman's been going round like a lost soul since she received those letters about Bert and Jack. She must be going through agony. It was bad enough losing her husband, but to lose her son as well . . .' Nellie's eyes misted over and Doris, who was watching her, knew that the older woman was thinking of Lenny.

Afraid that Nellie was about to get maudlin, Doris rose swiftly and was about to follow Emily upstairs when her eye again caught a movement outside the window. With an exclamation of annoyance she strode over to the door, saying, 'There is someone out there. Some silly sod mucking about, I bet.' But when she opened the door there was no-one to be seen. And when, with Emily, she left the house some time later, Doris kept looking up and down the street, feeling nervous but not knowing why.

Tommy crouched behind an old battered armchair that had been left out in the street. Come the morning, its owner would haggle with the rag-and-bone man for a few shillings, but for now it would serve as a hiding place until Tommy was sure that the coast was clear.

He had been looking through the window of number fifteen and had seen his son being picked up by Nellie Ford. He had had to force himself to stay silent, when what he wanted to do was rush into the house and take his son in his arms. But he couldn't. He couldn't put Emily or Doris, or Mrs Ford, into a position where they might get into trouble. There were stiff penalties for hiding a deserter, and much as Tommy yearned to enter the warm, cosy house, he couldn't put the women at risk.

When the two friends walked by on the opposite side of the road, Tommy had to put his hand over his mouth to stop himself from calling out to them. They stopped at Mrs Cotton's house first, and Tommy could hear their voices as they asked the elderly woman if she would like to visit Nellie for a while. When they passed under a lamppost he saw their faces clearly, and despite his best efforts a low groan escaped from between his dry, parched lips. They looked so lovely, so fresh and clean, and Doris . . . Well, he couldn't believe the change in her. She was still no match for Emily's loveliness, but she had an appeal all her own, and strangely it was Doris upon whom Tommy fixed his attention, rather than the mother of his child. He watched until they disappeared from view, and then, every bone in his body aching, he inched his way along the street until he came to his own house. Then he hesitated. What was he going to tell his mother? Dear God! How could he tell her Andy was dead? She'd go mad, completely mad. She had idolised his brother, and none knew that better than he. He lifted his hand to knock, then froze, his arm slowly dropping back down to his side. What if she turned on him! What if she started screaming? But he couldn't stay out here on the street. Somebody was bound to come along sooner or later, and then what? He couldn't pretend to be home on leave, not the state he was in. There was no lamppost in front of his house, but the one further down the street reflected enough light to show his unkempt, dishevelled appearance. The sound of a door banging nearby brought his hand up to the brass knocker and, taking a deep breath, he knocked twice.

'All right, all right, I'm coming.' His mother's disgruntled voice came to him clearly, bringing with it a sick feeling of apprehension. When the door was opened cautiously, Tommy quickly stepped into the small, gloomy hall saying lightly, 'Hello, Mum.'

Ida Carter's jaw dropped in stunned surprise. Then, a glimmer of hope appearing in her eyes, she looked towards the street and was about to step outside, when Tommy's voice stopped her.

'Andy ain't with me, Mum.' Tommy's tone was flat and weary, and as he stumbled painfully into the front parlour, Ida was close on his heels.

Dropping into an armchair by the fire, Tommy leant his head back gratefully against the soft upholstery.

'Where the bleeding hell have you come from?' Ida, her face muscles pulling and stretching in disbelief, came to stand by the armchair. Then, her eyes narrowing suspiciously, she moved to the wall and turned up the gas lamp. A startled gasp caught in her throat as she looked at her son properly. His army overcoat and trousers were filthy and his face hadn't seen a razor or a bar of soap for a considerable time. His dark hair was matted and lank, and where he had undone the buttons of his coat, she could see the bloodied uniform beneath.

Clutching the collar of her blouse, she dropped into the armchair opposite Tommy and said fearfully, 'Yer've deserted, ain't yer? That's why my Andrew ain't with yer. Yer've gone on the bleeding run an' left yer brother behind, ain't yer?'

Tommy winced at the scornful tone in his mother's voice. Somewhere at the back of his mind, he realised that his mother had dropped the posh vowels she normally used with her neighbours, but the fleeting thought vanished almost before it had begun to take shape. In a voice that was filled with tears he said, 'Please, Mum, it ain't like that. Look, can yer make me a cuppa? I ain't had nothing to eat or drink fer days. Please,

Mum, just let me get me breath, an' I'll tell yer the whole story.'

Ida was about to refuse, then reluctantly she got to her feet and stamped off noisily into the scullery.

Left alone, Tommy stared sightlessly into the flames, his mind wondering how he was going to tell his mother that Andy was dead. Oh, God! He pleaded silently. Help me, please.

Unable to dwell on the painful task ahead of him, he let his mind drift back over the past few days. On the journey across the Channel he had kept up the pretence of being unable to understand what was going on around him. When a doctor finally came to examine him, Tommy had remained mute, refusing to acknowledge his presence. It was only when the doctor had said loudly, 'There's nothing the matter with this man, he can be shipped back once we land,' that Tommy had jumped in fear. The doctor had looked down at him with a mixture of annoyance and compassion, saying, 'I'm sorry, son, I can't pass you as being unfit for duty. You'll have to go back.'

Knowing he was going on the run, Tommy had waited until nightfall before making his way to the galley. Once there, he had stuffed his pockets with dry biscuits to take with him on his journey, before making his way back to the deck.

On landing at Southampton it had been easy enough to make a run for it amid the confusion of unloading the wounded. He had been given an old overcoat by one of the nurses on board the ship, and once out on the road he had been doubly grateful for the heavy garment, because it not only kept him warm, it also hid his blood-stained uniform. But he was still afraid that once the roll-call was taken and he was found to be missing, the police would come after him. With this in mind, he had kept away from the main roads as much as possible, trying to grab a few hours' sleep during the day and walking by night. But, knowing there were seventy miles between Southampton and London, and without any idea which direction he should be heading in, he wasn't sure if he was on the right track or going in the opposite direction. Finally, exhausted and driven to desperation, he had stopped a truck bound for Guildford. The driver had let Tommy sleep for a few hours, then, when his passenger had become evasive to his friendly questions, the middle-aged man had become suspicious, forcing Tommy to jump from the truck at the earliest opportunity.

Afraid of being asked more questions, he had trudged wearily for three days and nights, barely stopping to rest, until another lorry pulled up beside him. He had gratefully clambered aboard, his need for rest outweighing the fear of discovery. Whether the driver hadn't noticed his passenger's condition or was simply turning a blind eye for reasons of his own, he had gruffly told Tommy to get some sleep. And although Tommy tried valiantly to stay awake, in case the man was going to drive him straight to the nearest police station, he was too exhausted to keep his eyes open. The next thing he knew he was being roughly shaken awake. Jumping up in fear, he had found himself in Liverpool Street with the lorry driver leaning over him, but all the man said was, 'Mind 'ow yer go, son.'

Tommy had leapt from the cab, throwing a hasty 'Thanks, mate' over his shoulder. Once on familiar territory, he had cut down side turnings, with the collar of his overcoat turned up around his ears just in case he bumped into someone he knew.

It was during the last part of his journey that the wall that Tommy's mind had thrown up around Andy's death began to crumble. And, as he relived his brother's last moments, he felt the hot tears scalding his cheeks. And when he had gazed into Emily's window and seen his child, he'd had forcibly to choke back another spasm of tears, for he feared that if he were to let them fall, he might never be able to stop.

The warmth of the fire was making him drowsy, and with a reluctant struggle he sat up straighter, waiting for his mother's return. Glancing down, he looked at his feet encased inside the heavy army boots. Months spent in the water and mud-filled trenches had rotted the leather, destroying any protection they might once have offered. Gingerly Tommy bent down and took the boots off, revealing threadbare socks and blistered, torn feet. Wincing with pain, he tried to take the socks off, but they were stuck fast into the open sores. His hands too were chaffed red-raw from the weather and from scrabbling in and out of ditches. The biscuits he had taken from the ship's galley had long since been consumed, and now he was weak with hunger and thirst. Every part of his body ached, but most of all he ached with the stark, raw grief of knowing that he would never see his brother again. Never again laugh with him, or argue, or just simply enjoy the warm, comfortable feeling of knowing that he was close by.

'Oh, Andy, I don't half miss yer, Bruv. What am I going do without yer . . . I feel like . . . like half of me is missing, like I've been chopped in two, an' . . . an' I'll never be put back together again.' The whispered words floated in the silent room.

Tommy looked up as his mother reappeared, her face tight and grim as she banged down a mug of tea on the arm of the chair. Without a word he picked up the steaming mug, then winced as the scalding tea burnt his cracked lips. He didn't look up, but he knew

273

that his mother was watching him, condemning him, accusing him for leaving his brother; and this without even knowing that Andy was dead. He glanced down, then quickly averted his eyes from his blood-stained tunic. He had carried a part of his brother home with him. Andy's blood – and the captain's. Maybe he was dead as well now. If so, then Andy would have died for nothing.

Tommy closed his eyes, praying silently as he tried to gather his courage for the ordeal ahead.

'Oh, Mum, I need yer. I need yer now like I've never needed yer before. Not even like when I was little, an' trying ter do anything I could ter please yer, ter make yer notice me, ter give me a cuddle, like yer did with Andy. Please! You're me mum, can't yer see I'm hurting, dying inside. I need yer, Mum, don't turn yer back on me. Please, Mum . . . Please!'

'Well, I'm waiting.' The curt, harsh tone held only impatience, and Tommy knew that he really was alone now. His hand trembling, he laid the mug down by the fireside, then turned towards the woman who was looking at him as if he'd just crawled out from under a stone. And it was that look . . . that almost contemptuous glare, that infused a spark of anger in Tommy's tortured mind.

His eyes dull, he ground out slowly, 'Yeah, I did desert, but I was half out of me head at the time. Still, it's no more than yer'd expect from me, is it?' The glance he shot his mother made the silent woman jump, but almost immediately she recovered and continued to stare at him, her eyes openly hostile.

Tommy swung his head in despair.

'Aw, what's the use? Yer ain't interested in anything I do, yer never have been. Well, I'm sorry ter disappoint yer, but yer won't have the pleasure of seeing me in front of a firing squad, 'cos I'm going back. I'll have a good night's kip, an' a decent meal down the chip shop – don't worry, I won't ask yer ter cook me a dinner. I wouldn't want ter put yer out,' the hurt was forcing him to adopt a tone similar to his mother's. Then, without stopping to think, he added, 'An' I'll stop an' spend some time with me son before I go back, an' all. At least I'll get a warmer welcome over at Emily's . . .' He trailed off as he realised what he had said. He watched as his mother's eyes widened in disbelief, then, just as he was going to put his hand out to her, she gave a short, abrasive laugh.

'Huh, so it's yours, is it? And there was me thinking she'd dropped on her back fer that old geezer she worked fer. I always said she was no better than she oughter be, fer all her airs an' graces. And her mate, too. They're well matched, the pair of them, a couple of slags if ever I saw them. And you went with one of them – or did yer have them both? It wouldn't surprise me. Nothing yer've ever done surprises me. Thank gawd I've got one son ter be proud of. He didn't turn tail and run, did he? Not like you. Oh, no, not my Andrew. He'd never desert and bring me shame, he . . .'

It was too much for Tommy. A wealth of anger combined with grief surged through him, and before he knew what he was saying, he leant forward in the chair and bawled into Ida's face, '*He's dead. Andy's dead. D'yer hear me, Mum. He's dead*. That's why I ran. I couldn't bear it. I was half out of me mind, so I turned and ran, and I've been running ever since . . . Mum . . . Mum . . . !' His voice dropped back to its normal pitch, his eyes now filled with silent pleading for a kind word, a gentle touch of reassurance. Any sign of compassion would have lifted his spirits, but the woman opposite him seemed to have turned to stone.

Ida Carter sat frozen, her face bleached white from the shock of hearing those words. It couldn't be true, not her Andrew. Yet she knew. Deep inside her, she had known something was wrong the minute Tommy turned up without Andrew. For those two had been inseparable since the time they were able to crawl. Oh, God! What was she going to do? Why wasn't she crying? Why wasn't she howling her grief from the rooftops, because that's what she felt like doing? Why couldn't it have been the other one? *Him.* Why couldn't he have been the one to die? It wasn't fair, it wasn't fair. And he had lived long enough to father a son. Even if he went back and was killed, he would still have left something of himself behind. Whereas her Andrew would never have the chance now. A slow, burning rage began to sweep through her body, blocking out everything except the need to lash out, to hurt someone as she was hurting, and by doing so keep at bay the grief that was threatening to tear her apart.

Getting to her feet, she looked down at Tommy's bowed head and, her upper lip curled as if witnessing something foul, she snarled, 'Why couldn't it have been you? If one of yer had ter die, then why couldn't it have been you!'

Tommy blinked back the hot tears stinging his eyes. He should never have come. He must have been mad to think he could get any comfort from his mother.

'I'm going ter bed fer a couple of hours, then I'll be on me way, so yer don't have ter worry about ever seeing my face again. Goodbye, Mum.' He walked painfully towards the stairs, then he stopped. Without turning, he said softly, 'I loved him too, Mum. An' . . . an' just so as yer know, I wish it had been me too, 'cos right now I don't know how I'm gonna go on living without him.'

Ida watched the ragged body climb the stairs. Then,

her face grim, she snatched her coat from the back of the door and went out into the cold, dark night.

''Ere, I wonder what all that's about?' Emily and Doris had just returned from the pub to find everyone in the street and a black Maria parked outside the Carters' house. Pushing through the small crowd, the two women looked across the road, their arms linked against the freezing wind. Pulling her black cloche hat further down over her ears, Doris said brightly, 'Maybe old Ma Carter's been caught entertaining gentlemen on the quiet. I always said there was something funny about her,' but her voice held a note of uneasiness. Then she jumped violently, as did Emily beside her, their expressions turning to horror as the familiar voice, charged with anguish, carried from the open doorway.

'NO . . . NO, I'm gonna go back on me own. Look, . . . listen ter me, will yer? I was gonna go back in the morning. Ask me mum, she'll tell yer, Mum . . . Mum . . . !' Tommy was being dragged from his home by three burly policemen, their faces grim. Twisting and turning, Tommy fought the men, his eyes frantically seeking out his mother, who was standing just a few feet away in the shadows. 'Mum, Mum, fer Gawd's sake, tell 'em. Help me, Mum, help me.'

As Tommy continued to struggle violently, one of the policemen yanked his arm up behind his back and thundered, 'It's no use shouting fer yer mum, son. She's the one who turned yer in – isn't that right, missus?' The policeman stared hard at Ida, his expression one of disgust. Gasps of surprise and outrage came at them from all sides, and Ida tightened the shawl around her chest defiantly. Then Emily and Doris were fighting with the officers, trying to prise Tommy from their grasp, their high-pitched cries piercing the still night air.

'Let him go, yer bastards, let him go.' Doris was pummelling a broad back with her fists, her long brown hair swirling round her face and shoulders as she tried desperately to loosen the policemen's hold on Tommy. Emily too was crying with rage, as she took several swipes with her handbag at the officers. A helmet was knocked off in the struggle, and as the man bent to retrieve it, Emily planted a well-aimed kick at his backside.

'Now look, you'll only get inter trouble if yer carry on,' a red-faced officer called out grimly as he tried to keep a hold on his struggling prisoner and avoid the women's blows at the same time. 'This man's under arrest fer desertion, an' there's nothing any of yer can do about it. So go home, all of yer.' Relinquishing his grip on the prisoner to his fellow officers, the sergeant swore loudly as he gripped Emily's flailing arms and pushed her away into the crowd. Immediately Doris was on his back, but before she could do any harm she found herself being thrown off and landed in the gutter with a resounding thump. Panting for breath, the sergeant bellowed angrily, 'Now I won't warn yer again, you two.' He pointed a warning finger at the two women, who glared back at him without fear. 'Any more of it, an' yer'll find yerselves locked up fer the night. Now clear off, an' let us get on with our job.'

Panting hard, the other two officers dragged and pulled Tommy to the waiting vehicle. Then Tommy suddenly stopped struggling, his anguished gaze fixed on his mother.

'Why, Mum? Fer Gawd's sake, why? I know yer never loved me like Andy, but I'm yer own flesh an' blood. How could yer, Mum . . . How could yer?'

Ida returned the gaze without blinking. Then she felt her heart leap in surprise. For the eyes that stared at her were a mirror-image of her own. A sudden shudder went through her. How had she never noticed that before? But then she had never spent much time looking at this son. She had always avoided contact with him as far as possible.

Would she have felt differently about him if she'd noticed the similarity before? Suddenly her body felt deflated. It didn't matter now – nothing mattered any more.

The sound of the wailing siren filled the air, causing her body to jerk in startled surprise. Angry, muttered words floated around Ida as her neighbours glared at her with animosity, their combined voices becoming louder by the minute. She returned their stares, her eyes picking out individual faces in the crowd, the majority of whom she had never had time for. But there was Dot Button, and Mrs Riley from number eighteen, thinking she was something special just because she had a couple of moulting chickens in her back yard. Her eyes flickered over the faces, then darted back to the slim, attractive woman holding a wrapped-up bundle close to her chest. Ida blinked, then swallowed hard. That was her grandson whom Nellie Ford was holding so possessively. If the father had been Andrew, she would have wrenched the child from the woman's arms. But it wasn't – it was Tommy's, and that being the case . . .

She felt strangely light-headed, and then Doris, her face ravaged with tears, pulled her round and spat in her face, 'Yer vicious bitch. Yer miserable, stinking, vicious bitch. I hope yer rot in hell fer what yer've done tonight.' Then she lifted her arm high in the air and brought the flat of her hand down across Ida's face.

Ida staggered back under the violent blow, then she seemed to compose herself. Turning her head slightly, she cast one last look over the bevy of women glaring at her in silent condemnation and shrugged. Sod 'em. It wasn't any of their business. When a hard lump of mud hit her squarely in the back, she jerked momentarily and then, her head held high, she walked sedately to her house, entered the hallway and shut the door heavily behind her. Back in the warmth of the parlour she stood uncertainly, as if she couldn't remember where she was. Then her eyes dropped to the worn boots lying by the fireside and she smiled.

'How many times must I tell yer to put yer boots away, Andrew? Oh, never mind, I'll do it,' she tutted lovingly. She bent down and put the boots tidily by the side of the armchair and began to sing softly:

> What's the use of worrying,
> It never was worthwhile . . . Sooo,
> Pack up yer troubles in an old kit bag,
> And smile, smile, smile.

Banking the fire up, she moved the two armchairs further away from it and made her way to the scullery. Still humming, she turned the gas pipe on the oven to full blast. Then, kneeling down, she rested her head inside the oven and closed her eyes.

CHAPTER TWENTY-ONE

It was over. The war to end all wars was finally over.

And when the news reached London, tug-whistles sounded, followed by the booming of foghorns from large berthed ships along the Thames. Maroons were fired from the Tower of London, paper-boys ran through the streets with special editions and many factories were shut down for the day. People ran wildly into the streets, cheering and hugging perfect strangers, united in a fever of excitement and happiness. Public houses opened their doors all day, and churches held special Masses for those who chose to celebrate with prayer. All through November and December the soldiers' homecomings were welcomed with Union Jacks hanging from upstairs windows and streams of bunting tied across the streets.

It was now July 1919, eight months since the war had ended, but it hadn't ended for Tommy Carter, who had spent those months, and the preceding year, in Wormwood Scrubs, after being court-martialled for desertion in the face of the enemy. He had been sentenced to death by firing squad, and whether the sentence would actually have been carried out, had it not been for the intervention of Captain Matthew Winter, would never be known.

Tommy had been in prison for six months before the captain, who had been hospitalised in France during that time, discovered Tommy's fate and immediately set about doing all in his power to have Tommy pardoned. This, however, proved to be impossible. It wouldn't do, he was told, to grant a pardon to a soldier who had deserted, whatever the circumstances. To take such an act would be to open the floodgates for thousands of soldiers with like minds.

Nevertheless, the perseverance of the captain led to the matter being raised in the House, and within days the newspapers had got hold of the story and had made a field-day out of it. Captain Winter's moving account of how Thomas and Andrew Carter had risked their lives to save his – their heroic action resulting in the death of Andrew Carter, shot dead by a sniper's bullet just yards from the safety of his own lines – had stirred the nation. The papers went on to state that Thomas Carter, devastated by the death of his twin brother, had temporarily lost his reason, but that once his senses had been restored, the young soldier had had every intention of returning to duty at the earliest opportunity. This claim had been corroborated by neighbours and by the officers who had arrested him.

It had all made very good headlines, but what captured the nation most was the fact that it had been the soldier's own mother who had turned him over to the police, before the unfortunate young man had the chance to return to France of his own volition. The wave of sympathy turned to a public outcry at the decision to execute Thomas Carter, forcing the authorities to reconsider. Another debate was raised in the House, this time resulting in a second trial being ordered.

The trial was still in progress when peace was declared, and with no reason to make an example of Tommy Carter, and bearing in mind public opinion, the charge was commuted from desertion to going AWOL and his sentence reduced to two years, with three months deducted for good behaviour.

During his stay in prison Tommy had, at times, tee-tered on the brink of a nervous breakdown. And on the day that his mother was buried in a pauper's grave, he nearly let himself be swept over the edge. Because, even knowing that she had betrayed him, he had still nurtured the hope that one day she would come to love him as she had loved Andy.

The only thing that had kept Tommy sane was know-ing that every visiting day would bring Emily, Doris and his son to see him. He had had other visitors – Mrs Ford and Mrs Button had visited twice, and Captain Winter on several occasions – but it was his life-long friends whom he most looked forward to seeing; and his son, of course.

But today he was being set free, and Emily and Doris were going to meet him and take him home to the Fords' house until he found a place of his own; at least, that's what Emily had thought was happening. But it now seemed that she was wrong, for Doris, her face slightly flushed, was telling her that she'd found a couple of furnished rooms to let, and she was going to ask Tommy to share them with her.

They were on the bus travelling towards Wormwood Scrubs when Doris dropped her bombshell. Emily, trying to keep a hold on her two-year-old son, who was endeav-ouring to escape her grasp, could only look at her friend in hurt disbelief.

Both women had made a special effort to look nice for Tommy's release. Emily was wearing a pale blue blouse and a straight navy skirt that came to just above her ankles, and black shoes with gold buckles. Doris's blouse was bright red in colour, with a frill that ran down the front and tucked neatly into a black skirt.

'Don't look at me like that, Em,' Doris muttered, turning her head towards the window. 'You know it would never work out . . . I mean, all of us living together under the same roof. Besides, there isn't enough room.'

Keeping her voice light Emily said, 'And does Tommy know of your plans, Doris, or are you going to surprise him, too?'

'Aw, Em. Don't be like that, please. And yes, he knows. I wrote an' told him I'd found a place fer us . . . but, whether or not he'll want ter come with me . . .' She lifted her shoulders. 'Well, I'll soon find out, won't I?'

She looked at Emily for reassurance and her friend, the hurt showing plainly in her face, said, 'You don't trust me, do you, Doris? You're afraid I'll make a play for Tommy, or vice-versa. That's the real reason you want to get Tommy away from me, isn't it?'

Doris turned a shame-faced look on Emily and shook her head.

'I'm sorry, Em. Honest, I really am.' Fiddling nervously with the clasp of her handbag, Doris chewed on the corner of her bottom lip. 'I know yer don't feel like I do about Tommy, but . . . but, if we're all in the same house . . . Well, yer never know what might happen, an' . . .'

'And you'd rather take temptation out of my way. Is that it, Doris? And what about Joseph? Do you plan to keep Tommy away from his son too?' Emily asked angrily. The toddler sitting on her lap heard the tone in his mother's voice and began to whimper, and Emily, filled with contrition, turned her attention to her child.

Gathering Joseph up into her arms, she stroked the dark hair soothingly, her mind in turmoil. To say that she felt stunned by Doris's news was an understatement, yet she knew in her heart that it was for the best. She loved Tommy, and always had, but only as a friend. But she wasn't sure how he felt about her. And with the child as a common bond . . . She buried her face in the child's hair to cover her confusion, and it wasn't until they had alighted from the bus that she turned to Doris and said shakily, 'Maybe you're right, Doris. But you should have said something before now. It came as a shock. And my mum's got everything ready for him. I mean, she's set up the bed Mrs Button gave her in the front room, and partitioned that space with a heavy curtain so he'll have some privacy. Well, you know all that, don't you? Because you helped with the preparations, and never said a word. Oh, Doris, you should have told us. It wasn't fair to let my mum do all that work for nothing.'

'It might not be for nothing, Em. Like I said, I don't know if Tommy will want ter share a place with me . . . But if he doesn't, well, I'll take the place fer meself, 'cos I couldn't stand it if he turned me down. I . . . I can't take the chance of being hurt again.' They were nearing the prison gates now, and Doris, pulling at Emily's arm, stopped walking and pleaded, 'D'yer understand, Em? I just can't face it again.'

And Emily, although the hurt was still rankling, made a supreme effort and gave a sardonic smile.

'It's all right, Doris, I understand. Though I would never have made a play for Tommy, I don't feel that way about him. But if it makes you easier in your mind . . . well, you do what you must.' Hitching the child further up in her arms she added, 'Where is this place you've found?'

Doris looked down at her feet before replying guiltily, 'It's in Ilford. Well, just on the borders really. It's more London way than Essex.'

The smile on Emily's face faltered and, when she replied, she couldn't stop a steely ring entering her voice.

'Really! Well, you're certainly not taking any chances, are you, Doris?' Then she was striding off, leaving Doris to follow miserably in her wake.

There were a few people milling uncomfortably outside the iron-studded wooden gates, their eyes fixed firmly on the ground beneath their feet. One couple, a middle-aged man and his wife, moved quickly to one side as Emily and Doris approached. And Doris, seeing their furtive look, let out a loud laugh.

'I don't know why yer looking so worried. We're all in the same boat, ain't we? Unless yer think we've come ter have tea with the warden.'

'Doris, behave yourself,' Emily reprimanded her friend, knowing that Doris was simply letting off hot air.

Looking at her watch, Emily saw there were still another fifteen minutes to wait. Tommy wouldn't be released until eleven-thirty. So she set her son down on the ground and, gripping the small hand, proceeded to walk him up and down the gravelly path.

Doris watched the two figures, her face filled with misery. Kicking up small pebbles among the gravel, she came over to stand beside Emily, saying apologetically, 'Look, Em, I know yer mad at me, an' I don't blame yer, but well . . . Yer see, I thought you and the captain were gonna – you know – I mean, he did ask yer ter marry him, didn't he? And that would've made everything all right. Only he ain't said anything ter yer since he came back, has he? And he's had plenty of chances. So yer see, Em, yer can't blame me fer worrying, 'cos . . .'

Emily spun round, her face flaming.

'Because what, Doris?' she demanded, her chest heaving with angry emotion. 'You make it sound as if I'd grab Tommy just because he's available. Why don't you just find a knife and stick it into my back, Doris? You might as well, because you've done everything but.'

Doris stepped back, her own temper beginning to rise, her mood made worse by knowing that she was in the wrong. Then they both heard the sound of a car approaching and Emily instinctively scooped Joseph up out of harm's way. She felt her face begin to burn, and a sudden rush of hope leapt into her heart as she recognised the occupant of the gleaming black Daimler.

'Hello, Emily, and you too, Miss Mitchell.' Matthew clambered awkwardly out of the motorcar. 'I see I'm early. I wasn't quite sure if it was eleven or eleven-thirty . . . Still, I'm in time, that's the main thing.'

As he came to stand by them, Emily felt her heart begin to pound. She had seen him on several occasions during the past year, as Doris had so tactlessly pointed out, but not once had he made any mention of that day in the park when he had handed her his front-door key and asked her to marry him. She had long since returned the key, and the weekly sum of five pounds had been stopped at her insistence. The relationship between them seemed to have reverted to what it had been before she left the house in Gore Road; and Emily felt angry and upset that he had raised her hopes concerning their future together. She had expected better of him than that.

But she couldn't fault Captain Winter on the way he had battled on Tommy's behalf, because it was his tireless efforts that had brought Tommy's case to the notice of the public and, together with the help of Fleet Street, he had succeeded in obtaining Tommy's release. She looked down to where Matthew was crouching in front of Joseph, tickling the young boy's neck and ears, much to her son's amusement. Yet it seemed to Emily as if he were deliberately using her child to avoid talking to her.

Well! He needn't worry. She had too much pride to go begging for favours from him – or anyone else for that matter. She would concentrate on Tommy, for this was Tommy's day and nothing must be allowed to spoil it.

Tommy was coming home – only he wasn't, was he? Not if he fell in with Doris's plans. And if that happened Emily would lose two very dear friends, because she couldn't see Doris visiting too often, unless . . . Unless you were safely married, a voice mocked at her. Emily jumped as if those last words had been spoken aloud, and when Doris and Matthew looked towards her quizzically, she laughed shakily and said, 'My nerves are all on edge today. I'll be fine once we get back home.'

Any further talk was cut short by the sound of a loud click as a lock was turned, and each of them, in their own way, took a deep breath and waited for Tommy to appear. Three men stepped through the Judas Gate and each was quickly embraced by those waiting for them.

And then Tommy was stepping out, his features gaunt, as was his body, dressed in the ten-shilling blue-striped suit that he had bought for his demob. He stood still, one bony hand gripping a brown paper parcel that contained his only belongings, his eyes filled with an emotion he couldn't quite put a name to. Then he was being enveloped by soft arms and fresh-smelling bodies, as the two women threw themselves against him. He let the parcel fall unheeded to the ground, and when his son was put squirming into his arms, Tommy let out a low groan and, burying his face in the soft neck, let the tears flow unashamedly.

Matthew, feeling somewhat excluded, stood to one side and watched the poignant scene, and found that he too was having to swallow hard against the rise of emotion within him. He looked up and found himself staring into the tear-filled eyes of Tommy Carter; one of the men who had saved his life, the other having forfeited his own in the heroic dash across the battlefield in France.

Pushing the two crying women gently to one side, Tommy, still holding his son tight against his chest, came up to Matthew with his hand outstretched.

'Thank yer, sir. I know it was you who saved me from the firing squad, an' got me released earlier than I was supposed ter be, an' I just want yer ter know how grateful I am fer all yer help.'

Matthew jumped back as if scalded, a terrible feeling of inadequacy stealing over him. Here was this man thanking him, when it was because of him that Tommy Carter had lost his brother and been incarcerated within those forbidding gates for twenty months. Twenty months of being branded a coward and a deserter, locked up alongside conchies and treated with contempt by prisoners and guards alike, and for the first part of his sentence not knowing if he was going to be lined up against a wall and shot. Yet the man showed no sign of animosity towards Matthew. The warm handshake and accompanying words were genuine, and Matthew couldn't help but bow his head, when he remembered the thoughts he had harboured against this man for being the father of Emily's child.

It was because of his own guilt that Matthew had deliberately stayed away from Emily and stopped his tongue from spurting forth words of love. He had already deprived this man of his brother, he couldn't, in all conscience, take away the mother of his child too. Swallowing hard, he managed to say, 'It was the least I could do, Tommy. After all, it was because of me that you landed in this mess, and I'm so very sorry for your loss. I can't imagine what it must be like to lose a brother, and in your case he was your twin as well, and you must have suffered dreadfully. I can't help feeling responsible, but as for your thanks – well, I couldn't have done it without the help of the newspapers. It is them you should be thanking.'

'Rubbish!' Tommy interrupted, a trace of his old self breaking through. 'They were only after a story. Mind you, I thought they would have sent someone to meet me terday, but obviously I'm yesterday's news, and that's the difference, sir. You're here now because yer care, an' . . . and I'm grateful fer that. And yer mustn't feel guilty about what happened, sir, 'cos we would have done the same fer anyone. Only not everyone would have stood by me, like you have. So, once again, sir, thank you. An' don't hold it against yerself any more, 'cos the way I see it, yer saved me life; so that makes us quits.'

Matthew blinked and hastily looked down at his highly polished shoes. Yet Tommy's next words cut through him like a knife.

'I'm gonna get married, sir . . . At least, I will if she'll have me. I ain't asked her yet. It's a bit awkward ter explain, 'cos everything's sort of jumbled up in me head at the moment, but I've got ter do the right thing by Emily, only that'll mean hurting someone else. Life's never simple, is it, sir?' The thin shoulders rose in a gesture of bewilderment, and Matthew, looking into the haunted blue eyes, experienced an overwhelming feeling of sadness. It would be a long time before Tommy Carter laughed again.

Matthew had imagined that he had prepared himself for all emotions, yet when Tommy said, with a plea in his voice, 'Wish me luck, sir, I'm gonna need it,' Matthew's head jerked back on his neck, the sudden movement causing a stab of pain across his chest. The bullet had lodged in his left lung, and although it had been successfully removed, the injury continued to cause him trouble, and he knew, despite the doctor's kind words, that he would never be as strong as he'd once been. This was yet another reason to keep away from Emily. No woman would want to be saddled with an invalid for a husband; an invalid and a pauper. Well, near enough. And all because of that vixen, who had wormed her way into his Aunt Rose's heart and somehow cajoled the elderly woman into making a new will, leaving the family home to her scheming cousin. But Cynthia Denton hadn't been content with just the house; she had wanted more, and had set out to achieve her goal in any way she could.

When Matthew had been discharged from hospital, he had gone first to visit his aunt and, finding her in fragile health, had decided to stay with her for a while until she recovered her strength. And, barely a week after he had moved in, that blasted Denton woman had tried to get into his bed. The memory of it still caused him to shudder. He had said some dreadful things to Cynthia, and she hadn't forgotten them.

The last thing she had said before leaving his room was, 'You've made a bad mistake, Matthew, and a bad enemy. I'll make you pay for this. It may take a while, but when the time comes, you'll wish you'd never been born.' And she had been as good as her word. She had begun to take his aunt on shopping sprees, buying anything that took her fancy and running up exorbitant bills. And when the money that his uncle left had been exhausted, Cynthia had persuaded Rose to use her nephew's name to purchase further goods and borrow money. His poor aunt's mind had long since become fuddled, and she had acquiesced to everything that Cynthia asked without a murmur. Matthew had paid the bills for his aunt's sake, but he had warned Cynthia that if she continued to use his name, he would have no option but to take out a notice in the papers disclaiming any responsibility. It wasn't until his aunt's death in April, three months ago, that Matthew had learnt of the huge debts she had run up.

He had already paid out thousands of pounds while his aunt was alive, but on her death her creditors had clamoured for payment, insisting that they had allowed the elderly woman free rein on the strength of Matthew's good name. He had been forced to sell his home in order to pay off the debts; it was either that or declare himself bankrupt, and he couldn't bear the shame of that.

The Daimler was the last object of value that he owned, and he had hung on to that like a drowning man, in order to pick Tommy Carter up from prison and take him home in style. But tomorrow! Well, tomorrow would take care of itself.

Forcing a smile to his lips, Matthew shook Tommy's hand warmly.

'Indeed I do wish you luck, Tommy. You deserve it more than any man I know.' There followed an awkward silence, and both men were relieved when Joseph began to cry for his mother, for in an instant Emily had joined them, taking the wailing boy from his father's arms.

'There now, there now,' Emily cooed. 'Whatever's the matter with you? It's only your dad, silly.' Lifting a smiling face to the two men, Emily said gaily, 'He's probably hungry.' Then, rooting in her bag, she produced half a rusk biscuit and handed it to the child. Instantly his tears stopped, and with a lop-sided grin of triumph he shoved the treat into his mouth.

'Well, we'd better be off, sir, an' thanks again, for everything.' Tommy had taken the child back, ignoring the soggy biscuit that was being pressed against his suit. Matthew was rendered dumb for a moment as he looked at the trio. They seemed to belong to each other, and even when Doris came to join them, it was Emily, Tommy and the child who stood out in his mind. It was only when they began making noises about getting the bus back that Matthew sprang into life.

'Oh, goodness, don't be silly. I have the car here. There's plenty of room for all of us.'

Emily looked at Doris doubtfully, all differences forgotten for the moment. She knew that Doris had hoped to talk to Tommy alone on the bus journey home, but she couldn't turn down Matthew's offer of a lift. It wouldn't be fair to Tommy, who looked as though he could do with a bit of comfort; at least, that was the reason she gave herself.

Doris saw Emily's raised eyebrows, as if asking her a question, gave a half-hearted smile and shrugged. She would have another chance later on. And if Tommy said no . . . Well, at least she would know where she stood. But there was still Emily to consider, and Doris knew that she would never truly be happy if her friend wasn't. So, before getting into the car, she nudged Emily in the ribs and made several nods of her head towards Matthew, which made Emily's face burn even redder.

Piling into the car, the two women and the child sat in the back seats, while Tommy joined Matthew up front. And when the car finally came to a stop outside number fifteen Fenton Street, Matthew refused the offer to come in for a drink, stating that he had prior plans for the afternoon. Doris, seizing her chance, took hold of Joseph and steered Tommy into the house, leaving Emily alone with Matthew.

On the journey from the prison they had all talked freely, each one damping down their individual emotions for the time being. Now that she was on her own with Matthew, Emily suddenly felt awkward. Then Matthew, resting his arm along the back of the leather seat, turned

293

to where Emily was still sitting in the back and said, 'I know I've said this before, but I'm very sorry about Lenny. He was a brave man. How has your mother been coping?'

Emily's body jerked slightly with nervousness as she replied, 'Oh, she has good days and bad. It's the not knowing exactly how he died, or where he's buried, that's tearing her apart. But I don't suppose we'll ever know exactly what happened. I only pray that his death was quick and without pain.' Matthew noticed that Emily hadn't made any mention of her father. But having heard about the dead man's character, that was understandable.

When another silence descended on them, Emily cleared her throat and said, 'I was very upset that Mrs Denton didn't tell me Miss Rose had died. I . . . I would have liked to have attended the funeral; I was very fond of your aunt, you know, in spite of what happened. Do . . . do you see much of her now – I mean, Mrs Denton?'

Matthew's eyes hardened at the mention of the hated name, but he wasn't going to whine to Emily about his problems. He still had good friends, who would help him out until he got back on his feet again. But it was going to be a long, hard haul. At least the law firm he had worked for before the war was eager to have him back. He had intended to take early retirement, especially in view of his present medical condition, but now . . . !

'You said you had sold your house the last time we met. Have you found somewhere else?'

'What? Oh, not yet,' he managed to sound casual. 'I'm staying with some friends for a while, until I find something more permanent.' That at least was true. But he couldn't sponge off his one-time school friend for ever, not now that the man's wife was expecting their first child. 'And as for Mrs Denton, I've seen her only twice since my aunt's funeral, and I have no plans to renew our acquaintance.'

Looking at his watch, Matthew gave an exclamation of surprise and said, 'Lord, I didn't realise it was so late. I have to go, Emily. Take care of yourself, my dear.' The dismissal was evident and Emily, her face stiff with hurt, nodded curtly.

'Yes, I will. Goodbye, Captain Winter.'

Then she was gone. And Matthew, his face set, drove off feeling very old and alone.

The tea Nellie had prepared had turned into a welcome-home party, for Tommy had always been a favourite with the women in the street, and now more than ever they wanted to show the young man how highly he was thought of. Dot had baked a cake, though how she had come by the ingredients with this new ration business, no-one knew, or bothered to ask. And the tin of salmon that Nellie had bought for sandwiches had stretched a long way. As she said to Dot afterwards, 'Talk about the loaf and five fishes.' But all the women had brought some contribution to the party, and in true East End style it had turned into a knees-up. And when Tommy, looking painfully thin and haggard, had laughed out loud for the first time during the hokey-cokey, there wasn't a women in the house who didn't feel a tear come to her eye.

But now it was morning, and Tommy and Doris were leaving for good. The three of them had talked far into the night, after Nellie had gone to bed, and it had all been decided. As Doris had packed her belongings, she had looked up at Emily and asked if Matthew had said anything to her before he left, and Emily, trying to smile, had answered, 'No. Well, nothing about us, that is. Our parting was very civilised.'

To which Doris had exclaimed loudly, 'Civilised be

blowed. Yer can be too much of a lady, Em. If it had been me, I'd 've given him a right mouthful.'

Now Emily was facing Tommy as he stumbled over the words he couldn't say last night in front of Doris. His body was trembling slightly, as were his hands.

'I meant what I said before I went away, Em. D'yer remember, I said I'd stand by yer if anything . . . Well, yer know what I mean.' His head drooped for a moment, then he went on, 'I was gonna ask yer ter marry me, only I didn't get the chance, not with yer mum an' Doris with us all evening. An' then when we was talking last night, it seemed as if . . . Well, you and Doris sort of took over, an' I let meself go along with the plan ter move out with Doris, but . . .'

'It's all right, Tommy, I understand. And it's very good of you to ask, but . . . I don't feel that way about you; not the way Doris does.' Taking hold of the almost skeletal fingers, Emily said softly, 'She loves you very much, Tommy, and I know it's really none of my business, but I have to ask. Do you feel the same way about her? And, more importantly, are you going to marry her? Oh, I know she says that she doesn't care what people think of her, but Doris is a lot more sensitive than she makes out.'

Tommy's body sagged with relief, a glimmer of a smile lighting up his face.

'I'm . . . I'm not really sure of anything at the moment, Em. I'll need time before making any decisions, so let's leave it fer now, eh, Em? What I do know is that I feel comfortable with Doris, an' I won't have ter worry about using the wrong knife an' fork, or being picked up on me grammar . . . Oh, Gawd, Em, I didn't mean . . .'

Despite the fact that she didn't want to marry Tommy, it still came as a blow to discover that he was relieved he wasn't going to be pressurised into marrying her.

'Oh, Tommy, I'm not that bad, am I?'

'No, no of course not, Em.'

The denial came quickly, a little too quickly, and Emily turned her head to the open door saying, 'Doris is waiting for you, Tommy, but don't forget your promise to visit. I want Joseph to know his father.'

Now it was Tommy's turn to look hurt. 'Aw, Em, I'd never turn me back on me own son. I know what it's like, remember?'

Then they were hugging fiercely.

'I'll be back next Saturday ter take Joe out fer the day. I thought maybe I'd take him over the park to feed the ducks, if that's okay.'

'Of course it is. Now go, before Doris comes and drags you out.'

A few minutes later it was Doris's turn to say her goodbyes, and although both women had silently vowed not to break down, the moment they hugged each other goodbye the tears began to fall.

'Oh, Gawd, look at us. Silly pair of cows, we'll be seeing each other next week. I mean, it's not like me an' Tommy are moving ter the moon, is it?'

But Emily couldn't answer. She was too full of emotion to speak, because, in spite of Doris's assurances, she knew that things would never again be the same between them.

When the door finally closed, Emily stood by the window watching the two figures walking away. And when a pair of arms came round her shoulders, she buried her head on Nellie's shoulder and sobbed, 'Oh, Mum . . . Mum.'

And Nellie, gently stroking the auburn hair, could find nothing to say except, 'I know, love. I know.'

CHAPTER TWENTY-TWO

'Do you want anything up Mare Street, Mum?' Emily was putting Joseph into his pram, and the young boy was bouncing up and down in delighted anticipation of going out. 'Sit still, you little devil.' The gentle admonishment brought a gurgle of unintelligible words from the dark-haired child. 'Yes, and the same to you, you little monkey.'

'I can't think of anything I need, love.' Nellie came into the room, wiping her wet hands down the front of her apron.

Straightening up from the pram, Emily looked sternly at her mother.

'Now, don't go tiring yourself out, Mum. It's your day off, so put your feet and rest.'

Nellie came over to the pram and tickled her grandson under the chin, a broad smile lighting up her face as the child giggled happily.

'Now have you ever known me to sit around doing nothing during the day? Besides, it's the only chance I get for a good clean.'

Yet when Emily and the child had left, Nellie didn't

return immediately to her chores, but sat down on one of the hard-backed chairs and took a small photo from her apron pocket. It had been taken on Lenny's fifteenth birthday and, as she stared down into that smiling face, she felt the familiar lump forming in her throat. Sometimes she might go for a whole day without thinking of her son, but not often. If only he'd had a decent burial, at least then she could have grieved properly. As for Alfie – well! She wasn't going to be a hypocrite. He had made her life hell, and she wasn't sorry he was gone.

Sniffing loudly, she put the photo back in her pocket and was about to rise when there was a knock on the front door. Thinking it to be Dot, she opened the door with a smile, then gave a small exclamation of surprise at the sight of a woman surrounded by five children looking at her nervously.

'Excuse me, Missus, but is yer name Mrs Ford?'

'Yes, I'm Mrs Ford. How may I help you?'

'I'm not sure if I've got the right address,' the woman continued apologetically, and her next words almost brought Nellie's feet from the floor. 'Did yer 'ave a son called Lenny?'

Clutching at her throat, Nellie threw out her arm and said weakly, 'Please, come in. Oh, please . . . come in.'

Pushing the pram past Woolworths, Emily stopped outside a small café and hesitated. She'd been out for a good few hours, and the September sun was extremely hot today. Quickly making up her mind, she lifted the small boy out of his pram and, after being served, managed to carry a cup of tea to a nearby table without spilling any.

'There now, you stop here, while I go back for the cakes, Joseph . . . On second thoughts, I'd better take you with me,' she said, eyeing the steaming cup.

She was breaking off a piece of currant bun for the boy when a woman stopped by her table and said hesitantly, 'Excuse me, Miss, but didn't yer use ter work fer Rose Winter?'

Startled, Emily looked up into a face she had seen before but couldn't remember where.

'Yes, I did, but that was over two years ago.'

The woman uttered an exclamation of triumph.

'I knew it. I knew it was you, the minute yer walked through the door.' When Emily continued to look at her in puzzlement, the woman cried, 'Oh, we only met the once, but I never ferget a face . . . You was moving out, just as I was moving in, remember? In Gore Road, I sort of took over your job, an' that was the worst mistake I ever made.'

A glimmer of recognition came to Emily.

'Of course, how silly of me. But as you say, we only met the once, and it was a very brief meeting. Oh, please, won't you join us,' Emily said, pulling out a chair from under the table.

'Well, I don't mind if I do, Miss. Thank yer kindly.'

As soon as the woman sat down, Emily regretted her hasty invitation. She hadn't a clue what she could talk about with this comparative stranger, but she needn't have worried on that score, for Fanny Lawson had plenty to say.

Seating herself comfortably, she began, 'Well, it's nice ter see yer've got on, Miss, 'cos I felt dreadful about taking yer job, especially since yer was . . . well, expecting like. He's a lovely little lad, an' no mistake. Who does he take after, Miss, you or yer husband?' Inquisitive, kindly eyes peered at the small boy, who was in the process of demolishing a currant bun.

Emily stiffened. Thinking the woman was simply being

nosy, she said curtly, 'I'm not married, Mrs Lawson. Now, if you'll excuse me, I have to be on my way.'

'Oh, oh, Lor, Miss. I didn't mean any 'arm, Miss, honest.' Emily couldn't help but notice the genuine remorse in the woman's voice, and she relaxed somewhat.

'That's perfectly all right, but I really do have to get home, unless . . . !' Emily had the impression that there was something on the woman's mind, then she remembered her earlier remark. Keeping her voice casual she said, 'What did you mean, about it being the worst day of your life when you went to work for Miss Winter?'

Immediately the woman became all bustle, declaring, 'Well now, I'm not one ter gossip, Miss. An' I don't want yer thinking I'm out ter cause trouble, just because I was sacked, 'cos I ain't like that.'

Emily eyed the woman keenly.

'Of course not,' she said soothingly, then probed gently, 'Is it something to do with your late employer, or has Mrs Denton done something to upset you – apart from dismissing you, I mean?'

The name of Cynthia Denton acted like a red rag to a bull. Bristling with indignation, the plump figure exclaimed, 'Oh, that one. She's a devil, a devil, Miss. She drove that poor old lady ter 'er grave. An' I'll tell yer another fing, Miss. The doctor, well, 'e was surprised when she passed away, 'cos, she might 'ave gone a bit peculiar in the 'ead, but she was in good 'ealth, an' we all expected 'er ter live a good few more years than she did, poor soul.'

Emily sat back in her chair, stunned by what she had heard. Then, very carefully she said, 'Mrs Lawson, you're surely not suggesting that Mrs Denton had anything to do with Miss Winter's death, are you?'

A look of fear sprang into the woman's eyes.

'Lor, Miss, now I never said any such fing, did I? A

body could get inter awful trouble spreading rumours like that.'

Quick to reassure her, Emily leant across the table and said, 'If I feel I have to act on whatever you tell me, I promise you that your name will never be mentioned. You have my word on it. But I was very fond of Miss Rose, and I'm sure Captain Winter would be very . . .'

'Oh, dear, Miss. The poor captain wouldn't be able ter do anyfing, not the state he's in, poor soul. An' that's the real reason I wanted ter talk ter yer, Miss, 'cos I've been that worried. I haven't 'ad a wink of sleep fer days now, thinking about 'im alone in the 'ouse with that woman!' Emily stared at her in alarm, but before she could say anything, Fanny Lawson was off again in full flow.

'He came round ter see 'er, an', ooh, yer should 'ave heard them, Miss. Yelling an' shouting, both of them. I don't know what it was all about, but the captain, 'e suddenly took ill, but she wouldn't let me call a doctor fer 'im. Insisted, she did, that he didn't need one, when anyone could see the poor man was really ill. Anyways, I didn't see 'im again that night, but I 'eard someone moving about in the attic. I asked 'er, Mrs Denton, if the captain was all right, an' she nearly bit me 'ead off.

'Anyway, the very next day she sacked me. That was nearly a week ago, but, oh, Miss, I've been that worried, an' when I saw yer come into the café . . . Well, Miss, I was never so pleased ter see anyone in me life. I mean, he might 'ave left by now, but 'e did look bad, an' . . .'

Emily sat very still as the woman rambled on, and as the words flowed, she felt her anger slowly building to an overpowering rage.

Joseph shrieked with delight as the pram rolled at break-neck speed over the cobbled pavement. A few times he was almost catapulted onto the ground. Almost, but not quite, for Emily, although still gripped by rage, had her eye firmly on her child and each time he rose in the air, her hand automatically shot out, pushing him back into the safety of the pram.

When she first dashed into her home she thought for a moment she had charged into the wrong house, for staring back at her were five rather grubby children, and a woman she'd never seen before. Emily was about to speak, when Nellie came in from the kitchen exclaiming joyfully, 'Oh, hello, love. This is Mrs Anderson. She very kindly came with news of Lenny.'

For a wild moment Emily thought her brother was still alive, and Nellie must have seen it in her daughter's face, because she immediately added, 'Oh, no, love, he . . . he's dead, but at least now I know how he died. He . . . Oh, please, Mrs Anderson, would you repeat to my daughter what you told me.'

The visitor shuffled awkwardly on the hard-backed chair, then, lifting her gaze to the tall, auburn-haired woman, she related the news she had recently told the mother.

'Well, Miss, it's like this. Me 'usband was fighting out in France, an' he got hit. 'E thought 'e was a goner, 'cos there weren't any stretcher-bearers, on account of the mud; they couldn't get ter the wounded, yer see. Anyways, like I said, me 'usband thought 'e was finished, then this young man sort of appeared out of nowhere, bundled my 'Arry onter a stretcher, an' dragged 'im back ter the first-aid post. An' when the orderlies went out ter fetch 'im in, yer bruvver, I mean,' she looked from Nellie to Emily as if in apology, ''e was gorn. 'E must've gorn back ter try an' rescue someone else, only . . . only 'e never came back.' The woman lowered her eyes.

'How . . . how did you know where to find us?' Emily asked quietly.

'Well, it was like I told yer muvver,' she nodded in Nellie's direction. 'Me 'usband an' yer bruvver didn't 'ave time fer a chat, there was bombs an' bullets going orf all over the place, but they did manage ter exchange names on the way. An' when my 'Arry got outta the 'ospital, 'e tried ter find 'im ter say thanks, but it was such a muddle over there, an' 'Arry didn't know what regiment yer bruvver was with, so 'e had ter leave it. But 'e never fergot 'im. 'E was in hospital fer ever such a long time, over a year it was, but as soon as 'e came out, 'e started to make enquiries like. It took ever such a long while, but 'e found out. Then 'e was frightened ter come 'ere. 'E thought yer might 'old it against 'im . . . I mean, if yer knew yer son 'ad died because of 'im. But like I said ter 'im, "'Arry," I said, "yer've gotta go an' tell 'is poor muvver what 'appened, 'cos 'e was an 'ero."' The woman paused for breath, and when she looked at Emily and Nellie again her eyes were bright with tears. 'An' 'e was, yer know, 'e was a 'ero, 'cos nobody else risked going ter get the wounded in. Your son saved me 'usband's life, an' . . . and I'm heart sorry he was killed, 'cos I would've liked to meet 'im . . . Oh, dear . . . Oh, I'm sorry.'

Instantly Nellie was by her side comforting the woman. Emily, too, came to the woman's side and rested a hand on the heaving shoulder. And when she looked up at her mother, she saw Nellie smile. It was a watery, emotional smile, but it was genuine. Lenny would never come home, but at least they now knew how he had died. As the woman had said, Lenny had died a hero, and if he had to die, it was a death he would have been proud of. Emily and Nellie were both reliving Lenny's last moments in their minds, and though the images brought sadness to their hearts, it was a sadness tinged with joy. For Lenny's last moments on earth had been those of a man; a very brave man.

It was nearly an hour later when Emily left the house. They had all enjoyed a good cry – the children too joining in, bewildered by the sight of the adults weeping and holding each other. But now Emily had to concentrate on another matter. Her face and body steeled with determination, she marched purposefully across Victoria Park, the memory of Mrs Lawson's words adding strength to her already highly charged state of mind.

As she strode through the iron gates of the park, she came to an abrupt halt at the sight of the removal van parked outside the house in Gore Road. With a cry of anger she ran across the road, calling out loudly, 'Wait, there's been a mistake. Just wait a minute, will you?'

Two men, wearing brown overcoats, were in the process of lifting the piano into the back of the van when they heard the voice calling to them. Puzzled, they looked at the tall, attractive woman for an explanation.

Panting for breath, Emily gasped, 'There's been a mistake. The furniture is staying where it is.'

The elder of the two men tipped back his cap and scratched his head, perplexed.

'We've got our orders to shift the furniture. It's all been bought an' paid for, Miss.' Pulling a large sheet of paper from the breast-pocket of his overcoat, he held it out for Emily to see. 'Look, all bought an' paid fer, like I said. There's been no mistake, Miss.'

Emily grabbed hold of the man's arm, pleading, 'Please, I can't explain right now, but can you wait before removing anything else? Please, it's very important.'

The man looked into the lovely blue eyes and relented. 'All right, Miss. But we can't hang around all afternoon. We've got other houses to visit.'

'Bless you,' Emily cried, then she was running up the stone steps and into the house.

Stopping only to make sure that the downstairs rooms

were empty, she quickly ran up the carpeted stairs, calling out loudly, 'Mrs Denton. Mrs Denton, where are you? I need to speak to you urgently.'

Within seconds Cynthia Denton appeared from the bedroom that had once belonged to Miss Rose. Emily swept her eyes over the slim figure, noting at once the expensive beige summer coat and the large, black floppy hat that almost covered the right side of her face. Behind Cynthia, in the bedroom, Emily's eyes fell on two trunks and several suitcases, obviously packed and waiting for removal.

'Well, well, if it isn't the serving girl. Have you come back to reminisce over old times, or were you hoping to get your old job back?' Cynthia Denton's gaze swept disdainfully over Emily's plain white blouse, fastened at the neck with a marquise brooch, and her black hobble skirt. 'If so, then I'm afraid you've wasted your time, on both counts, Miss Ford.' One eyebrow was raised mockingly. 'How did you find out I was selling up? Through the East End grapevine, I suppose. If that's the case, then I suppose you already know that my late cousin left me the house in her will. Wasn't that kind of her? But I've decided not to stop on. The house has too many memories and . . .'

'Where is he?' Emily demanded. 'Where is Matthew?'

'My, my, Matthew, is it? I'd no idea you two had become so close. Have you come to take him home with you, to that poxy little back-street hovel where you live?' Cynthia was smirking, carefully pulling on a pair of white linen gloves, one finger at a time. 'Still, beggars can't be choosers, and I suppose he'll be grateful for a roof over his head, wherever . . . Oooh . . .' The smirk vanished as she found herself being pushed into the large living-room, then a violent shove sent her sprawling across the dark green settee.

'You bitch! You wicked, cruel bitch. I know all about you, and what you've done, and by God you're going to pay for it! And to answer your question about taking him home, he *is* home, and here he's going to stay.' Emily glared down at the hated figure, her chest heaving with anger. 'I don't know why you asked him to come here, how you tricked him into seeing you, and I don't care. What I do know is that he's very ill, and you . . . you evil, wicked bitch, you've deliberately kept him here out of spite, so that . . .'

Cynthia sprang to her feet, snatching up her black hat from the floor as she did so. As if nothing had happened, she carefully fitted the hat back on her bobbed hair, her actions unhurried. Then, walking towards Emily, she drawled, 'Matthew is free to leave whenever he chooses. I haven't tied him up, or locked him in some dark room, but he doesn't seem that anxious to leave. Of course, that may be because he has nowhere else to go, but that isn't my concern. And I didn't trick him into coming here; why on earth should I? He came to see me of his own accord – some silly notion he had about contesting the will. Really, the lengths one will go to when one is desperate. And he is desperate, poor man. Oh, I confess there was a time when I might have been interested in him, but that was before dear Rose passed away.'

She began to walk round the room, now bare except for the settee and one armchair. 'I already have a tidy sum put by, and of course there is the money from the sale of the house to be considered, plus the few pieces of jewellery that Rose left; mine now, of course. Yes, indeed, I shall be very comfortably off in the future.'

Her manner suddenly changing, she turned menacingly to where Emily was standing white-faced by the door and sneered, 'If it's Matthew you've come for, then take him and get out, you're welcome to him. God! As if I'd waste my time on a pathetic specimen like he's become. If I want a man, I'll choose a strong, capable one, not a man who can't even cough without choking his lungs up. And you think I've kept him here for my own pleasure! He's no use to any woman now – but take him, please.'

When Emily didn't move, Cynthia bunched her hands into fists and hissed, 'Now I've been very patient with you. Obviously that was a mistake, so I'll put it to you plainly, in words you will understand. Get out of my house, you little whore, before I . . .'

Emily gave a harsh laugh.

'You're a fine one to be calling me a whore. I wasn't the one who climbed into bed with a man who was so sick he was barely able to fight you off. But he managed to, didn't he? It's said that in times of crisis, people acquire a strength they didn't know they possessed, and by God, finding you next to him must have given Matthew that strength. It must have been like finding a snake crawling between the sheets . . . Now, I'll ask you one more time. Where's Matthew? Is he still here, or have you thrown him out with the furniture?'

Making a sound almost like an animal, Cynthia snarled, 'He's in the attic, or what's left of him is. I haven't seen him for days – he could be dead, for all I know, or care. Now, I'll give you just fifteen minutes to leave, alone or with Matthew, I don't much care which. If you don't, I'll call the police and have you both forcibly removed.' As she said these last words, Cynthia put out her hand and pushed Emily to one side; and that was her biggest mistake.

Forgetting all that Mr George had taught her, Emily let out a cry of rage and launched herself at the mocking figure. Grabbing handfuls of Cynthia's hair, she pulled and tugged without mercy. Then her own hair was being yanked so hard that Emily imagined it was being pulled out by the roots. Screeching and shouting, the two women fought like wild animals, rolling around on the carpeted floor, each determined to get the upper hand. Neither of them heard Matthew calling to them to stop, until he stepped forward and tried to separate the writhing bodies.

A foot came out and caught him hard in the stomach, and with a gasp of pain he staggered backwards, his hand going out to grab at the nearby armchair to prevent himself from falling to the ground. It was Emily who first became aware of his presence. Bringing up her clenched fist, she drove it straight into Cynthia's face, causing the woman to loosen her grip on Emily's hair. Crawling on all fours, Emily inched her way towards Matthew.

'You'll pay for this, you little trollop,' Cynthia screamed wildly. 'I'll have the law on you for this, you see if I don't.'

Gently lowering Matthew into the armchair, Emily rounded on the furious woman and yelled, 'You do that, Mrs Denton, and I'll have a story to tell them as well. Like how Miss Rose died so suddenly, when she was in perfect health. I'm sure the police would be very interested in what I have to say.'

Cynthia came to an abrupt halt, her eyes widening in sudden fear. Then she pulled herself upright and said scornfully, 'You're mad. The doctor examined her. He found no suspicious circumstances in her death, he . . .'

'No, but he wouldn't have been looking for any, would he?' Emily shouted back. 'But if I were to voice my suspicions, they'd have to check, wouldn't they? I wouldn't be surprised if they exhumed her body. I've heard that they do that if there's even a suspicion of foul play. But that shouldn't concern you, should it? After all, if your conscience is clear, you have nothing to worry about, have you, Mrs Denton? It all depends on whether you're willing to take that chance.'

Cynthia's face was contorted with rage, but it wasn't until she screamed, 'Damn you for an interfering little slut, damn you to hell' that she raced from the room.

Emily stood stunned by Cynthia's reaction, then a sickness rose in her throat. Dear Lord! So Fanny Lawson had been right in her suspicions. She felt suddenly weak and drained.

'Emily, what . . . What's going on . . . ?' Matthew, his face ashen, gripped her hand feebly.

'Sshh, my dear. It's nothing for you to worry about. I'll see to everything. You just rest and get well again. There's just one more thing I have to see to, then I'll get the doctor to have a look at you, and then we can talk.' Smoothing back the lank, dark hair from his forehead, Emily bent and kissed the clammy brow.

The noise of something heavy being dragged down the stairs brought her swiftly to her feet. Racing down the hallway, she saw Cynthia desperately trying to drag the trunk down the stairs, and with a quick bound Emily was running down stairs and barring her way.

'Oh, no. Oh, no. You're not taking anything from this house, Mrs Denton. You'll leave the way you came; with nothing but the clothes on your back.'

Like a trapped animal, Cynthia's eyes darted back and forth as if looking for a way to escape, then she blustered belligerently, 'That's a lie. I brought two suitcases with me when I came here and . . .'

'And the whole lot went straight into the rag-bag. Everything you have now was bought with the Winters' money, and I'll be damned if I'm going to let you walk out the door with those cases. Everything in there belongs by right to Matthew, and I'm going to make sure you'll never profit by what you've done.'

Dropping the cases with a thud, Cynthia looked at Emily with loathing.

'Look, I'm leaving. You can have the wretched house, and it's not because I've anything to hide, either,' she added defiantly, but she couldn't meet Emily's cold stare. 'I just don't want Rose dug up. I think too much of her memory to allow her grave to be desecrated . . .'

'Huh! Tell that to the pigs.' Emily heard herself repeating an old saying of Dot Button's.

Nervously pulling at her gloves, Cynthia muttered fearfully, 'What are you doing to do?'

Emily stared back, her face grim.

'I don't know yet. I'll have to talk it over with Matthew, but if I were you, I'd find a place to hide. And for the rest of your life you'll live in fear of a knock at your door one day; either that, or you'll end up swinging from a rope. And it would be no more than you deserve, you evil bitch.'

Cynthia glared at Emily, her eyes filled with pure hatred. Then, turning abruptly on her heel, she ran down the stairs and out of the house.

When Emily followed, she was just in time to see the slim figure disappearing round the corner. Heaving a sigh of relief, she addressed the removal men in a trembling voice. 'I'm sorry you've been messed about, but could you put all the furniture back, please. You'll be reimbursed for your troubles, of course.'

Ignoring the grumbles of the men, she raced back upstairs to find Matthew looking out for her, his face filled with anxiety.

'What on earth's going on, Emily? I don't understand.'

Dropping to her knees, Emily looked up at him and said softly, 'I'll explain later, my love. But there's one question I have to ask you.' She took a deep breath and added, 'You once asked me to marry you. Does that offer still stand?'

A glimmer of hope sprang into Matthew's eyes.

'B . . . but, what about Tommy? And . . . and I'm sick, Emily, and old. You can do much better than me . . .'

Placing a finger on his lips, Emily gazed at him in adoration and whispered, 'Tommy's with Doris. And you'll get better, I'll see to that. Now, answer my question. Do you want to marry me?'

Matthew looked down into those blue eyes and nodded weakly.

'Oh, yes, my dear. More than anything else in this world.'

'Then it's settled. As soon as you're well enough to carry me over the threshold, we'll be married.'

Holding onto his hands, she laid her head in his lap and closed her eyes happily. She had come home. Tomorrow she would go to the police, but for now she just wanted to savour some time with the man she loved.